"I know it's fake but thank you, Ty.
Thank you for giving it to me."

And I couldn't stop myself, his eyes so close, that look in them, my arms moved from around his shoulders, my hands framed his face, I leaned up and whispered, "Thank you." Then I pressed my lips to his.

I meant to give him a soft kiss of gratitude. This was not to say I didn't want to give him a long, hard, wet kiss of something else. But when my mouth hit his, he didn't give me the chance to give him a soft kiss of gratitude. Instantly, his fingers slid up into my hair, cupping my head and his mouth opened over mine making a demand. Mine complied. His tongue spiked into my mouth and I liked the taste of it, I hadn't had it in what seemed like a decade, I missed it and he tasted so fucking good my body pressed into his and not just because his arm around me grew super tight.

His torso was on mine, his hips beside mine, his long, heavy leg moved to tangle with mine as his tongue moved in my mouth. I wrapped one arm around his back, one around his shoulders, my hand moving to cup the back of his head and hold him to me.

God, he couldn't kiss. He could *kiss*.

Acclaim for Kristen Ashley and Her Novels

"A unique, not-to-be-missed voice in romance. Kristen Ashley is a star in the making!"

—Carly Phillips, *New York Times* bestselling author

"I adore Kristen Ashley's books. She writes engaging, romantic stories with intriguing, colorful, and larger-than-life characters. Her stories grab you by the throat from page one and don't let go until well after the last page. They continue to dwell in your mind days after you finish the story, and you'll find yourself anxiously awaiting the next. Ashley is an addicting read no matter which of her stories you find yourself picking up."

—Maya Banks, *New York Times* bestselling author

"There is something about them [Ashley's books] that I find crackalicious."

—Kati Brown, DearAuthor.com

"Run, don't walk...to get [the Dream Man] series. I love [Kristen Ashley's] rough, tough, hard-loving men. And I love the cosmo-girl club!"

—NocturneReads.com

"[*Law Man* is an] excellent addition to a phenomenal series!"

—ReadingBetweentheWinesBookClub.blogspot.com

"[*Law Man*] made me laugh out loud. Kristen Ashley is an amazing writer!"

—TotallyBookedBlog.com

"I felt all of the rushes, the adrenaline surges, the anger spikes...my heart pumping in fury, my eyes tearing up when my heart (I mean...*her* heart) would break."

—Maryse's Book Blog (Maryse.net) on *Motorcycle Man*

lady luck

Also by Kristen Ashley

The Colorado Mountain Series

The Gamble
Sweet Dreams
Breathe
Jagged
Kaleidoscope

The Dream Man Series

Mystery Man
Wild Man
Law Man
Motorcycle Man

The Chaos Series

Own the Wind
Fire Inside
Ride Steady
Walk Through Fire

lady luck

KRISTEN ASHLEY

FOREVER

NEW YORK BOSTON

This book is a work of fiction. Names, characters, places, and incidents are the product of the author's imagination or are used fictitiously. Any resemblance to actual events, locales, or persons, living or dead, is coincidental.

Forever
Hachette Book Group
1290 Avenue of the Americas, New York, NY 10104
forever-romance.com
twitter.com/foreverromance

Originally published as an ebook by Forever Yours in December 2012
First trade paperback edition: June 2017

Forever is an imprint of Grand Central Publishing. The Forever name and logo are trademarks of Hachette Book Group, Inc.

LCCN: 2017933244

ISBN: 978-1-5387-4436-9 (trade pbk.)

Printed in the United States of America

LSC-C

10 9 8 7 6 5 4 3 2 1

Acknowledgments

A big shout-out to members of my Facebook page for helping me with this book.

When I was at a loss as to what my hero should drive, Rebekah Oliva had the fabulous idea that Ty should own a Viper. So he does. I'm not sure in real life if Ty would fit in a Viper but, lucky for me, in my books I can make anything happen.

But my cousins Jane and Lew Foster thought Ty should drive a Land Cruiser, and since Carla Griffin, Lisa Bachlet Smith and Josephine Ingram all quickly agreed, I decided Ty should have two rides. So he does.

Not to mention, during my name-fests on my Facebook page, Beccy Golding gave me the awesome last name Champion, which I used. I also used Erika Wynne's suggestion of Dewey, Penny Peers's suggestion of Elijah and Kellie Shircliff Purdy's suggestion of Zander.

And last, another shout-out to Lisa Bachlet Smith, who thought "Ty" was a good name for a hero. I read Lisa's suggestion and loved it. So my Ty was born.

And I love him. I hope you do too.

CHAPTER ONE

A Miracle

My cell rang, I snatched it off the passenger seat, looked at the display and it said, "Shift calling."

I sighed.

I flipped it open, my other arm twisting so I could look at my watch.

Twelve oh two.

Shift was impatient, as usual.

"Hey," I said into the phone.

"He out?"

My eyes went out the passenger-side window, through the two guard towers, down the long tunnel created by two sides of high, cinder-block-walled fence topped with razor wire circling through lines of barbed wire, the heat sweltering on the day making the air down that open empty tunnel wave and shimmer.

"Nope," I answered.

"Fuck!" Shift clipped. "What's takin' so fuckin' long? He's supposed to be released at noon."

"Shift, it's noon oh two," I told him.

"Yeah, so?" he asked back, sounding pissed and impatient. "They're releasing him from prison. I doubt he's sticking around for a going-away party."

I doubted that too.

"I'll call," I promised.

"They got seven minutes," he threatened, and I stifled a sigh.

This was Shift. He was a thousand miles away. He was a full-time pimp slash drug dealer and part-time asshole. Though, that said, he put far more effort into being an asshole than his other occupations.

And he thought he had some sway over the California Corrections Department.

"All right," I said.

"Call me the minute that brother breathes free air," he bit off and hung up.

I flipped my phone shut wondering, for the seven thousandth time, why the fuck I was doing this.

I came up with no answers except for the fact that when Ronnie was murdered, he'd left me with one thing.

Shift.

I would have preferred a vast estate, a fortune in jewels or, perhaps, nothing.

I got Shift.

And although after Ronnie died I wanted nothing to do with that part of his life, I wanted to move on, turn my back on it all, Shift wouldn't allow that. If Shift got his talons in you, they went deep, attached straight to the bone, the tips sprang open into claws that sunk into your marrow and didn't let go. Not for anything.

And Shift had his talons in me. I didn't want it, didn't invite it but there they were.

The good news was, he didn't often scroll down to my number on his phone.

The other good news was, when he did, the shit he asked for was usually not that hard to do and it was never illegal. He knew me. He knew where I stood. He knew there was no fucking way I'd get involved in any of his garbage.

But he also knew I loved Ronnie more than anything in this world and Ronnie—for reasons only known to Ronnie—loved Shift only slightly less than he loved me. Though, I had to admit, sometimes then and now, I wondered if he loved me slightly less than he loved Shift—but I didn't often go there.

So he knew I'd take Shift's back.

Unless Shift tried to get me dirty. Then he knew I'd throw him right under the fucking bus even if I had to take my life in my hands to do it.

So he avoided that. Not that he cared about my life, just that I might succeed before he took me down.

The other good news was, Shift loved Ronnie more than anything in the world so he didn't play me... too much.

The bad news was, he was in my life and therefore I was sitting outside a prison in southern California in my 2011 electric blue Charger with the two wide, white racing stripes that went up the hood, over the roof and down the trunk and spoiler waiting for a man named Ty Walker to be released from prison.

Shift did not give me a full brief about this assignment. He told me to be sitting right where I was at noon, to wait for Walker, to call him the minute Walker got released and then to take further directions from Walker. He also told me Walker would know it was me and my Charger waiting for him.

I took a week's vacation to do this. I had nothing else planned for my vacation and Shift was footing this bill so I thought... whatever. I thought this mainly because that was the only thing I *could* think. Shift didn't take no for an answer very often and Shift freaked me out. He loved Ronnie, this was true, they weren't blood but they were closer than it. But Shift was not right. Not at all. There wasn't something missing in Shift that most other human beings had. There were *multiple* somethings missing. And all the things that were missing were the good things like compassion, humor, decency, honesty.

He knew about loyalty. He knew brotherly love. That was all he knew. Other than that, he had no morals that I'd witnessed. None.

And Ronnie was dead.

When Ronnie was alive, he stood between Shift and me and he stood between Shift, his world and my world.

But Ronnie was dead, and I didn't suspect loyalty and brotherly love for a dead man would stop Shift from doing what he had to do to get what he wanted, including from me.

I didn't have to balance this line often but it was there. I knew I could push him and I also knew just how far I could push him. And, for whatever reason, me picking up Ty Walker was important to him. Important enough that I knew Shift's loyalty to Ronnie would vanish if I pushed him too hard and then I'd topple over that line.

I didn't need that shit.

So there I was, waiting for a soon-to-be ex-con to walk out of prison.

I sat in my car in the hot sun, no breeze flowing through my opened windows, thinking that it seemed like I spent a lifetime doing this kind of crap to steer clear of shit. It was exhausting. I was tired of it. Bone tired. And scared. Because I knew the odds were against me that I could stay clear of it. With Shift in my life and my number on his phone, someday he'd need me to do something and it would be something where I'd get hit with shit.

I had to get out.

I glanced at my watch to see it was twelve oh seven then I glanced down the tunnel again and something was moving through the shimmers. That path was long and the heat on the day was immense so I didn't see much but something made me keep watching.

And as the thing moving through the shimmers formed into a man, I kept watching as my breath started sticking in my throat.

Then the man kept getting closer, coming into focus through the heat waves, and my breath grew shallow as my body got still.

I didn't blink. I didn't move. I just watched that man coming at me and my car.

He got even closer and my body moved for me. I didn't tell it to move, it just did. Without taking my eyes off him, my hand reached for the door handle, released it and I unfolded out of the car, losing sight of him only when the roof was in my way for less than a second.

Shit.

Shit, shit, *fucking shit*!

He was huge. *Huge*. I'd never seen a man that big. He had to be six foot five, six foot six, maybe even taller.

His shoulders were immensely broad. The wall of his chest was just that. *A wall.* His hips were narrow, his thighs enormous. He was muscle from neck down, pure, firm, defined muscle. I saw it through his skintight black t-shirt, his tattooed arms, his jeans that tightened on his thighs as he moved.

His hair was black and clipped short on his head, another tat drifted up his neck.

His jaw was square and strong. No stubble. Clean-shaven. His brow was heavy, his eyebrows black, arched and thick but the left one had a line through it, a scar that matched the smaller one under the eye.

But this scar did nothing, not one thing, to mar his utterly perfect features. Strong, straight nose. High, cut cheekbones. Full lips. His eyes were shaped like almonds, turned slightly down at the sides and ringed, even when he was the width of my car away, I could still see, by thick, curling black lashes.

That said, his face, though sheer male beauty, was blank. Scary blank. Expressionless. Completely. His eyes were on me standing in my opened door watching him round the hood and turning with his movements. But there was nothing in those eyes. Nothing. Void.

It was terrifying.

Ronnie and Shift didn't hang out with good people. They were the dregs of society, but even dregs had dregs and the dregs of the dregs were who Ronnie and Shift hung out with. Again, it didn't happen often but it wasn't like I hadn't come into contact with some of these people. And I didn't like being around them but I learned a long time ago to hide that.

But this man, Ty Walker, was something else.

I did not think he was the dregs of the dregs. Or even the dregs.

I just had no idea *what* he was except downright terrifying.

I made an almost full circle as he cleared my door and walked half a step in, pinning me between him and the car, and I had to tilt my head way, way, *way* back to look up at him.

It was not an optical illusion, a trick of the heat waves. He was *tall* and he was *huge.*

And also, his eyelashes were long and curly.

Extraordinary.

I'd never seen eyes that shape, lashes that thick and curly. I'd never seen any single feature on any living thing as beautiful as his eyes.

He stared down at me with his beautiful but blank eyes and my only thought was that he surely could lift one of his big fists and pound me straight through the asphalt with one blow to the top of my head.

"Uh…hey," I pushed out between my lips, "I'm Lexie."

He stared down at me and said not a word.

I swallowed.

Then I said, "Shift wants a call the minute you're out. I, uh…"

I stopped speaking because he leaned into me with an arm out and I couldn't stop myself from pressing my back into the car. But he just pulled my cell from my hand, straightened as he flipped it open, his gorgeous eyes staring at it as his thumb moved on the keypad. Then he put it to his ear.

Two seconds later, he said in a deep voice that I felt reverberating in my chest even though he was three feet away, "I'm out."

Then he flipped the phone closed and tossed it to me.

Automatically, my hands came up and I bobbled it but luckily caught it before it fell to the asphalt at our feet.

"Keys," he rumbled, and I blinked.

"What?"

His big hand came up between us, palm to the sky, and I looked down at it to see his black tats and the veins sticking out on his superhumanly muscled forearm.

"Keys," he repeated.

My eyes went back to his beautiful ones.

"But…it's my car."

"Keys," he said again, same rumble, same tone, no impatience, no nothing, and I got the sense he'd stand there all day fencing me in and repeating that word until I complied.

I swallowed.

Hmm.

I was thinking I didn't want to spend the whole day in the hot sun having a conversation with a mountain of a man where his only contribution was one one-syllable word.

"They're in the ignition."

"Passenger seat," he replied, and I wondered if he knew any verbs.

I didn't think it wise to ask this question. I nodded and noticed he didn't move. There was a slip of space on either side of him between door and car but only a small slip. He didn't intend to get out of my way.

I turned sideways, sucked in my gut and squeezed by him, the front of my body skimming the hard side of his, the back of it skimming the car door.

I got free and moved around the trunk to the passenger side.

He'd adjusted the seat and folded his big bulk into the driver's side by the time I angled in the passenger side.

The second I pulled the door shut, my precious baby roared to life.

He didn't put his seat belt on or wait for me to do so as he skidded out, wheels screeching against asphalt and we took off through the waves of heat down the road in front of the prison.

Shit.

* * *

"Two," Ty Walker rumbled at the woman who was wearing a yellow waitress dress, white cuffs on her short sleeves, a little white apron, a little white cap on her head, the whole outfit belonging in a sitcom from the '70s.

She had her head tilted way back and she was staring up at him blinking rapidly, easily read expressions moving across her face. Awe. Fear. Titillation. Curiosity. Lust.

"Two," Ty Walker repeated when she didn't move then he added, "Booth." Then he finished, "Back."

She kept blinking.

I stepped in front of him and waved my hand in hopes of getting her attention.

She blinked a couple of times and her head tipped down so she could look at me but it was still tilted back because I was also taller than her and I would be even if I wasn't wearing platform sandals.

"Hi," I said chirpily. "Can we have a booth at the back of the restaurant?"

She stared at me, her eyes flicked up to Walker then they came back to me and she nodded. She turned to the hostess stand, grabbed a couple of menus and hustled through the diner to the back where there was an open booth. She slapped the menus on the table and Walker rounded her and sat with his back to the wall. I slid in on the other side.

"Thanks," I said, smiling at her.

"Coffee," Walker said over me. "Now."

She nodded quickly.

He kept speaking. "Bacon, crispy, double order. Sausage links, double order. Four pancakes. Four eggs, over medium. Four slices of bread. Hash browns, double order. After the coffee."

She blinked at him and it hit me that was the most he'd said since our hourlong ride from the prison to this diner consisted of no talk at all. And it also hit me that maybe he actually *didn't* know any verbs since he still hadn't used any but one and that was to tell Shift he was out. Even so, he'd only used two words to do that.

Then she looked at me.

"I don't know what I want to eat yet but a Diet Coke would be sweet. I'll take a look at the menu. If you can get my guy here his food, though, that would be good," I said to her. "He's, uh… hungry," I finished, pointing out the obvious since he ordered enough to feed four.

"We have Diet Pepsi," she whispered, her whisper holding a tremor of fear, like me not getting Coke would send Walker into a violent rage the bloody results of which would make network news.

"That works too." I smiled at her again.

She nodded and rushed away.

I looked at Walker. He was looking out the window.

Then I looked at the menu.

She came with the coffee first and I ordered a tuna melt and curly fries. She came back with my diet. Then she came with his food before my tuna melt. Finally, she delivered my sandwich.

By this time, Walker was almost done with his food.

And, I will note, he said not one word throughout.

As I chewed a fry, I figured it was time for me to suck it up and attempt conversation if just to find out what was next.

"Is it good?" I asked as he shoved pancake into his mouth, thinking to ease into it.

His eyes cut to me.

What he did not do was speak. He just chewed and swallowed while forking into pancake and, once he swallowed, he shoved more pancake in.

Then his eyes moved through the diner and didn't come back to me as he continued to scan his surroundings.

I tried again, deciding on a more direct approach as, clearly, this guy was not into idle chitchat.

"So, um…what's next on the agenda?"

He looked at me again. Then he speared a sausage link with his fork, brought it to his well-formed lips and bit it in half with even, very white, extremely strong-looking teeth.

He did this and he didn't answer.

So I kept trying. "It would kinda be nice to know, uh…what we're doing and, um…where we're going," I told him.

He ate the rest of the sausage link.

He again didn't answer.

"Uh…Ty—" I started, but he finally spoke and when he did, he spoke over me.

"Name," he rumbled.

"Name?" I asked, confused.

His beautiful eyes didn't leave me and he also didn't explain.

"You mean *my* name?" I asked.

Again, he continued to stare at me without saying a word.

"Lexie," I told him, guessing that's what he meant and not pointing out I'd already introduced myself.

"Full name," he said then speared another sausage link.

While he bit off half, I answered, "Alexa Anne Berry."

He chewed. He swallowed.

"Priors?" he asked, and I felt my brows draw together.

"Sorry?" I asked back.

"You got a record?"

I was surprised at this question for two reasons. One, he'd used his first verb, and I had convinced myself he only knew caveman-speak. Two, it was a weird question.

"No," I answered. "No record."

Or, at least, not one that wasn't sealed. What could I say? There was a reason Ronnie was my boyfriend since high school. I'd been wild. It was just, back then, he wasn't. Then I stopped being wild, he'd started and he did it better than me. I had a juvenile record but that didn't count. Or I told myself that.

His gorgeous eyes did a head to chest and back again and his head tipped very slightly to the side.

Then he asked, "Sweep?"

"What?" I asked back and also I was back to confused.

"You get picked up in a sweep? Somethin' that didn't stick."

I shook my head, still confused. "A sweep for what?"

"Solicitation," he answered, and my back went straight.

That's when I knew he thought I was one of Shift's girls.

I leaned in and whispered on a slight annoyed hiss, testing the boundaries, I knew, but pissed enough to do it, "I'm not a prostitute."

And I couldn't believe he'd ask it. I mean, did I *look* like a prostitute? *No!* And I'd been around enough of them to know. Sure, one could say the ribbed white tank and low-rider, khaki shorts I was wearing weren't the height of fashion, but they weren't slut clothes.

Even if I was wearing (very cute, in my opinion) tan, wide-strapped platform wedges (that still took me nowhere near his height).

It was hot out there!

And I wore high heels. It was what I did. It was who I was. A lot of women who weren't prostitutes wore high heels. Even with shorts.

"Shift knows two types of women, whores and junkies. You a junkie?"

"No," I snapped and sat back. "Jesus, of course not."

Now he was really ticking me off because I'd been around junkies too and I *really* didn't look like any of them. My hair was clean, for one. And I'd had it trimmed not a week ago. I had body fat, for another. Maybe a wee bit too much so, seriously, not a strung-out junkie.

"Shift knows two types of women, whores and junkies," he repeated. "Which one are you?"

"Neither," I bit off.

"Shift knows two types of women, whores and junkies," he said yet again. "He sent you which means he knows you so which one are you?"

Okay, now I just *was* really ticked off.

Therefore I replied, "You can ask it again and again, Mr. Humongo, but the answer doesn't change."

This was the wrong thing to do. I knew it when he instantly dropped his fork on his plate and both hands flashed out, catching mine by the wrists. He pulled them and, incidentally, *me* to him across the table, my arms insides up. His chin tilted down and his eyes did a scan of my upper extremities.

He was looking for tracks.

Asshole.

I made a mental note that he might be large but that didn't mean he couldn't move fast.

Then I yanked at my hands.

He didn't release them so I hissed, "Let me go."

He let me go and grabbed his fork. Then he ate the rest of the sausage.

I sucked in breath thinking maybe I should have pushed this particular favor with Shift, as in, put my foot down, refused to do it and took my chances.

Just driving across a few states, picking up some guy from prison, taking him wherever. That's what I thought it was.

It was never just that with Shift.

I should have known better.

"Toes," he muttered, dropping his fork and going after a piece of toast.

"What?" I asked, going after another fry but finding myself not hungry though thinking that my situation was uncertain and therefore I should probably eat when I had the opportunity.

His eyes came to me.

They were light brown. I just noticed that. The shape and the eyelashes had taken all my attention so I missed that they were light brown. This was a little surprising considering his skin tone said he was a mutt and that mutt definitely included African-American. There was Caucasian in him, I was guessing, but no more than half. His skin was as perfect as the rest of him but dark-toned and not with Italian olive undertones but definitely black. Whoever's genes formed him, they gave him the best of the both of them. At least in the looks department. Personality was seriously up for debate.

"Shoot up between the toes," he explained, and my thoughts went from the color of his eyes, the perfection of his skin and his luck with heredity to our annoying conversation.

"I told you, Walker, I'm not a junkie. I've never shot up anything, on my arms, between my toes, *anywhere*," I stated then bit into the fry maybe a little angrily but still, what the fuck?

And further to what the fuck, why was he asking me these questions?

He studied me, eyes still blank, nothing working back there or nothing he'd give away. But his gaze didn't leave my face.

This lasted a while. It lasted while he chewed on his toast and I made a dent in my fries. It lasted long enough for me to wish he'd scan the restaurant or stare out the window again.

Then he declared on a low, knowing rumble, "You spread for him."

I stopped avoiding his study of me and looked back at him. "What?"

"Surprising," he muttered, going back to his fork and his pancakes.

I guessed as to his meaning and informed him, "I'm not Shift's bookie."

His eyes shot from his pancakes to me.

"Come again?"

"I'm not Shift's bookie," I repeated. "I don't do a spread for him."

He stared at me.

Then he whispered, "Jesus."

"I work retail," I told him.

He stared at me more.

"I'm a buyer," I continued. "At Lowenstein's department stores."

He continued to stare at me.

Then he asked, "How'd he tap that?"

"What?" I asked back.

"A buyer for a fuckin' department store. How'd Shift tap that?"

I shook my head again, my eyes narrowing and I repeated, "What?"

"Why do *you*," he tipped his head at me as if I didn't know who he meant by "you," "spread for him?"

"I'm telling you, I'm not his bookie. He doesn't place bets with me. And anyway, what bookie would run an errand for a guy like Shift?"

Jeez, maybe he had a hearing problem.

He leaned toward me and said quietly, "Spread." I opened my mouth to reply but he went on, "Your legs."

I blinked.

Then I got him.

My back went straight.

Then I snapped, "I don't *sleep with Shift.* Gross! Are you crazy?"

He sat back and stared at me again. He dropped his fork, grabbed his cup of coffee and stared at me while he took a sip. Then he kept staring at me as he put his coffee cup back.

I was over the staring so I told him, "This conversation is bizarre. Maybe you might want to say what's on your mind or ask what you want to know, like, straight out and try not to annoy me seeing as I'm not a prostitute, junkie, bookie or sleeping with Shift or anyone like him but instead I'm a buyer at a mid-to-upscale department store."

"All right," he agreed immediately. "What the fuck are you doin' here?"

"Shift asked me to do him a favor."

"And how does a buyer for a department store know Shift?"

"We had a mutual acquaintance. That acquaintance died," I replied, just as immediately. "Unfortunately, the relationship didn't die with that acquaintance because Shift's an asshole. He sometimes invades my life and asks me to do stuff. It's healthier and less of a pain in the ass to agree. So, he asked me to do this, he's footing the bill and I'm here."

"No marker?" he asked.

"As in Shift calling in one?" I asked back.

"Or you givin' him one," he replied.

I shook my head. "I don't want anything from Shift so, no. I've never asked and there will never be a time when I'll need to call on Shift to do *anything* for me. There's no marker involved."

"But you're still here."

I was sitting across from him so I didn't think that merited a response.

"People don't do somethin' for nothin', 'specially bitches like you," he noted.

I ignored him calling me a bitch, something Shift and his crew did frequently. I also didn't get into what kind of "bitch" he thought I was.

Instead, I stated, "You obviously know Shift."

"Unfortunately," he answered, and this surprised me. First, it indicated we had something in common. Second, it was a five-syllable word. Third, Shift acted like this guy was important to him in some way. It occurred to me only then that when he phoned Shift, they didn't have a heartfelt conversation about his joy at his newfound freedom. In fact, except for Shift (probably) greeting him, he'd said two words to him.

I found this intriguing.

I also didn't get into that.

As far as I was concerned, I was going to drop this guy off wherever he wanted to go (and I hoped that wasn't northern Canada) or, more to the point, let him drive himself wherever he wanted to go. Then I was going to go back to my apartment, my job and my frequent musings about pulling up stakes and getting far, far away from Duane "Shift" Martinez.

What I did do was take a chance.

And the chance I took was sharing, openly and honestly.

So I leaned forward and said quietly, "We're connected, Shift and me, not by my choice. I do not want him in my life but he wants to be there and he stays there. He can make things difficult for me just being Shift. I know this. I avoid this. And the way I avoid this is, when he calls me and asks me to do something, I do it. He knows where my boundaries are and, so far, he's respected them. I'm not stupid. I know he'll push those boundaries and I know I have to get out from under this before he does but it takes a lot of shit to start a new life and I only have half of that shit. The half being me *wanting* to start it. The money, the job, the destination, all that I *don't* have. So, until then, he calls, he asks, I do and he stays in the shadows of my life instead of taking center stage and fucking everything up. Hence," I threw out a hand, "I'm here. Simple as that."

His beautiful eyes held mine.

Then he grunted, "Phone."

I blinked.

Then I turned to my purse, dug in, pulled out my phone and handed it to him.

He took it and slid out of the booth, saying, "You finish, pay the bill. Meet you at the car."

Then he walked out of the diner.

Ty

"Jackson," Tatum Jackson said in Ty Walker's ear.

"Jackson, Walker," Ty Walker replied.

Silence for a long moment then, "Shit, fuckin' hell, Ty?"

"Yep."

Another pause then, "Shit, brother, you out?"

"Yep. Today."

Another pause before, "Ty, fuck, Wood told me it was soon but I didn't know it was today." He paused again then quietly, "Fuck, Ty, good to hear from you, man." Another pause then, "Where are you?"

Walker didn't respond to that. Instead he said, "Got somethin' I need you to do."

More silence then, "Talk to me."

"Alexa Anne Berry. Dallas resident. Buyer at Lowenstein's department store. I need everything you can get on her."

"Walker, I'm a bounty hunter, not a PI," Jackson reminded him.

"You got resources. You got connections. I'm askin' you to use them."

Pause then, "Who is this woman?"

"I'm marryin' her tomorrow."

Silence.

Walker broke it. "You do this for me, I owe you."

"You're getting married?" Tate Jackson asked, disbelief clear in his tone.

"Yep."

"Tomorrow?"

"Yep."

"No joke?"

"Nope."

"Fuckin' hell, brother, who is she? How'd you meet her?"

"Doesn't matter. You gonna look into her?"

Pause then, "I'll do what I can do, Ty, but I don't know how much I can pull together before tomorrow."

"Doesn't matter. We're gettin' married tomorrow. You find shit, I'll deal with it."

"Don't you know her?"

Ty Walker thought about the woman he left behind in the booth.

He didn't know her. Not at all.

He knew she had great fucking legs, fantastic fucking tits, a generous, round ass and more fucking hair than he'd ever seen on any woman's head. It looked thick, it looked soft and he knew it'd feel good trailing on his skin. He knew she spoke with her eyes *and* her face even before words came out of her mouth. He knew he wanted to taste her pussy and he knew he wanted it in a way that he'd want it even if he wasn't in a situation where he hadn't tasted any pussy for five very long fucking years.

And he knew he was going to marry her tomorrow.

"I know enough," Walker answered.

Silence.

Then, "Ty, brother, is this a big setup? Can you delay? Give me a chance to—"

"I'm not asking for marriage counseling, Tate," Walker said low. "I'm askin' a favor. You gonna do that for me?"

Silence then, "You know I will."

Walker knew he would.

"You comin' home?" Jackson asked.

He felt his blood heat and his voice was like the rumble before the break of thunder when he whispered, "Oh yeah."

More silence.

Jackson heard the rumble and Tatum Jackson was far from stupid so he knew what it meant.

Therefore Jackson stated, "You're not gonna let it lie."

No he fucking wasn't. He was not going to fucking let it lie. No fucking way.

No *fucking* way.

He didn't answer.

Jackson went on, "Best thing you could do is let it lie. It's done. Move on. You come home, Wood'll take you on. You don't want that, we'll find you something. You got friends, brother, and you know it. We'll set you up."

This was easy for him to say. Five years of his life hadn't been stolen then flushed down the toilet. He didn't have a record. He wasn't an ex-con needing to lean on friends for a fucking job. He didn't rot in a cell, sharing air with scum, eating shit food, no pussy, no beer, told when he could sleep, when he could eat, when he could play ball, when he could work out, what he could wear, what he could read, watch on fucking television. No choice. No freedom. None. Constantly looking over his shoulder. Forced to use his fists to make his point and keep the jackals at bay.

All that shit for five years.

Five years.

Only to come out and have a tall, leggy, rounded, beautiful woman with a fantastic ass wearing a tight tank, short shorts and sexy shoes back away from him and press herself into a car just because he leaned in to grab her fucking phone when that shit would *not* happen with *any* woman five years ago.

Yeah. Easy for him to say.

"I'll talk to Wood when we get home," Walker told him.

"That'd be good," Jackson said quietly. "And it'll be good to see you."

Yeah. It would be good to see Tate. And Wood. And even Krystal though that bitch was a pain in the ass and she was a pain in the ass mostly because she was a bitch. Still, if she liked you, she was good people. If she liked you, she was the best people you could have. And luckily she liked him and she'd done what she could. So had Tate. So had Wood. So had Pop, Stella and Bubba. But none of them could do anything to stop the shit storm swirling around Ty Walker.

"I'll look into Alexa," Jackson said.

"Lexie," Walker corrected.

"Come again?"

"She calls herself Lexie."

"Right," Jackson muttered, a smile in his voice, not getting it but thinking he did.

"Catch you at Bubba's in a few days," Walker said, referring to the bar Tate owned with Krystal.

"Lookin' forward to it, Ty," Jackson replied.

Walker flipped the phone shut.

Then he scanned the parking lot.

He saw the car that picked them up a mile from the prison.

Shit tail. Total shit. How did these fucking guys take him down? They were all part idiot.

Except Fuller. Fuller was all asshole. All asshole with a badge. Not a good combination.

His eyes moved from the car into the diner. Lexie was at their table, paying the waitress while smiling at her.

He took in that smile.

The bitch had a fantastic smile. Nearly as good as her tits, not as good as her ass and nowhere near as good as her legs. Still, it was good.

She finished paying and walked toward the doors, hitching her purse strap up on her shoulder with one hand, her other hand going into her hair at her forehead, pulling the thick, shining, waving dark mass back, lifting a huge bunch of it at the back of her head and shaking it a couple of times before dropping it only for it to fall into and around her face again, settling on her shoulders and streaming down her back.

He felt his cock twitch.

Fucking magnificent.

Shift chose well. Who knew that useless, piece-of-shit motherfucker had the likes of Lexie on tap? It was a miracle.

He watched her move and noticed she walked in those shoes like she was barefoot. Her hips swayed with her strut, the lifting of her arms moved her tits and, when he could tear his eyes off her, he saw the two men sitting at stools at the counter watched her every move, swiveling around so they wouldn't lose track of her.

Looking back at her he noticed she was oblivious. Completely.

Walker had not said no to Shift sending a girl in his stable but he had said no junkies though considering Shift was a useless, piece-of-shit motherfucker, Walker expected he'd have to take what he got or, if she was unacceptable, scrape her off and find someone who would serve his purposes. It would be a frustrating delay. He had work to do.

But she had to be right.

And it went without saying Lexie Berry was right.

It didn't sit well with him that she was on Shift's hook and how she was on it. In fact, what she said to him at the table he still felt like it clogged his throat. She had no love for Shift. Just fear he'd fuck up her life or worse, and obviously she knew him enough because that useless, piece-of-shit motherfucker would do it and before he did it, he wouldn't blink.

What he didn't get was how she ever got connected to Shift. No light shined in the world of Duane Martinez and light shone off Lexie Berry like a beacon.

But he'd find out or, more accurately, Tate would do it for him.

He would have preferred one of Shift's whores who would know her place and do what she was told. Walker had a feeling Lexie Berry was not going to do that. Clearly, the sass she was holding in check when she met him had broken through if the attitude she threw at him and her Mr. Humongo comment was anything to go by. But Walker knew he, like the vast majority of the human population who happened to have dicks, would put up with a whole fuck of a lot from Lexie Berry, and he happened to have a dick.

Just as long as she did what she was told in the end, even if she gave him shit before doing it.

And there was no denying the cover Lexie Berry could provide was a far sight better than one of the girls in Shift's stable, considering the few he'd seen. Fuller would look into her, Walker had no doubt. But if she was a whore, there would be little question now that Ty Walker would accept whatever he could get. Pussy was pussy, Walker had always liked his pussy and everyone knew that. Too much, it would turn out. But now, his future limited in a way he'd never have foreseen just because he liked his cunt, he'd have to take what he could get.

So Lexie Berry was definitely a miracle.

As she made it to the door, she'd been looking down, digging into her purse and when she pushed through, she lifted her head and came out into the sunshine squinting her eyes but pulling out a pair of shades. She flicked the arms out with a practiced movement of her wrist and shoved them on her nose.

There it was. The shades, the purse, the shoes, they all said buyer for a mid-to-upscale department store. The tank and the shorts she could get anywhere but those shades, that purse and those fucking shoes said class.

Yeah, Lexie Berry was a miracle.

Her shades hit him, her head tilting back for them to do so and when she got close, she asked, "Ready?"

As answer, he beeped the locks, opened the door and folded into her sweet ride.

CHAPTER TWO

Be Happy

"Mr. and Mrs. Walker, king-size bed, not by an elevator or any fuckin' vending machines."

I pressed my lips together to keep quiet.

We were in Vegas, the slot and video poker machines ringing behind us as we stood at the reception desk and Walker checked us in.

It was very early morning. The sun was shining and it was already so hot out there, I broke into an instant sweat the minute I unfolded out of my Charger, and this happened even though we were under an awning so the sun wasn't directly hitting me.

Luckily, we only stood out there for long enough for Walker to grab the huge-ass, black duffel Shift had put in my trunk and warned me not to open or "hell would be paid" and then heft out my roller bag and drop it to its wheels on the pavement. He walked away, leaving my bag where he put it. I yanked up the handle, followed him to the valet rolling my bag behind me. He exchanged keys for ticket, pocketed the ticket and entered, destination: reception desk.

We drove all night. For some reason, since our destination was obviously Vegas, Walker took what turned out to be a circuitous route that added hours onto our travel time. He did not explain this to me, any of it, where we were going or why we took that route. Conversation was nonexistent. I listened to my iPod and slept a bit.

Now he was checking us into *one* room with a king-size bed. And he was doing it under Mr. and Mrs. Walker.

I did not think this was good.

"How many nights will you be staying, sir?" the desk clerk asked.

"Three," Walker answered.

Oh shit. Three? Three nights?

What were we going to do in Vegas for three nights?

"Excellent." He picked up a form and put it on the counter. "If you could fill that in and give me a credit card—"

"Cash," Walker rumbled, and the clerk looked from his computer to Walker.

"That's fine, sir. But we like to have a credit card on file just in case you use the minibar, should you like a movie—"

"Cash," Walker repeated.

The clerk blinked up at him, clearly having been lost in a fog of customer service and seeing just about everything in Vegas, he was used to blocking it out. Now he was fully taking in Walker and processing what he saw, all of what he saw and just how much of it there was.

He swallowed, his Adam's apple bobbing then he started, "It's policy, sir, to—"

I stepped in mainly to move this along because I knew Ty Walker would repeat the word "cash" until we were physically ejected or the clerk gave up. And I needed to, first, see what the hell was up with him getting us one room, second, attempt again to figure out what was happening and my part in it, third, take a shower and fourth, sleep in a bed or, better yet, buy a swimsuit and sleep by a pool.

I dug in my purse saying, "I'll give you my card. You can have it on file but when we check out, we'll pay in cash. Cool with you?"

The clerk's relieved eyes slid to me and he nodded.

"Room safe," Walker stated at this point.

"Of course," the clerk murmured on a bow of his head toward Walker. "All our rooms have safes."

Walker stared at him half a second then his eyes did a sweep of the immediate area.

I handed the clerk my card, filled out the registration form, took my card back and the clerk handed Walker our little envelope with its keycards, wisely not noting that my credit card said Alexa Berry and not Alexa Walker. After I filled out the form, as he processed us, I tried not to think where Ty Walker would get cash to pay for a swanky Vegas hotel room considering he walked out of prison not twenty-four hours ago with nothing (that I knew of) but the clothes on his back. He didn't even have one of those big plastic Ziploc bags in his hand holding his belongings that recently released prisoners on TV shows were given.

Nothing.

But that duffel.

A duffel packed by Shift.

Shit.

"Room six twenty-three. You'll find the elevators over there." He pointed to his left but Walker was already walking that way.

I smiled at the clerk, expressed mumbled words of gratitude, grasped the handle on my bag and followed Walker.

He tagged the button before I got there and I stopped close to him.

"Hubby, we need to chat," I said quietly.

His chin dipped into his neck to look down at me, his face still as impassive as ever and then his head turned and he looked over his shoulder.

When he kept looking, his eyes honing in on something and staying there, I turned to look too.

He was looking at a man who was standing at the reception desk. He was super slim and when I say that I mean bag-of-bones thin. It was a wonder his clothes stayed on him, he was so skinny. He had light brown hair with a hint of red in it but he didn't have much of it. It was thin everywhere, seriously light on the top and clipped super short. He wore glasses. His features were pointy. Considering he wasn't much to look at, I was surprised to see his clothing was of very good quality and suited him as best it could given his physique.

And he was looking right at Ty Walker, as bold as you please, checking in at the reception desk but staring at Walker at the same time looking knowing in a way that made something unpleasant crawl along my skin. If he sneered, I wouldn't have been surprised. But it did surprise me that this obvious weakling was so bold considering he was a third of the man standing at my side (and a third was being generous) and the man standing at my side could easily break him in half.

But he was.

In-your-face bold.

How weird.

"Do you know him?" I asked as the elevator chimed and then it happened.

Ty Walker touched me for the first time. That was, the first time he touched me when he wasn't looking for needle tracks at the same time annoying me.

His fingertips went into the small of my back and they pressed forward so I moved into the elevator rolling my bag behind me. His hand dropped away, he turned to face front and automatically I did too as he leaned to the side, tagging the six button. After those few annoying seconds an elevator stays open for whatever reason it does, the doors slid closed.

But I barely registered any of this.

Because I could feel five hot marks burning into the small of my back where he touched me. The touch was light and it didn't last long but I still felt them burning. They were like a brand searing into my skin.

As the elevator went up, I waited for them to fade. I wanted them to fade. But they didn't fade. They stayed burning hot and deep, and I'd never experienced anything like it. I didn't even know what it was. I just knew it was profound. I knew it was life-altering. I knew somehow that, even if the burn was to fade, I'd never forget that elevator ride my whole life.

The elevator stopped, the doors slid open and, my mind still on the burn, I didn't think as I followed him out, down the hall to a room. He used the keycard and entered, not holding the door open for me.

Mindlessly, I pushed the door open as it started to close and followed.

The door closed behind me.

Walker dumped his duffel on the low, wide shelf opposite the bed that was meant for luggage, one side of that shelf going up with three drawers under it, a big, flat-screen TV on top of it, the other side doing the same with a cabinet under it probably containing a minibar, an attractive leatherette holder on top holding the TV remote.

He immediately zipped the duffel open. I came to a halt at the mouth of the hall that led into the room and righted my bag on the floor at my side.

My mind went off the slowly fading burn of his touch at my back as it registered on me it was a nice room, really, *really* nice. It was large, larger than I expected, larger than I knew hotel rooms could be. The furniture was stylish, the wood gleaming, all of it obviously exceptionally clean. There was a downy comforter with an attractive cover on the huge bed, not a thin bedspread. There were even toss pillows. Two sweep-lined armchairs at either side of a table at the back in one corner by the window. A standing lamp rounding out the seating area. An elegant desk with a lamp on top facing the room at a diagonal in the other corner.

In fact, I'd never been in a nicer room.

Actually, I'd been in very few hotel rooms at all in my thirty-four years.

Ronnie had promised a lot of good times in fabulous places and, before he gave me his empty promises, there was a time in our life when his future was so bright, this room would have been a joke to us. Our future held travel all over, and everywhere we'd have the best of the best. The best rooms. The best food. The best champagne. The finest clothes. Sweet rides. Big houses. Cleaning ladies. We were going to live large. He told me I would drip gold. He meant it. He loved me that much, I would drip gold. He would make that happen for me.

Then he fucked it all up.

I didn't need gold. I just needed him. But still, he fucked it all up in the end. He fucked it up so badly, I didn't even have him.

I came out of my reverie when I heard something hit surface and my eyes focused on Walker.

Then I felt my eyes get wide.

He'd dug into the bag Shift packed for him and he was currently putting fat rolls of crisp, fresh bills wrapped tight in rubber bands on the wood above the minibar cabinet attached to the luggage shelf. The first roll had a twenty on the outside of it. The second, another twenty. The third, a fifty.

At the fifty, my breath started sticking in my throat.

The fourth, more twenties.

Then he came out with a gun clip, and it clattered on the wood by the bills as he dropped it there.

My breathing stopped.

Another gun clip. Another roll of fifties. A box of ammo. Another roll of twenties.

Then a gun.

I sucked in air.

"Um, darling?" I called on the exhale. "I'm thinking we need a family meeting."

Just his head turned, his body stayed bent over the bag and his light brown, almond-shaped, curly-lashed eyes hit mine. As usual, he did not speak.

I tipped my head to the unit. "What's with the bank and the firepower?"

His eyes stayed on me. Then he straightened and turned to me.

I braced in order not to flee though I didn't know why I didn't attempt escape. Probably because he'd proved his hands were fast and I didn't want to find out if his legs were just as fast.

He still didn't speak.

I carried on. "I mean, I'm no parole officer but it's my understanding ex-cons aren't allowed to be armed."

He finally spoke. "You don't have a record."

I felt my head jerk at the same time I was certain my eyes bugged out.

Then I breathed, "What?"

"Hit trouble, the .38 is yours."

At this juncture, I felt it was time to share.

I took two steps toward him and stopped.

"As I told you during our last and only conversation, Shift knows my boundaries. Any trouble we could," I lifted up my hands and his beautiful eyes moved to them as I did air quotation marks and said, "hit," then I dropped my hands and his eyes came back to mine as I continued, "that would require a .38 and half a dozen wads of cash is not within my acceptable boundaries."

He stared at me.

Then he walked the four steps to me (that, for my legs, would probably be around seven) and I found my purse being slid off my shoulder. I watched with no small amount of concern as he dug in it and was somewhat relieved when he pulled out my phone. He turned, tossed my bag across the room to the bed then turned back to me, flipped the phone open, used his thumb and put it to his ear.

I waited as it rang. So did he. Then he flipped it closed, opened it again, hit more buttons and put it to his ear.

I waited. So did he. Then he flipped it closed, opened it and repeat.

I waited. So did he.

Finally, he spoke. "It ain't Lexie, scum, it's Walker. What the fuck?"

I pressed my lips together because his face might still be blank but his voice was low and rumbling. Or lower and more rumbling than normal. I didn't know him very well but I felt this indicated extreme unhappiness.

"Yeah, with her, yeah," he growled into the phone confusingly (at least to me), paused then stated in a further growl, "Yeah, the bag ain't light." Another pause then, "She don't know jack." Another pause then, "Jesus Christ, you're worthless."

He flipped the phone shut and tossed it on the unit where it clattered. Then he looked at me.

"Family meeting," he said.

I was suddenly not feeling like having a family meeting.

I had no choice.

"He told you dick, didn't he?" he asked.

I nodded and wished he'd take a step back but still, I answered, "I'm sensing I didn't get a full briefing."

"What'd that piece of shit tell you?"

"That I was to pick you up and take you where you wanted to go."

"That's it?"

I thought about it. Then I amended, "Well, actually, his words were that I was to pick you up at noon, call him when you were out and take further directions from you."

And I had assumed by directions he meant directions to wherever Ty Walker called home or wanted to make his home. But I was thinking I assumed wrong.

"That's it?" he repeated.

Yep, I was wrong.

"That's it," I replied.

He pulled in breath through his nose, crossed his arms on his chest and his eyes locked with mine.

Then he told me what I'd already figured out. "He didn't give you a full briefing."

"Great," I muttered.

"He owes me," Walker stated, held my eyes but tipped his head to the desk to indicate what was on it. "Big," he finished.

I nodded.

He continued to hold my eyes and then he jerked his chin out at me and said low and quiet, "Big."

Oh *shit.*

"What?" I whispered as I took a step back.

"Don't move," he ordered, and I stopped because his order was firm and serious and I didn't want to test how firm and serious he was. "He didn't make it worth your while, I'll deal with him. So I'll make it worth your while."

"What..." My voice sounded choked so I swallowed then started again, "Make what worth my while?"

"You and me are getting married."

My head jerked again even as the rest of my body froze.

Then I said shrilly, "*What?*"

"I need a wife. You're her."

Oh shit. Shit. Shit. Fucking *shit*!

"Um..." I started, my heart hammering, the one room and marital status of check-in explained, my need to flee overpowering, my sense of self-preservation keeping me rooted to the spot but I got no further, he started talking.

"He didn't take care of you, I will. You need out from under him, I'll make that happen. You marry me, I pay you fifty thousand dollars. At the end, I deal with the divorce. Once it's done, you're clear. I'll see to it we're untied. All you'll have to do is sign the papers, you'll never see me again and I'll also see to it that wherever you decide to go, Shift doesn't follow."

"The end of what?" I asked.

"My business."

"What business?"

"That's need to know and when you need to know I'll tell you what you need to know."

In other words, I'd likely never know all of it just what I needed to know.

"The gun . . . the money?" I asked.

"I just got let outta prison. I wasn't in there while the Pope considered my sainthood. I got enemies."

"Oh God," I whispered.

"You're covered," he told me.

I'd heard that before and now the person who promised me that was dead and the person he promised to cover me from was the reason I was standing right where I was.

I shook my head. "I don't think—"

"I got no time and I got shit to do. You're gonna bail, you can walk out that door. I got nothin' to offer you but cash and my word. I can see you pickin' me up from prison, my word don't mean dick to you, but I'm tellin' you right now—and it's up to you to believe it or not—my word is solid. No harm will come to you and nothin' from my business will blow back on you. You'll be my wife, you'll act like my wife and you'll do it until this is done. That's it. Then we go our separate ways."

"I'll act like your wife?" I asked quietly.

He shook his head once. "You wanna let me into that pussy, I'll take it. No increase in money, I don't pay for pussy. That you give if you got a mind to give it. You don't, I'll find what I need elsewhere and that won't blow back on you either."

This was not exactly the romantic, tender marriage proposal every girl dreamed of.

"Ty," I started, lifting up a hand, palm out then dropping it. "I've been . . ." I hesitated. "I've managed to . . ." I stopped again.

"Jesus, spit it out," he rumbled.

I nodded and spit it out. "That world has been at the edge of mine a long time, pushing in, and I've managed to steer clear. I don't know what this business of yours is and I don't know you and I already have the leftover bullshit that comes from broken promises. I don't need more."

"I told you none of my shit would blow back on you," he reminded me.

"And I told you I've heard that before and here I stand," I reminded him.

He stared at me, still unreadable, but something about him made me think that he wasn't blank, he was alert and assessing and he gave no indication of it but it *felt* like he was reading me down to my bones.

Then he said quietly, "Shift has fucked you."

"I know," I said quietly back, and he had. Shift knew this. He knew Walker wanted this. He sent me anyway. He blew right through my boundaries, lying to me and putting me in the clutches of a huge, terrifying, taciturn, freshly released ex-con with enemies and a gun.

"This time, you walk out that door, nothin' bites you," Walker told me. "You go back to him, he'll find a way to fuck you worse and how he does it, you might not be walkin' out the door."

I pressed my lips together then unpressed them and whispered, "I know."

"I can get you clear of that."

I had to admit, that was definitely something to consider.

He kept talking. "Fifty G's will set you up anywhere you wanna go. I'll take care of Shift."

He held my eyes. I noted his were unwavering. He was hiding from me, I knew it. Though I figured you learned a poker face in prison, probably not healthy to wear your heart on your sleeve. But he held my eyes, he didn't look away, whatever he was hiding was his to hide from the world, not something he was specifically hiding from me.

And he was also not in my face. He wasn't pissed. He wasn't shouting. He wasn't threatening. He told me I could walk out and

I believed him. In fact, everything he told me, I believed. I'd been around a lot of the dregs, Ronnie saw to that, so I had a highly tuned bullshit detector. Whatever this man was, he was not bullshitting me.

And he could get me clear of Shift, I knew it. I knew it because Shift was scared of him, I could see this now. That was the reason behind the frantic phone call. He wanted to make sure Ty Walker got what he wanted and liked what he saw. He'd played me to make sure Walker didn't lose it and take what Shift owed him a different way.

And he was right, I pulled up stakes, fifty thousand dollars would set me up.

And I'd be clear of Shift.

And away from that life, clean and free.

Clean and free.

Finally.

"How long would this, um... business last?" I asked.

I didn't know if I was seeing things but I could swear it looked like his body relaxed even if the change was so slight it seemed like an illusion.

"Don't know," he answered.

"I have a job," I told him.

"You want clear of Shift, you gotta leave Dallas. You leave Dallas, you leave your job. Might as well do it now."

This was true. It sucked because I liked my job. I'd been working at Lowenstein's for nearly ten years. But I always knew I'd be leaving it one day, either when I gave up on Ronnie or when Ronnie made a break for it and took a chance on us and, more recently, to get away from Shift.

However...

"I didn't give notice."

"Emergency," he said.

"What?"

"Emergency leave of absence. You gotta look after your sick mom. Your mom don't get better, you don't go back. Shit happens. They'll deal."

"I don't have a mom."

He went silent and did that blank but still alert and assessing thing.

Then he said, "Your dad."

"I don't have one of those either."

Again, I could swear something happened to his body even though I couldn't be sure but this time it wasn't relaxing, it was tensing.

"Don't give a fuck who it is. A grandparent, whatever—"

I shook my head indicating I didn't have grandparents either.

He stared at me.

Then he whispered, "Jesus."

"Long story," I muttered.

He went silent again and stared at me.

This went on awhile.

Then he said, "I told you, got shit to do. I don't have time to give you a chance to consider your options. It's now or never. Walk out that door or stay and become Mrs. Walker."

I pressed my lips together.

Then I took the nanosecond he was giving me to consider my options.

Then I sucked in breath.

Then I asked, "Can I have the first shower?"

Ty

Lexie's phone rang as he walked out of the phone store. He yanked it out of his back pocket, turned it and saw the Colorado area code on the display, a number he knew. He flipped it open and put it to his ear.

"Yeah?"

"Bad news, brother," Tate's voice came at him, and Ty pulled in breath.

Tate had been hard at work, not a surprise.

That was because Tatum Jackson always had his back. He probably didn't sleep last night in order to have Walker's back.

"Yeah?" he repeated.

"Your woman, she likes clothes."

Walker's chest released.

"Already know that," he lied. He didn't know it but the weight of her bag meant she stuffed that fucker so full, the instant she opened it, it would explode all over the room.

Luckily, he'd given her her instructions and took off so he wasn't around when that happened.

So he reckoned it was a good guess.

And now he knew Jackson had pulled her credit.

Guess confirmed.

He listened to Tate's low laughter.

Then, "I bet."

"That all you got?" Walker asked.

"Yep. She's clean. No record. Four speeding tickets the last five years and a shitload of parking tickets. Your woman's got a need for speed and thinks she can park anywhere she wants and she does."

Walker would have guessed that too considering her ride. Not many women with classy shades, shoes and purses had rides that sweet. Hinted at a wild side. He thought it explained her connection with Shift but apparently it was something else.

"She carries debt, not a lot of it," Jackson continued. "Over two credit cards a little over a thousand dollars. All payments current though. She rents. Works steady. Saw her DMV picture, brother. The state employee who took that should win an award. Best driver's license picture I've seen in my life."

Lexie was photogenic. Also not surprising. Though, probably the picture was actually shit, she was just so beautiful even a shit photo looked good.

Though the debt, not good. Not smart. She should have worried less about clothes and more about getting herself out from under Shift's thumb.

"Sucks about her folks though," Jackson went on.

Fuck.

He found shade and moved under it.

Then he demanded, "Talk to me."

Silence then, "You don't know?"

"Don't know what you're gonna tell me," Walker evaded.

Pause then, "Right." Another pause then, "She's clean. Her parents were not."

Fuck.

He was silent. Jackson kept talking.

"Caught that, did a little digging and called a couple of guys. They're digging too. I'll know more but what I got, they were junkies. Made the news in Dallas thirty-four years ago. She was born in a crack house. Mother so gone, don't know she even knew she had a kid and probably a miracle the baby survived and wasn't fucked up, considering what the mom was doin' to her body. Someone in the house was together enough to phone emergency. They went in, got her, placed her with her grandparents. Don't know what went down after that until I get callbacks but I do know the mom OD'd five years later. Dad died four years after from internal injuries when he got his ass kicked by a loan shark."

He was right, it was definitely *fuck*.

"She was placed with her grandparents?" Walker asked.

"That's why I'm diggin'. It was the mom's parents. Death records show the grandma died when your girl was six. The grandpa died when she was thirteen. I don't have access to those kinds of files but my work takes me to Texas, got some people I know so I've contacted those who can access the files or know people who do. May take a couple of days."

"What about her dad's parents?"

"That was easy. Traced him, found out they died in a car accident when he was sixteen."

"Aunts? Uncles?"

"Mom, an only child. Dad had a sister but she didn't step in. Don't know why."

Foster care.

Walker looked across the street to their hotel thinking about

Lexie and her shades and high heels and short shorts and bright smile in foster care. Then, thirty-four years later, finding her shit tied to the likes of Shift.

Fuck.

Jackson spoke in his ear. "Ty, you're marryin' this girl, you don't know this shit?"

"Both of us prefer to look to the future," he lied again though he had no clue what Lexie preferred. However, that statement was pure bullshit from him. He was living in the past and would until mistakes were rectified.

Then, if he had a future, he'd look to it.

"That's good news," Tate said quietly, misreading him and Walker thought it was good this conversation was happening on the phone. He'd learned a lot in prison but he didn't expect part of that was pulling shit over on Tatum Jackson. "Though, that's true, why am I doin' what I'm doin'?"

"Can't be too careful."

"She know about you?"

"She picked me up outside the penitentiary yesterday."

Silence then Tate started digging, this time somewhere else.

"You meet her in Dallas before you came home and that shit went down with Fuller and Misty?"

"Yep." Another lie.

"Again, brother, seen her picture. How the fuck you leave that behind?"

"I think me bein' an idiot was proved in a courtroom, Tate."

This was no lie.

"Don't wanna stir up demons, Ty, but that shit, it's not on you, and everyone in town knows it. That was all Fuller."

He knew that. Oh yeah, he fucking knew that.

He didn't respond.

"It was me they targeted, fuck, anyone would have gone down," Tate told him. "Don't get buried under that shit. Rise above."

Again, Walker didn't respond.

Jackson waited for it then gave up.

"I'll keep diggin'. Call you back. It's tomorrow. When's the wedding?"

"She's shoppin' for a dress."

Or at least he hoped she was. He gave her a wad of cash and he had the valet ticket. The ticket was not insurance. All he had was hope she wouldn't bolt, but he wouldn't blame her if she did. The fact that she didn't walk out the door when he gave her the chance still surprised him. It sucked but he had Shift to thank for her not leaving. She was desperate, he played on that. He didn't like it but it worked in his favor and he had a mission, he was focused, so he used it.

That said, this was done, he'd set her up and, she was smart, she'd go onto a life where she never again had to make desperate, fucked-up decisions like marrying an ex-con she didn't know.

His response got a low chuckle from Jackson then, "I'm sure she is." Pause then, "I suspect she's good people, you're marryin' her so I'm glad she gave you a second chance, saw through that shit, knows what she's gettin'."

She had no fucking clue.

Time to move on. So he did, out from under the awning and down the sidewalk toward the jewelry store.

"How's Jonas?"

"Growin' so fast, Laurie can't keep him in clothes."

"Laurie?"

Pause then, "Fuck, man, forgot. I got married."

Walker stopped dead and he heard someone behind him let out a squeak and scuttle around him but he didn't move.

"No shit?"

A definite smile in his voice before, "No shit."

"The woman from the news," Walker stated.

"Yeah."

He tried to remember if he'd seen any photos of her when all that shit went down with Tate and that serial killer who had kidnapped his woman and stabbed her with the intent to rape her with that knife before he killed her, which, luckily, he didn't get around to doing. They'd reported it on television and during a variety of sports commentator shows, considering Tate had had a very short-lived career as a linebacker in the NFL.

He'd watched it in the joint, seen photos of Tate, none of his woman.

But he didn't care if she was butt ugly. She wasn't Neeta, Tate's old bitch from high school and on and off for what seemed would last an eternity. Fortunately, it didn't, and Tate got shot of her and could talk about being married with a smile in his voice. Unfortunately, Neeta had been one of the victims of the serial killer Tate tracked down. Neeta was so much of a pain in the ass she was the definition of a cunt, just a shade better than Misty but not by much. Still, no one deserved what went down with her.

Except, maybe, Misty. And he knew thinking that made him a dick and he didn't fucking care.

"Told her about you," Jackson said in his ear. "She's already conspiring with Maggie, planning a celebration for your return."

Fuck.

"Not necessary," Walker said as he started walking again.

"Don't fight it, Ty. When Laurie's in the mood to be friendly, no one can stop her. And you know Maggie."

Terrific.

"And, trust me, she cooks for you, you'll wonder why you even considered fighting it," Tate went on.

At least that was something.

He pushed open the doors and hit the plush interior of the exclusive jewelry store. The clerks looked up at him and he noticed two go pale. They were the men. The women had a different reaction.

They always did. Though they'd rethink their reaction if they knew he was an ex-con and what he was sent down for.

He didn't care. All he cared about was it was air-conditioned. Spending five years in a correctional institute in southern California, he'd had enough hot to last a lifetime. It sucked it was the beginning of summer. Even his hometown of Carnal in the Colorado Mountains would get hot.

But when winter hit... heaven.

"Gotta buy a ring, Tate," he muttered into the phone, going direct to one of the women who was smiling slow, turning fully to him, not knowing she was about to make one fuck of a commission.

"Right," Jackson replied.

"Got a new number. This is Lexie's phone. I'll text it to you."

"Right," Jackson repeated.

"Later."

"Later, and Ty?" he called.

"Yeah."

"Congratulations, brother. Be happy."

"Right."

Walker flipped the phone shut.

CHAPTER THREE

Signing Bonus

I SAT IN the passenger seat of my own car, the glossy violet and ice blue cardboard folder that carried our wedding photos and a large envelope with our marriage certificate was sitting on my thighs, a huge bouquet of roses was in my hand, the Vegas traffic was heavy, Walker was driving us back to the hotel.

We'd been married by Liberace. Not the real one, obviously, since he'd passed. A fake one. I didn't know you could be married by Liberace. I knew Elvis would marry you. Liberace, no.

I found this hilarious, totally loved it. If I knew you could be married by Liberace, even if I was head over heels in love with the man I married and thinking I was starting a life that would last forever, I'd blow off the traditional and go for Liberace in a chapel festooned with violet, ice blue and a liberal hand with silver gilding. It was freaking awesome.

But I wondered why Ty Walker chose Liberace. I didn't think he got a kick out of it because, as far as I could tell, he had no sense of humor…or any emotion, really. It was likely because it was the first wedding chapel we happened upon so he swung the Charger in.

When we arrived inside, the vestibule was packed. Two brides all kitted out in big dresses.

One had at least two dozen friends and family around her, groom in a tux, girlfriend in a bridesmaid dress, another male in a tux—wedding party. This was planned. They'd picked Liberace specifically. Their posse had come with them, vacation and big event.

The other bride and groom had about half a dozen friends around them, the bride's gown clearly off the rack and not fitting properly and her hair was a mess as was her makeup. Her groom was wearing shorts.

She'd probably donned that gown in the car. They'd been partying and were about two sheets to the wind, teetering on three. Not planned. Spontaneous but happy. Good times that may, or may not, be regretted in the morning. I couldn't tell. Right now they seemed giddy with happiness but it could be giddy with booze. They'd wake up tomorrow and realize they'd done the one thing that could happen in Vegas that didn't stay in Vegas. And looking at their loopy, drunken grins, I hoped they didn't care.

Walker walked me up to the desk that had a huge display of real wedding bouquets and shelves of boxed confetti in every color behind it and also behind it was a diminutive woman with loads of dyed dark hair ratted out into a hairstyle the likes of which I'd never seen and, not to be mean or anything, I hoped I'd never see again. She also was sporting an excess of bulky rhinestones, which adorned her at ears, neck, wrists and fingers, and so much makeup it was unreal. It wasn't a look I'd choose but she worked it, except the hairstyle.

"Love is in the air!" she cried when we stopped at the tall counter that was topped with glass under which were photos of happy couples, the bride and groom sandwiching a smiling-like-a-lunatic Liberace sporting an enormous, lilac-hued pompadour. These pictures intermingled with printed menus of wedding packages. "We've got a wait of about half an hour, a bit more. I hope that isn't a problem," she went on.

"Nope," Walker replied.

"Excellent," she breathed, clasping her hands in front of her then she took us both in. "What'll it be? Menu's on the counter. We got a basic version then add-ons or you could go with the deluxe package. And, I tell all my lovebirds, whatever you do, go for the bubble machine even if it's just as an add-on. Nothing says joy like bubbles," she advised.

I pressed my lips together to stop from giggling but even though I thought she was funny, I couldn't exactly argue with the fact that nothing said joy like bubbles. I'd just never thought of bubbles like that.

She looked behind us then at us. "You need witnesses?"

"Yep," Walker answered.

She leaned in. "We throw that in, freebie."

Walker just stared at her.

"That's great," I said.

"Basic," Walker said, and her smiling, love-is-in-the-air eyes went up to him and her face fell a little.

"Oh," she whispered.

"Cash," he added.

She gave him a top to waist and muttered, "Right." Then she moved to the cash register.

My eyes moved to the bouquets.

After Walker told me what I needed to know for now and gave me thousands of dollars to make it so, I'd braved the Vegas heat and gone shopping. I was exhausted. I wanted a shower and a nap but he was intent on getting this done and I figured, if we did it then it would be over, I wouldn't have a mind filled with whether or not I'd made the right decision or kicking myself for getting played by Shift rather than upping stakes and getting the fuck out of Dallas about thirty seconds after we laid Ronnie in the ground.

And as I tried on dress after dress trying to find one to get married in, I thought about the men in my life.

By the way, the first dress I'd been instructed to get I'd found right away. A wedding dress, not so easy. And, incidentally, I'd done a detour from Walker's instructions in order to buy a bikini. A hopeful effort that I might eventually get to veg beside a pool where every girl knows she can let the sun bake away her life, however crazy it is, and I needed that for certain.

In thinking about the men in my life, I started at the beginning and counted them down.

First, there was my grandfather. A decent enough guy if you didn't know him. Not so decent if you did.

Total shit at being a dad.

This was evidenced by the fact that my mother was a mess. He hadn't learned any lessons from what went bad with her before taking me on. This was because, first, he didn't want to learn and, second, he was the kind of man who always thought he was right so he didn't think there was anything *to* learn.

My mom flying off the rails was therefore all on her. Not on the fact that her mother was a weak woman cowed by an overbearing man and her father was more interested in football than fatherhood and expected the women in his life to toe the line and wasn't best pleased, and showed it, when they didn't do what he wanted even if he hadn't expended the effort to explain what he wanted.

There you go. Enough said about Granddad.

Then there was Ronnie.

And, enough said.

Then there was Shift.

Definitely enough said.

Now there was Ty Walker, an admittedly gorgeous and weirdly honest yet still unforthcoming ex-con who went to a pimp to get himself a wife for reasons unknown.

Again, enough said.

Evidence was suggesting in the man department I should give up while the giving up was good.

So, upon finding my wedding ensemble, an extortionately expensive dress full price that had been marked down twice and I knew why—only a buyer would see it on the hanger and know it was fabulous—I decided to give up while the giving up was good.

In other words, this would be my only wedding. I was done with men and that done could be displayed in neon lights, that was how done I was.

And I had a fabulous dress, great shoes and Ty Walker's diamonds.

And since this was it for me, I wanted a bouquet.

"Can you, uh… add on a bouquet?" I asked the lady. "Ring it up separately. I'll pay for it with my credit card."

Her gleeful eyes came to me and she cried, "Absolutely, darlin'!" Then she threw out an arm indicating the bouquets like she was the gowned eye candy on a game show. "You pick."

I looked at the bouquets and instantly spotted the one I wanted. "Top row, second one in."

A huge, close bundle of blush-colored roses mixed here and there with gorgeous ivory ones. Nothing else. Just roses pressed together tightly. Elegant. Gorgeous.

"Fabulous choice," the woman approved.

Moving to the bouquet, she plucked it out and I saw the spray of stems was bound with a wide, ivory organdie ribbon tied in a big bow. She turned and offered it to me.

I took it and she announced, "One hundred and fifty dollars."

Oh my God. One hundred and fifty dollars? There were a lot of roses, probably two dozen, maybe even more, they were gorgeous, each one sheer perfection, but still.

I stared down at the bundle, muttering, "Um…"

"Add it," Walker rumbled, and my head jerked back and to the side to look up at him.

"You don't—" I started.

His eyes tipped down to me. I shut up.

"All righty, lovebirds," the woman chirped.

"Photo," Walker stated, and I looked from him to the now-beaming woman.

"Five by seven or eight by ten?" she asked.

"Two. Of both," he answered.

"No problem," she stated. "Anything else? Confetti?" She did the game show thing with her arm again, indicating the boxes of confetti behind her but eyeing my dress. "We got pink."

"No," Walker said firmly.

She bit her lip and I waded in. "My man isn't a confetti type of guy."

And this I knew to be true. Earlier, he'd returned to our hotel room while I was in the bathroom getting gussied up for the big event. When I came out, he barely looked at me even though I was coiffed, made up and had the dress on (but my feet were bare) before he passed me and went into the bathroom saying, "Delivery will come. Accept it. Tip. The boxes on the bed are for you." Then he disappeared in the bathroom.

No, "Honey, you look fabulous," which I wasn't expecting but his eyes didn't even flare. Nothing. My dress was fantastic. It fit like it was made for me. It was sexy yet elegant and my hair had totally behaved for once and it looked amazing. All this but nothing from Ty Walker. I could have been wearing a potato sack.

So definitely not a confetti guy. I was surprised he wanted pictures.

After he went into the bathroom, I'd gone to the boxes on the bed but the minute I spied them, my step had gone hesitant.

That was because the boxes on the bed were a very distinctive color and they were tied by white satin ribbons. And there were four of them.

I'd sat on the bed and slowly opened the first one, finding it hard to breathe.

It was a set of earrings. Diamonds clustered in the shape of a flower. Gorgeous. Not huge. The sparkle and setting saying it all. The fact that the post was screw-in laying testimony to how expensive they were. They were not earrings you'd want to lose because the doohickey fell off the back.

The second box held a necklace, a delicate white gold chain on which was suspended a flower cluster of diamonds that matched the earrings. The pendant was larger than the earrings, eye-catching but not ostentatious.

The third, a diamond bracelet made up of the same flower clusters. It was extraordinary, and it had to be at least five times as expensive as the earrings and necklace because it was all diamonds linked with thick, white gold links.

I put the first two in and on but couldn't do the clasp on the bracelet one-handed because it was too complicated.

Then I turned to the last.

The last box I knew what it was by the size. And when I opened it, I saw I was right.

A diamond engagement ring, princess cut, stone not even close to small, white gold, the stone elevated, double rows on an open curve guiding up to it set with an array of much smaller diamonds but a whole lot of them.

I stared at it thinking that Ty Walker was not fucking around.

I held my breath as I slipped it on. Lost my breath when it caught on my knuckle. Deep breathed as I panicked that it would be too small, then it slid over my knuckle and down where it sat at the base of my finger snugly. It wouldn't ever fall off. Perfect fit.

"Shit," I whispered, staring at the beautiful ring that looked really fucking great on my finger.

A knock came at the door. I jumped then hurried to the door to find a man stood there holding a hanger on which was a zipped-up suit holder, and he was balancing four boxes in his other hand.

"One-hour tailoring," he announced.

There you go. In Vegas, you could get anything.

I smiled at him and let him in. He put down the boxes on the top of the cabinet unit, hung up the hanger in the closet. I gave him a ten, he smiled and hustled out. I went to the boxes, white cardboard sides but clear plastic top. I sifted through them. Four dress shirts. One deep gray, one deep lavender, one deep blue and the last a light, dove gray.

The shower went off but Walker didn't come out so I stopped sifting through his stuff and went about my final preparations. In other words, perfume, deodorant, lip gloss and shifting things I needed from my purse to my new satin clutch with the rhinestone clasp that matched my shoes.

When he came out, I was sitting in a chair putting on my spike-heeled, deep blush, satin, open-toed sandals with the wrapped heel and ankle strap that had a rhinestone buckle.

My fingers arrested on the buckle when my head came up and I saw my new fiancé wearing nothing but a towel.

I was right. All muscle. Lots of it, all of them big.

I was also right. Perfect skin as far as the eye could see.

That was, the skin not inked but even the inked skin was perfect because the ink was awesome.

He had a lot of tats. Lots of them.

Or, more to the point, he had two tats but one that curved, slanted and swirled doing all of this while covering a lot of space. From the top of his left forearm, up, covering his upper arm, up, curving over his shoulder and up his neck, curling around his shoulder to his back and across his left lat. At the front snaking across his chest, pec, midriff, abs, most of this halfway across his massive, muscled torso, some of its awesomeness slithering even farther to invade the right side of his upper body. More went around his left side to lead to more on his back and even more meandering down to disappear tantalizingly into the towel. The other tat was a line of intriguing symbols that ran from his inner right wrist curving around to end at the top of his outer forearm.

The big tat was amazing, a work of art. The smaller tattoo was not as cool but still fascinating. That said, I was too overwhelmed by all that was him and how beautiful every inch of it was to pay discriminating attention to the tats.

He was digging into the bag Shift packed and pulled out a pair of black underwear.

When the underwear appeared, my head dipped straight back down to my shoe. It took a while to get them fastened because my fingers were trembling. By the time I looked up, he had on a pair of dark gray suit pants and was shrugging on the dove gray shirt.

"I need your help with the bracelet," I said, and my voice sounded funny, scratchy.

His eyes came to me and he jerked his chin up but kept buttoning his shirt.

"Uh...just wondering," I went on as I stood. "What's with the bling?" Then I lifted a hand and touched the diamonds at my neck.

"Man in the lobby?" he returned.

I nodded, knowing who he was referring to.

"Watchin' me. Watchin' you."

I nodded again. I knew this though his confirmation of it still made my gut get tight. I also figured it explained the circuitous route we took to Vegas. That man was tailing us. Walker knew it and was either trying to shake him or play with him.

"Knows me," he continued.

I nodded again.

"Knows how I am with my women."

I nodded again but at this news I felt my chest expand so much I was finding it hard to breathe.

"He'll expect bling," he finished.

Learning this, for the first time in my life I had to make a conscious effort to suck in air.

I searched for then found my voice. "This is a lot of bling and I don't know—"

"Signing bonus."

I blinked then asked, "What?"

"Yours to keep. Signing bonus."

My chest deflated but I felt a strange warmth invading my insides.

"Ty," I whispered.

He finished buttoning his shirt, went to the bed, tagged the bracelet and came to me. He bent low, grabbed my wrist and lifted it. I held it up as he clasped it on, all business, and he did it like he'd done it before. Often.

Then his hands went away but his eyes came to mine.

"My business is important to me. You're facilitatin' me gettin' on with that. I appreciate it. Signing bonus."

Without another word, he walked to the desk and rifled through a bunch of bags there that I hadn't noticed, what with diamonds and impending nuptials and all. He pulled out a glossy, distinctive-colored bag, the same as the boxes still scattered on the bed, and out came two more boxes. One, he opened, unearthed cuff links and put them in his cuffs. The other, he opened, pulled out whatever was in it and put it in his trouser pocket. I would find out later that was our wedding bands.

Then he went to the duffel, pawed through it and pulled out socks.

Five minutes later, he was adjusting his collar under his suit jacket as we walked out the door.

Twenty minutes later we were at the Liberace chapel of love.

A little over five minutes after that, Walker was handing over cash for a wedding, a bouquet and photos.

One minute after that, his hand came to my elbow, fingers curling around, that strange, intense heat hit my skin where his fingers touched and he led me to an open corner. A small space but the only space void of happy, soon-to-be linked-for-eternity (maybe) lovebirds.

His hand dropped and my mind centered on the touch that still burned the skin around my elbow. Then my eyes caught on something and I forced myself to focus.

Across the way, there was a silver gilt–framed, full-length mirror and in it, Walker and I were reflected.

I was wearing a blush-colored, silk crêpe, to the knee, snug-fitting sleeveless dress, the bodice a wide vee that showed lots of chest and hints of cleavage, the material skimming over the points of my shoulders to dip into another vee that exposed my back to the bra line. My hair was down and I'd curled it in chunky curls so there was a lot more of it than normal and normally there was a lot of it. My shoes were fantastic. My diamonds, more so. Much more.

Even being such a big guy, he wore his suit well. The one-hour tailors had done a good job. The suit wasn't shit, not at all. And it fit him perfectly. It was fabulous, it was expensive. Maybe not top-of-the-line Italian but nothing to sneeze at including the shirt, the material of which was very fine, the tailoring, for one hour, spectacular.

My heels were four inches. I was five nine so my heels put me at six foot one. He still towered over me. I had ass, I had tits. I was not petite or slender, not even close. His mass still dwarfed me.

The bouquet I held looked like it was made for my dress. The shoes I'd found, the same. I had a sixth sense when it came to shoes. It took me an hour and a half to find the dress. The two pairs of shoes I found, tried on and purchased in twenty minutes.

I couldn't help but think we looked good together. If you had showed me his picture and told me to build his perfect mate, I would have said, first, lithe, graceful African-American with a long neck, slender arms, elegant hands and a short-cropped afro that exposed her perfect skull. Second, I would have said a California girl, tan, blonde who looked like she spent her days surfing and her nights fucking his brains out.

But seeing us, we worked. And seeing us in that mirror, I couldn't help but think we not only worked but we worked in a big way.

I turned to him and tipped my head back.

"Thanks for the signing bonus," I whispered. "And the bouquet."

His eyes dipped to mine. Then he jerked up his chin before he looked over my head and scanned the room.

Thirty-seven minutes later, we were in the chapel with Liberace.

Ten minutes after that, Walker was rumbling at Liberace to stand aside as the photographer angled for our picture, a picture he wanted Liberace to have no part in. Liberace looked crushed. I gave him a dazzling smile to help with his despondency and was pleased to see this worked.

Walker yanked me into his side with an arm around my shoulders and pointed his blank stare at the camera. I wound my arm around his waist, tilted the front of my body, pressed it into his side and aimed my dazzling smile at the photographer. The photographer snapped our photo.

Ten minutes after that, rhinestone lady handed us the folder with our photos and our marriage certificate.

A minute after that, we were in my car.

Which brings me to now. Married. With a bouquet in my hand and wedding photos and a marriage certificate resting on my thighs.

And I was thinking, the minute Ronnie had his scholarship yanked and copped a plea I should not have been the girlfriend who stuck by her man.

I should have dumped him and moved on.

But I didn't.

And now I was married to a man I didn't know who had a gun, a history where he was in the position for Shift to owe him big and was the kind of man who casually bestowed what had to be very expensive diamonds on "his woman."

But even though all this was irrefutably true, there was also no denying Ty Walker and I just had one kick-fucking-ass wedding.

The Charger growled up the front of our hotel. We did the valet gig then I followed Walker into the hotel. I clocked the bag-of-bones guy the minute we entered. He was hanging around, waiting, watching, and he clocked us about two seconds after I clocked him.

That tightness took hold of my gut and instantly, without me telling it to do so, my hand transferred the folder, envelope and my clutch to press them between my arm and my body, freeing my hand so I could take hold of Ty's. I shoved my fingers between his, lacing them together and I edged closer to him.

His chin tipped down even as he carried on walking and his fabulous, arched eyebrows went up half a centimeter.

"Bag of Bones," I whispered, pressing into the side of his body even as we moved.

"Come again?"

"Bag-of-bones dude. Your shadow."

His fingers tightened in mine and he stopped us in front of the elevator, leaning forward and hitting the button but not looking around.

He came back and I got even closer.

He stared at the elevator doors but muttered, "You tagged him."

"You didn't?" I muttered back.

"Yeah. Just surprised you did."

"He's hard to miss."

"Part idiot," he mumbled.

"Hmm," I mumbled back.

You'll be my wife, you'll act like my wife and you'll do it until this is done.

That's what he'd said.

That was the deal.

That was what I needed to do to get clean and free.

And that was why I curled into him, letting his hand go but moving mine to his chest and sliding it up, up, *up* until it curved around the side of his neck.

That neck bent and his eyes hit mine.

I went up on tiptoes but needed more inches so he was going to have to help.

"We just got married," I whispered.

He stared into my eyes but said not a word.

"I'm carrying a wedding bouquet."

More staring and more silence.

"Ty, he's watching."

He continued to stare into my eyes, silent but his hand hit my waist, gliding around in a touch so light, if it didn't trail a burn I could have convinced myself it wasn't there. He pressed me into him and bent his neck, giving me the inches I needed.

Then his mouth was on mine.

And when it was, I flashed back to our wedding kiss. Something, after it was done, I promised myself I would bury. Something, with this flashback, I knew I never would.

Our wedding kiss wasn't chaste. It wasn't removed. It wasn't void of emotion.

It was an arms-crushing-me-to-his-body, heads-slanting, mouths-opened, tongues-invading, toes-curling, knees-weakening, bones-dissolving, deep, wet, hungry, carnal *kiss.* It seemed to last forever but that forever was not near long enough.

Just then, that memory fresh, sharp and resurfacing in a surge even though I tried to bury it, his warm, sleek skin under my hand, his lips hard on mine, my fingers tightened on his neck, my front pressed tight to his and my mouth opened of its own volition.

His tongue snaked out and touched the tip of mine.

Warmth washed through me in a flood.

The elevator dinged.

His head came up, his arm disappeared but his hand closed around mine and he dragged me into the elevator.

He tagged the button. Then his arm came back, joined by his other one. My body collided with his. His head came down, mine was already tipped back, my free hand sliding around his shoulders, my hand holding the bouquet moving around his arm, the stuff under my arm fell unheeded to the floor of the elevator and his mouth hit mine. My lips opened, giving him instant access.

He took it.

My bones dissolved and I held on tight.

The elevator doors closed.

* * *

I put the folder, envelope and clutch that Walker had collected from the floor of the elevator and handed to me after our kiss on the table by the window in our hotel room. Then I carefully set the bouquet on its side on the table.

I turned and saw he was at the desk, flipping through the leatherette binder there. He picked up the phone, hit two buttons and put it to his ear.

I stood there and watched as he said into the phone, "Yeah, room six twenty-three. Bottle of Cristal, two glasses, now." His head was dipped down and one long finger was touching the leatherette binder as he went on, "Two bowls of clam chowder. Two prime rib dinners, one potato loaded, the other one all the shit on the side." He flipped a page. "One cheesecake. One chocolate truffle cake with whipped cream. One panna cotta. One hot fudge sundae. And another bottle of Cristal. Deliver that in an hour. No. An hour and a half." Pause. "Right."

Then he hung up and looked at me.

That was when he asked, "You like prime rib?"

I burst out laughing.

When I quit laughing, he was staring at me, deadpan.

"Uh…yeah, thanks for asking," I answered, still smiling because I couldn't help it. He was hilarious even if he didn't think so. Then I finished, "Belatedly."

He made no response, pulled off his suit jacket while moving, tossed it on his duffel, walked to the bed and sat down.

I realized I hadn't had anything to eat since my tuna melt. I'd sucked back two lattes while shopping because I could go without food, at a push. Caffeine, no way in hell.

And I was starved.

"An hour and a half?" I said to his back as he pulled off his boots.

"A man marries a woman like you in a dress like the one you got on, he'll want champagne but he won't be thinkin' about food. Still, he'll want her to have something special so he'll be makin' sure she does," he said to his boots.

My hand went to the table to hold myself standing because it wasn't an extravagant compliment but that didn't mean it wasn't a supremely effective one.

And he'd noticed the dress.

And these meant a lot to me, both of them did. The compliment and the fact he noticed my dress. I didn't know why, they just did. And when I say it meant a lot, I mean it meant *a lot.*

I swallowed.

Then I forced out, "That might be so but—"

He stood and turned to me, hands going to the buttons on his shirt. "Bag of Bones?"

"Yeah."

"Good guess, he's down the hall and watchin'."

My gut tightened again.

"Really?"

"Really."

That's when I thought, *Oh, hell with it.*

So I tried, "Why?"

He stared at me as he unbuttoned his shirt. He got it totally unbuttoned. Then he walked to his duffel.

He didn't answer.

I sighed.

Then I turned to the table and picked up my bouquet, walking behind him as he pawed through the duffel and I went to the bathroom. I stoppered the sink, filled it with water and set the bouquet in it, wishing I had scissors so I could give the stems a fresh cut in order for them to drink hearty. I didn't want that bouquet to die. Not yet. Not tomorrow. Not the next day. I wanted to keep it alive for as long as possible. And it wasn't because it cost a hundred and fifty dollars. I didn't know why it was. I just knew I did.

I decided I'd take my steak knife and saw off the stems later.

I walked back into the bedroom to see Ty on the bed, eyes aimed at the TV, which was on but muted, no sound at all, baseball game. He had not taken off his shirt and a wide (but not wide enough) expanse of his chest, abs and tats were on display. His feet were bare. His long, muscled legs stretched out. Ankles crossed. His back was to the headboard, one arm lifted, hand behind his head.

That big beautiful body reclined in bed, the big-man energy that normally flowed from him turned low but not turned off, his gorgeous eyes on the game, his fantastic features no less fantastic at rest. I wondered, what the fuck?

Why go to a pimp for a woman when you looked like that? When you could take the elevator downstairs and find at least a couple dozen women on the floor playing slots who would jump at the chance to pretend to be your wife and you wouldn't have to give up fifty grand or a secondary fortune in diamonds.

"Uh…Ty—" I started, but as I spoke there came a knock on the door.

He angled off the bed and I moved across the room. A waiter came in with a tray on which was a silver bucket, a bottle of champagne draped in a crisp linen napkin, two glasses on the sides. He put it on the table by the window.

"Would you like me to open it?" he asked, tipping his head back to look at Walker.

Walker shook his head.

The waiter grinned a knowing grin, smiled at me and headed back to the door, Walker following him. Walker came back alone and went right to the champagne. He opened it with a practiced hand and poured a glass, handing it to me, another one for him.

"To connubial bliss," I toasted as a joke, lifting my glass, but his eyes cut to me.

Nope, no sense of humor.

He put the glass to his lips and threw back half the contents while I watched his corded throat working like I was watching a master at a canvas.

He dropped his chin and hand, grabbed the bottle, refilled and moved back to the bed, resuming his position but without the hand behind his head.

I took a sip of my champagne and walked to the side of the bed.

"Um…Ty," I called, and his eyes went from the game to me. "Can I ask you a question?"

"Yep," he answered, but I knew this meant I could ask but that didn't mean he'd answer.

I took in a breath. Then I went for it.

"I don't want to point out the obvious but... you're hot."

He stared at me but didn't speak. I didn't either.

Finally, he asked, "Is that a question?"

I shook my head and explained, "What I mean is, why Shift? You could—"

He cut me off. "Five years ago, yeah. Now, no."

"What's that mean?"

His eyes went back to the game.

End of subject.

I took a sip of champagne and my eyes drifted to the game. They drifted back to him and I tried again.

"Ty," I called, and he looked back at me but said nothing. So I continued, "I'm supposed to play your wife. That's gonna be hard, I don't know shit about you."

He stared at me again then said, "Give-and-take."

"What?"

"Give-and-take," he repeated. "You give, I take. Then I give and you take."

"You mean, I tell you about me, you tell me about you?"

He didn't answer but held my eyes so I took that as a yes.

I could do this. I had nothing to hide.

"What do you want to know?" I asked.

"You pick what you wanna share. I pick what I wanna share."

Totally doable.

I nodded to him to indicate that, took a sip of champagne then put a knee to the bed and moved in, sitting on a hip and leaning into a hand, knees bent, legs to my side.

"You know Ronnie Rodriguez?" I asked.

Again his eyes held mine for a moment before he answered, "Name's familiar."

I nodded again. He watched baseball. He was a man. It was a long time ago but these two things told me Ronnie's name would be familiar.

"Basketball. Indiana University. Full scholarship."

I stopped talking when he jerked up his chin and stated, "Scholarship yanked. Brother was juicin', sellin' juice to teammates and pimpin' his basketball groupies to his fraternity brothers."

Yep. That was Ronnie. Stupid. Or stupid when he wasn't with me, and he wasn't.

I was in Texas, he was in Indiana making fucked-up decisions.

He needed steroids like he needed a hole in the head. Hoop dreams. Shit life. Projects. Desperate. Wanted a life where all that was a faded memory. Wanted his mom and sisters seen to, his girl dripping gold. Wanted to make sure it happened and wanted insurance. Scholarship yanked and since he was dealing and pimping and ended up doing time for both, he was banned. He was destined for the NBA. Everyone said it. He wasn't even going to get his degree. He was going to go for it the minute he was eligible. Then he fucked it up.

"We started seeing each other when I was fifteen and stayed together until four years ago, and it was over when he took seven bullets from a rival dealer who wanted Ronnie's turf. His mom and I chose closed casket seeing as two of those bullets he took to the face," I shared.

Walker had no response to me sharing this shocking and tragic news of a talented man who lost it all in a hideous way. Then again, Walker had walked out of a penitentiary the day before. He'd probably heard it all.

"After he did time in Indiana, he got out, came back to Dallas and was loose partners with Shift. Ronnie was about the girls, Shift about the dope," I told him. "But it was Shift's dope that got Ronnie dead."

Walker again had no response.

I took a sip of champagne and turned my head to face the TV but didn't see the game.

And then, for some bizarre reason, reclined on a bed in Vegas with a man I didn't know, I shared shit I'd never shared with anyone but Ronnie's mom and his two sisters.

"I loved him, crazy loved him," I said quietly. "Thought I could live the life, straight and narrow, prove to him it wasn't that bad. I didn't have a degree. I wasn't a hotshot basketball player. But I did it, though it was a struggle. Ronnie didn't like struggle and he didn't like to see me doing it. Lost his dream, lost his way, hooked up with Shift who he'd known for God knows how long, Shift dragged him down further. I never gave in but I also never gave up." I took another sip of champagne then whispered, "Should have given up."

"Never pimped you?"

At his question, I turned my head to face him again then shook it.

"Miracle," he muttered.

"Ronnie wouldn't let anything touch me."

"You're wrong."

I blinked. "What?"

"Might not have wanted your mouth around another man's cock but he didn't give a shit about you."

My throat closed as what he said penetrated but I pushed past it and began, "I—"

"Didn't give that first shit."

"Ty—"

He interrupted me again. "Dope, that's a choice, a weak one, but a choice. Girls who suck cock and spread for cash, they don't choose that life, a shit life chooses them. Desperation. Any man who uses that to make a living doesn't give a shit about women. *Any* women."

"That isn't true. He had me. He had a mom and two sisters he loved. But he saw no other future," I defended lamely. "And he promised me he took care of his girls."

"He lied."

My back went straight. "You don't know him."

"He lied."

"You don't know that," I snapped.

His back came away from the headboard and his torso twisted to face me. "Woman, he sold cunt. You value your cunt?"

I closed my eyes and looked away, giving him his answer.

"Right," he whispered.

I opened my eyes, looked at him and whispered back, "He gave a shit about me."

"He...did...*not*," Walker enunciated every word clearly. "The only reason he didn't pimp you is because he knew you wouldn't be pimped. He got the barest fuckin' inklin' he could sell you, he'd have done it. Now, I got a dick and I assume he had a dick so, seein' as he and I have that in common, I'll tell you, your pussy was *my* pussy, I would not be sellin' pussy, not that I'd do that shit anyway. I would not be sellin' dope and I wouldn't do that shit either. What I would do is make fuckin' coffee drinks if it meant you could wear your heels and feel good about sleepin' in my bed. He didn't do that. This means he did not give one shit about you."

He stared into my eyes and I let him. Then I looked back at the game.

While doing that I experienced a miracle, and that miracle was the fact that I didn't get crushed under the weight of the full understanding I never, *ever* let myself comprehend that Ronnie Rodriguez was a pimp, a dealer, a loser, selfish, morally void and just plain stupid. He may have started out loving me but the minute he decided to piss his future away when he fucked up in Indiana, he stopped loving me or anyone and I was blind in love and wanted so badly to belong to something, anything, *anyone*, I never let him go.

"I'm an idiot," I whispered to the game.

"You're human," Walker said to me, voice firm, and I looked back at him to see he was reclined again against the headboard.

I tipped my head to the side. "So, no sympathy for Ronnie for making fucked-up decisions, but me, I'm just human?"

"You loved him and didn't want to give up on him. That is not wrong. He didn't love you and didn't give a shit about anyone but himself. That *is* wrong."

I shook my head. "That doesn't jive, Ty."

"Oh yeah. It does," he returned. "Think I explained I have a dick. Think I told you what I'd do if your pussy was mine. I was fuckin' up and you weren't givin' up on me, I hope to Christ I'd be the type of man who'd pull my head outta my ass and earn that devotion. Makes him worse, he didn't and left you to the wolves. But you givin' that devotion, that isn't wrong."

"It was stupid."

"So, you know when the limit's up on love?" he asked, and I felt my chest depress as the profound weight of his question hit me.

"No," I whispered.

"Right. No. No one does. Not you. Not me. No one. You loved him, you believed in him. Far's you were concerned, he didn't take those hits, the day after, he coulda got his head outta his ass and done right by you. You held onto that belief. Nothin' wrong with that except the fact that he never manned up, and that's on him not on you."

It was my turn to stare at him and I did this trying to come to terms with the fact that he was sage.

Then I told him. "I think I'm done sharing."

To that, he muttered, "I bet."

And to that, I replied, "Your turn."

He jerked up his chin and stated immediately, "I'm thirty-six. Never been married. I'm a licensed automotive mechanic…or I was. My dad's alive, a drunk and an asshole. My mom's alive and a bitch 'cause her husband's a drunk. Or maybe he's a drunk because she's a bitch. Whatever, they define dysfunction and I been livin' with that shit since I had memories. My dad's parents hated my mom and died doin' it. They had reason. My mom's parents returned the favor with my dad but their reasons, in the beginning, were different and total bullshit. They're alive and I had not one thing to do with them when I was a kid, their choice, and not when I grew up either and that choice was mine. I got a younger brother who's a pain in everyone's ass. He's thirty-three and been married four times, got five kids and my guess, he marries women and makes babies 'cause he gets off on bein' a pain in the ass and wants to spread that shit around far's he can. Good news is, he moved to Los Angeles and that proved far enough away, his talent with being a pain in the ass didn't reach. I grew up in Carnal, Colorado and I just got done doin' a nickel for a crime I didn't commit in a state I never stepped foot in until I was extradited there to stand trial."

Then he stopped talking.

I waited.

He shared no more.

So I asked, "That's it?"

"That's it."

"I shared more than you," I pointed out.

"How you figure that?"

"Okay, I didn't share more but mine was more personal and included me coming to terms with something I've been avoiding coming to terms with for nearly twenty years. Those terms are uneasy terms and I'm still processing but still. You shared a lot and some of it was big, as in *way* big, but there was no detail and hence that's *not* it."

"Said give-and-take, didn't say it would be equal. You picked. I picked. That's fair."

It was not.

And because it wasn't, I asked, "You didn't commit the crime you served time for?"

"Nope."

"What happened?"

His eyes moved directly to the game.

"Ty," I called, and his eyes came back to me. "What happened? How could you—?"

"What'd I say?" he cut me off to ask.

"What?"

"What'd I say?" he repeated.

"About what?"

He held my eyes. Then, low and more rumbling than normal, he stated, "That's it."

And that, obviously, was it.

"Next time we play this game, you get to go first," I declared and watched with intense fascination as his lips curved up the minutest bit.

Then they uncurved and he muttered, "That's fair too."

His head turned to the TV.

I got off the bed and went to the champagne.

Ty

Walker's eyes moved from the TV to Lexie.

She was curled on her side facing him, hands under her cheek, knees tucked nearly to her middle, still wearing her classy but sexy pink dress but she'd finally taken off the classy but sexy shoes. Her eyes were closed. She was out.

He studied her thinking she was probably the only woman he'd ever known in his vast experience of women who could pull off classy and sexy while being married by Liberace.

Actually, truth of it was, she was the only woman he'd ever known who could pull off classy *and* sexy at all.

Then he studied her thinking that Ronnie Rodriguez was one serious dumb fuck and this was not evidenced by the fact that he lost the sweet life God saw fit to grant him through providing him with immense talent on a basketball court. But instead, it was evidenced by the fact that the classy, sexy pussy lying asleep at his side in a king-size bed in Vegas was lying asleep at his side in a king-size bed in Vegas and not curled into a living, breathing Ronnie Rodriguez who didn't spend every ounce of energy earning the privilege of having the classy, sexy pussy right then lying asleep at Ty Walker's side.

On that thought, he moved off the bed, went to the table and grabbed the tray on which Lexie had stacked their used dishes. While walking to the door, something caught his attention and his head turned. He looked into the bathroom and stopped.

Her bouquet was in the sink resting in a couple inches of water.

Seeing it, he balanced the tray on one hand and felt his back pocket. Finding the keycard still there, he walked out the door. He set the tray on the floor by the door and scanned the hall. Then he walked down it. At the end, he looked right and saw it on a narrow table between the elevators. He went to the vase with the fake flowers on top of the table, yanked out the flowers, put them on the table and walked back to their room, putting out the Do Not Disturb sign.

In the bathroom, he pulled the bouquet out of the sink, let out the water, used a glass to fill the vase and shoved the stems in it.

Then he walked out of the bathroom, around the bed and set the flowers on her nightstand.

He undressed and didn't blast the AC like he wanted to considering she was not covered. He just slid between the sheets and turned out the light.

CHAPTER FOUR

Total Goof. Total Cute.

Ty

THE NEXT MORNING, Walker slid the keycard into the slot, waited for the green light, slid it out and walked into their hotel room. He hit the bedroom area and saw the maids had been through, bed made, vacuum marks on the floor.

No Lexie. But a note on his pillow. The maids likely made the bed and placed it back where Lexie put it.

He tossed the sweaty towel he was carrying on the bed, walked backward, opened up the closet, crouched to the safe, opened it and scanned it.

All good.

He closed it and walked back into the bedroom to the note.

He picked it up and read it.

Hubby,

At the pool. If I don't return by nightfall, it's your marital duty to rescue me. If it goes that late, this means I've passed out on a lounge chair in Vegas in summer so my advice is to stock up on aloe vera before you launch the rescue effort.

Lexie

Walker stared at the note thinking that Alexa Berry…

Strike that.

Alexa *Walker* was fucking funny.

Then he stood there staring at the note thinking how much he liked the name Alexa Walker.

Then he stood there staring at the salutation of the note and thinking the bitch was a goof but also thinking he liked that.

Then he stood there staring at the handwriting of the note and memorizing her scrawl, which was not girlie or precise but spiky, the cursive words often disconnected and they had no slant. She didn't lean this way or that. She sat comfortably in the middle.

Finally, he folded the note and dropped it to the bed. Twenty minutes later, having showered away the sweat from his workout, shaved, dressed in jeans, a white tee and his boots, he went to the bags on the desk, grabbed his new shades and then he went to the note on the bed and shoved it in his back pocket. He grabbed the keycard.

And he went to the pool.

His first thought after hitting the late-morning Vegas sun was that he did not want to be in the hot-as-fuck late-morning Vegas sun. Five seconds later, halfway through a scan of the bodies around the pool, he forgot about the hot-as-fuck late-morning Vegas sun because his shades had pinpointed his wife.

String bikini the color of raspberries. Hair still in that mass of thick, wild curls but bunched up at the top back of her head, long locks having escaped and trailing down her neck. Skin glistening with suntan oil. Mostly exposed body better than he expected and he'd expected her body to be pretty fucking great. She had her shades on and tipped down to a magazine spread in her hands, her knees bent, soles of her feet in the lounge, towel draped over the back.

He moved toward her and tagged Bag of Bones at her ten o'clock making Walker wonder if he'd been wrong about the guy. He'd suspected closet gay. Since the fucker had chosen to trail Lexie and not Walker, maybe not.

She sensed him when he was twenty feet away. Her head came up and he knew she knew Bag of Bones was there because, the second her shades hit him, her gorgeous face split into a blinding smile.

She flipped her magazine closed and tossed it to a table beside her that held a rapidly melting iced coffee drink.

Five feet away, she called, "Hey, hubby."

There it was again. Fucking goofy but the way she did it, he had to admit, also fucking cute.

He jerked his chin up and the instant he arrived at her side, her hand shot out, closing around his and tugging. He didn't resist her pulling him down to sit on the side of her lounger as she shifted her hips and legs so her bottom half was resting at an S on its side in order to give him room and she curled her thighs around the back of his hips.

"Woke up alone. Where'd you go?" she asked, her hand still in his, her head tipped back to look up at him and he was glad he was wearing sunglasses because, at her question, his eyes moved from her tits to her face and he didn't think she noticed.

"Workout."

"Dude," she said low, her mouth still curved up at the ends.

Dude. Yeah, total goof.

"Dude?" he prompted when she said no more.

"We're in Vegas," she stated.

"Yeah," he agreed.

"Is it legal to work out in Vegas?" she asked, her head tipping, the bunch of hair at the back of it shifting with the movement.

"They got a gym so I'm guessin'...yeah."

This got him another bright smile then her shades did a head to lap and back again before she observed, "You aren't in swim trunks."

"Lexie, I'm half black. My tan is permanent. I don't need to work on it."

"Right," she muttered, still grinning.

It was then he cast his mind back to try to pull up Ronnie Rodriguez. Rodriguez had fucked himself the middle of his sophomore year but saw a shitload of playing time the season and a half before he did it. Therefore Walker could pull him up but not much except the fact the brother was lean, tall and black. How he got the last name Rodriguez, Walker didn't know. Then again, Shift had the last name Martinez and he, too, was black. Maybe it was some Texas thing.

What Walker did know was that a lot of white bitches didn't mind playing with black but they sure as fuck didn't take it home to daddy, and black was black even if it was full, half or a nuance.

He also knew Lexie didn't have a daddy but if she did, she'd take black home and, he figured, with her sass, daddy didn't like it, she'd tell him to go fuck himself.

On this thought, he asked, "Had breakfast?" and she shook her head.

He turned his and saw the outside restaurant at the side of the pool.

Then he looked back at her. "I'm hungry."

"Me too," she agreed, let go of his hand and moved instantly.

Rolling off the lounger, she bent low and grabbed some clothes she'd shoved under it. She pulled on a tight tee-fabric halter top the color of her swimsuit and a pair of black short shorts. Then she sat, bent forward and started strapping on a pair of black sandals with tall, wedged heels.

Something barbed pressed into the skin at the back of his neck and he tore his eyes from his new wife to look three loungers away.

There he saw a man who definitely spent a lot of time working on his tan. Oiled up. Tight black swim trunks. Gold at his neck. His shades aimed at Alexa Walker's cleavage exposed to his view as she was bent toward the guy.

"*Yo!*" he barked, felt Lexie's surprised movement rather than saw it but also saw tight trunk man's shades jerk up to his face. Walker shook his head slowly. The guy quickly looked away.

The barbed feeling faded.

Lexie stood and came into his line of sight.

"What was that?" she asked quietly.

"I'm standin' here," he answered.

Her head cocked to the side. She was confused or maybe she didn't notice the guy. He was guessing the second as he'd noted she didn't notice men's attention, something which she got a lot of.

But he did.

He moved around the lounge, got close to her and tipped his chin down to lock shades.

"He was starin' at your tits."

Her head slowly turned to the lounger holding tight-trunk man.

It turned to him, tipped back and they again locked shades.

Then she muttered, "Euw."

Total goof. Total cute.

Fuck him.

"Yeah, that for you. For me, my woman is puttin' on her shoes, I'm standin' right there, you do not fuckin' stare at her tits."

"Oh," she whispered.

"Right. Oh." He jerked his head at the lounge. "You gonna get your stuff?"

She shook her head. "No, I'll leave it to keep my place. I'll keep an eye on it from our table."

That was acceptable so he moved.

She moved with him and did what she did the day before, grabbing his hand and lacing her fingers with his. She held on tight. Bag of Bones was watching and she was earning her fifty K.

They were seated at a table where he could keep an eye on her shit. She sat in the seat next to him at the square table instead of opposite. A scan of the pool and restaurant showed that Bag of Bones was gone, probably because the morning Vegas sun was torture on his pasty white skin.

They ordered and he was doing another scan to see if Bones was back when he felt her fingers on his hand. His head tipped down to see her hand was at his, which was resting on the table, and she was thumbing his wide, white gold wedding band.

"He's gone," Walker informed her.

Her hand moved away quickly and her head shot back to look at him, both movements indicating that for some reason he'd startled her.

"What?" she asked quietly.

"Bones. He's gone."

Her shades immediately moved to scan the area and she whispered, "He was here?"

Something sharp pierced straight through the left side of his chest.

Then he asked, "You didn't tag him? He was out here when I got here."

Her shades came back to him. She shook her head and said, "I thought he was following you. Why's he following me?"

"You didn't tag him," Walker repeated, this time a statement, not a question.

She shook her head again and said, "No. No. I…" She paused. "Oh my God. How creepy. Why's he following me?"

She didn't tag him.

She'd smiled bright at him. Called him her goofy name. Kept smiling at him. Tugged him to her lounge. Held hands with him almost the entire time he was with her and thumbed his wedding ring in a way that she'd been absorbed in it and he'd startled her when she saw she had his attention.

What the fuck?

As that question came to his mind, their coffee came, saving him from having to guess at an answer and giving him an opportunity to set aside an explanation as to why Bones was following her. The time would come when the need to know she needed to know was that she'd be looked into. Now was not that time.

"Today I got shit to do," he told her as she poured milk into her coffee.

She nodded. "That's cool. I'm gonna bake."

"You got shit to do too."

She went from spooning sugar into her coffee to looking at him. "What?"

"In two days we're headin' home. *My* home. Carnal. You got a job to quit and a life to shut down. You need to start on that."

Her shades stayed locked with his.

Then she muttered, "Oh God, I didn't think about that."

"Tomorrow can be your vacation day. Today you sort shit out."

She went back to spooning sugar in but she did it nodding. He counted as her hand moved. She took four sugars. No wonder she had that ass.

"You got people who can help you or do we need to carve out time, drive down and sort that?" he asked.

She stopped stirring, put her spoon aside, took a sip then put her cup down while looking at him.

"Ronnie's mom and sisters will kick in for me. I tell them I'm moving out from under Shift's thumb, they'll rent Dallas Cowboys Cheerleader outfits and do cartwheels around Cowboy Stadium."

"They probably should save that energy and use it to pack your shit and send it to Carnal."

She laughed softly then muttered, "Yeah, Ty, you're probably right."

"You need movers, they get quotes, you tell me. I'll get them the money. I'll also give you the address."

Her head tipped to the side. "The address?"

"To my house."

"Your house?"

"My house."

"What house?"

"My house in Carnal."

"You have a house in Carnal?"

"I went to prison but doin' it don't mean I was stripped of all my possessions. I went, Maggie saw to my shit."

He watched with interest as her shoulders went straight and she asked, "Maggie?"

"Maggie," he confirmed.

"Who's Maggie?" she asked, and her tone was one he hadn't heard from her yet. Not sass. Not attitude. Not annoyed. But the edge was sharp. Leaning toward pissed not in the sense that women get pissed. In the sense that women get *pissed.*

"My former boss's ex-wife. Though, he got his head outta his ass, saw what he fucked up and now they're attempting a reconcile. So, I guess I should say, the last year, Maggie *and* Wood been seein' to my shit."

"Wood?"

"Maggie's ex. The man who owns the garage I used to work at."

"Oh," she whispered.

"We get home, you'll need to take a look. Your shit's better than my shit, move your shit in and we'll move my shit out. It's not, have your people get rid of it, bank the cash."

Her shades held his.

"Um... again, how long's this business gonna last?"

"Again, I don't know. But what people gotta see is you and me startin' a life together."

She hesitated. Then, "Right."

He stared at her. Then his eyes went to her left hand sitting in her lap. The band embedded with small diamonds sitting tight under the engagement ring served as a reminder that yesterday cut deep into his reserve. He had a marker of fifty K to pay. He had a life to restart. He had business to see to. He had to find a table.

Then he noticed her lips were pressed together, he guessed as to why and reminded her, "Time to bolt is over. You're wearin' my rings."

Her head jerked and she declared firmly, "I'm not going to bolt."

The tightness in his chest he hadn't noticed until he heard her words released.

"How did, um…Maggie and Wood take care of your shit?" she asked.

"Rented my place. Paid my bills. Banked the extra. Vacated the tenants a month ago when I asked 'em to. Stored my shit when I went down, took it outta storage and dumped it at home. Sorted through it to pack the shit I needed, sent it to Shift for him to add what he owed and give it to you."

"That was nice of them to do."

"They're nice."

Her lips tipped up.

Their food was served.

Unlike with her tuna melt, but absolutely the same as when their room service was delivered last night, she dug in. No bullshit nibbling, pretending she didn't need food to survive. She'd ordered a Belgian waffle. And she liked what she ordered and didn't give a fuck if he knew it.

Alexa Walker was a beautiful, classy, sexy, part goof who liked her food.

And Ty Walker liked all of that.

Too much.

Christ, pussy had fucked his life and here he was, two days out of the joint and sitting under a fucking umbrella in the Vegas heat next to pussy who'd had dick fuck up her life and he wanted in there so fucking badly he could almost convince himself he already tasted her on his tongue.

Jesus, he needed another shower. And not because he was eating eggs, bacon, sausage and toast in the Vegas heat but because he needed to take his fist to his cock or he'd likely do something he seriously regretted and that something would mean she'd bolt and he'd never see her smile again.

Her voice cut into his thoughts. "What's your place like?"

"Condo," he answered.

Her laugh made him turn his shades to her. "You're not much on specifics," she remarked.

"What's there to say about a condo?"

She kept her shades on him for several seconds.

Then she murmured, "Point taken," while smiling at her waffle.

Yep, he had to get the fuck out of there. Soon.

"You start sortin' your shit, you need me, I'll leave my new cell number in the room."

"Okay."

"That second dress you bought, you're wearin' tonight."

He felt her eyes on him but he shoveled in more food.

"Okay," she said.

He swallowed and stated, "Soon's I eat, gotta go. You charge this shit and the tip to our room."

"Okay," she repeated.

He focused on eating. She fell silent, maybe reading his mood.

The instant he finished, he sucked back the dregs of his coffee, turned to her and in case Bones was watching from somewhere, he nabbed her behind the neck, pulled her to him, pressed his lips to hers hard, let her go, got up and walked away licking his lips.

They tasted like whipped cream, strawberries, waffles and Lexie.

Fuck.

Lexie

I walked out of the bathroom gussied up in what I thought of as my slut dress. Ty's instructions had been "Two dresses. One to get married in. One that'll get attention."

I'd never dressed to get attention. I liked clothes—buying them and wearing them—but I'd never owned a dress like this and I hoped the one I picked would be the ticket.

I walked into the bedroom to see Ty doing the cuff link thing again. This time he was wearing the deep lavender shirt with a pair of dark blue suit trousers. My eyes took in his male beauty then they slid to my nightstand.

I'd woken up to my bouquet in a vase precisely where it now stood. Upon waking, after seeing Ty's side of the bed was mussed but empty, processing the fact that I slept on top of the covers in my wedding dress, those flowers in that vase were the second thing I saw after I rolled.

And the minute I saw them, I'd frozen, blinking the sleep out of my eyes, convinced I was seeing things.

Unless Vegas had bouquet fairies as well as one-hour tailors, there was no one but Ty who could have located a vase and put my bouquet in it while I slept the sleep of the dead. And, when I realized I wasn't seeing things, I didn't know what to think about Ty locating a vase and putting my bouquet in it. I didn't know him all that well but from what I did know, this seemed a very un-Ty-like thing to do. Therefore, I lay in bed and stared at those roses for what had to be five minutes trying to figure out what I thought.

I got out of bed not knowing.

But I also got out of bed with a warm feeling deep in my gut that felt really, *really* good as well as thinking that this fake marriage business wasn't going to be that bad.

Sure, he didn't talk much.

Sure, when he did, most of it was crude, but it wasn't like I wasn't used to that from Ronnie, Shift and their crew. In fact, Ronnie, Shift and their crew were worse.

Sure, there were important ways he was closed off. Then again, we barely knew each other. Sharing our deepest, darkest secrets within forty-eight hours of meeting was not something to be expected. I had no idea why I poured my heart out to him last night. What I knew was, when I did, although he didn't exactly handle me with care, he was honest. He shared his opinion and I just happened to like his opinion no matter that the realization it made me come to didn't feel all that great. Not to mention, he'd shown himself to be wise.

Sure, he seemed to have no sense of humor but he also didn't get ticked when I laughed when he didn't find anything funny. And he didn't have *no* sense of humor. His lips curled up last night. I saw them.

He also didn't like smarmy men with gold chains staring at my breasts and since I didn't like that either, I thought it was very cool that he barked at the gross guy who was checking me out making that gross guy stop checking me out.

And he had a way with a compliment.

And last, he was a really fucking good kisser.

The last part was the part where I wouldn't go. Not yet. I knew I wanted to sleep with him. I knew that the minute I laid eyes on him. Hell, *every* woman who laid eyes on him knew that. I also knew I was a thirty-four-year-old woman who'd had one boyfriend and thus one lover in her life and he wasn't very good at being the former and (not to speak ill of the dead), although I had no experience of another, he was hit and miss at the latter.

I had since had a four-year dry spell and my life decisions had led me into a fake marriage with an ex-con who contended he was wrongly imprisoned but wouldn't elaborate. Furthermore, just the day before I'd decided to give up on men and it probably wasn't the brightest move to go back on that decision after knowing the man for just over two days. I was thinking maybe I should play this smart and not jump into the sack and give him my "pussy."

"You sort your shit today?" he asked, and my eyes moved from the bouquet to him.

He was looking at me, my face, not the dress. This was disappointing because I really wanted to know if I'd done what he needed me to do but I wondered if it was like yesterday where he wasn't going to give it away until he was ready.

About half an hour ago, I'd heard him come back while I was in the bathroom. He'd been gone all day but called twice. Once to say have lunch without him. The other to say have dinner without him. He did not tell me where he was or what he was doing. I also did not ask.

"Ella's all over it," I answered.

Ella, Ronnie's mother, was also kind of like my mother since she was really the only one I ever knew. She took me under her wing when I was thirteen and her daughter Bessie and I became best friends. Then she kept me there even after I hooked up with Ronnie and treasured me being there because Ronnie had slipped over the edge but she knew I was the only thing that kept him from free fall.

That was, until he went into free fall.

When I explained things to her earlier that day, I skipped the ex-con slash picking him up from a correctional institute slash fake marriage bit and just told her I'd lied about going on vacation and was instead hooking up with a friend who was helping me move to Colorado. I'd explained the lie by saying I didn't want anything to get back to Shift. Since Honey, Ella's other daughter, was sweet as her name but not the brightest bulb in the box and had a connection with Shift that had more to do with history and missing her brother than brains, I didn't want to take any chances.

Ella, birthing Honey and still living with her even though thirty years had passed since the blessed event, understood. She'd also been beside herself with glee. She had a key to my place and she was what I told Ty. All over it.

Then I'd called Margot at work. I'd given her the same story with the same omissions. She knew about Shift. She knew my dilemma. We'd often had conversations about how I could get out, move on, start a new life. She'd been worried about me for more than the four years I didn't have Ronnie as a buffer, stretching that out to the eight I'd known her. In other words, when she started at Lowenstein's. She wasn't a big fan of Ronnie though she was a good enough friend not to mention it (too much) or give me her disapproving look (that often) or, when I'd bitch about him, she did not say "I told you so" with anything but her eyes. Last, she did not lose her mind and point out how stupid I was when I gave him another shot. Like me, she'd worked her way up from clerk and she wasn't the head honcho of HR at Lowenstein's but she was the assistant head honcho. She promised she was going to smooth the way.

And, incidentally, she was beside herself with glee too.

The truth was, all of this seemed pretty easy. So much so, I was feeling like a major idiot that I hadn't tried it before.

Then again, I didn't have a condo to move into, a huge scary man to have my back and a nest egg of fifty K to fall back on before.

"Ella Ronnie's mom?" Ty asked, and my attention focused on him again.

I nodded. "She's already been to my place, started sorting and has called three moving companies to get quotes."

He nodded once. Then he went to his suit jacket that was lying on the bed.

I walked across the room to my shoes while talking. "Work seems kosher too. My friend Margot, who works there, is going to explain things to the HR director." I sat down and slid my foot into a strappy, stiletto-heeled silver sandal. Then, again, right out of my mouth popped more honest sharing. "Actually, this is all so easy, I'm kinda feeling like a moron that I didn't do it before."

"Shift hadn't fucked you this bad, you didn't have anyone that scared his black ass shitless and you didn't have fifty large to fall back on before."

I tilted my head back and grinned at him. "Those are all the reasons I talked myself out of feeling like a *total* moron and into only feeling *kinda* like one."

He stared at me for long moments. Then, without comment, he went to two money rolls he'd obviously at some point pulled out of the safe. One was a fifty roll. The other was a twenty.

My attention went back to my shoes. I was done around the time I heard the door open on the closet. I watched him drop the now-less-fat rolls back in the safe. He closed the door to it and the closet and turned to me.

"Ready?"

I stood and put my hands to my hips.

"I don't know, am I?"

I meant I didn't know what we were doing, where we were going and why I needed an outfit that would get attention and, not knowing any of that, I couldn't know if I was ready.

But at my question his eyes traveled down the length of me to my toes and back again. They did this slow, taking their time, missing nothing, and I felt their path like a touch on my skin. As they moved, I saw my dress in my head. Navy, clingy silk jersey, pleated down the side seam creating diagonal gathers across the dress, one shoulder was bare, the other arm sleeveless. It hit me four inches above my knee, showed no cleavage but still tons of skin and it was so form-fitting it left very little to the imagination.

When his eyes locked on mine, he spoke and his voice was a very deep, low rumble. "Yeah. You are definitely ready."

And as he spoke, I noticed his eyes were different. Not void, not shuttered. The first emotion he'd shown me in two and a half days.

And that emotion was carnal.

I felt my body go electric.

I fought against the surge and whispered, "Thank you, Ty. But I meant I don't know what I'm all gussied up to do tonight so I can't know if I'm ready."

He answered immediately. "High-stakes poker."

I stared at him, not getting a good feeling about this. I'd never gambled before, not in my life. I didn't do this because I didn't work hard for my money to throw it away.

Ronnie gambled. He bet on basketball games all the time. Convinced, since he had played them, he had the inside track. He didn't lose all the time but he also didn't win all the time. It seemed ridiculous to me and scary because Lady Luck didn't swing Ronnie a break very often and I was always waiting for her to pull the rug out from under him and stop with the balancing act as pertained to his gambling. Luckily (heartbreaking pun intended), he died before she could do that.

"High-stakes poker," I repeated.

"One hundred K buy-in."

I blinked. Then I asked hesitantly, "Um... are you good at poker?"

"Very."

"Really?"

"Woman, you're wearin' over thirty thousand dollars proves that true."

I blinked again. Then I breathed, "Really?"

"Yeah."

"No, I mean, really, I'm wearing over thirty thousand dollars?"

"And the answer is still yeah. Your engagement ring alone is nearly half that."

"Oh my God," I whispered, suddenly feeling my engagement ring burning a circle around my finger. I mean, it wasn't like I didn't know all he gave me was expensive, including the wad of cash he dropped on the bed to buy my outfits, which were not couture but I didn't buy them at Target either. I just didn't know it was *that* expensive.

"What?" he asked when I didn't move.

"What?" I asked back.

"Yeah, Lexie, what?"

"What as in... what, you give all your women this kind of bling?"

This gave new definition to "very" good at poker.

"No. None of my other women signed a marriage certificate, took my name and gave up their whole life for me and by the time they earned bling, I'd known 'em more than a day and they *still* hadn't done anything that important to me."

I stopped breathing and apparently I did this visibly because I got my second reaction from Ty Walker (if you didn't count the lip curve last night). His eyes narrowed.

"Jesus, woman, you gonna pass out?"

That's when my breath came back at the same time *my* eyes narrowed. "Excuse me, Ty, I've never worn thirty thousand dollars."

"Yeah you have. Yesterday. But, sayin' that, I'm guessin' at the cost of your shoes."

"They were on sale."

"Well, thank Christ for that."

I stared at him. Then I burst out laughing.

Ty didn't find anything funny.

"Babe, we got a game to get to. I spent a day makin' the connections to get a chair. But, the doors close, the deck's cut, they don't let anyone in."

My hand went behind me to the table again to hold myself up when he called me "babe." Again, I had no idea why, it was just that it was casual, it was an endearment and for many men, it was throwaway. They said it to women they didn't even know.

Ty Walker was not that kind of man. He was not casual. He didn't do anything throwaway. Every move he made, every word he said had meaning. I knew this down to my bones.

"Lexie..." He was now growling.

"Um...one thing," I said quietly.

He sighed audibly.

I kept going. "*I* don't know how to play poker."

"That's good because women don't sit this table."

I was back to staring at him. Then I asked, "So what am I supposed to do?"

"Get attention."

"What?"

"Poker isn't all about the cards. Poker's mostly about attention. You got a woman whose legs are like yours, tits are like yours, hair is like yours and ass is like yours, all she's gotta do for me is sit there and half the men at the table won't be concentrating on their cards. They'll be thinking about your legs, tits, hair and ass, how much they want 'em and just what they'd do to get 'em."

"I appreciate the compliment, Ty, but I don't think I'm all that."

"You got a dick?"

I felt my mouth twitch.

Then I answered, "No."

"Trust me."

I really had no choice. It wasn't my money anyway so I decided to do that. Trust him.

But I asked, "So is this always your tactic, bring in some woman that gets attention?"

"I've never had class with a rack and an ass like yours so, no. We need the money so tonight I'm tryin' somethin' new."

There it was again. Another supremely effective Ty Walker compliment.

My fingers pressed deeper into the table.

Then I asked, "Do you lose concentration when a woman you want is in the room?"

"I hope not or tonight we're fucked."

And there it was again. My fingertips slid out and my palm pressed into the table.

That was when he asked, "We gonna go or you wanna stare at me some more?"

I sucked in breath. Then I walked to him. He stood where he was and watched. When I made it to him, I got close, tipped my head way back and put my hand flat on the wall of his chest.

"All right, hubby, let's go kick some poker ass."

He stared down at me. Then he shook his head.

Then he muttered, "Christ, you're a goof."

He moved to my side, put his hand to my back and propelled me to the door and since his hand was on me, I was concentrating on it so I didn't have a smartass retort to the goof comment.

I just moved with my husband out the door.

* * *

I learned a few things quickly after the poker game began. First, if you weren't playing it (which I never had so maybe even if you were, I wouldn't know), poker was mind-numbingly boring. Second, Ty was not as good as he thought he was.

This game was like one of those games you saw in movies. I knew this when we didn't go down to the gambling floors, we went up to the top floor. I also knew this because two men in dark suits were standing outside the double doors at the end of the hall we walked through to get into the game. Further, I knew this because when we entered, every character from a movie was there.

The oldish Texan with a Stetson and a big-haired blonde in strapless, clingy, cut-up-to-*there* gold lamé dripping off his arm. Two men in ill-fitting but nevertheless expensive suits (in other words, it was time to lay off the carbs and that time was about six months ago) that looked like they could easily be made men in the Mafia. A slender, handsome man in an expensive suit that *did* fit him well, very well, and I thought there was a good chance he was a secret agent. And a swarthy man chomping a cigar, sporting a beer gut fit for two and probably being on vacation from his oppressive rule of some small, South American country.

Lastly, I knew this was like those poker games from the movies because there was a bar, with bartender, and the casino had provided a black-vested, white-shirt, black-bowtie-wearing dealer and a swish poker table with all its accoutrements.

The dealer eyed me and Blondie, had a quiet word with Ty and the Texan and then Ty came to me and told me I was relegated to the couch against the back wall.

Then he bent his head, lips to my ear and whispered, "Cross your legs. Often."

After this, he went to a chair at the table where big piles of multicolored chips were sitting.

I sat and the bartender got me a French martini after I ordered it. I did this because of my surroundings, not that I ever drank one. I drank beer. The martini just popped into my head and sounded like something a woman wearing a slinky dress who was relegated to a couch during a testosterone-only poker game would drink. And I found out it tasted really good.

Then, for over an hour, I sipped my (two) French martinis, crossed and uncrossed my legs frequently but not frequently enough to seem silly like Blondie was fidgeting at my side, making me wonder if she might have a movement disorder. As I did this, I tried not to fall asleep and watched with increasing alarm (the only thing that kept me from falling asleep) as Ty's piles dwindled.

Twice, he'd reached into his inside suit pocket, thrown bills on the table that were snatched up by the dealer faster than you could blink and new chips were stacked at his place. Twice, those stacks shrunk.

He had two chips in front of him that I was staring at in a vain effort to make them multiply spontaneously and the mound of chips in the middle was about three times larger than any other game.

It was then I felt something slither along my legs, my eyes slid to the left and I noticed the secret agent's head was slightly turned my way, his eyes downcast and I knew they were on my legs.

"Lexie."

I heard Ty's rumbling voice call my name. I jumped and called, "Yeah, honey?"

"Come here," he ordered, his back was to me and he didn't turn around.

I looked to secret agent guy and saw his gaze was now alert and on Ty.

I set my drink on the side table, got up, moved quickly to the poker table and stood at his back right. "You need something, Ty?"

His neck twisted and his head tipped back. "Give me your necklace, baby," he said softly.

My breath started sticking in my throat but his eyes held mine and they were not impassive. They were communicating. I just had no freaking clue what they were saying.

I didn't want to lose my necklace. I liked it but I liked that Ty gave it to me and why.

But he told me to trust him.

I had to trust him.

So I lifted my hands, unclasped the chain and brought it down, watching it and the pendant pool in Ty's upturned palm.

He instantly tossed it on the pile of chips and I felt my stomach clench. Then, directly after, he tossed in his last two chips.

Then he said to the table, "Thanks, babe."

I stood there not knowing what to do.

For reasons unknown to me, my hands lifted and I unscrewed one earring and set it by his wrist on the table. Then the other. Then I fiddled with the clasp on my bracelet, managed by a small miracle to get it unhooked all on my own and I placed it by the earrings. This done, I bent low, leaned in and kissed the hinge of his jaw. I straightened, squeezed his shoulder, looked over his head at secret agent guy and aimed a smile at him.

I turned and walked back to the couch, ignoring Blondie smiling slyly and superiorly at me.

Five minutes later, Ty won that huge pot. Fifteen minutes later, he won the next one. The one after, he lost. He won the next three.

The night wore on, I ordered another martini and sipped it because dinner was long past and I didn't want it to go to my head and I watched Ty win big.

When it was clear things were breaking up, Ty's pile had to be about five times bigger than when the game started. Men moved. Blondie pushed herself up and shuffled forward. I uncrossed my legs then recrossed them on the other side.

Ty jerked his chin at the dealer while the Texan stood and said in a loud mutter, "Not sure you'll be welcome to sit another game, Walker."

"Don't 'spect so," Ty replied, sounding like he couldn't care less and standing, his side to the table, his neck twisted until his eyes were on me.

I was to go to him.

I went to him.

Goodnight-type words were exchanged and I did a scan of the occupants of the room as I walked to Ty. The swarthy man looked mildly annoyed. The Texan looked pissed; then again, his piles had dwindled the most when Ty started winning. The rest simply looked like they were tired and ready to call it a night.

I stopped close to Ty and the minute I did, he took hold of and then lifted my wrist, tagged the bracelet off the table and latched it on. He put a hand to my hip, put pressure on and my body moved until my back was to him. The pendant dangled in front of me then disappeared downward.

That was when I heard him murmur, “Lift up your hair.”

I did as I was told.

He clasped my necklace on, tingles sliding up my scalp and down my spine when his fingers brushed against my skin.

The hand came back to my hip turning me to face him, he again lifted my wrist, twisted it and deposited my earrings in my palm.

“Don’t bother puttin’ ’em in. We get back to the room, we’re goin’ straight to bed.”

I felt my body go electric again. I licked my lips and nodded.

His eyes cut through the room. He did a few jerks of his chin. I aimed a tired smile around, his hand went to the small of my back and he led me to and out the double doors.

CHAPTER FIVE

Breakfast

THE NEXT DAY, I sat baking in the sun on a lounge chair by the pool, sweat mingling with my suntan oil, my eyes directed to the Kindle in my hand but my mind was not on my Kindle.

It was on Ty.

Last night he won four hundred and fifty thousand dollars playing poker.

Four hundred and fifty thousand dollars.

This boggled the mind. I didn't know what to do with this. It was so huge, it was impossible to process.

But that knowledge wouldn't be the only thing that boggled my mind last night.

Playing it cool, I hadn't asked him until we got to the room how much he won but I did it the minute the latch clicked on the door. He answered as he strode into the room, shrugging off his jacket.

I stood in the little hall, stunned motionless.

Then I'd walked into the bedroom to see him draping his jacket on the chair by the window.

"Four hundred and fifty thousand dollars?" I asked.

"Yep," he answered.

"Four hundred and fifty thousand dollars?" I repeated.

Ty didn't respond that time.

"I can't believe you won that kind of money," I stated because I couldn't.

"Don't get excited," he replied, taking out his cuff links and acting like he wasn't excited. But then again, he rarely acted like he was anything.

Still.

Four hundred and fifty thousand dollars was exciting and should be, even for Ty.

Therefore I stared at him and I did this for a while.

Then I asked incredulously, "How can I not be excited? That's a lot of money. And you won that money. In Vegas. In a poker game that came right out of a movie. And that…is…*fucking*…cool!"

His eyes came to mine. "It wasn't cool. It was easy. They were amateurs. The only one who knew what he was doin' is Navarro, and Navarro was more interested in your legs than the game."

This surprised me. It surprised me but it didn't take the wind out of my sails though it did make me curious.

"They were amateurs?" I asked.

"Think they're big shots, they aren't. Navarro was the only professional sittin' that table."

"Which one was Navarro?" I asked but I thought I knew.

"Slim. Black hair. Eyes sliding to the couch about a hundred fuckin' times."

I was right, I knew.

"So amateurs play for those kind of stakes?"

He nodded as he dropped his cuff links on the desk and said, "The rest of those men got money to burn. Hobby. That's why they let me play them. They don't let just anyone sit a table. My boy that got me in the game told them about me. They knew my history. They thought I was an easy mark. Had money, not much, but enough, and they were willin' to take it. I spent an hour losin' and they lost interest in me since they thought they took me, forgot to pay attention. Amateur mistake. Navarro knew what I was doin' the minute I started doin' it, and that includes walkin' in the room with you."

This didn't make sense. "If he's a professional, why did he lose his concentration?"

His eyes came to me. "I won big but I'm seein' with that question you were payin' attention to me, not the game. He won bigger and that's how good he is. Half his mind on the game, half on your legs and he still took them for almost nine hundred large."

"Oh," I whispered, thinking nearly a million dollars was cool too but I wasn't in a room with a man who won nearly a million dollars. I was in a room with Ty and what he won was *more* than enough. Then I asked, "What did Stetson guy mean when he told you that you wouldn't be invited to sit another table? Was he just pissed you won?"

"The Texan figured out I played him and wasn't happy about it because he thinks I'm dirt. I'm an ex-con, but even if I wasn't, I'm half black and have been all my life so I can smell it when a man don't like color. That man don't like color so he thinks I'm beneath him, ex-con or not and ex-con only makes it worse and also makes him think he's right, all the reasons he's convinced himself it's okay he don't like color. He's in his sixties and still tappin' twenty-somethin' ass because his money and status can buy him that kinda tail. Still, I played him. He doesn't like that. But he didn't like me the minute

I walked in with you. Man like me shouldn't have class like you. Mouthed off to save face and remind me of my place."

I felt angry heat hit my chest as I whispered, "That isn't cool."

He shrugged. "Happens all the time. A mechanic who's got color or he doesn't hits a high-stakes game, they don't know my reputation or they do and think they can best me, I take their money, they get pissed."

"So, is he going to block you from sitting another game?"

"I'm not gonna be sittin' another game."

I stared at him, thrown.

Then I asked, "What? Why not? You just won nearly half a million dollars."

His eyes held mine and he explained, "Lexie, that shit sucks you in. You don't control it, it controls you. I just spent five years essentially in chains. I don't need to be chained to somethin' else."

I felt my breath start sticking in my throat because he meant this. He had no intention of getting sucked in in order to live large doing something that wasn't exactly illegal (though I wasn't sure about that) but still was slightly dubious and definitely unpredictable. Testing Lady Luck who was unforgiving and living a life that wasn't under his control.

I liked this. A lot.

Too much.

Ty went on, "I sat that game for a reason. That money's got a purpose. That money finances the business I need to see to. I got a life to restart. That money will help me restart it. Now I got the money, don't need to sit another game."

In other words, it wasn't about bling, great shoes and one-hour tailoring of expensive suits.

Tonight had a purpose, he'd seen to it and he was moving on.

Yes, I liked this. A lot. I liked it even though any business that required nearly half a million dollars was dubious too.

"Well, I'm glad you got what you needed, Ty," I said quietly, and he stared at me, face expressionless but, again, it felt like he was reading me. Finally he jerked up his chin.

Then he started unbuttoning his shirt.

I moved to the unit and dropped my earrings on it, took off my necklace and put it there too then struggled with my bracelet, managed to unclasp it and laid it with the others.

I went to my bag, which had exploded on the floor at the end of the luggage shelf. I dug in, got my drawstring shorts and the little tight tee I wore to bed and moved to the bathroom. I secured my hair in a messy bunch on top of my head, changed, washed my face, brushed my teeth, moisturized and walked out carrying my dress and shoes. I hung the dress, dumped the shoes and saw Ty in bed, back to headboard, sheet up to his waist, chest and defined abs on display, eyes on the TV and they didn't come to me even as I moved about the room.

Even though I hadn't been in the bathroom very long, the air in the room seemed about ten degrees cooler than when I went in and the AC was audibly pumping. Therefore, I wasted no time in moving around the bed and sliding under the covers beside him. Last night, after a huge meal and almost a bottle of champagne to myself, I fell asleep watching TV and slept on the covers. Tonight, sliding into bed beside him felt strange. And part of this strange had to do with wondering what he was wearing under the sheet.

I sucked it up, rolled to my side facing Ty, up on an elbow in the pillow, knees curled and I pointed my eyes down my body to the TV.

"Put your jewelry in the safe," Ty muttered, and my gaze slid to the unit then back to the TV.

"Thanks," I whispered back then I noted softly, "You mentioned something about when a mechanic hits a high-stakes game. Obviously, you've played before."

To my comment, his response was, "Give-and-take?"

My gaze moved from the TV up his large frame to his beautiful eyes that were on me.

"Sure," I whispered.

"I played, yeah. Not often but I did it. My dad drank his paycheck so growin' up, wasn't used to havin' a lot but found I'm a man who likes nice shit. You like it you find a way to get it. I discovered I got talent at a table, I found the way."

Okay, suffice it to say, this I *didn't* like. Ronnie liked nice shit too and he found a way to get it. And I was seeing I should have noticed this about Ty earlier.

Firstly, he wore jeans and tees well but he wasn't a stranger to nice suits and expensive cuff links. Secondly, that morning when I saw his shades, I knew he didn't pick them off a tall, upright, plastic rack displaying a hundred other pairs of five-dollar sunglasses. They cost some cake and he wore them with jeans, a tee and boots like he was used to wearing two-hundred-and-fifty-dollar sunglasses. Thirdly, practically the first thing he did when he hit Vegas after getting released from prison was go shopping and drop tens of thousands of dollars. The bags on the desk he still hadn't emptied weren't just bling and shades.

Therefore, I remarked, "I noticed you don't have an aversion to shopping."

"Also don't got an aversion to work or gettin' my hands dirty," he returned.

"What?"

"I like nice shit but I don't mind workin' for it and as much as I like it, not gonna fuck myself in order to get it."

"So..." I hesitated then went for it, "you playing poker didn't have anything to do with you being wrongly imprisoned?"

His eyes held mine.

Then he said quietly, "Didn't say that."

There it was. Shit.

"That's why you won't play anymore after tonight," I whispered, disappointed that he'd semi-lied.

"No," he replied. "The men who marked me to go down needed a fall guy. I took money from one at a table. He got pissed about it so I got his attention and became his fall guy."

"So you playing poker had something to do with you being wrongly imprisoned," I stated.

"No," he repeated. "I just happened to be at the wrong place at the wrong time getting the wrong kind of attention. Someone else won that night, it woulda been him. I accidentally brushed him as I walked by him buyin' a beer at a bar, he didn't take kindly to that, that woulda bought me the same shit. They didn't care who they targeted, they just needed someone to target. It didn't have to do with poker. It had to do with them needin' a fall guy. I got in their sights, that's who I became."

At his explanation, the fact he gave it to me and the fact that it proved he hadn't lied earlier, I felt my breathing steady and hadn't realized it had become slightly labored.

Then I went for it again. "How did that happen, um…exactly?"

He shook his head. "Done givin'. Now I take."

Well, at least I got something.

He continued, "You asked, you got. Now I ask."

"Okay," I agreed.

"Told me you don't got a mom or a dad. No grandparents. You got any people?"

I shook my head.

"None?" he pushed.

I kept shaking my head but affirmed, "None."

"How can you have no people?"

"I do. Ronnie's family."

"They aren't your people."

"Yes, Ty, they are."

He held my eyes.

Then he asked, "They raise you?"

"Kind of."

"Not an answer, Lexie."

I blew out a sigh.

Then I pulled my knees to my belly, wrapped my arm around them and told him my story.

Or parts of it.

"My mom and dad died when I was young. Long story. My dad's parents died when he was sixteen. Car crash. My gran died when I was six and granddad when I was thirteen. My dad had a sister but by the time Granddad died, well…let's just say, I was a handful and she didn't want any part of that so she didn't take any part of it."

I stopped. Ty said nothing so I kept going.

"Obviously, because of that, although she lives in Dallas, I don't see her and when I say that, I mean *ever.* Life was shit for me. Granddad wasn't all that great. I was thirteen, acting out and just needed someone to give a shit. She didn't. I got put into a home for girls then was farmed out into foster care. Foster care took me to a new school, I met Bessie, Ronnie's sister, we became BFFs—something, by the way, we still are. They lived in what could be considered one step up from the projects and that was a small step but, trust me, no matter how fucked up that was, their home was better than foster care. So I spent a lot of time there."

Ty held my eyes the entire time I was talking and kept hold of them as I continued.

"My foster carers still got paid so they didn't give a shit where I spent my time and ate my meals. Ronnie's dad took off, whereabouts still unknown, so Ronnie grew up watching his mom struggle to put food on the table and spending most of his time avoiding local boys who were trying to recruit him into a gang. He was also the man of the family. He took that seriously but, obviously, didn't do it smart."

I took in a deep breath and went on with my voice much lower.

"As far as Ronnie was concerned, there were two ways to take care of his women. One, the NBA. Two, what he ended up doing. Problem with that was, Ella wanted not one thing to do with money earned the way he earned it. This caused dissension. I was the link that kept this dissension from going into meltdown. Ella never took any of Ronnie's money but at least I managed to keep him in the family fold. And I was definitely part of the family fold and would have been even if I ended things with Ronnie. We broke it off, I would have got his family, not him, and when he died none of that changed. So, seeing as that's the way and the fact that they were the only real family I knew, they're my people."

When I quit talking, Ty just stared at me and said not a word.

So I asked, "Are we done with give-and-take?"

"Yeah," he answered but his eyes didn't move back to the TV and the way he was staring at me, as normal, impassive but yet I still felt the intensity of his stare, my eyes didn't move either.

This also made me prompt, "What?"

"I don't get it," he replied.

I felt my brows draw together and I repeated, "What?"

He looked to the TV muttering, "Nothin'."

"Ty," I called and he didn't look at me but still I repeated, "What?" He continued not to look at me so I asked, "What don't you get?"

Then his eyes sliced to me and he proceeded without hesitation to rock my world.

"You're part goof, all class. Never walked in a room, any room, with a woman on my arm, any woman, who's got your looks, your style, the kinda beauty you got and the light that shines from you. So I don't get it. I don't get how a woman leads a life full of shit and comes out of it bein' part goof and all class. That shit's impossible but there you fuckin' are. Part goof, all class."

I felt my breath coming fast but managed to whisper, "I'm not part goof."

"You're right. I was bein' nice. You're a total goof."

"Am not."

"Babe, you call me 'hubby,'" he pointed out but my breath came faster because he called me "babe" again.

"You *are* my hubby."

"No one says 'hubby,'" he told me.

"I do," I told him.

"All right, I'll rephrase. No one but a goof says 'hubby.'"

"Is that written in stone somewhere?"

"It should be."

"So, you don't like it."

At that, his body twisted minutely in my direction, his chin dipped down a half a centimeter, his eyes locked with mine and I quit breathing.

And his voice was a very low rumble when he stated, "I didn't say I didn't like it."

"Okay," I breathed.

"I like it." He kept rumbling.

"Okay," I repeated breathily.

"You're still a fuckin' goof."

I kept silent.

"And I like that too," he finished, readjusted microscopically and his eyes slid to the TV.

I decided my best course of action at that juncture was to point my eyes at the TV too, so I did. Then I struggled to regain control of my breathing. I managed this feat. When I did, I wondered again what he was wearing under the sheet. I struggled to quit wondering and also managed that, but barely. Then I allowed the fact that he liked me calling him "hubby" and that I was a goof (he thought) to penetrate. I tried to stop myself from allowing the fact that I liked that he liked those things and I also liked all the other things he said to penetrate.

I failed at that.

Then I pulled the covers up high on my shoulder because the room was fucking freezing, and I managed to fall asleep in a bed with Ty Walker.

I woke up and he was gone. This time, he left a note on his pillow that said:

L

Gym.

T

I studied it with sleepy eyes and for some bizarre reason, memorized his slashes. And that was what his handwriting was. Dark, heavily pressed slashes. Even where there should be curves there were slashes.

I got up, got ready to hit the pool, wrote him a note and, for some other bizarre reason, I folded and tucked his one-word note into a pocket in my wallet.

I went to the pool and ordered a latte from a passing waiter hoping Ty would show eventually so we could have breakfast together. And I didn't allow myself to think about this hope or the fact that my eyes moved to the doors to the pool on far more than a rare occasion, hoping I'd spy him striding out of them. In fact, not lying in bed with him after he won half a million dollars and told me I was a goof and beautiful, I was able to disallow myself from doing a lot of things.

Though one of those things wasn't stopping my eyes from wandering hopefully to the door time and again.

Shit.

It hit me I was hot, as in very hot, and that was something I didn't expect I'd be after I woke up with a frozen nose in the deep freeze that was our room. It also hit me that the morning was wearing on, Ty was not showing and I was hungry.

It was time to find my husband.

But I'd do that after a cooldown.

I set my eReader aside, took off my shades and tossed them aside too, got up and moved to the edge of the pool. I waited for my opening in the busy pool, bent my legs and dove in.

The cool waters hit me like a slap and felt great. I loved the water, loved swimming. Ronnie had promised me a beach house but obviously never delivered on that promise. In fact, until I took a significant detour the day before showing up to pick up Ty, I'd never been to a beach. But I built the time in to hit La Jolla. I didn't have a lot of time but I built it in, parked the car and took an hourlong walk on the beach before climbing into my car, driving to the town outside the prison and checking into a motel to spend the night before I had to pick up Ty.

And even though that beach was packed, it was the most peaceful hour I'd had in my entire life. It wasn't bliss, it wasn't even happiness. It was quiet contentment, warm sun, soft sand, the sound of the waves and the beauty of a horizon filled with blue.

Now that I had my life back, I was going to carve in a vacation at the beach. Maybe, after Ty's business was done and I was free, I'd go to the beach.

Maybe I'd try to talk him into going with me.

Shit.

Pushing this thought aside, my stomach told me it needed food and I struck out to the ladder at the side of the pool. I pulled myself out and the sun glinted, sending a bright flicker that caught my attention and I looked to my left hand and saw my wedding rings.

I felt my mouth curve into a smile.

When I realized my mouth had curved into a smile at the mere sight of my wedding rings, it turned down into a frown.

Shit.

I pushed that thought aside too when my feet hit deck, my eyes went to my lounge chair and it took a lot for me to keep moving to it when I saw the man stretched out in the one next to mine.

Navarro. Navarro wearing nice slacks, one of those shiny, expensive polo-necked shirts and shades that cost more than Ty's. Shades, incidentally, that were pointed at me and they were pointed at me in a way that I knew they'd been set in my direction for a while.

I was dripping wet and not feeling good about him being there as I moved to the opposite side of my lounge from him, quickly grabbed my towel and held it full length to the front of me, eyes on him, hands in the towel pressing it against the lower half of my face.

His shades were still on me.

I dropped my hands to my neck and pressed my bent arms against the towel into my body.

"Hey," I said.

He unfolded from the chair and stood opposite me.

"Hello, Lexie."

I pressed my lips together then asked, "Something I can do for you?"

"Actually, yes."

I waited even though I didn't want to. I also wondered where the fuck my husband was. How long was he going to work out? He had a great body but hell, I'd been out here at least an hour and he was gone before I woke up.

"And that would be?" I prompted when he said nothing more.

"Would you mind, perhaps, coming with me so we can find someplace to talk in private or, maybe, meeting me somewhere later?"

I felt my back go straight because I didn't expect this and also because I didn't like it.

"Yes, I would mind," I answered then I asked, "Does this have to do with Ty?"

He shook his head. "No."

"Then why are you here?"

"I have an offer to make to you."

I didn't like this either and felt my eyes narrow. "And this doesn't have to do with Ty?"

"No. It has to do with you."

Me? How could it have to do with me?

"Um… dude, I don't know you," I pointed out.

"I'd like to change that."

Oh. *That* was how it had to do with me.

Shit!

"Uh… not sure you know this but I'm married and the guy I'm married to is Ty."

"I do know this."

What the fuck?

I didn't ask that. Instead, I nodded my head. "So, you know that, now I'll tell you that Ty and I are here for fun and we're going home tomorrow. This isn't our circle so our paths aren't going to cross."

"This…" he paused, "*circle* isn't often mine either," he replied. "My circles are varied and I'd like to speak to you about the possibility of introducing them to you."

Shit, shit, fucking shit.

"I think I already answered that," I reminded him.

"Lexie, I'm asking you for the opportunity to speak with you privately so I can fully explain what I'm offering."

I stared at him.

Then I said, "No."

"I'm not sure you—"

I shook my head and stated, "I said no. I'm married to a good man who makes me happy and I see you're handsome and dress nice but when a woman marries a good man who makes her happy, she doesn't fuck with that no matter what she might be offered."

He studied me through his shades and he did this for a while. So long, it made me uncomfortable and it made me want to grab my shit and go, leaving him there but, more importantly, finding Ty.

Before I could do this, he informed me, "I suspected this would be your answer."

I blinked at him then asked, "If you did, why'd you ask?"

"Because when a man sees another man who has a good woman who will stick with him no matter what she's offered, he wants that for himself. There are not many women who look like you who would make that choice." He grinned. "So it was worth a try. Everything worth something is worth a try."

"Well, you tried and I've decided I'll take your effort as a compliment rather than finding it annoying but now I need to find my husband because I'm hungry and I want breakfast."

He nodded. Then he lifted a hand in a vague gesture of a farewell wave.

After giving me his wave, he said, "I appreciate your time."

"Whatever," I mumbled and he again grinned, turned and sauntered away.

I watched him go thinking he gave the impression my response was all the same to him and then I clocked Bag of Bones watching Navarro move toward the doors to the hotel.

Shit again!

I toweled off, squeezed the water out of my hair, pulled my shirt and shorts over my wet suit, gathered my stuff and hightailed my ass to our room thinking the whole way there that I'd been right to give up on men while the giving up was good. Imagine walking up to a woman you didn't know but did know was married and propositioning her.

Insane.

I slid in the keycard at our door, waited for the green light, slid it out and walked in. The minute I did I heard the shower going as well as the television blaring. Automatically, my eyes moved to the bathroom door and then I stopped dead.

The bathroom door was open. I had a view to the mirror and reflected in the mirror was Ty in the shower.

That was enough. All the beauty that was Ty, naked in the shower, was enough to make me stand there statue-still and stare in lost but avid fascination, but that wasn't all there was.

Because Ty wasn't just taking a shower.

He had one powerful arm lifted, hand pressed to the tiled wall, his neck was bent, the water beating against his head, neck and back, his skin was glistening, his eyes were closed, his other fist was wrapped around his cock and stroking.

And I had it then…indisputable proof that every inch of him was beautiful.

Every inch.

And there were a lot of them.

A lot.

I knew I should back out, go get myself a latte, leave him to his business and come back but I couldn't move. I couldn't move because what met my eyes was beautiful and it was so unbelievably sexy, I was instantly turned on more than I'd ever been in my life.

In…my…*life.*

I couldn't breathe. I couldn't think. I could only see and feel what was happening to my body watching him doing what he was doing. Then I had to fight the overwhelming desire to drop my stuff, pull off my clothes, join him in the shower, wrap my arms around him and press my body to his back while he finished.

Or talk him into finishing a different way.

I got hold of myself, backed up and, as silently as I could, I opened the door and scuttled through.

Then, wet hair, tacky body, wet seeping through my clothes, armful of stuff, I found the nearest coffee cart, bought two lattes and juggled them and my things as I went back to the room.

I stood outside and pounded on the door with my foot, shouting, "Hands full, hubby! Help me out!"

I waited approximately three point five seconds before the door opened and Ty stood there in faded jeans and nothing else.

My mouth went dry.

It was then I realized I should probably have gone back and jumped in the pool and, maybe, stayed there for a decade.

Visions dancing in my head, by a sheer miracle I pulled it together enough to push through the door and walk by him all the while babbling.

"I got you a coffee. I need breakfast but before, I need to tell you what went down by the pool and then I need a shower so maybe we should do room service because my hunger is eating through my stomach lining and I could use taking off a couple of pounds but I don't want my system filled with stomach acid in order to do that."

I stopped, turned, dumped everything in my arms on the floor by holding my elbows out to the sides then I shoved a hand his way, offering him a takeaway latte.

His eyes were on the stuff now scattered on the floor then they moved to the latte.

"It isn't fancy," I declared and his eyes moved from the takeaway cup to mine. "Full fat. Considering the amount of muscle you lug around, your metabolism has to be akin to Superman's so you can hack full fat. And no syrup because I've noticed you have a sweet tooth but I haven't noticed if you lean toward anything specific. You seem to like it all and you're a huge badass. I didn't want to get it wrong and incur disfavor so the basic will just have to do."

When I finally quit babbling and he could get a word in edgewise, he asked, "Are you all right?"

No. No. It was safe to say I was *not* all right. I'd seen my husband masturbating in the shower. I'd never seen anything more beautiful in my life. And I was standing in a hotel room probably looking like garbage when he was three feet away from me looking like the definition of male beauty and I had a near-overpowering urge to jump him and fuck his brains out.

So no, I was not all right.

I didn't share any of this but I still answered, "No."

His hand came up and he took the latte from me, ordering, "Talk to me."

"I was at the pool," I told him and then sucked back some of my own latte wondering if Ty would find it amiss if I hit the minibar and poured a few mini-bottles of rum into my coffee. Say, seven of them.

"Yeah, I know. You left me a note," Ty prompted when I said no more.

"A pool, incidentally, that you didn't join me at."

"Lexie, told you, got no need to hang out in the sun."

"I know you told me that but there's a meal to be consumed, it's called breakfast and it's the most important meal of the day."

"You're hungry, eat."

"Aren't you hungry?"

"They got a counter at the gym. Had a protein shake after I worked out."

My eyes narrowed. "You have a phone, you didn't think to call me and tell me you were covered so I could take care of myself?"

"No, I didn't, seein' as you're a grown woman. I assumed you could take care of yourself or, say, phone *me* you wanna know what's happening, not charge into the room throwing sass."

My back went straight.

"Throwing sass?" I asked.

"Throwing sass," he answered.

"What the fuck does that mean?" I snapped and, surprisingly, his brows drew together and he shared a reaction with me and that reaction was puzzlement with an edge of annoyance.

"It means, you barged in here yammering and then threw a fit about me not joinin' you at the pool, which I told you I didn't do, and you bein' hungry when anyone knows, they're hungry, they should fuckin' eat, and not phonin' you when your phone's right fuckin' there." He pointed to the phone that fell to the ground when I dropped my stuff. "And you got fingers so you can also dial me. That's throwin' sass."

I glared at him.

He kept talking. "I also told you this was your vacation day so I got back, saw you were at the pool and left you to it."

"You left me to it?"

"Uh... yeah."

"Yeah?" I snapped.

His eyes changed at my snap and it was new to me but I read it right away.

Confusion and annoyance gone. Now he felt anger.

He proved that by biting out, "What the fuck's your problem?"

"My problem, Ty," I started, not giving one shit about the fact that this huge man was obviously angry and angry enough to let it penetrate the impenetrable shields he kept up to cover his emotions, "is that I wanted to have breakfast with my husband, not be *left to it.* What, were you gonna leave me out there all day?"

It was then I noticed his body had gone still but I was still angry.

And I knew why I was angry.

I was angry because I was reacting to something different. Something important. Something big and it had nothing to do with breakfast and everything to do with life being total shit and me never being able to latch onto anything good, anything clean, anything right.

And I sensed, no matter what secrets the man standing in front of me had, he was all three of those things. Therefore right in front of me I had something I wanted and there I was, in a position where I couldn't let myself have it, not until I knew I was right.

But I wanted it, not later, but right then and that pissed me way the hell off and I was taking all that out on him.

"Hello?" I called. "Did you hear me?"

He spoke and when he did it was soft in a way that made *my* body go still.

"You wanted to have breakfast with your husband?"

"Well, yeah," I replied. "We did that yesterday. It was nice. I mean, I'm the kind of person who can be alone and I have no problem doing that but why be alone when you can be with someone you like being around? And we're in Vegas and we have a vacation day. It isn't often you get to be in Vegas on a vacation day so you should live it up. If you don't want to hang at the pool, that's cool. So we have breakfast, go shopping, go to some crazy Vegas museum or do the Star Trek Experience. I heard that's cool and not just for geeks. But whatever we do, we should do something. And all of this, by the way, was something we could have discussed over," I leaned in to drive my point home, "*breakfast*."

He stared at me and I let him.

Then he rocked my world again and he did this by saying in a different kind of soft voice, "Baby, you wanna have breakfast with your husband, all you gotta do is pick up the phone and dial. I'm covered, you eat, I sit with you and drink coffee. But you want me, anytime you want me, that's all you gotta do."

I didn't speak and again I couldn't breathe and there were a lot of reasons for that. The first, he called me "baby," which was the second time he did that but the first time he did it without an audience. The first time he did it in that soft voice. The first time he did it just him and me and I felt that word rushing through my blood with a warmth I never wanted to leave. Second, his soft voice was the most beautiful thing I'd ever heard in my life. And third, him telling me anytime I wanted him, he was a phone call away was the kind of thing I'd wanted my entire life and never—not ever—had and there he was, giving it to me.

"Lexie," he called.

"Navarro propositioned me at the pool," I blurted to cover all the profound feelings I couldn't quite deal with feeling right then and he gave me yet another reaction.

His torso jerked back, his brows snapped together, his eyes narrowed and his big-man energy swelled to fill the room.

"What the fuck?" he whispered.

"With Bag of Bones watching," I went on.

"What'd he say?" he asked, but each word lashed out like a whip.

"I didn't let him say much of anything. He said he wanted to talk privately about an offer he'd like to make me. I said I didn't wish to talk privately with him and reminded him I was married. He did a little pushing. I made it clear I wasn't interested. He gave up and walked away."

Ty stared at me.

"Still," I continued. "It was an asshole thing to do."

Ty kept staring at me but he was doing it like he didn't see me.

"Ty?" I called.

His eyes focused on me.

"Throwin' sass," he muttered.

"What?" I asked.

"You're not hungry. You got cornered when I wasn't at your back and that's why you're pissed."

"Well, no," I said. "We were in a public place. He didn't push it and told me he knew the answer I'd give him but it was worth a try. Anyway, I can take care of myself but I thought you should know. I thought you should also know Bag of Bones was part of our audience. I don't know what's going down with him but, well...whatever it is, you should know."

He stared at me again and I didn't mind because I was used to that.

Then he moved straight into rocking my world yet again and I minded that because you *never* got used to that.

"It's good you're not pissed but I am. I fucked up. I used you last night to help me get somethin' I needed and doin' it made you visible, which put you where you were this morning. And I don't like where I put you this morning. That's on me and I also don't like that that's on me. But it happened and right now all I can do is promise you that won't happen again."

It was my turn to stare at him.

Then I pointed out, "But isn't this whole gig for me to be available to—?"

He shook his head. His arm swung out to the side, he set his coffee down by the TV then crossed his arms on his chest. "I told you when I laid it out for you, none of my shit would blow back on you. This morning, my shit blew back on you."

"Ty," I said gently. "It wasn't that big of a deal."

"It's good you think that, Lexie, but I don't agree."

I tried to assure him, "He was relatively gentlemanly about it."

"I don't give a shit how he was about it. I don't like the idea of you bein' out there alone and a man like Navarro thinkin' he can get in your space. Your space is your space and you get to decide who's in it. At the very least, Navarro should think your space is *my* space and *I* get to decide who's in it. Either way, he got in your space, that does not make me happy because him doin' it means I gave you my word and then I broke it."

"You didn't break it, Ty. You can't be responsible for his actions."

"I tell you to cross your legs often?" he shot back.

I pressed my lips together.

"Right," he clipped.

I walked the short distance between us and put my hand on his bicep.

"Honey, you aren't responsible for his actions."

His chin was in his throat as he stared down at me but he didn't reply.

"I shouldn't have said anything," I muttered, looking away.

But I looked back and that was because I had no choice but to do so when Ty's big hand cupped my jaw and forced my face to his.

"Don't keep shit from me," he ordered quietly.

I nodded and whispered, "Okay."

"For however long this lasts, you play wife. That's all you do. You don't put up with shit from anyone and especially not because of me."

"Ty, guys hit on women they're wearing wedding rings or not. What he did was the same thing. Who's to say that, he didn't see me last night but saw me at the pool, he wouldn't have done that anyway?"

"*I'm* to say it because last night he saw you watchin' me lose, your face givin' it away that you didn't know that was the way I was playin' it but you still laid your jewelry at my side without hesitation and kissed my jaw before you walked away. He saw a woman take her man's back. He's a guy who's got no shot at findin' a woman like that because the women that gravitate toward men like him are not your kind of woman. And he wants what I got. I showed him that. So, he might like what he sees by the pool but he took a shot at it because I showed him what's behind the tits, ass and legs. He can get tits, ass and legs anytime he wants. What he can't get is what's behind yours."

There it was again. A Ty-style compliment that couldn't be beat.

"Ty," I whispered.

"It won't happen again."

"Okay, but you need to know, I'm not mad at you for that. I don't even *care* about that. I'm not actually mad at you about anything. I really am hungry and wanted to have breakfast with you."

"Okay, I know what you need me to know but I need to know you get it that it won't happen again."

Good. Clean. Right.

Right there. In front of me.

Shit.

"I get it," I said softly.

His hand dropped.

I instantly missed it.

"Okay," he said and took a step back so my hand had to drop. "Get in the shower. I'll order room service and get you fed. While you eat, we'll decide what we're gonna do on your vacation day."

I nodded but asked, "Are you going to let me pick what I want for breakfast?"

And again, he gave me a gift. His lips tipped up a half a centimeter.

Then he replied, "You didn't let me pick my coffee."

So maybe he also had a sense of humor.

Good.

One step closer to knowing what I thought he was was real. An important one.

"Fair enough," I muttered, smiling at my feet and turning to my bag.

He got on the phone and I gathered my stuff as I listened to him ordering me blueberry pancakes, which sounded really good. Then again, I was super hungry so pretty much anything would sound really good.

I went into the bathroom, shut the door and turned on the shower.

In the shower, I listened and heard the TV even over the water.

So I knew a door, a wall, a shower and the TV would drown out me doing what I needed to do.

So I did it.

After, I felt much better.

Even so, I knew what would make me feel even better.

But I wasn't going to go there.

Not yet.

Ty

Ty lounged on the bed, eyes on the TV and mind in the shower.

That was how he heard it when Lexie made herself come. It surprised him. He wasn't expecting it, the noise was slight but also unmistakable and unbelievably hot.

He closed his eyes and muttered, "Fuck."

A knock came at the door.

His wife's breakfast.

CHAPTER SIX

Amos Moses

Ty

"Amie, what you wanna do..."

The Charger was growling down the highway, the sun shining bright, Lexie sitting beside him, hair flying all around her face, feet to the dash, knees bent near to her chest, heels popping up, legs swaying, hands on her thighs slapping, mouth open singing some hick-ass, country rock song at the top of her lungs which was the only way he could hear her considering that shit coming from her iPod connected to the car stereo was blasting out the speakers.

It was day two of their road trip and they were two hours out of Carnal. The drive from Vegas was a one-day haul but she'd wanted to take a detour and spend the night in Moab.

And, seeing as he was currently thinking with his dick, he'd given her what she wanted.

Thinking on it, after she told him she wanted to have breakfast with her husband, he would have given it to her. But after spending her vacation day in Vegas with her, he would have walked to Moab at her side if she'd asked.

It was official. He was fucked.

As they talked about what to do while she stuffed her face with blueberry pancakes after her shower, all the shit she wanted to do in Vegas he did not want to do.

But then she dropped the bomb that she'd never been to Vegas. After that, she'd dropped the bomb that, the day before she picked him up from prison, she'd taken her first trip to a beach. She'd then dropped another bomb that, although her job took her to LA and NYC for buying trips, she'd had her promotion to head buyer for only a year which was when she started traveling for work, these trips were manic and she had zero time to sightsee.

Further, considering she was hooked up with Ronnie, they didn't enjoy romantic couple's retreats at exotic locales. Pimps, apparently, didn't get vacation time. The only other places she'd been were Austin, Texas, when she went on a very long joyride in her twenties with Bessie, and Atlanta, Georgia, where Ronnie's people were from and where they'd sometimes spend Thanksgiving or Christmas.

So he'd followed her ass to fucking M&M World and dealt with her crushing disappointment that the Star Trek Experience had closed down. They'd stood in the heat three times to watch the Bellagio fountains spraying to music. They'd toured casino after casino. She'd played kids' video games (*not* adult gambling video games) while he watched. She'd scoured gift shops giggling herself stupid half the time and pretend-begging him to buy her tacky crap.

And, when she wasn't looking, he did, buying her a t-shirt at Paris Las Vegas and a snow globe at Treasure Island, both of which, he made certain to note for future reference, when he gave them to her, she was more excited about than the diamonds.

And last, they'd walked up one side and down the other of practically the whole fucking Strip after the sun set so she could take in the lights and the sights.

And as they did this, she opened up and let it all hang out.

Lexie forgot all about give-and-take and just gave.

She did this by telling him about Ella, Bessie and Honey. About her friend Margot. About her other friend Nyssa. Yammering through lunch, through dinner, as they walked only to interrupt herself, point at something and shout, "Ohmigod, *look at that*!"

She also did this by holding his hand and when she wasn't doing that, her fingers would curve around his elbow and hold on. As she walked, she got so close to him, he could feel her skin brushing his. If they were standing, she stood leaned into his side. If they were seated, she sat close. When she talked, she'd touch him, shove his shoulder, grasp his hand, shake his arm, bump her body into his depending on what she wanted, to get his attention, because she was laughing and wanted to share her humor, because she was fake annoyed at him for teasing her or to point something out.

Walker had never met another woman like her, her casual affection, ready sense of humor, openness, her clashing ability to seem confident in her surroundings at the same time excited by them. Day three of knowing her and there she was, no bullshit. And he realized that was what he had since the beginning from Lexie. No bullshit.

And all day, Bag of Bones was nowhere to be seen. This was her. This was what she gave free and without expecting anything in return. All give, no take.

That night, she'd been out within seconds of her head hitting the pillow.

Walker didn't get to sleep for hours.

The next morning he learned more about Lexie and this was she could be a pain in the ass. She took forever to get ready, freaked out about leaving something in the room so she checked under the bed twelve times and opened all the drawers even though neither of them had put shit in them and making him check the safe twice even though nothing he put in there he'd fucking forget.

And, fuck him, after they checked out and were waiting for the Charger to be brought around, he thought of it and he couldn't stop himself from thinking it was cute.

They got in the car and the battle instantly began.

She didn't like "fake cold"—what she called air-conditioning. He didn't like the windows down. Compromise, she got the windows down first, he got AC after the clock struck one thirty. Then she hooked up her iPod and tortured him with her music. He told her he thought it was shit. Compromise, when the windows were opened, they played her music. They listened to what he wanted to listen to when he jacked the AC up.

They hit Moab and the bitch flipped for it, making him find a store so she could buy a camera, something he didn't allow her to do, the buying it part. He bought one for her, an expensive digital camera, and when he did, she gave him something else, something new. Her face got soft, her eyes went warm and she leaned her tits into his arm, tipping her head back and smiling at him huge, shining the full force of her light on him and, swear to Christ, he'd been blinded.

At that, he wished he'd watched her open her diamonds.

Then she made him drive her all over the fucking place. At her shout, he'd stopped a dozen times so she could take pictures and anytime another breathing being was close, she asked them to take a picture of him and Lexie together. She'd drag him in front of something, curl into him and smile bright into the camera like she'd hit Heaven, not Utah.

They'd checked into a hotel, went out and had dinner, came back and ordered up a movie. It was an action film and she sat sprawled at the end of the bed shouting at the screen the whole time and when the hero finally kicked the bad guy's ass, she'd actually yelled, "Take that, sucka!"

Sucka.

Proof positive she was a total fucking goof.

That night, too, lying at her side in bed, Walker had trouble finding sleep.

Now they were in the car, two hours into day two on the road, two hours away from home. She'd done the whole freak out at not leaving anything behind but she'd also taken twice as much time getting ready.

Yesterday, she'd worn her Paris Las Vegas tee, some shorts and some flip-flops.

Today, her hair was done wild and sexy. She had on a pair of nice, army green short-shorts and a sexy-as-hell, loose-fitting, apricot tee that caught on her tits just right and left her back exposed. A drape at the bottom of the back, one string tied in the middle to hold the fabric together and you could see her cream-colored bra strap. She'd added the sandals she'd been wearing the day he met her, the first time he'd seen her wear the same pair of shoes twice. And last, gold hoops at her ears and a bunch of thin, gold bracelets at both wrists.

What she was tricked out for, he had no idea. He didn't ask. He didn't have a chance. She was busy checking under the bed and opening and closing drawers.

He left her to it and dragged their shit down to the reception desk and out to the Charger after he checked out. She met him there, throwing sass about him being impatient and how "We can't just swing by if we left something. FYI, Utah is a whole different *state* than the one you live in, Ty."

He decided to concentrate on putting the car in gear rather than responding.

She opened her window, put on her music and his torture began.

Two minutes later she told him she was going to "Die in five minutes if I don't have coffee."

He swung into a convenience store. They went in and she bought a two-liter cup filled with joe and a pack of breakfast Ding Dongs. He bought a cup of coffee about a quarter the size of hers and a stale bear claw from the donut display. After bite three, he decided he couldn't deal with the stale and threw it out his open window.

To this she snapped, "Ohmigod, Ty! What the fuck?"

"It was stale," he told the windshield, trying not to smile because he'd learned from her tone, which he'd heard before, that this was going to be good.

"So! You just littered."

"It's food so it isn't litter."

"You're telling me food is omitted from the official definition of litter?"

"Yeah."

"All-Knowing Ty Walker, also known by his superhero alter-ego, Mr. Humongo, has memorized the definition of litter?"

Yep, he was right. This was good. Even pissed, the bitch was funny.

"They make you do that kinda shit in prison."

"They do not."

"Babe, five years in one building, they gotta do something to keep us occupied."

"You're full of shit," she mumbled, he looked to her and saw her shove an entire Ding Dong in her mouth.

Ding Dongs.

Christ.

Total goof.

They hit the highway, she jacked up the music and he experienced the unusual desire to beg someone to drive ice picks in his ears so he wouldn't have to listen to it.

Then she started singing while sipping her coffee, just like the day before, at the top of her lungs with occasional car dancing.

And again. Total goof.

The country-rock song finally died and she snatched up the iPod to consider his next agony.

"Baby?" he called, and he felt her eyes on him.

"Yeah?" she replied, her sweet voice soft, another tone he was getting used to and this was because the last couple of days it had started to come at him often.

"Do me a favor?"

"Sure."

"In a second, I'm gonna pull over, get out my gun and give it to you. When I do, shoot me with it."

"What?" she whispered.

"I'm facin' another hour and a half of your music. I'd rather be dead."

Silence then, "Shut up."

"No, seriously."

A smile in her voice then a repeated, "Shut up."

He bit back his own smile.

Then he heard her say, "Actually, a pit stop wouldn't be amiss at this juncture."

He glanced at her then back at the road. "What?"

"I need to use the restroom."

He sighed.

Two-liter cup of coffee.

Jesus.

"We been on the road two hours," he pointed out.

"You are correct but that doesn't change my need to use the facilities."

"Next time, you get a coffee the size of mine."

"I have a small bladder."

She didn't have a small anything, thank Christ.

"You drank a two-liter cup of coffee."

"It was hardly two liters, Ty."

"A liter and a half."

"Are you *trying* to be a pain in my ass?"

"No," he straight-out lied.

"I'm rethinking my 'I do,'" she muttered and he grinned at the windshield not knowing his wife had her head bent to her iPod selecting his next torment and missed it and also not knowing she would have given *him* fifty K in order to see it.

Straight-on hillbilly music filled the car and some had-to-be white man started singing about a man called Amos Moses.

"Jesus," he groaned and when he did, he heard his wife giggle.

Since he was listening to hillbilly music, he wasted no time finding a restroom for her but as he hit the exit off the highway and Lexie bent to strap on the sandals she'd taken off, he looked in the rearview mirror, saw the SUV follow and his mouth got tight.

Bag of Bones had disappeared at the Utah–Colorado border and the SUV had taken his place. Fuller's California connection was off duty. The local boys had been sent in.

They expected him to make trouble, they wanted to make trouble for him or they wanted to make a point. No matter what the fucking reason, he didn't like it.

He hit a gas station and decided to fill up so as not to totally waste this waste of time so he guided the Charger to a pump. He was angling out his side as Lexie folded out of hers when his phone rang. He pulled it out of his pocket, looked at his display, flipped it open and put it to his ear.

"Tate, can you hang on a second?" he said into it, eyes on Lexie strutting to the building.

"Yeah," Tate replied.

He took the phone from his ear, whistled, Lexie stopped and turned to him.

"Money," he called across the fifteen feet that separated them.

"I got it," she called back.

"Money," he repeated.

"Ty, I got it," she repeated.

"Woman," he growled and knew by the slight upward shift of her chin she'd rolled her eyes to the heavens behind her shades then she strutted to him.

He shoved his hand in his back pocket and slapped some bills in the opened palm she'd stretched over the car door.

Her fingers curled around it and her hand moved away as she asked, "Do you want anything?"

"No, and you don't either."

Her head tipped to the side just as her hip hitched the opposite direction.

"I don't?"

He knew that tone too. It was the danger tone.

"Lex, I'd like to get to Carnal before Christmas."

When he started speaking, her head jerked for some reason and she waited a second before she responded.

"We'll be there before Christmas."

"Not if you drink another two liters of coffee."

"It wasn't two liters, Ty!" she snapped loudly.

"Just pay for the gas," he ordered.

"We need snacks," she informed him.

"We don't need snacks."

"Okay, let me rephrase, *I* need snacks. We're on a road trip. It's a moral imperative to have snacks, the worse for you, the better," she explained.

"Christ," he muttered.

"Do you want anything?" she asked.

Had his wife been in another dimension the last thirty seconds?

"You seriously askin' that shit?" he asked back.

She stared at him through her shades. Then she decided out loud, "I'll stock up, just in case."

Then, before he could say a word, she strutted away.

He put the phone to his ear to hear Tate flat-out laughing.

He waited for him to stop and then he waited for him to talk.

And when he talked he said, "I fuckin' love this."

Walker remained silent.

Tate didn't. "You two take that show on the road?"

"There a reason you're callin'?" Walker returned.

"Yeah, but first, with what I heard, I'm guessin' you're on your way to Carnal."

"You'd guess right."

"How far out are you?"

"Depending on what snacks Lexie hauls back to the Charger, we could be there in a coupla hours, we could be there next week."

"Good news," Tate muttered through a distracted chuckle.

"The reason you're callin'," Walker prompted, moving to the gas cap.

"Right, how much time we got before she comes back?"

"We're in the middle of fuckin' nowhere but still, she's in a building where there's shit to buy so probably a lot," Walker answered as he jerked the nozzle out of the gas pump and fed it into the car.

"Didn't know you'd be home so soon so this could wait but while I got you, might as well give you what I got."

Walker pressed the buttons on the pump, got the zeroes on the display then pulled up the handle and set the lever. He turned his back to the car and leaned into it, scanning the area, finding the SUV, clocking the driver, clocking that he knew the driver and controlling his blood pressure when he saw who it was while saying, "Talk to me."

"Last coupla days, got a lot of info on Alexa Berry."

"Walker," he corrected automatically.

Silence then through an obvious smile, "Walker." Then, quietly, "Congratulations, man."

"You sayin' that means the shit you got isn't shit that's gonna suck," Walker noted.

"Opposite in regard to Lexie."

Walker bent his neck, studied the toes of his boots and listened.

Jackson spoke. "She's got a juvie file. Considering her history, not surprising. Nothin' big. Vandalism. Disturbing the peace. A couple of times picked up for shoplifting. Started when she was around twelve, ended abruptly when she was fourteen."

Around the time Ella Rodriguez entered Lexie's life and gave his wife her first taste of having a motherly type woman who gave a shit.

"Right," he muttered.

Tate went on, "Found out what happened after the granddad died. Home for girls then foster care."

Walker knew that so he didn't respond.

He heard Jackson take in a breath. Then he asked cautiously, "You remember that ballplayer Ronnie Rodriguez?"

"I know about Rodriguez," Walker told him as he heard the lever disengage. He yanked out the nozzle and shoved it back into the pump.

More caution with, "Lexie forthcoming about his chosen profession?"

"Pimp. Drug dealer. Occupational status changed when he took seven, two to the face."

"She was forthcoming," Tate muttered. "The news I got for you, and it surprised the fuck outta me, I got a call from a vice cop, Dallas

PD. Don't know this guy, didn't ask for the call. He heard I was snoopin' and he called me wonderin' why."

Walker felt that barbed sensation at the back of his neck and his eyes went back to his boots but he didn't see them. He was focused on Tate.

"What'd you tell him?" he asked.

"The truth," Jackson answered. "That she married a good friend of mine, that friend had been jacked in the past and I was taking his back."

"You give this cop a name?"

"No, considering his interest in your new wife."

The barbs pressed in.

"What's this fucker's name?"

"Detective Peña. Angel Peña."

Fuck.

"You get a bad feeling about this guy?" Walker asked.

"No, but she's not *my* wife. She was, then fuck yeah."

Fuck.

Walker looked from his boots to the horizon still not seeing anything and he shared quietly, "She hasn't mentioned him."

"Reckon she wouldn't. Don't think he's on her radar. But she sure as fuck's on his. He's taken an interest in Alexa Berry now Walker. The good news is, this was a natural progression seeing as he had an interest in Rodriguez before he caught sight of your wife."

"Explain," Walker rumbled.

"He had a lot to say about Rodriguez. Gotta tell you, man, heard about her association with him, wasn't pleased to hear those two were paired and you were in Vegas marrying her. That was until Peña called and gave me the full brief on Lexie, who, by the way, he's surprised as fuck to find out is in Vegas gettin' hitched."

Walker didn't like that. Not at all. Some vice cop who knows Lexie enough to be surprised. Some vice cop who hears someone asking around and gives a shit enough to pick up the phone.

He didn't fucking like it at all.

Tate continued, "He liked Rodriguez. Had a lot to say about him and a lot of what he said was good."

At this news, news that took him off guard, Walker pulled in a deep breath but didn't speak.

Jackson went on, "Said he didn't get why Rodriguez was in the game, never understood it. Talked to him often. At first it was because he sensed Rodriguez would flip, wanted to groom him to become a CI, then he did it because he sensed Rodriguez might straighten his shit out. They struck up a relationship. Rodriguez gave him time but not info and during these times Rodriguez shared he had a variety of pressure from his family and his woman to leave that life. Peña took an interest in him, sought out Lexie and tried to work with her to work Rodriguez."

"He explain to you the interest?" Walker asked.

"Yep. Called him an ace pimp, you believe that shit, though the way Peña said it, even after all this time, sounded like he couldn't believe that shit either. Peña said the man treated his girls like gold. From the start, a john jacked them up, that john got a visit. Another pimp tried to lean on them, that pimp got a visit. He protected their turf, gave them a high percentage of their take, they got roughed up or knocked up, he took care of their medical bills and he never took freebies. Girls all over Dallas leavin' their men to join his stable, he took all comers and beat back the pimps who came lookin' for them. When he died, far's Peña knew, he had fifty-seven girls in his stable."

Jesus. That was a lot of women.

And Walker was not feeling good hearing that Lexie's claims were true about Rodriguez. He'd convinced her different. And apparently he'd been wrong.

Jackson kept talking.

"Rodriguez and Lexie told Peña that he steered clear of Lexie and when I say that I mean they didn't live together, never got engaged, she didn't take any of his earnings, most of the time they met it was on her turf so he rarely brought her around his business. Not only didn't she take money from him, neither did his family. It was separation of family and business, strict. This caused Rodriguez to be conflicted seein' as he was doin' that shit to provide for Lexie and his family. So his main motivation for doin' it wasn't a motivation. This is what confused Peña, seein' as he kept doin' it and, from what both Rodriguez and Lexie told Peña, the pressure he was gettin' to stop was far from light. By his report, Lexie threatened to end it with Rodriguez about once a week. How he talked her around, Peña didn't know but he did. And Peña was even more confused that he went down and he went down not because of the girls but because of dope."

"He'd partnered with a dealer," Walker told Tate.

"Yeah, Peña explained all about Duane Martinez. *All* about him."

"What's that mean?"

"Far's Peña could tell, Rodriguez propped up Martinez. He mighta had some cracked respect from Peña but still, Peña said Rodriguez wasn't the sharpest tack when it came to relationships. Apparently, this Martinez guy is downright blunt when it comes to everything. Rodriguez didn't have enforcers. Rodriguez did time. Rodriguez was an athlete. Rodriguez could take care of himself and his girls and he did. Personally. Peña says Martinez used the association with Rodriguez as a shield. He says he has no evidence Rodriguez dealt dope, never had any, and he looked deep. He had his stable, he stuck to his stable. But Martinez and Rodriguez were tight, brothers from the 'hood, and Rodriguez gave his brother protection."

"Went down doin' it," Walker muttered, his eyes sliding to the station seeing Lexie at the counter. She was yammering and smiling at the clerk who was smiling back in a way that, Walker suspected, she went on for two minutes longer, the man would get down on a knee no matter the diamonds on her left finger.

"Maybe not," Jackson said into his ear and Walker's gaze went unfocused.

"Maybe not what?"

"Martinez inherited Rodriguez's stable."

Walker felt his chest start to burn.

"What?" he asked quietly.

"Peña has no proof but everyone knew who did what with those two. And Rodriguez was well liked by everyone but other pimps. The tragic hero. Losin' his scholarship was part of it. He was famous in his 'hood and not livin' the dream didn't make that fame fade, just changed its nuance. Further, this guy was a badass. Acted as his own enforcer, never got bested. That kinda reputation holds a lot of sway. That said, according to Peña, he was just a nice guy. His word was gold. He was a diplomat. A peacemaker. A master at balancing while standin' on a fence. There was a sit-down, he was often called on to mediate. People trusted him. He was solid. A rival dealer needed to take someone out, he wouldn't aim for Rodriguez even if he was providing protection for his brother partially because Rodriguez was well liked and this would be unpopular, mostly because Martinez is *not* well liked."

Walker kept his eyes locked on his wife as he asked, "Peña thinks Martinez ordered the hit?"

He asked it but he knew. He knew men like Shift. He knew. That piece of shit would do it and still cry at the funeral.

"That's the word on the street, according to Peña. Murder never solved but that shit spread wide and Martinez moved up the ranks. You gotta be one cold motherfucker to take down your brother in order to take over his stable. He recruited soldiers and got a different kind of protection. But Peña says there's more. Says Martinez was resentful of Rodriguez's success on the basketball court then his respect on the street and his way with his girls. Especially seein' as he hit the game late, after he came back from Indiana, and Martinez had been in the game for years by that time. Says Rodriguez was blind to that shit. Wouldn't hear a word against Martinez and that was what Peña was using to sever the ties and get him to go straight. Peña is convinced Rodriguez stayed in the game to have his brother's back. Rodriguez never explained why those were ties that bind and why they bound him so tight he'd risk losin' his woman and family, but Peña figures something in their history connected them and Rodriguez was the kind of man who took loyalty seriously. Unfortunately, Martinez was not."

Walker watched Lexie push through the door, juggling two white plastic bags filled full with what he suspected were not apples and bananas and a cardboard container holding two huge-ass beverage cups at the same time flicking the arms out on her shades and shoving them on her face.

"Lexie's comin'," he warned Tate.

"Right," Tate replied.

"Fast, tell me if I got a problem with either Peña or Martinez."

"Shits me to say it but yes to both. First, Peña says that he's got the feeling that Martinez has got some hold on Lexie and he's been in contact with her the last few years after Rodriguez went down, offering help, keeping an eye on things. She's been, he reports, uninterested and Peña thinks she's got her head in the sand and just wants to move on with her life clear of that shit. He's worried about it and he's in the position to know if he should be worried. Now, whether Martinez's reach goes outside Dallas, that'll take me makin' a few more calls."

Peña was right. Shift fucked Lexie. Huge. The question was, setting up Lexie for what she was doing for Walker, did he think he was done with her?

Walker would have to explain to him that he was.

Lexie was halfway to him, smiling bright, her hips swaying as she walked not having any idea just how much and for how long her world had been controlled by a piece-of-shit motherfucker. And now that she was free, he hoped she'd die not knowing it.

He jerked up his chin to her and muttered into the phone, "The cop?"

"Wasn't in the same room with him but gotta say, his interest was borderline unhealthy. It magnified when I told him she was tyin' the knot. Though, she's in Colorado with you and he's not on her radar so there's fuck-all he can do."

That wasn't true and Walker knew it. You got on the bad side of a cop, the reach was long. He knew it because six years ago, he experienced that reach stretching from Colorado to California.

Lexie was at the passenger door looking over the roof at him and aiming the straw of one of the drinks to her mouth. She captured it between her lips and sucked as her head tipped to the side.

"A second, baby," he murmured to her and watched her release the straw as her mouth got soft. She nodded then juggled her shit as she opened the door and started to fold in. To Tate he said, "He seem frustrated or pissed at this news?"

"Nope, just interested. Maybe relieved but I couldn't tell. I don't know dick about this guy, still, he's holdin' a torch and that torch is burnin' bright. Since I don't know him, don't know if he doesn't give a shit he gave that up or if he's also not the brightest bulb. Could make a few calls, get some inside information and do it on the quiet. See what you got on your hands."

"Run with that."

"Right. You want me to look into Martinez?"

"I'll deal with him."

Silence then, "Ty—"

"That time I spent in Dallas?" he asked then didn't wait for an answer. "Became acquainted with him."

"Right," Jackson said, making guesses that were probably not accurate.

"It'll be cool," Walker assured him.

"Okay, brother."

"Lexie's back and we gotta hit the road."

"How much shit she buy?"

"We'll hit Carnal next week," Walker answered and Jackson chuckled.

Then Tate muttered, "Full of shit," and finished, "I'll see you tonight at Bubba's."

"Bubba's," Walker agreed. "And, Tate?"

"Yeah?"

"Thanks, brother."

"You got it."

He heard the disconnect, flipped his phone shut, shoved it in his back pocket, returned the gas cap, angled into the car and shut the door.

"Fritos or Cheetos?" Lexie asked before his ass was fully settled in the seat and he turned to her.

"Neither."

"Okay. Pork rinds or Corn Nuts?"

"Babe, please tell me you didn't buy pork rinds."

She grinned at him then declared, "Barbeque flavored."

He shook his head and faced forward, twisting the key in the ignition.

She transferred the cups into the cup holders while he pulled out, telling him, "I got you a Coke."

"You gonna bitch when I toss it out the window?"

"Yes," she replied instantly.

He sighed but only to stop himself from smiling.

"Everything cool on the phone?" she asked quietly.

"Yeah, good. Tate, a friend of mine in Carnal. You'll meet him, good man."

"Good," she said, now her sweet voice was soft and, having dumped her bags to the floor, she nabbed the iPod.

Walker braced.

Five seconds later, 50 Cent's "Disco Inferno" filled the car.

"Baby," Walker whispered to the windshield through a smile.

And it was a smile that his wife caught. The first one she'd ever seen and he had no idea that seeing it meant that for the next two hours she gave him Outkast, Eminem, Jay Z, House of Pain and Snoop Dogg somewhat losing her way playing some TLC, Beyoncé and Black Eyed Peas but he didn't complain about the last.

At least none of them sang about a man called Amos Moses.

Lexie

I rode the high of the beauty of Ty's smile for at least an hour then my mind reminded me of Ty calling me "Lex" in that casual but immensely sweet way, a name no one called me. A name that was all his. So I rode that for the next half hour. After that, I rode the high of the last couple of days, a high so high it felt like I could coast it forever.

Even though these things filled my mind as I endeavored to find as much hip-hop and R&B for Ty as I could on my iPod (I liked it but I couldn't say I was often in the mood for it so the selection wasn't all that great, something I needed to rectify), I still managed to see the stunning beauty of Colorado. Most especially when we drove by the Colorado National Monument. Something I decided we had to come back and take a closer look at. I also wanted to go back to Moab. Driving around in a car was one thing but, although I was nowhere near an outdoorsy type of gal, it was the kind of place you had to get out and walk around in order to see as much of it as you could pack in, something we didn't have time to do.

I was riding so high on all things Ty it came as a surprise when we passed the sign that said, "Welcome to Carnal." When I saw it, my mind instantly cleared and I came alert, looking around Ty's hometown.

It wasn't what I expected. One long main street, starting with the tidy, flower-festooned Carnal Hotel (which, regardless if it was tidy and flower-festooned, it was more of a motel than a hotel) on the left and ending with a big mechanics garage on the right with residential areas leading off the main street, which were compact rather than sprawl.

Ty was jeans and tees but he was also suits and cuff links so I knew his hometown could be anything. Still, I didn't expect it to be what it was. Small, seemingly quiet but obviously populated and not a single building had been built in this decade or the last or the one before that.

I liked that.

It was also surrounded by tall Colorado hills which were surrounded by taller Colorado mountains, neither of which I had seen except in pictures before that day and both of which I instantly loved.

The town was ordinary, settled, you'd drive through it and probably not pay much attention.

And I liked that too.

Ty drove us by the mechanics where the town and the residential area abruptly died away with only a few houses dotting the valley.

About half a mile out of town, he turned left and drove into the hills where, after a short while, we hit thick pine and aspen. Not too long after that, he turned right into a road I wouldn't have noticed if he hadn't turned there. Another short drive that was all pine and aspen on both sides broken intermittently by boulders, this suddenly opened up to a development that was far newer than the town we'd just driven through.

Whoever planned and built it, they did it with care. It was a bunch of three- and four-story buildings dotted up a steep, winding incline. All an attractive red-brown wood and lots of windows. All with abundant decking to enjoy the views. All with their own short, private drive at the mouth of which was a mailbox.

The houses weren't close together but they were also not far apart. Quite a few of the pine trees and aspens between the houses had not been disturbed when they built so they provided even more privacy. Every single one was taken care of but there were a few that really were taken care of with big planters and flower boxes filled with blooms and trailing or spiking greenery. A couple of flagpoles with American flags. Some with decorative accents on the outside like iron kokopellis, terra-cotta suns and fancy outdoor lights and some with very attractive deck furniture.

It was awesome and I figured that Maggie and Wood lived there and we were there to pick up the keys to Ty's condo. This meant I'd been right to take extra time getting ready that morning. If I was coming home like Ty was, I'd want to see family and friends right away. I figured Ty would want to do that too and I would be with him when he did so I wanted to look good for him when his posse met me.

He drove to the very top of the development, turned left into the private drive of the last of the houses in the development. This one was a little bit more removed from the others and having pine and aspen at its sides, one side a steep decline that eventually led to another house, the other side leading into nothing but the steep, heavily wooded incline of the hill.

He stopped the Charger in front of a large, two-car garage and beside the garage was an open space and on top of all of this were three stories with a large-ish deck jutting out over the open space. The open space was big enough to park another car or, maybe, snowmobiles or ATVs. There was a set of wooden steps with open slats inside the space, these positioned beside the garage.

I released my seat belt and leaned forward, tipping my head back to look at the tall building, seeing the wraparound deck and noting that, if that wrapped around the front, it would have a spectacular view to Carnal and the hills and mountains beyond.

"So," I said to the windshield as I heard Ty's door open but he hadn't yet angled out. "Are we here to pick up your keys?"

"Come again?"

I tore my eyes from the house to look at him. "Are we here to pick up the keys to your condo?"

"This is my condo," he replied, and I blinked as surprise flooded through me. Surprise mingled liberally with excitement as he went on, "Maggie's left the keys so we can get in."

"This isn't your condo," I told him stupidly and he stared at me a second.

Then he said, "It is."

"No it isn't."

"Lexie, it is."

"It can't be. This isn't even a condo," I informed him.

"It is," he replied.

"No, it isn't. It's a house."

"Woman, it's a condo."

"It is not," I argued.

"It is in Colorado," he replied.

At this news, the surprise shifted out, the excitement took over and my happy gaze slid back to look up at the condo.

Then I whispered, "Wow."

To this he muttered, "Goof," and exited the car.

I followed him, still looking up at the house and thinking this did it.

I knew.

The last couple of days I'd given a lot of head space trying to determine if the signs I was reading were correct. That in a crazy, wild way life had finally led me somewhere sweet.

It had led me to a beautiful man who had his issues but then again, everyone did. That didn't mean he couldn't be generous, gentle, thoughtful and, yes, I discovered, also funny.

He was great at teasing, he found my buttons and enjoyed pushing them but in a way that wasn't nasty but intimate and increasingly familiar.

When I talked, he listened. He didn't pretend to, he just did. No matter what I was blabbing about, he found it interesting and I knew that to be true. I didn't know how I knew, I just knew.

He was patient. He was gentle. He was calling me "babe" and "baby" more often but, even so, he still didn't do it like other men, throwaway. These words had meaning to him, I sensed I'd become these to him or he wouldn't have called me those names. I was *his* babe, *his* baby and those were things I wanted to be.

He was also using his soft voice with me more often. Sometimes for reasons I didn't know him enough yet to understand, whatever mood he was in making him do it. Sometimes he used it when he was teasing me. It didn't matter. I liked it.

He still didn't give much away but I had a feeling all this stuff *was* giving something away. Giving something to me. Something big. Something important. Something good and clean and right. Something I liked having and wanted more of.

And now there I was in a Colorado condo development outside

a small, quiet, settled town surrounded by beauty and my place of residence was going to be a kickass crib, three stories of house with spectacular views.

He'd gone to the trunk and swung his duffel over his shoulder and nabbed my bag. I carried the bags with the snacks in them, thinking I'd clean out the car later, after a tour of his house. I negotiated the gravel under my feet with some difficulty in my high-heeled wedges and found him around the side, bent to a border of rocks that edged some attractive, clipped shrubs. He flipped a rock over, did something to it with his thumb then opened it.

Fake rock where Maggie hid the key.

He put the rock back, grabbed my bag he'd set beside him and headed to the stairs.

I followed him.

We hit deck and I peered around the narrow wooden walkway at the side of the house seeing I was right. The one-story elevation gave views over the tops of the trees to the town and the vista beyond and the walkway led to a wider deck at the front of the house.

Awesome.

I went to stand behind him at some wood-framed glass double doors the opposite of which I could see some wide vertical blinds, which were closed. Ty unlocked the door, pushed it in and shoved aside the blinds, entering, and I pushed in close behind him.

The minute one foot hit floor over the threshold I heard a cacophony of cries including, "Welcome home!", "Surprise!" and "Congratulations!"

Ty had gone solid in front of me and I automatically stepped to his side.

When I did, I didn't take in the interior of his house but instead all I could see were a bunch of people, a bunch of balloons, a bunch of streamers and two huge banners. One had stars printed on it around the words, "Welcome home," and the other one had a profusion of two facing doves with linking wedding bands at their beaks printed on it with the word, "Congratulations!"

This was all I took in before a tall, extremely well-built, freakishly attractive man wearing a shit-eating grin approached Ty, took his hand and shook it while moving in to give him a back-pounding man hug. At the same time a gorgeous blonde woman with legs nearly as long as mine came right up to me, pulled me into a tight hug and said in my ear, "So nice to meet you, Lexie. I'm Laurie. Welcome home."

Welcome home.

A shiver slid over my skin, a shiver the likes I'd never felt but I knew instinctively it was not a bad one.

And thus it began.

I was divested of my bags as Ty got hugs and handshakes, I got hugs and cheek kisses.

I met Tate, the freakishly good-looking man, and Laurie was his wife (of course).

And I met Maggie, a pretty, petite brunette and Wood, another freakishly good-looking man with black hair and a goatee.

Also I met Bubba, a man nearly as huge as Ty (but not as solid) with light brown hair and a good ole boy smile and his wife, Krystal, a petite, busty woman in a tight tank top with flaming red hair and assessing eyes.

Then there was Pop, an older man with a beer gut and a gray beard, Stella, a full-on biker babe with dark hair highlighted with streaks of blonde and Deke, a blond mountain of a man who was as solid as Ty and even scarier.

And I further met Jim-Billy, another older man wearing a beat-up baseball cap and a broken smile. Broken because he was missing a tooth. And Ned and Betty, an upper-middle-aged married couple who approached me together declaring they were a unit and they liked it that way.

Rounding out this pack was Jonas, a handsome boy being thus seeing as he was Tate's son who was, I guessed, twelve, maybe thirteen. And, finally, Maggie and Wood's two kids, a pretty little girl named Addison and a cute little boy named Noah.

After the introductions I realized we were in a kitchen, a big one and a modern one. Then I realized it seemed like a big one because it was, but also because the entire floor of the house was open plan, the kitchen feeding into a huge living room that had floor-to-ceiling windows at the end with a view to a large, jutting front deck and the panorama beyond.

The kitchen had a massive island on which were big bowls of chips, smaller bowls of dips, platters of fried chicken, bowls of coleslaw, mountains of mashed potatoes and gravy boats of gravy. Among the food there were stacks of baby blue paper plates decorated in white doves like on the banner, the wedding rings on the plates silver, matching napkins and cups filled with blue plastic cutlery. Last, there were several small vases filled with flowers here and there and in the middle was a delicious-looking homemade cake that had a plastic, traditional wedding top bride and groom stuck in the middle of it.

I was led to the island sandwiched between Maggie and Laurie and I heard the door to the fridge open as there was chatter and laughter all around. The hiss of beer caps snapping off filled the air and I found one in my hand. My eyes went to Ty who was opposite the island from me and I watched Wood shove a beer into his hand while grinning.

Ty's head started to turn in my direction but Laurie filled my vision before his eyes could meet mine.

"Tate was tasked with finding out when you were arriving home," she told me. "Being a man and not understanding the delicate intricacies of party planning, he failed in this endeavor and we only had two hours."

"Thank God we already bought all the decorations," Maggie noted, moving in at Laurie's side. "No way we'd have time to get to the mall and back again." She grinned up at me. "You can find practically anything in Carnal but, gotta admit, the party supplies leave something to be desired."

"This is, unfortunately, true. Carnal needs less biker shops and more party stores," Laurie agreed then looked back at me. "Anyway, this means it's fried chicken and the fixin's from the grocery store but they do it really good. Jonas loves it. He can eat a family pack all by himself. And I gave Shambles an emergency cake order and he got it ready just in time."

Shambles? I didn't think I'd met a Shambles.

I wondered if that was someone there's nickname but I didn't get to ask because Maggie again spoke.

"We were going to get the bakery in town to make you a real wedding cake but that was if we had more than two hours, which we obviously didn't. But we tried anyway and they said they couldn't do it," Maggie told me. "But they had a cake top so it looks kinda stupid. But, stupid or not, it says what it needs to say."

"Betty went to Holly and did the flowers," Laurie added.

"Stella took charge of the kids and did the decorating," Maggie went on.

Suddenly I felt my left hand taken in a tight grip and lifted. I looked down to see the flaming-haired Krystal thumbing my wedding bands.

She jerked my hand up high in front of me, stating, "Pure Ty. Look at these fuckin' rings." She shook my hand at the two other women. "He hasn't changed. No half measures for that boy. Jesus. You could buy a house with these rings."

That wasn't exactly true (though they certainly would be a hefty down payment) but I didn't get to inform her of this, again because of Maggie.

"*Ohmigod!*" Maggie shrieked, and I struggled against taking a step back in reaction to the noise but couldn't do it because she snatched my hand out of Krystal's and dragged it close to her face. Then her head tipped back to look at me. "Those are *gorgeous*!" Still holding my hand, she twisted her torso and shouted across the island, "Ty! These rings are *gorgeous*!"

Before I could look to Ty to see his reaction to Maggie's shout, Krystal spoke again.

"I bet you didn't have to say a word. I bet those rings were all Ty. Which makes you the only female on the planet who didn't have to give her man some instruction when it came to an engagement ring,"

Krystal noted correctly, and I looked down at her. "He may drink beer but that boy is pure champagne."

Before I could comment on this, another voice came.

"Laurie." It was Jonas calling from the side of the island. "Now that they're here, can we eat? I was starved an hour ago and I've been sniffin' chicken for *forever*. Can we break the seal or what?"

And before Laurie could answer, yet another voice came.

"Mommy!" Addison shouted from the other side, and she was jumping up and pointing at a bunch of boxes extravagantly wrapped in wedding paper resting on a side counter. "Is it time for presents?" she asked.

"No, honey, not just yet. After we have cake," Maggie answered but I was staring at the presents.

Presents.

Presents, cake, fried chicken and decorations.

I pulled my hand from Maggie's and took a step back as my eyesight grew fuzzy but through the haze I heard the cheerful buzz all around. Smelled the chicken. Felt the vibe of friendship that had a hint of relief but more happiness and even love.

Good. Clean. Right.

Ronnie's best friend was Shift. Shift did not arrange for Ronnie to have a welcome home party when he got let out of prison in Indiana and came home to Dallas. None of Ronnie's friends did; neither did his family. This was because he'd fucked up and although we were happy he was home, his future was in the toilet. He'd flushed it down his damned self and that wasn't anything to celebrate.

But also, outside of Shift, all of Ronnie's decent friends (who turned out to be not so decent) deserted him after he got home and the crew he found wasn't the cake, banners, decorations, fried chicken and gift-giving kind. They took. They didn't give.

"Lexie, you okay?" I heard Laurie ask, and I took another step back, my eyes moving in the direction of Ty but I didn't see him.

I didn't see him because it hit me that Ronnie had never had this but I didn't either.

I had good friends but there was nothing to celebrate for me with Ronnie in my life. He hated it, I knew, but he knew it, as I did. He was a shadow blocking out the sun of my world. He wasn't about happy chatter and good friends rushing around in a two-hour window to do something beautiful. If he'd lived and I'd given in one of the gazillion times he tried to talk me into marrying him, our people would have gone through the motions but the chatter wouldn't be happy, the buzz not filled with love but instead obligation and maybe even doom.

But more than that, I never thought I *would* have this. Growing up the way I did, dreams like this died early. You learned not to hope for too much when you experienced the bitter taste of disappointment as early as I did.

These people doing this said it all about Ty. It said I was reading those signs right. No one did this kind of thing for an asshole or a loser. They did it for someone who was worthy of it.

And my marriage to Ty might have started out fake but this… this was real. These people cared about him, a lot, and they were wasting no time bringing me into the fold.

And he'd given me this.

I'd never had anything so beautiful.

And I couldn't handle it.

"Ty," I vaguely heard Maggie call. "Somethin's wrong with—"

I took another step back and my arm went out to find purchase because if it didn't, I was going to go down. I knew it. My head was swimming, my vision was blurred and my system couldn't process what was happening.

I felt a burning sensation at the small of my back, the beer slid out from between my fingers and I heard a deep rumble in my ear saying, "Lex."

I turned and saw a wall of black.

Ty's tee-shirt.

I lifted my hands and my fingers curled into the material right before I did a face plant in his chest, my legs gave out and I burst into tears.

His long, powerful arms closed around me and they did this tight.

"Baby, what the fuck?" I heard in my ear.

"I can't...this isn't happening...I can't process...presents...cake...chicken," I stammered crazily then tilted my head back, saw him through blurry eyes and whispered, "Ty, honey, you know good things don't happen to me. They don't happen to me. I can't take this. I don't know what to do with it."

I lost sight of him because the wet was too much to see through so I shoved my face in his chest again and my body shook against his with my sobs.

Then I was up in his arms and I automatically adjusted, pressing my wet face in his neck, wrapping my arms around it. We were moving but I was deep in the throes of a massive crying jag, didn't see where we were going and wouldn't have cared anyway.

I felt myself settled in his lap as he sat somewhere, his arms moving to wrap tight around me but I kept my face in his neck, my arms around it, though I pushed my torso deep into his, held on hard and kept crying.

Eventually, one of his hands drifted up my back, under my hair to curl hot around my neck.

"Lexie, baby, calm down," he whispered in my ear.

I nodded but kept crying.

His fingers squeezed gently. "Baby, you gotta get a handle on this."

I nodded again and sucked in a broken breath. Then I sucked in another one.

Then, face still in his neck, I mumbled, "I'm sorry. I just never...something like that..." I took in another broken breath and whispered, "It was unexpected."

"Got good friends," he murmured.

I nodded again because he did. He had good friends. The kind of friends you didn't just get. The kind of friends you earned.

And I didn't know what to do with that either.

I kept my face in his neck and held on.

Then I took in another breath, this one didn't break and my voice wasn't trembling but it was quiet when I said, "I'm glad you have that."

"Me too."

I held on awhile longer.

Then I swallowed and admitted, "Maybe I am part goof."

"Total," he replied on another squeeze of his fingers at my neck with a corresponding squeeze of his arm around my back. "Total goof."

"Not total. Part."

He didn't reply.

I drew in a last breath through my nose and finally pulled my face out of his neck. His head came back and his chin dipped down so he could look at me.

And God, *God*, he had beautiful eyes and their beauty increased exponentially when they were close up.

"Sorry," I whispered.

"Don't be," he whispered back.

"I know..." I started, stopped, pulled up the courage and started again, "I know it's fake but thank you, Ty. I never expected to have anything that nice and it *is* nice, no matter what. So thank you for giving it to me."

He didn't speak but his eyes changed, one of those changes I didn't know, didn't yet understand but this one was meaningful. They all were but this one was more meaningful than the rest.

A lot more.

And I couldn't stop myself, his eyes so close, that look in them, my arms moved from around his shoulders, my hands framed his face, I leaned up and whispered, "Thank you."

Then I pressed my lips to his.

I meant to give him a soft kiss of gratitude. This was not to say I didn't want to give him a long, hard, wet kiss of something else. And just what I wanted to give him and what that would lead to had also been filling my head space the last couple of days but that wasn't where I intended to go just then. Not yet. Not with a house full of people downstairs waiting to eat fried chicken.

But when my mouth hit his, he didn't give me the chance to give him a soft kiss of gratitude.

Instantly, his fingers slid up into my hair, cupping my head, and his mouth opened over mine making a demand. Mine complied. His tongue spiked into my mouth and I liked the taste of it, I hadn't had it in what seemed like a decade, I missed it and he tasted so fucking good my body pressed into his and not just because his arm around me grew super tight.

Then I was twisted, on my back in what was, I noted vaguely and was unbelievably happy for, a bed. His torso was on mine, his hips beside mine, his long, heavy leg moved to tangle with mine as his tongue moved in my mouth. I wrapped one arm around his back, one around his shoulders, my hand moving to cup the back of his head and hold him to me.

God, he couldn't kiss. He could *kiss*.

And spending days and days with his beauty, his generosity, his teasing, his attention, his fabulous body, hearing his deep, rumbling voice, trying to find sleep beside him in bed at night, seeing him stroke himself in the shower, knowing he could use his mouth, I wanted that. I wanted all of it. I wanted it naked and moving on me, *in* me.

I wanted all of him.

To tell him this, I pressed up into his body. His arm slid up my back then moved out so his hand could slide down my side from pit to waist, his thumb extended so it brushed light against the side of my breast. Just that simple touch sent shocks of electricity between my legs so strong, I thought for a second just with that, his weight on me, my arms around him, his leg tangled with mine, his tongue in my mouth, I was going to come and do it hard.

But I suddenly found myself on my feet by the side of the bed, teetering because I didn't know how I got there and the loss of all the beauty I'd just had was a brutal shock. I only remained standing because Ty's big hands were cupping my jaws, his thumbs moving through the wetness still on my cheeks but his big body was held distant, the few feet between us seeming like miles.

"Christ, I'm sorry," he whispered, and I blinked up at him in profound confusion.

"What?" I whispered back breathily.

"I'm sorry, Lexie. That won't happen again. I promise you, it won't happen again."

I blinked again. His hands dropped away. I felt the loss of them like a blow and I watched, I…actually…*watched* as he closed down. Completely. He snapped the shutters tight and the Ty I'd been getting to know disappeared behind that impenetrable wall that had been up when he'd walked out of prison five days ago.

"Bathroom's in there, you wanna clean up," he told me, jerking his head to the side. "Take your time. They're cool. They'll get it. Come down when you're ready."

And without another word or glance, he walked away.

And I stood there in what I realized was a huge bedroom, watching him disappear down a flight of stairs wondering what just happened and hoping it wasn't what I thought it was.

Hoping at the same time knowing that it was.

Because good shit didn't happen to me.

Lady Luck played with Ronnie and she also played with Ty, giving and taking, not in equal measure but they got their chance to taste sweet.

But she didn't like me.

Not at all.

CHAPTER SEVEN

Still Feeling Hollow

I OPENED MY eyes and saw Ty's pillows beside mine, the down depressed from his head resting there but his head wasn't resting there as it hadn't been the morning before or the morning before that or the morning before that.

I knew it was stupid but I looked for a note on the pillow, his nightstand, my nightstand. But there wasn't a note as there wasn't the morning before or the morning before that or the morning before that.

I flopped to my back on the bed and looked at the wood-paneled and beamed arched ceiling.

I should probably be thankful I had a few days of it. A few days of sweet. A few days of teasing and soft voices and endearments.

But I wasn't.

Because if you don't know how good something can be, you don't know how bad you'll miss it when it was gone.

I sighed, stared at the ceiling and let the last few days sift through my brain.

When I finally got back to the party, everyone was a bit watchful and a bit friendlier (if that could be believed), handling me with care though doing it without prying. I tried to relax and pulled on my game face. I was a newlywed married to their Ty, happy, giddy and about to help my man put the past behind him and start a new life.

The good thing was, with that many people, all of them wanting Ty's time and to get to know me, distance from him didn't seem unusual so I nursed that as best I could. He was in huddles. I was in huddles. Sometimes, we'd find ourselves in the same huddle and his arm would move casually around my shoulders and I'd smile bright and listen hard so I didn't miss anything but mostly so I wouldn't dissolve into tears again.

And those tears I was holding back were because his arm slid casually around my shoulders, tucking me to his side, a place I liked to be but no matter our physical closeness, he was gone. I saw it in his impassive face, which he didn't give only to me. He was going through the motions and I wasn't the only one to notice this. Tate caught it early on, Krystal not long after and Wood not long after that.

But they didn't say anything. They watched but said not a word. We ate. We drank. We cut the cake, which Ty flatly refused to do in a traditional wedding way no matter how much everyone was teasingly trying to push him to do it. I ended up doing it, saying stupid shit about how the superhero Mr. Humongo was above cutting cakes and didn't use the laser beams he could shoot from his eyes for trivial purposes, making people laugh and doing all this in an effort to cover for him.

Then we opened presents. Like Ty, his friends were generous. A whole set of brand-new, stylish, expensive stoneware including serving platters, bowls, creamer and sugar, the whole enchilada. It was awesome, the tops and insides a shiny, dusky sky blue, the backs and outsides a gorgeous matte dark gray. Also a whole set of beautifully shaped glasses including drinking, wine and even martini glasses. And a whole set of unusual but kickass cutlery. And, last, a new KitchenAid coffeemaker.

"Ty's got good shit but he's a man. Men buy expensive TVs and mattresses. They do not think of stoneware," Maggie explained to me after I'd opened everything (Ty also didn't open presents). Then to Ty with a wicked smile she said, "Goodwill, honey. That's where your old stuff is. Kiss it good-bye."

Ty sighed. I forced a laugh that I hoped didn't sound forced.

"And Tate told me Ty told him you liked your coffee," Laurie whispered in my ear, surprising me with this news. "So I sent Pop and Jim-Billy to the home store to get you a good coffeemaker so you'd be covered."

There it was again. Good people. Generosity. Thoughtfulness. Kindness.

I smiled at her and it wasn't forced but my eyes were again wet.

Her return smile was warm and she gave me a hand squeeze. I knew she saw the wet but thankfully she didn't mention it.

Presents didn't herald the end of the party though. Night fell and they kept on going. I liked them. They were fun, their vibe was good enough to cut through my worry but I still wanted them to go so I could talk to Ty.

They eventually did but by that time I was slightly drunk, dead on my feet and Tate, Wood, Bubba and Deke sent their ladyfolk home with others and they moved to the front deck with Ty getting close to me and saying, "Go on up. I'll be up later," then not waiting for an answer and following the men.

It was time for a man huddle. I knew a woman never messed with that. And with those men, I knew she never, *never* messed with it.

So I went on up and fell asleep before he came up.

I woke up with him gone and no note. Midmorning, my cell rang and it was him saying he had the Charger, was "seein' to shit" in town and didn't know when he'd be back. I didn't get that single word in edgewise before he disconnected.

I spent that day getting used to his house and phoning my girls in Dallas to see how things were progressing.

Ella told me three boxes of stuff were already in the post, shoes and clothes. She was still sorting and would get back to me.

I gabbed with Bessie, handing her the same story with the same omissions I gave her mom, skirting pointed questions because Bessie could smell bullshit a mile away and finally steering her into talking about herself, telling her I didn't want to think of that shit and wanted us just to act normal.

I felt shit about doing this. She was my best friend and I never kept anything from her but with the way things were with Ty and me, I didn't have it in me to go into full disclosure.

Bessie gave in but I knew she didn't like it nor did she buy it. She was worried about me. That made me feel more guilt but I set it aside. I was feeling too much, something had to go and Bess had been through the thick and the thin of it with me. She'd stick through a new thin.

I also called Margot and she told me that she'd talked to the HR director. A woman who had been there since the doors opened five decades ago (slight exaggeration). A woman who hired me. A woman who supported my four promotions. A woman who talked the CEO into taking a chance on me as head buyer even though I'd been assistant buyer for only a year and a half and never been allowed on a buying trip (the old head buyer was a bitch, which was one reason why she was asked, nicely but firmly, to leave). This made me the youngest head buyer in Lowenstein's history.

And, last, she was a woman who had no idea about Ronnie or

Shift until Margot told her. Therefore she was a woman horrified, not that she'd employed me, but that I'd had to live with that. She was also stunned (in a good way) that I'd never let that leak into my work. And when Margot transferred my call to her she was a woman who told me I was brave. She admired me. She wished me all the luck in the world and she'd be happy to give me a stellar recommendation when it was needed. "You just call, shugah. Me and Lowenstein's will be there for you."

After hanging up with her, I realized I'd forgotten that Texan women liked strength, the quieter, the better, Texan women liked survivors and Texan women stuck together.

I should have remembered.

There you go. Thanks to Margot I left a bridge unburned and thanks to Ella I had clothes and shoes coming. Two good things.

When Ty said he didn't know when he'd return, he meant he was going to return when I was asleep.

And he did.

He was gone again when I woke up. No note. No Charger. Another midmorning phone call.

At my greeting, he said this, "At the garage, Wood took me back on. I start today. Boys are goin' to Bubba's after so I'll be late. Wood knows we just got the Charger right now so he'll pick me up for work tomorrow so you'll have wheels. Later."

Then he disconnected. That was it. He disconnected.

I'd said, "Hey, Ty," and that was all I said.

And he did, indeed, get home late. I'd tried to stay up but I couldn't. I wanted to talk to him or maybe, at that point, yell at him and I wanted that bad. Bad enough to stay up as long as I could. But I couldn't stay up long enough, that was how late he stayed out.

And again the next day I woke up and I did it early but no Ty, no note and that morning, no call. No call that afternoon. And no call that evening when five o'clock went to six, six went to seven and seven slid past eight.

And at this point, I was pissed. He was supposed to be a

newlywed too. I didn't know what his business was and maybe he was seeing to it. Any man let out of prison would want to get on with his life, I guessed, so starting a job would be good. I could see that. But disappearing for an entire day? Going out with his buds for drinks after work, drinks that lasted into the wee hours? Not coming home until way late? How did any of that say newlywed?

What the fuck was up with that?

This anger stopped me from calling him because I worried I'd shout at him over the phone and I didn't want to do that. I didn't want to do that because if I did, it was easy for him to hang up. When I shouted at him, I wanted it to be hard for him to get away from what I was saying.

At a quarter to nine, he came home in sweaty workout clothes, long shorts, skintight, sleeveless shirt, carrying a workout bag and two plastic grocery bags.

"Yo," he said to me at my place on the couch watching TV.

Uh…yo?

Three days with the definition of minimal conversation, he comes home when I'm awake and he says, "Yo"?

He dropped the workout bag, turned to the counter, dumped the grocery bags on it and started to take stuff out of them.

I turned the volume down on the TV, rolled off the couch and approached the kitchen asking, "Where have you been?"

He turned slightly to me, *very* slightly, looked down at himself, glanced at me then turned back to the counter.

Although I knew these actions were a form of communication, he didn't respond verbally.

I sucked in a calming breath so I didn't unleash hellfire.

Then I started, "Ty—"

"Wiped," he cut me off. "Gonna make a shake, hit the shower and hit the sack."

It was then I saw he had a package of strawberries, a bunch of bananas, a pot of yogurt and a big, plastic vat of something I didn't know what it was. He pulled the blender to him and started to peel a banana.

"Um…we need to talk," I said, putting my hands flat on the island where I stood opposite him, the island between us, Ty at the counter at the back wall.

"'Bout what?" he asked.

About what?

"Where do you want me to start?" I asked back as he dumped the banana into the blender then opened the strawberries.

"Don't care. Just start. Like I said, I'm wiped so, sooner we get it done, sooner I can hit the shower."

I stared at him as he pulled the stems off of the (unwashed) berries and started to add them to the banana.

"Ty—" I whispered and he turned to me.

"Spit it out. I'm not fuckin' with you. I'm not in the mood for this but if you got something to say, say it."

I swallowed against a throat that was closing and this was because, suddenly, I wasn't pissed anymore.

I was something else.

And that something else was understanding that I'd been wrong that day we'd arrived in Carnal. He hadn't shut down after our kiss. This wasn't the closed Ty. This was a different Ty. This was an asshole Ty.

And it hurt to know that there *was* an asshole Ty.

"I…" I started, not knowing what to say. He went back to his strawberries and I tried to start with something easy. "I don't know what you want me to be doing."

He didn't respond. He finished with the strawberries, leaned way to the side, opened a drawer, grabbed one of our awesome new spoons and went after the yogurt.

"Ty," I called. "I can't spend my days hanging around and watching TV. What am I supposed to be doing?"

"Starting a life," he told the blender, spooning in yogurt.

"How?" I asked.

"How?" he asked the blender.

"Yeah, how?"

He opened the big vat, dug in with his hand, came out with a scoop full of powder and dumped it in the blender saying, "What people do. You want a job, get one. You don't want one, I can cover you. Deal with your shit in Dallas. Buy groceries. Clean the house. Do what people do."

He screwed the lid on the vat of powder and went to the fridge. I watched him get a big handful of ice and go back to the blender and drop it in. Then he went back to the fridge, got the milk (Maggie had kindly stocked us up) and splashed some of that in. He put the milk beside the blender, shoved the lid on top and fired it up. He stopped it, took the lid off and drank directly from it.

I didn't speak throughout this. I didn't know what to say. And I didn't like the feeling that I was right there and he was acting like he didn't know I was even on the same planet.

He was halfway through his shake when I said quietly, "Something's changed."

He turned to me and leaned his hips into the counter.

"Yeah," he agreed. "Something's changed. We're here. This starts. No fuckin' around. I got shit to do, it's important and I gotta focus on it. Vacation's over. Time to earn your fifty K."

He threw back more shake like he hadn't just delivered a verbal blow to the gut. And this blow was reminding me about the fifty K, something, for some stupid, insane reason, I thought we'd gone beyond, making us something we obviously were not.

Even so, to remind him of who I thought we had become, when he dropped his arm, I whispered, "That wasn't nice."

His blank but still beautiful eyes leveled on mine. "Never promised I'd be nice."

"You'd been being nice," I reminded him.

"Yeah," he affirmed then said, "Mistake. Told you in Vegas, been in chains five years, don't need anything chaining me."

Blow two.

"I'm not chaining you," I told him, my voice trembling.

"Woman, you're pussy and never met pussy that didn't come with a chain. Some of them are heavier than others. Don't wanna find out how heavy yours is."

Another blow. That one savage.

"I can't believe you just said that," I whispered.

"Well, I did," he replied then threw back the last of the shake, put the blender on the counter and left the milk, banana peel, strawberry stems and everything where it lay as he headed to the steps saying, "Hittin' the shower then goin' to bed. Wood's comin' again in the morning to get me. Man who was lookin' after my ride's bringin' it back tomorrow. Probably see you tomorrow night."

Then he was up the steps and gone.

I stood at the counter seeing nothing. Then I moved around the island and cleaned up his mess. After I did that, I went back to the TV.

I didn't go to bed until way late and I did this only after spending a good deal of time wondering if I was going to do it at all. And that wondering included whether I should sleep on the couch or whether I should write him a note, tell him to go fuck himself and shove his fifty K up his ass, get in my car and go.

For some reason, I went up to bed.

Now was now.

I stared at the ceiling realizing that I was hurt and angry, both in equal measure. Ty had opened to me and showed me something beautiful then for some fucked-up reason all in his head, he'd snatched it away from me.

And I had two choices. Either I break my back and work him to pull that back out again, help him to deal with whatever he was dealing with, get him to trust me, show him that whatever demons he was battling, he could let them go and I could give him a good life. Or I could do my job, collect my fifty thousand dollars and move the fuck on.

I considered these choices.

I loved Ronnie. I loved him a lot. I loved the way he could make me laugh and the look in his eyes when he looked at me, even early on, when his future was bright. He'd look at me like he couldn't believe his luck.

I loved that he gave me a family.

I loved our quiet moments when I could forget our lives were a complete mess and that shadow he cast blocked out the sun. No matter what Ty said about Ronnie, and he was probably right, still, I knew there was something there for Ronnie, something he got from me. And I liked giving it to him so I did it even longer than I should.

But even though I had years with Ronnie and only five good days with Ty Walker, I knew, if he let me in, I could love him more than Ronnie. With all that I gave to Ronnie, all the devotion, every last chance, I still knew I could love Ty more. I didn't know how I knew it but by the time we hit the "Welcome to Carnal" sign, I knew it down to my bones.

But I didn't need this shit anymore. I'd broken my back and laid a man in the ground who couldn't have an open casket because his face was blown off even though I'd spent years begging him to leave that life behind. A life that could lead to that and it did. Now I was with a man who bought a bride and needed hundreds of thousands of dollars to take care of some unknown business. A man who could give me something beautiful, snatch it away and calmly stand opposite me and talk to me about my pussy coming with a chain.

I didn't need that shit.

I'd been right while searching for a wedding dress. I'd been wrong about changing my mind.

I needed to give up while the giving up was good.

Deciding (again) to do that, I dragged myself out of bed and went to the bathroom.

The interior of Ty's house was more awesome than the exterior. He didn't have a lot of stuff but what he had was excellent quality, stylish and expensive. This was probably why he didn't have a lot because, before his life was interrupted, he'd been patiently accumulating, buying the best, happy to wait until he could afford the next addition because it had to be right. What he wanted. The "nice shit."

I didn't know if he bought the condo at build but either he or the people who ordered it had to have chosen every upgrade. Gleaming marble tile in the bathrooms. Shining oak floors. Fabulous slate floors in the kitchen. Top-of-the-line appliances. Granite countertops in kitchen and in bathrooms.

The top bedroom was the entire floor though stuttered, the balcony off of it running the entire length but being the roof of the second floor. There was a staircase going through the middle of the house on the upper two floors, which meant that there were three sections of the top bedroom. A wide back where the furniture was and two big areas on either side of the staircase that were void of anything. It had floor-to-ceiling windows too and the balcony off had a wooden railing.

Completing this area were a huge bathroom with a big, oval tub that could fit two, a separate shower, a toilet in its own room and a very long counter with two basins and a huge mirror lit by fantastic, cool-as-shit lights as well as a large walk-in closet.

Ty only had a bed, two nightstands and two dressers in that room, one dresser tall, one long with a mirror. All this was handsome but sparse. There wasn't even a rug to cover the floorboards under the bed. In fact, there were no rugs in the house because he obviously hadn't gotten around to buying rugs.

There was an enormous amount of space left over. You could put couches and chairs up there. Have a TV space and a reading space, one on either side of the stairs. Deck furniture on the balcony with thick cushions. I'd pick lounges.

It was already fabulous but it could be spectacular.

I would, no doubt, never see that. I was pissed at Ty but I still hoped that he did whatever he had to do and then went back to building his life and filling it with "nice shit."

The middle floor of the house had two bedrooms either side of the stairs, both with their own much smaller baths. Both had small balconies jutting out, made of decking. Neither had anything in them. Nothing. Except for some stuff stored in the closet of one, they were totally empty.

At the back of the middle floor sandwiched between the bedrooms was a smaller room that Ty used for an office. It was the only room in the house that was carpeted. He'd furnished it. Big, fantastic desk, big-backed, black leather swivel chair but the computer had obviously been purchased prior to his being sent to prison. It was at least five years old, maybe older. Still, it was there and I'd discovered it had Internet, I just didn't know the passwords to access it.

Mental note to ask Ty.

The bottom floor was all kitchen and living room with a narrow boxed cutout on one side that housed a powder room with a door close to the living room and a big walk-in pantry with a door close to the kitchen. There were floor-to-ceiling windows at the long, wide deck that jutted out farther than the balconies above them, which, with the floor-to-ceiling windows and the room being open plan, made the deck feel like it was a continuation of the first floor. Since beyond that was uninterrupted nature until the view hit town, this gave that floor the feel that it went on forever.

Completing this open vibe and sharing of nature and adding tons of light when the sun was up, there were a generous amount of windows all around. This included a huge picture window over the sink at the back wall that had a great view too, a view into the woods. It wasn't as phenomenal as the view in the front but it was good enough to make me look forward to doing dishes.

The open-backed stairs to the upper level cut into the middle of the space, the railing made of beautiful wood that was full of character, the steps carpeted in short-pile cream wool with sparse brown and gray speckles. The stairs were so awesome they were a feature on their own. The view was fabulous but if I got a look at those stairs cutting through the room, I would have said yes to this house.

There was another flight of stairs that led down to the utility room that was at the side wall of the garage. These were at the side of that level, leading from the kitchen and surrounded by another railing of the same wood.

He had a deep-seated, very large, cushiony, black L-shaped sectional, a flat-screen TV and a shelving unit that held a top-of-the-line stereo with speakers built into the house giving surround sound even on the upper levels and out on the decks. There was also a stone hearth fireplace. Further, there were four unusual but awesome stools at the lip end of the counter of the massive, square island. Like the rest of the house, there were no rugs and tons of room to add more furniture.

The fireplace would look great with some cool candleholders around it. The cream cabinets and black granite countertops in the kitchen would look fabulous with cream KitchenAid standing appliances. Ty only had a blender which was cream so that was why I knew cream would look good. Then, of course, there was the coffeemaker, both, seeing as he liked "nice shit" and his friends undoubtedly knew that, were KitchenAid.

There was a lot you could do with his house. A new wife, a real one, would be in throes of ecstasy if she was carried over the threshold to this place.

On that not-so-happy thought, I washed my face, brushed my teeth and headed down to the kitchen.

No coffee in the coffeemaker. No note on the island. Ty just gone.

I made coffee and I used his strawberries, bananas and yogurt, cutting up the fruit and covering it with yogurt in the bowl. I poured myself a cup of joe and wandered out to the front deck that also had no furniture.

I set my coffee down on the railing after taking a sip then shoveled fruit and yogurt in my mouth while staring at the sun shining bright on Carnal, the green pine-covered hills beyond, the purple mountains beyond that.

I let the warm morning sun shine down on me and I decided how to start my life.

Ty's furniture was way better than mine. Mine was cheap and I'd had it for nine years so it wasn't in the best of shape. But my bed was newer, decent and would fit in one of the rooms on the middle floor. I'd need a bed when this was done. And he had plenty of room. My shit could be stored in his other room. And I'd bought my new computer only three months before. We'd get rid of his and he could get a new one when this was done and I went away.

I'd call Ella, tell her what to get rid of and what to send. I'd buy new of what I needed when my real life started.

She said she was gently nudging Honey to move into my place and take over the lease and surprisingly Honey was considering this. Then again, Ella was not immune to motherly emotional manipulation. So not immune, she'd become a master at it and therefore she was coaxing Honey to cut the apron strings she'd latched onto by using helping me out as incentive. And Honey was sweet. She'd want to help me out. This meant Honey could use my furniture if she wanted to until she got set up.

I also needed a job. Ty might be able to cover me but I wasn't going to let him. He lived his life, did his business, I'd do mine.

So I needed a paper.

People would expect his new wife would make his house a home. And I was his new wife. I thought his decks needed flowers and furniture. So I'd see to that. If I had to live here for however long, I was going to enjoy the view and not do it standing at the railing.

I also had a town to discover. Maggie's groceries were running out. I needed to do an inventory, toilet paper, cleaning supplies, laundry stuff (the washer and dryer being in a kickass utility room in the garage). He had friends and they'd probably wonder where I was. I couldn't stay up here forever. That wouldn't be doing my job.

I needed to break the seal, go into Carnal, see and be seen.

And thinking on laundry, I needed to do some. For me. For Ty.

Another thing to add to the list.

My plans set, I finished my bowl of breakfast, set it on the railing and stood there sipping my coffee, staring at the view, having eaten and still feeling hollow.

I finished my coffee and still wasn't full up.

And I knew I could eat a bathtub full of fruit and yogurt and not feel full.

This was because I was not the kind of girl who ever got to feel full. I knew that. I just had to learn to stop forgetting it.

I grabbed my bowl and went into the house to find my phone and call Ella.

I had things to do.

I had a life to fake starting.

Ty

Ty Walker hit the button on the garage door opener, the door slid open and he saw the Charger parked there. He'd taken an opener with him that day knowing Max would be bringing him the Viper. He'd put one in Lexie's car and obviously she'd found it.

The Viper growled into the garage, the sound of the vehicle reverberating in the closed space. He shut her down, opened his door and folded out.

It wasn't late. He'd planned to see to some business after work but he often still had a tail. They were sticking close. They hadn't approached, made their intentions clear, they weren't watching all the time but they were watching. It was too soon to try to shake them when they were. They'd know he was doing it. They'd be more alert.

He didn't need that.

Still, when they weren't, he'd made his connection. He'd handed over a fuckload of cash and he hoped like fuck Dewey would be hard at work. Not because of the cash. In normal circumstances Dewey would bolt with the cash, disappear for half a year doing whatever the fuck and whatever the fuck would undoubtedly include sitting a game or five dozen of them and he'd come back broke.

No, he hoped Dew would be hard at work because he knew

Walker would find him if he bolted and when he did, Walker wouldn't be happy. Dewey knew to avoid that.

But more, Dewey was a friend, had been since junior high and Walker hoped to God Dewey would fight the urge and do right by Walker.

So it was just after six. After work, he'd gone to the gym to work out.

And now he was home.

And so was Lexie.

He started to the door that led to the utility room and the interior stairs. By the door the garbage bins were standing side by side, the top of one having slid partially off. On his way to the door, automatically, he grabbed the handle to secure it but he caught a glance at something familiar inside the bin through the small opening left by the lid. It was familiar enough to capture his attention. He pulled the lid entirely off to see what it was and stopped dead.

Big bags filled with party trash on bottom. Lexie's wedding bouquet on top.

It was looking tired, petals falling off, blooms drooping, but she'd carefully carried that thing to the Charger when they left Vegas and made sure the stems were in water the minute she could when they were in Moab. When they got to Carnal, he'd lost track of it. She could have brought it in the house but he didn't remember seeing it.

All that care, now it was in the trash. Not precious. Nothing but garbage.

He slowly lowered the lid to the bin and pressed until it clicked closed. He leaned into his hand on the bin and closed his eyes.

Then he opened his eyes and moved through the door to the utility room.

The minute he hit the open doorway to the stairs, he smelled it.

Garlic.

She was cooking.

He climbed the stairs, rounded the railing and saw her in the kitchen.

She didn't know he was there. She had her iPod earphones in and was standing at the back counter doing something.

She was wearing a tight yellow tank and her Army green short shorts.

She was not swaying, kitchen dancing or singing.

And that was when he knew that Lexie, who could throw bright even when she was asleep, had shut out the light.

Fuck.

Fuck!

She turned. Moving to the stove at the side wall, she caught sight of him in her peripheral vision, her body did a small jerk then her head turned and her hand came up to pop out an earphone.

"Hey," she said.

"Hey," he returned, walking in and dumping his workout bag on the opposite side of the island from where she was.

She watched him do this then she turned her back on him, picked up a wooden spoon and started to stir something in a skillet.

"I did some laundry today," she told the skillet. "If you've got anything you want cleaned, just dump it in the utility room on your way to work tomorrow."

He didn't respond. Instead he leaned a hand on the counter of the island and watched her.

"I'm making spaghetti if you don't want one of your shakes."

"I'll do both," he told her.

"All right," she replied, put the spoon down and reached to a box of spaghetti that was sitting beside the stove on the counter.

"You go grocery shoppin'?" he asked.

"Yeah," she answered, dumping spaghetti into a big pot. "You need anything, write it down and leave it for me. I'll go into town and get it."

Walker again didn't respond.

He didn't respond because he'd fucked up and he didn't know how to fix it.

Days before, seconds after she told him she wanted to have

breakfast with her husband and he liked hearing her say that, he liked it too fucking much, he fucked up. Then he kept fucking up. Then he kept fucking doing it. He knew it and he couldn't stop.

Then, the instant she pressed her mouth to his, her soft body in his lap, overwhelmed with emotion and sharing that with him, he lost control and he knew he couldn't do that. And the only way he could manage to keep control was to stay the fuck away from her, her sweet smiles, her soft voice, her brightness, that fantastic fucking body. He couldn't hold up. So he stayed the fuck away from her and spent a lot of time thinking about how to encourage her to stay the fuck away from him.

Putting that plan into action last night, he'd *really* fucked up.

"Lexie—" he started but she moved quickly, not looking at him and heading toward the stairs while talking.

"Do me a favor and don't let that boil over. I gotta go check the dryer."

Then she was rounding the stairs and she didn't even give him her face when she went down, but instead kept her eyes on her feet.

When he lost sight of her thick, shining hair, he dropped his head and stared at his hand on the counter. Then he moved, mixing some protein powder with water, he drank it keeping an eye to the stove making sure the pot didn't boil over. She came back up the stairs with her arms full of folded clothes, went to the stove, checked on things then walked to the stairs and up them.

She didn't look at him. She didn't speak to him.

Walker downed the rest of his drink then stared at the cup while expending a goodly amount of effort stopping himself from hurling it across the room.

After he succeeded in this endeavor, he put the cup in the sink, went to the stove, turned everything to low and walked up the stairs.

She was closing a drawer when he got to their room.

"Le—" he started but she didn't even let him get her name out.

Without looking at him she headed toward him, eyes on the

stairs, interrupting him by asking, "You gonna have a shower first? I can keep your meal warm."

"You think you can worry about dinner in a minute and maybe look at me?" he asked back.

She stopped dead and her head tilted to look at him.

He looked in her blue-gray eyes and there it was. Or, more to the point, there it wasn't.

The light was out.

He sucked in breath.

Then he gave it to her. "I was an asshole last night. I got a lotta shit on my mind but that wasn't cool."

"Don't worry about it," she replied instantly.

He felt his throat start to burn.

"You were right last night," he told her. "We need to talk."

She shook her head. "No, it's good. It's all good, Ty. I have a plan. I've got everything sorted out with Ella. Margot fixed things for me at work. Ella's already sent some of my stuff. It'll be here soon, maybe even tomorrow. I'm going to get a job, don't know what, something. I bought a paper today. I'll have a look. Ella is going to have moving quotes tomorrow. I'll let you know. It's all happening. It's all good. So you can get on with..." she paused "...whatever you need to get on with."

She started to move by him but he caught her, wrapping his fingers around her bicep. She stopped and her head tipped back again.

"We got more shit to talk about," he said quietly.

She shook her head again. "No we don't."

"You know we do."

Suddenly she was nodding her head. "You're right, we do. I need to ask if it's okay if I use one of your rooms downstairs to store some stuff and if I can set up my bed in the other one. Oh...and if I can switch out my computer with yours. I bought mine three months ago. It's a good one."

That burn in his throat got hotter but he forced through it, "Do whatever you gotta do. I don't care. Now, we—"

She twisted her arm out of his hand and quickly moved around him, jogging down the stairs, muttering, "I have to check the spaghetti."

He took in a deep breath. Then he took in another one.

Then he hissed, "*Fuck!*" and followed her.

She was dumping spaghetti into a colander in the sink. He got close to her back and started to say her name again when suddenly the pot hit the countertop with a clatter, she whirled and took two steps back, lifting a finger and pointing it at him.

"*Don't!*" she snapped. "Don't you fucking come home and think you can give me a different Ty. Do not think you can *fucking* play me like that."

Ty watched her suck in a deep breath but even as she did, she gave him no opening and kept on talking.

"I don't know what the fuck you're dealing with and I don't care. I asked, you wouldn't tell me. I tried everything I knew to get you to let me in there," she jabbed her finger at his chest, "and you didn't let me in and now, Ty, I don't fucking care. You can ride the wave of whatever's controlling you but don't drag me along on that trip." She swung her arm out to the side. "Out there, I'll be what you're paying me to be." She pointed to the floor. "In here, it would be good if we could be civil to each other and you don't give me any of that 'pussy' bullshit of yours. And that's all for in here, Ty. Tonight, I sleep on the couch and I keep doing it until my bed gets here and then I'll move to it. You wanted to talk, there it is. I'm laying it out. You don't like that, you get your bling back and I walk. Think about it and enjoy the spaghetti. I'm going for a drive."

Then she turned, snatched her keys off the island and ran to and down the stairs.

Walker stared at the space where he last saw her and he did it for a long time waiting for the burn to fade from his throat.

This took a while.

Then he turned off the burner under the stove, the oven where the garlic bread was baking, walked upstairs and took a shower.

* * *

When Lexie got home at ten to eleven, Walker was flat out on the couch, eyes to the TV.

He didn't move when he heard her hit the room.

But he did speak.

"I'm takin' the couch, you take the bed."

No sound, no movement.

Then, "Fine."

He heard her go up the stairs.

He stared at the TV for a long time not seeing it. Then he lifted up his hands and rubbed his face. After that, he turned the TV off and tried to find sleep.

This took a while.

CHAPTER EIGHT

Got a Wife Who Knows My Every Move

Ty

Walker jogged up the outside steps after his morning run. It had been over five years since he'd run in Colorado. He wasn't used to it and the altitude had kicked his ass.

But it had also been over five years since he'd run free, alone, wherever he wanted his feet to take him, the road open for him to decide where he wanted to go. Not caged. Not limited. Not with eyes tracking his every move, so he didn't give a fuck the altitude kicked his ass.

He opened the door and instantly saw Lexie at the island, dressed, hair done, makeup on, coffee cup halfway to her lips.

Her boxes had come, her wardrobe selection increased and she'd wasted no time unpacking her shit and taking advantage of it and the results were right there. Thin tank-like tee the color of the inside of a honeydew melon with ragged, torn-looking straps, one falling off her shoulder. What he was sure were dark brown short shorts even though he couldn't see her legs but that was all she wore. Thick, dark brown leather belt with something stamped on the leather and a heavy silver buckle. And he knew by her height she was wearing heels.

It was Sunday, his day off, two days after she'd laid it out. He'd come home from work both Friday and Saturday, Friday, right after work, last night, right after his workout after work. She was civil. She offered him dinner. She made him dinner. She did the dishes. Then she disappeared to the top floor and he didn't see her again.

Her light was out.

And her eyes were on him now, and he saw she hadn't switched it on that morning.

And he didn't like her light switched off. He didn't like her keeping that light from him. And the fuck of it was, he was the asshole who'd switched it off in the first fucking place.

"Morning," she greeted, then her head went down and he saw she was scratching something on a notepad. She kept talking, her voice dead as it had been for three days, and he didn't fucking like that either. "I don't know if you noticed but I got the bottled water on that note you left me."

He'd noticed.

He'd also noticed she'd done his laundry.

He went to the fridge and got a bottle of the water she bought for him after he left a note about it, twisted the cap and sucked back a huge pull.

This he used as his affirmative response. He didn't speak often because he didn't feel he needed to speak when his actions could speak for him. At that moment, he also didn't speak because he didn't want to do something stupid. Something that would set her off. Something, anything that would make Lexie's light shine through. Which was what he wanted to do.

"All right, I'm going. I'll see you later," she announced, moving to the sink to put her coffee cup there.

"Where you goin'?" he asked.

"There's a garden center in Chantelle. Shambles told me about it. I'm going to get some flowers," she told the island where she went to grab her purse, which she did then she ripped off the top sheet on the pad. Her eyes skimmed through him and she finished, "Later."

She started toward the stairs, shoving the paper into her purse but stopped and turned around when he asked, "Who's Shambles?"

"The guy who owns La-La Land Coffee," she told him, started to turn back to the stairs but stopped and turned back at his voice.

"La-La Land Coffee?"

"The coffee house in town," she answered then started to turn again but stopped when he again spoke.

And he spoke when he shouldn't have. He spoke because he was a dumb fuck. He spoke because he couldn't hack it. Lexie shut off, not just off but shut off from him.

"You're not goin' to a garden center."

Her head tipped to the side. "I am. The deck needs plants."

"The deck doesn't need plants."

"Yes it does."

"It doesn't."

"Okay." She took one step toward him and the dead was gone from her voice. She was now speaking with strained patience. "You're a guy so you don't get this but when a man brings his new wife to his house, she does shit like plant flowers to put her stamp on it, make it her home, make it *his* home. People are going to expect me to do shit to put my stamp on your house and therefore, the deck needs plants."

To this, Walker replied, "It's Sunday."

Her brows snapped together. "You're right. It's Sunday."

There it was. Something. Not something big but confusion mixed with impatience.

He took it and without hesitation, fuck him, he went for more.

"So, a man gets outta prison, he gets himself a new wife, he brings her home, takes care of business by findin' a job to provide for her, his first day off, his wife does not go to the garden center to buy plants in an asinine effort to put her stamp on a house. She stays home with her husband while he fucks her brains out."

He watched the color hit her cheeks and her eyes flare and he liked it. It wasn't that Lexie light but it was something. Something more than confusion and impatience and he took it too.

Then he watched her straighten her shoulders before she returned, "You're right, Ty. A man who just got out of prison with a new wife, I can see this. I can also see him returning home right after work and getting his workout not at a gym but, as you put it, by fucking his wife's brains out. But you haven't been doing that. Even this morning," she threw a hand out toward the door, "you didn't engage in morning nookie with your wife but went for a run. You've established the pattern so, clearly, I'm not behaving outside the norm."

"Maybe I didn't fuck my wife this morning because I tired her out last night," he replied, and watched her hands shoot up in the air and drop as she lost patience.

There it was. He went for it. He got it.

More.

"Well, you didn't tire her out last night. You slept on the fucking couch!" she snapped.

"You drew that line, Lexie," he shot back.

That's when she lost it and how she lost it, she shredded the already frayed hold he had on his control. Frayed because she'd been picking at it from the moment he saw her standing beside the Charger outside in the hot-as-fuck southern California sun and, after she'd shut down, he'd kept picking at it.

"No, Ty, *you* drew it when one second you had your tongue in my mouth, your hands on me and me on my back in your bed and swear to God, *swear to God*, that was all you had to do. I was this close," she lifted a hand and held her thumb and forefinger an inch apart, "to climax just with that and the next second you took it all away from me. *All* of it, and you fucking know exactly what I'm talking about because the next second I was standing on my feet, you were two feet away but you might as well still have been in fucking California. And then I watched you shut down."

At her words, he felt his lungs seize but he managed to force out, "What?"

"You heard me," she bit off and whirled, saying, "Now I'm going. I'll be back in a couple of hours."

Oh no she fucking wouldn't.

"Don't walk away from me," Walker growled.

She didn't respond but she did keep walking away from him.

That was when Walker moved.

She was two steps down when he caught her around the waist and hauled her right back up. The back of her body slammed into his, he wrapped his other arm tight around her chest, turned, set her on her feet and marched her forward, his mouth to her ear.

"I said, don't walk away from me."

"Ty," she whispered. Now he had breathiness, surprise, maybe even shock and he'd take those too. Fuck him, he'd known her just over a week and he'd take anything from her.

Her hand came up and wrapped around his forearm at her chest.

He let her go at the waist, pulled her purse off her shoulder, dumped it to the floor and curled his arm back around her stomach, moving her the whole time, stopping her by the couch.

"Why'd you throw away your wedding bouquet?" he rumbled in her ear. She didn't respond, he gave her a careful shake with both arms and clipped, "Why?"

"It's just flowers," she whispered.

"It wasn't just flowers."

"Ty—"

"Why?"

"Why are you doing this?" she asked quietly.

He gave her another careful shake. "Answer me, Lexie. Why'd you throw your bouquet away?"

"It was just flowers."

"It wasn't."

"No, you're right. It wasn't," she told him softly. "Then, after you put me in my place, it was."

He closed his eyes and shoved his face in her neck.

He couldn't do this. For two days he told himself he could. This was better. This was safer. Not for him, for her. He'd let her in, *wanted* her to come in and she did. Then he saw the error of his ways. Then, being a dick, he'd pushed her back over the line he'd drawn to keep her safe from his shit, from him, and he'd made it clear she should stay there. She got his message, she couldn't miss it.

But Christ, he couldn't do it.

He had to have her light back.

"Let me go," she whispered.

"No."

"Let me go."

He moved his lips to her ear and whispered, "I hurt you, baby."

Her body went still in his arms and she whispered back, "Don't."

"I was a dick. I fucked up and hurt you."

"Stop it."

He tightened his arms and pressed his temple into her hair.

It was soft as well as thick and smelled fucking great. He wanted his hands in it. He wanted to feel it on his skin. He wanted to feel it all around as her mouth worked his cock.

"I'm sorry I hurt you, Lexie," he murmured into her hair.

"Please stop it."

He slid his hand from her arm, up her shoulder to wrap it around the side of her neck as he slid his temple down her hair so his lips were at the other side of her neck.

"You honest to God nearly came with only my mouth on yours?"

She gave a jerk at his change of subject but he didn't let her go. Instead, he held her closer.

"Let me go," she demanded.

"Answer me," he ordered in return. "All it took was my mouth?"

"Ty—"

"Answer," he growled into her skin.

"No," she hissed. "There was your tongue and your leg was tangled in mine and you also ran your hand down my side."

That was nothing. That was just Lexie, giving everything, taking nothing.

He smiled into her skin instead of groaned.

"That's all?"

"Can you let me go?"

"No," he answered. "I wanna see what it takes."

Her body stilled again. She read him. She read him clear.

"Ty—" she breathed.

He lifted his lips to her ear and whispered, "You gonna let me in there?"

"Stop."

"Or do I even need to *get* in there?"

"Ty."

"Maybe I can get you to give me that while you're standin' right here."

That's when he felt her shiver.

And that's when he knew he could.

So that's why he moved his mouth to her neck and touched his tongue there.

He felt her shiver again.

"Jesus, baby," he muttered against her skin.

"Please," she whispered.

He trailed his lips along her neck and asked, "Please what?"

"Let me go."

"Do anything you ask, 'cept that."

She didn't speak but he felt her chest rising and falling fast and his mouth worked behind her ear as his hand at her neck moved down her shoulder, her arm, to stop where his thumb could stroke the side of her tit.

And it did.

He heard her soft intake of breath but he didn't hear the release.

"Breathe, Lexie," he whispered into her neck.

"Ty—"

"You gonna give it to me right here?"

"Ty—"

His teeth nipped her skin and he prompted, "Yes or no, baby."

Suddenly she moved. Twisting in his arms, his head was forced to go up but it didn't stay up because both her hands were at the back of it, pulling it down so his mouth could hit hers.

But his mouth didn't hit hers.

Their mouths collided because she was surging up to meet him.

Her lips opened instantly and just as instantly, he swept his tongue inside.

Tasting her, Christ, his dick, already hard, jerked.

He had to have her and he had to keep his shit together. He didn't, this could go very badly, not for him, for her. And he didn't want that for her.

He twisted. Falling back to the couch, pulling her with him, he landed. She landed on him and he rolled her immediately so he was on top, slanting his head, taking more. She arched her back, wrapping a leg around his thigh, her fingers at his head holding him close, not about to let go.

Fuck, she was hot.

And she wanted him in a bad way.

Testing that theory, he pressed his hips into hers and she moaned into his mouth.

Yeah. She wanted him in a bad way.

And he had to give it to her, give it to her before he took anything because he knew, once he got started, having pussy for the first time in years, that pussy being Lexie's, he wouldn't last long.

He tore his mouth from hers, his hands moving over her with intent, his lips whispering against hers, "Baby—"

"Don't stop," she begged, her hands at his head trying to pull him back, get his mouth. She lifted her head and he pulled back an inch.

"I'm not stopping, Lexie, but listen, yeah?"

He watched her face, her eyes hooded, his hand moved over her stomach, down the front of her shorts and she licked her lips.

Christ.

Beautiful.

"I'm gonna give it to you," he murmured.

"Okay," she breathed.

"No, not like that. First, I'm going to—" His hand had slid between her legs, over her shorts and he stopped speaking because her eyes closed, her lips parted and her neck arched.

Jesus, was she coming?

He cupped her between her legs.

"Baby?"

Her neck righted and her eyes slid half open. "Why do you keep stopping?" The words were half a breath, half a snap.

He grinned. "I'm not."

"You're not kissing me and you're not touching me, how's that not stopping?"

"Jesus, wildcat, keep your shirt on. I need to tell you—"

"Hello? Ty?" she called, arching her back, pressing her hips in his hand, and he felt his hold on his control slip so he was hanging on by his fingernails. "I don't *want* to keep my shirt on."

"Lexie, you're not helping."

"Helping what?"

"Baby, I haven't had a woman in five years. This isn't fuckin' easy seein' as all I can think is I wanna bury myself inside you. Good for me but it's been so long, I take what I want, it's not gonna be good for you. You wanna cut me some slack so I can make sure I see to you before I see to me?"

She blinked. Then her eyes warmed and he watched, right there, an inch away as she flipped the switch and her light flooded out, bathing him in brightness.

Then a loud knock came at the door.

She froze under him and he stilled on top of her. His hand was still between her legs and his cock was still hard and he was about ten minutes away from finally making his wife *his wife* and someone was knocking on the fucking *door* on fucking Sunday *morning.*

"Jesus, fuck, you gotta be kidding," he muttered.

"Ty Walker! Carnal Police. Need a word."

The limbs Lexie had around him tightened but his head turned to look at the back of the couch.

He didn't see couch. He saw red.

"Jesus, *fuck*, you gotta be *fucking kidding*," he clipped then knifed off his wife.

"Ty, let me get it," she called from behind him.

"I got it," he growled, prowling to the door.

"No, honey, please." He heard her. She was up and on the move. He could tell by the way her feet hit the floor that she was rushing. "You need to let me get it."

He didn't let her get it. He walked to the door and tore it open.

Then he saw him.

Fucking *motherfucker.*

"What?" he clipped, and then he felt her at his back, close, pressing her body to him, just to the side so she could peer around.

"You're home," good-old-boy, asshole, so-fucking-dirty-he-was-filthy cop Officer Rowdy Crabtree noted.

"Yeah, you've known that awhile, Rowdy, seein' as you followed us to Carnal from the Colorado state line."

He felt Lexie press closer to his back.

Rowdy didn't respond, his eyes moved to Lexie who was peeking around his side.

"Mrs. Walker, nice to meet you, ma'am," he stated, dipping his chin.

Motherfucker.

"Uh...hi," she said softly.

Rowdy's eyes tipped up to Walker's.

"Pretty. You get her off the Internet, order her from prison or somethin'?"

Motherfucker.

Walker locked it down and asked, "You here for a reason, Rowdy?"

Rowdy nodded his head. "Yup. Just stopped by, makin' sure you checked in with your parole officer."

"Think maybe you could ask my parole officer that?" Walker asked.

"Didn't think a' that."

"Well, you did, you'd find out from him that I did."

"Well, that's fine. Wouldn't want you steppin' outta line, doin' somethin' stupid, needin' to go back and finish your time."

There it was. Under their thumb. He went right to it. Didn't even beat around the bush.

Fuck.

"Got a wife. Got a job. Got a life I'm pickin' up, Rowdy. Just seein' to my business and mindin' only my own. Might wanna try that sometime," Walker returned.

"Not possible for me, seein' as I'm an officer of the law. Sometimes I need to stick my nose places," Rowdy replied.

"Careful of that," Walker said low. "Junkyard dogs might bite it off."

His chest puffed up and he leaned in half an inch. "That a threat, Inmate Walker?"

"Not an inmate anymore. I'm free. Hooked up with my parole officer. Hooked up with a job. Got a wife who knows my every move. Not gonna step out of line. Someone thinks I do, sees somethin' they didn't really see, got someone at my back to tell it as it is."

And there he was. Right into it. Not beating around the bush.

And Lexie heard.

And she understood.

He knew this because she froze solid behind him.

Lexie got it. Rowdy, being Rowdy, didn't.

"Just doin' the good citizens of Carnal a favor, visitin' a new ex-con who lives local, makin' sure he knows he needs to mind his p's and q's."

"Did you say 'mind his p's and q's'?"

That came from Lexie.

Walker looked down at her but not before he caught Rowdy's eyes slice to her.

"That's what I said, ma'am."

"Okay," she whispered, but the switch was flipped, the light flooding out even though he couldn't see her face fully as it wasn't tipped to him.

Then she tipped it to him and he saw her eyes were dancing.

Then she full out smiled.

"P's and q's," she whispered and he felt her body start shaking against his and he knew she was about half a second away from bursting out laughing.

"Babe, get a handle on it," he warned.

"Okay," she choked out then her face disappeared because she shifted so she could shove it in his back.

That was when he heard her snort.

Fuck. She was a goof.

He looked at Rowdy who clearly didn't like being laughed at.

"My wife's a goof," he explained.

That got another snort and he felt her fingers fisting in his sweaty tee at the back.

"Not sure what's funny here, Walker, this shit's serious business," Rowdy snapped, and Lexie suddenly wasn't at his back anymore.

She was at his side.

And she was no longer amused.

"You're right. There's nothing funny about a police officer showing up on Sunday morning on the doorstep of a man who did his time and is trying to get on with his life, simply, it would seem, to harass and threaten him. That isn't funny."

"Lex," Walker whispered, sliding an arm around her shoulders and pulling her into his side.

She didn't take his warning. She kept throwing sass.

"And, by the way, the good citizens of Carnal threw a huge-ass welcome home party for Ty when he got back. They know he's here and they're happy he's home. So, I don't think you have to worry too much about the good citizens of Carnal. I expect they don't need your kind of favors."

Fuck.

"Lexie, shut it," he growled, and her head shot back so she could look up at him.

"Well, it's *my* Sunday too and Sundays are good days and he's ruining it. It's still morning! He's ruining it right off the bat," she snapped.

"Lexie."

"It's true."

"Yeah, babe, but get a handle on it. You stop yappin', he'll be gone and we can get on with what we were doin'."

Color hit her cheeks, her mouth formed the letter and said the word, "Oh," softly then she shut it and looked to Rowdy.

So did Walker. "We done?"

Rowdy scowled at him. "I think you get me."

"You're not talkin' in code though you think you are. I get you."

Rowdy continued to scowl at him. He moved his scowl to Lexie. Then he stomped to the steps.

Walker shut the door and locked it.

Lexie pulled out from under his arm, took three steps back as he turned and the minute his eyes hit hers, she whispered, "Got a wife who knows your every move?"

He didn't answer that. Instead he crossed his arms on his chest and advised, "Promised none of my shit would blow back on you. I can deliver on that but I see you gotta help me do it and the way you can help me is not gettin' in these motherfuckers' faces and settin' yourself up as a target. News, Lexie, no man likes a woman laughin' at him. More news, that man's an ugly fuck who'd thank his lucky stars he dips his wick in skank pussy. He'll like it even less when the woman laughin' at him looks like you."

She ignored that and repeated, "Got a wife who knows your every move?"

Walker remained silent.

She stared at him.

Then she said, "He's dirty."

Walker didn't reply.

Lexie kept going by guessing wrong, "He's the one who lost to you at poker."

Walker still didn't speak.

Lexie did. "You're paying fifty grand for an alibi."

Yep. He was right. She caught it.

He again didn't speak.

She again stared at him.

He watched her pull in a deep breath and when she let it go, she spoke softly.

"This is the only time I'll ask, the only chance you'll get to tell me. You think it's not my business, I'll know where I stand."

That wasn't a good opening.

She finished it. "What's going on, Ty?"

He didn't speak. She held his eyes. He still didn't speak. This went on a long time.

She dropped her head at the same time her shoulders sagged. Defeat.

She was giving up on him.

No, strike that, she was giving up on *them*.

Two weeks ago, sitting in his cell wondering who he'd walk out to, he would never have guessed he'd walk out to a *them*. But he did. Lexie knew it. So did he. He hadn't had her pussy yet but she gave him all the rest. He'd pushed it away. But right then, he knew she was giving him another shot. If he wanted it, he'd have it all.

And, him not taking that shot, she was giving up on them, and his silence and distrust was forcing her to do that.

And, fuck him, he couldn't take it.

"You know Tate?" he asked, her head shot up and her light flashed. Hope so bright it blinded him.

There it was. She was giving him another shot and she wanted him to take it.

And so did he.

So he took it.

"Yeah," she said quietly.

"He's a bounty hunter."

"Okay," she whispered slowly.

"Used to be a cop."

She didn't reply.

"For the Carnal PD."

He watched her body go still.

He kept talking. "His captain, Arnie Fuller, now chief of police, was an asshole. Tate didn't like workin' for an asshole. Fuller was also on the take. Tate liked workin' for a cop on the take a lot less than workin' for an asshole. He quit and became a fugitive apprehension agent."

She nodded slowly.

"Fuller likes to play poker."

Her eyes flared but she remained silent.

"He likes it but he's not good at it."

He watched her swallow.

"He's also got a lot of opinions he don't mind sharin'."

When he said no more, she prompted carefully. "And those would be…?"

He answered immediately. "He likes a certain kinda people. Only that kind. *His* kind. Which means other kinds, like gays, liberals, hippies, he don't like. He also don't like color. Top of the heap he don't like is color."

She closed her eyes slowly then opened them and locked hers with his.

"Fuller's got a brother," he told her.

She pressed her lips together.

Walker continued, "Cut from the same cloth, Fuller and his brother."

She stopped pressing her lips together and he saw her clench her teeth.

He kept going. "Fuller's brother is a cop in LA."

She closed her eyes slowly again but this time she dropped her head, reached out a hand, took a step back, her hand hit island and she leaned into it. Then she sucked in another breath, lifted her head, opened her eyes and caught his.

He went on, "Don't know yet why. Just know the California Fuller had a problem. His brother offered me up as a solution."

"Ty," she whispered.

"Got his boys in on it. Recruited outside help. I didn't have a prayer."

"How?" she asked quietly, still leaning into a hand, this news weighing on her. He could see the weight. She was barely holding up.

"There are about three clean cops in the Carnal Police Department, that's how."

"But... California? You said you'd never been there."

"My word against theirs. Rowdy Crabtree made a statement that he heard me talkin' in Bubba's about hitting a game in LA over Labor Day weekend. Witnesses in LA corroborated I sat that game."

"So?" she asked, pulling herself straight, expending effort to do it, having that effort to give because she was getting pissed.

Getting pissed for him.

"So, cop says I headed to LA, I headed to LA. Cop buys witnesses, pulls in favors or extorts statements, they got witnesses."

"LA isn't an hour away, Ty," she told him something he knew. "You can't pop over there, commit a crime and pop back no matter what witnesses say."

"Yeah, you're right, Lex," he replied. "But see, over Labor Day weekend, I hooked up with pussy named Misty. Hot snatch, all over me, she didn't let me up for air for three days. It wasn't the first time I had her, we were on and off. I liked what I got from her but knew she was trouble. Like it or not, Lexie, pussy can be trouble and it can be the worst kind. She's the worst kind. Thought I had it under control. She let me in, I took what she gave, I didn't give back shit except as many orgasms as she could squeeze outta me. Had no fuckin' clue she was also bangin' someone else. Now she's married to Chace Keaton. *Detective* Chace Keaton, Carnal PD."

Lexie sucked in a sharp breath.

Walker finished it.

"She was my alibi. The only person I saw the whole weekend. When I offered her up, they talked to her, she said I'd lied about bein' with her but also shared I told her I was hitting a game in LA. Can't prove it was her but there were prints found at the scene in LA. Someone had to lift mine. Not hard, Bubba's, Pop's garage, coulda got them anywhere. But she was here, in this house, for three days and she's a cunt and that weekend she was a cunt sent on a mission."

"That's why," she whispered, and he knew what she meant. That was why he knew pussy came with a chain.

"That's why," he confirmed.

She stared at him.

Then she stated, "You're going after them."

"Fuck yeah," he replied immediately.

She took her hand from the counter and straightened her shoulders and Walker thought this was an interesting reaction. He thought she'd bolt. He thought he'd see disappointment.

She wasn't giving him that.

"What are you going to do?" she asked, and he shook his head.

"Can't keep you clean, you know."

He watched her and he could see it working behind her eyes, he just didn't know what it was. He felt his body was tense. He was preparing to do what he had to do. Stay still and let her walk out of his life or go after her if she tried.

"So, as you do this business, someone finds out and asks questions, you're paying me fifty thousand dollars to cover for you," she said.

He pulled in breath.

Then he gave her what she needed and what he needed to give her.

"Your money is in my safe upstairs in the bedroom. Part of the reason I had to sit a game is to make sure I covered you as well as my business. Right now, you take the diamonds, I go get you the money, you pack your shit, you go and I let you. I can see what I'm doin' don't sit well with you. You've already had that kinda shit in your life, too much, kept yourself clean. I'm gettin' you dirty. This is your chance to stay clean. Take it and go."

She held his gaze and asked, "How is this getting me dirty?"

"Lexie, it comes down to it, I'll be askin' you to lie to cops."

"Ty, it comes down to it, I'll be lying to dirty cops, and everyone knows a double negative is a positive."

At her words, Walker felt his lungs seize, so bad, he couldn't breathe or speak.

He battled for oxygen as he watched her look around the kitchen, over her shoulder, taking in her surroundings.

Then she whispered, "Life interrupted."

"What?" he asked quietly.

Her eyes came back to him.

"You were what? Thirty years old? Thirty-one? You had a job. A house. Friends. And just because you're a half-black man who won a poker game, they took all that away for five years? Then when you get out, they follow you for days and show up at your door on a Sunday morning just to give you shit?"

The air came back into his lungs and it did this because her voice was getting louder and shriller. She was working herself up.

She was not getting pissed.

She just *was* pissed.

For him.

"Baby—" he started.

She leaned toward him and her eyes narrowed. "That is not cool, Ty. That is *not* cool." Then she slapped her hand hard on the counter of the island and shouted, "*I do not believe this shit!*"

Oh fuck. She was off.

He moved toward her but she stepped back, lifting up a hand.

"No." She shook her head. "Heads up, you don't know this about me yet but when I get mad, it's good to keep a distance and I'm… fucking… *mad.* I mean, *what the fuck?*"

She yelled this still backing up as he advanced thinking she was wrong. She got mad the other night. He'd learned then distance was good when Lexie went off. He just wasn't going to give it to her now because then, she was pissed *at* him, now she was pissed *for* him.

She suddenly stopped retreating and planted her hands on her hips. "All pussy doesn't have chains, Ty. This Misty bitch was a bitch. We're not all like that. I assure you. Okay," she threw out a hand then planted it right back on her hip, "we can be pains in the asses. I'll grant that. But *lying about your whereabouts*? And doing it in order to *steal five years of your life*?" She shook her head, her voice loud, sharp, seriously fucking pissed. "Unh-unh." She kept shaking her head. "No way."

He approached cautiously, got close and sifted his hands into her hair at either side of her head. Holding it back and resting his forearms lightly on her shoulders, he dipped his head close.

"Babe, get a handle on it," he whispered.

"That's why you don't trust me," she returned, not whispering, hands still on her hips, body held tight.

"Uh…yeah," he confirmed.

She nodded, the movement jerky, taking his hands with it. "Right. I can see that."

He felt his mouth twitch.

"Lexie—"

"We're not all like that, Ty."

He pressed the pads of his fingers into her scalp and murmured, "All right, babe, now—"

"And I'm going to prove it to you and I'm going to prove it to you by not going. You need someone to take your back during this business, that's me. I'm not going. I'm staying right here and giving you what you need."

He felt his gut clench at the same time that thing pierced through the left side of his chest.

"All right," he whispered through a pain that was exquisite.

She stared into his eyes and kept her hands on her hips. He stared into hers and watched the wet start to form.

And there it was again. She was giving him more because that wet was for him. And it was then he knew how she felt the day they arrived in Carnal, overwhelmed by something unexpected, something good, something she never thought she'd have. He knew how she felt because he felt it right then, looking into her eyes, her giving him that. Something good. Something, after that mud was flung at him and it stuck, he never thought he'd get a shot at. And there she was, his hands in her soft, thick hair, her eyes growing wet, giving it to him.

She fought it and beat it back and she did this by continuing to throw sass.

"Now, are you gonna go with me to buy flowers for the deck or what?"

He bent his neck and dropped his forehead to hers.

Then, his eyes holding hers, he muttered, "Yeah."

"I'll warn you, I've never done any gardening. They'll all probably die."

"Whatever," he replied, fighting a grin.

She looked into his eyes for a while.

Then she told him, "You need to shower. Do you need coffee? One of your powder thingies?"

Powder *thingies*.

Total goof.

"Coffee."

She nodded her head, again moving his hands.

"I'll fix it while you shower. Travel mug."

He closed his eyes and pulled in breath. Then he moved the lower half of his face and touched his lips to hers.

He let her go and walked to the stairs.

He was one step up when she called his name. He looked through the open slats and saw her at the coffeemaker, her body turned to the side counter, her neck twisted, her eyes on him.

When she had his eyes, she dropped the bomb.

"FYI, there's been no one since Ronnie. No one. For four years. You've got a year on me but, I figure, mostly we're in the same boat."

He fought the urge to move to her and drag her up the stairs to his bed.

Or, saving time and energy, take her to the couch.

Instead, he asked, "You gave me that, baby, what you want me to do with it?"

She looked to the coffeemaker and muttered loudly, "I'll leave that up to you."

Fuck.

He knew what he wanted to do with it. He also knew how he wanted to do it. He also knew he was going to do what he wanted to do.

But that was not for now. What he wanted to do would take time.

And control.

He didn't have any of the last left. And they had plants to buy.

So he drew breath in through his nose and walked up the stairs.

CHAPTER NINE

Lady Luck Was Feeling Generous

I WALKED DOWN the stairs behind Ty wondering what I'd been wondering the last twenty minutes while he took a shower, shaved and donned another black tee, faded jeans and boots.

Was I crazy?

Was I stupid?

Was I both?

Or was Lady Luck feeling generous for once and if I fucked this up, I'd piss her off?

We hit the utility room and Ty opened the door to the garage, stood clear of it but kept his hand on it, his long arm extended, keeping it open, he wanted me to precede him.

I did, took two steps into the garage, my mind cluttered. Then it uncluttered when what was hitting my eyes filtered to my brain. I stopped dead and stared.

This was because, parked across from my Charger, there was a kickass, badass, sleek, shiny, beautiful, *oh-my-God* black Dodge Viper sporting two narrow silver racing stripes up the hood and over the roof. Vaguely, it occurred to me it had to be there the other night when I'd taken off in a huff but that was how upset I was. I didn't see it.

Now I was seeing it.

Ty moved around me muttering, "We'll take the Snake."

My head jerked to him as he headed to the driver's side like he was walking up to a sedan.

My eyes drifted back to the car and, upon seeing it again, I felt a tickle between my legs.

Obviously, I enjoyed this tickle a bit too long because I heard Ty call, "Lex, what the fuck?" and my eyes went back to him.

He was standing in the open driver's door. He looked hot standing in the open driver's door of a Viper. He looked hot all the time but he looked *smokin' hot* standing in the open driver's door of a Dodge fucking Viper.

"Where did this car come from?" I forced out.

"Max brought it back to me the other day," he answered. "He was keepin' it in his barn while I was gone."

"It's yours?" I whispered.

"Yeah," he replied.

"It's yours," I repeated.

"Yeah," he repeated too. "What the fuck?"

"I knew you were good at poker but this…this…" I waved a hand vaguely at the car. "Did someone bet it or did you buy it from winnings?"

"I didn't get it playing poker. I won the pinks street racing."

I felt my mouth drop open.

Street racing?

"The guy sucked," Ty went on. "College kid up from Denver skiing. Came to a gathering, thought his car could do all the work, not his driving. Bet me, lost. I got the Snake. He got his bud to call a taxi to get a ride back to his daddy's condo."

I stared.

Then I asked, "You street race?"

"Not anymore."

"You used to?"

"Yeah."

"Are you good at it?"

He looked down at the Viper then back at me.

"You're good at it," I whispered.

"He sucked. Raced him in my Skyline GTR. *That* I won because I'm good."

"Where's that?"

"You're standin' in it. Sold it for a down payment on this condo."

"House," I corrected and his lips twitched.

"Condo, babe."

I studied him standing in the door of a kickass Viper, one hand casually laid on the top of the door, from his other hand dangled his travel mug of coffee. I didn't even know if he could fit his big body in that kickass car but, obviously, he could.

And as I studied him I thought Lady Luck was definitely feeling generous.

"Lex, you gonna get in or what?" he asked, his deep voice edged with impatience.

I was thinking "or what." I was thinking, my ass hit the seat in that car I might have a spontaneous orgasm. I didn't even want to know what would happen to me when he fired it up. And I wanted to save my orgasm for when Ty got around to giving it to me.

"You can't drink coffee in a Viper," I informed him, and his lips twitched again.

"Why not?"

"It's against badass, muscle car law."

He dropped his head and looked at his boots but I could swear I saw his shoulders shaking.

"And we also can't take it to a garden center," I continued. "The steering wheel will lock you try to pull it into the parking lot of a garden center. We have to take the Charger."

He lifted his head and even across the expanse, I saw his eyes were dancing.

"Get in the car, Lexie."

"But—"

"Ass in the car."

I stared at him. Then I moved across the garage to the passenger side of the Viper, muttering, "Don't blame me if she ejects us, we try to take her on errands at a garden center."

"Live wild, baby," he murmured, and folded his big body behind the wheel.

There it was. He fit. A miracle.

I gingerly aimed my ass into the passenger seat. I got the door closed and my seat belt on without incident. Ty hit the garage door opener and turned the ignition.

The Snake bit.

Another tingle, stronger. Nice.

I smiled at the windshield.

"Fuck," Ty muttered. My eyes slid to his, he was looking at me and when I caught his gaze, he shook his head. I smiled bigger.

He placed an arm around the back of my seat, looked over his shoulder and pulled out, still shaking his head.

She growled through the condo complex. I allowed myself to feel her then, when we were out of the complex, I pulled my shit together.

"Who's Max?"

"A friend, lives in Gnaw Bone."

"Gnaw Bone?"

"A town not too far away."

"There's a town called Gnaw Bone?"

Ty didn't reply because, obviously, there was.

So I asked, "Why wasn't he at the party?"

"Different set of friends," he told me. "Met him on a construction job in Wyoming. He was a good guy, we found we were both from around the same patch, solidified the connection. We stayed tight even though, back then, he wasn't around much. Now he's married with kids so he was around but I wasn't."

"Construction? I thought you were a mechanic?"

"Diversified. Job was short, hours long, money fuckin' great. Same kinda job took me to Dallas."

I took in a breath.

Then I tested the waters.

"And what led you to Shift?" I asked.

"Poker. I was in Dallas. Sat some games. He heard about me, thinks he's got a big dick. Called me out. I bested him. He went down and did it hard. Lied about collateral. Walked away from the table unable to pay up. That isn't my favorite thing. I needed to make my point. I did. He got my point. Promised a payment plan, started it. The job got done, I was back in Carnal, payments were supposed to keep coming and he knew they didn't, I'd be taking a vacation in Texas. I got framed, went down and Shift thought that was his good luck. Met a guy inside, he knew Shift, didn't like him, itchin' to teach him a harder lesson than the one I taught him. He's out in about a week. I got word to Shift, he didn't sort out his debt, he's first order of business when I got out. He gets a visit from me *then* he gets a visit from my friend. Shift saw the wisdom of sorting out his debt."

"Enter me," I whispered.

"Yeah," he whispered back.

"What'd you do to him?"

"You don't wanna know."

I looked to Ty. "Actually, I do."

He glanced at me then back at the road. What he didn't do was answer.

"Ty, I don't care about Shift. You know that."

He sighed before he stated, "Another reason to quit the game. Sometimes men fuck up, do that shit, you can't be the man who lets it slide. Not my favorite thing to do. With Shift, he's such a piece of shit, gotta say, I didn't mind but the effort it took. Didn't mess around, my message left him breathing if not standing. Delays getting my money I have to wait for the end of a hospital stay."

"I'm surprised about that," I said quietly to the windshield. "Ronnie usually took Shift's back."

"Can't offer you an explanation, baby," Ty replied quietly. "Didn't hear shit about Rodriguez when I was down there. That wasn't exactly my world but I'm at a table, I don't care whose money I'm taking just as long as they're good for it. Maybe he hid that shit from Rodriguez.

Losin' that bad, he'd not wanna spread that around. He'd wanna keep it quiet, save his rep from takin' that hit."

"Yeah, that sounds like Shift."

"'Cause that *is* Shift."

I fell silent and experienced the smooth ride of the car, listened to the growl of the engine, eyes to the wide, two-lane road ahead of us, the beauty of Colorado all around, thinking he'd shared. As I sat there silent, I waited but he didn't ask for his take. I'd asked him a question, he gave me the answer and there it was.

Yes, Lady Luck was feeling generous.

Hesitantly, scared shitless the Lady would turn on me and strike, I pushed my luck.

"So, you made friends in prison?"

"One," he answered and I felt the beat of my heart ease because he answered.

"Just one?"

"Not a social club, Lexie."

"Right," I said softly.

And, surprisingly, he kept talking. "Name's Julius. Julius Champion, you believe that shit."

"That's a great name," I told him.

Ty didn't respond.

"What was he, um… in for?"

"Manslaughter."

"Oh God," I whispered and then I heard it.

Ty chuckled.

My eyes moved quickly to him firstly because I was shocked and secondly because I didn't want to miss it.

It was good I didn't miss it, his beautiful lips curved, his face relaxed in humor, amazing.

Still.

"Manslaughter is funny?"

"No," he stated firmly, all humor gone, and my heart started beating hard because, before I left Texas, I knew this one thing about

Ty. Shift had shared this. Shift had delighted in doing it because that was Shift.

I knew voluntary manslaughter was what Ty had been sent down for.

And he would not find that funny.

"Sorry," I said.

"I was laughin', baby," he started gently, "'cause Julius walked into his sister's house and saw her man takin' his fists to her. He lost his mind and beat the life outta him. You sounded scared. Men, they got reason to be scared of Julius. He'd never hurt a woman. I know this 'cause, on the outside, he's got three. They're all devoted. They all visit him regularly. The bitches fuckin' carpool."

This was so crazy, and funny, I felt laughter bubble up and then it bubbled out. I watched Ty's lips tip back up.

My heart again eased.

I looked forward and asked, "Why do men have reason to be scared of Julius?"

"He jacks cars for a living."

My head swiveled back to look at him. "What?"

"He jacks cars for a living. Don't know much about his business but, according to him, there's turf wars. You wanna be successful, you gotta learn how to take care of yourself, protect your territory." He glanced at me then back at the road. "He's an inch taller than me and twenty pounds heavier. Man sees that and that man knows Julius knows how to use his fists and body, smart thing for any of them to do is be cautious. Smart thing for any of them who fuck him is be scared and run. Smartest thing is not to fuck him."

I looked back at the road. "Sounds like a good friend to have."

"He was. He took my back. I took his."

"How does he know Shift?"

"He's from Texas. Something happened, things got hot there, he moved his business to LA. Better trade for him there anyway. Took his family with him—he's a family man—sister got hooked up with an asshole. Julius took care of him and is doin' his time. It isn't his favorite thing to do but he didn't complain. Worth it to him. His sense of justice is whacked. His sense of loyalty isn't. I found the amount of loyalty he's got balances out the other."

"So are you going to keep in touch with him?" I asked.

"Never lose touch with Julius," he answered. "Sucks how we forged our bond but we did it and, you got a bond like that, you don't lose it."

"You liked him," I noted quietly.

"We were in prison, Lex, and he took my back. He's six foot seven and weighs two hundred fifty pounds. That's a good man to be at your back. But that place, it's populated but in there, you are alone, very alone. That is, you're alone unless you got a brother. We became brothers. We played ball together. We worked out together. We ate together. Honest to God, wasn't for him, probably woulda lost my mind."

My heart didn't feel easy anymore. My heart squeezed.

"Ty," I whispered.

"No fuckin' with you, bein' in there and why I was, it wasn't for Julius keepin' me sane, I woulda lost my mind."

"You don't have to talk about this," I told him.

"Yeah, I do, baby. I don't, I'd lose my mind. Learned that and how I did was from Julius."

My head turned to him and I saw his arm straight, fingers curled around the wheel, muscles bunched with tension.

"It's over now," I reminded him softly.

"Yeah," he agreed, and those muscles stayed bunched.

"You're going to a garden center," I pointed out. "Free to drive your kickass car on a Sunday to a garden center. It's over."

"Yeah," he repeated with no release of those muscles.

I reached out and wrapped my fingers around his bicep, saying gently, "It would suck, you bent that steering wheel into a U."

He took in breath and when he let it out, his elbow bent and the tension went out of his arm.

I slid my hand away and faced front again.

"You've had a wild life," I remarked.

"Grow up with crazy, folks screamin' at each other all the time, Dad fall-down drunk every other night and at twelve you think bologna is gourmet, you get free, you live wild."

"Bologna?"

"Yeah, big score, me and Ike got bologna."

"Ike?"

"Isaiah, my brother."

"And your full name?"

"Tyrell. No middle for either of us. Mom and Dad had used up their creativity coming up with first names. Lucky we got 'em."

I sighed. Then I muttered, "Bologna."

"Bologna," he repeated.

"For me, it was corned beef hash. Granddad got the gumption to put together some corned beef hash, I was in seventh heaven. Usually, he forgot I needed sustenance to survive and I made myself PB and J's. He also forgot to teach me the importance of dental hygiene so a diet of PB and J's led to me having seven cavities by the time I was ten. I'm not a fan of the dentist but I am a fan of dental hygiene, just, unfortunately, hit the game late."

"Corned beef hash is better than bologna," Ty remarked.

"Yeah, but as far as I can see, you have perfect teeth."

And he did, all white, strong, even. His teeth were as beautiful as the rest of him.

"Least those two gave me something," he muttered, and a giggle erupted out of me.

"Yeah, count your lucky stars, honey," I advised.

"I am," he returned, and his voice was soft, those two words had meaning and I knew what that meaning was.

I knew what it was.

I knew.

And what it was was proof Lady Luck was feeling generous.

And I knew then I was not going to fuck this up and piss her off.

No way.

* * *

I was right. A kickass Viper did not go to the garden center.

This was because, outside Chantelle, there was a Toyota dealership. And Ty slowed before the entry of that dealership, muttering, "Quick stop, baby."

I didn't care if we made a quick stop. He was calling me baby again. His lips were twitching. I'd even heard him chuckle. And he was sharing. I'd take a quick stop in hell to keep all that.

We were gliding through the lot when a man with light brown hair wearing an ill-fitting pair of slacks and sports jacket saw us, his face split into a huge smile and he ran, actually *ran* to where Ty parked the Viper.

Ty barely cleared his door and I was only folding out when the man was on him, shaking his hand, grinning like a lunatic, head tilted back looking at Ty like he was a top-paid professional athlete on a mission and there to clear out the lot of all their high-end models.

"Ty, fuck, Ty. *Ty!* I heard you were out. Fuck! Good to see you, man," he said, pumping Ty's hand

"Stan, yo," Ty replied, pulled his hand free, moved out of the door of the car, forcing Stan out too and he turned and looked at me over the roof. "My wife, Lexie, Lex, this is Stan."

"Hey, Stan," I called, slamming my door, but Stan was staring at me, mouth open.

Then he swung his open-mouthed stare to Ty.

"Buddy, *you're married?*" He looked at me then back at Ty and spoke again before Ty could answer. "To a *hot chick*?"

"Not gonna marry butt ugly, Stan," Ty muttered, and I pressed my lips together as I moved around the back of the Viper toward them.

"All right, to a *super-hot chick*," Stan slightly amended.

"Yeah," Ty replied as I made it to his side and his arm slid around my shoulders, pulling me into him. "Lucked out."

Lucked out.

Yeah. I'd take a quick stop to hell to keep this. I'd even stay for a cup of coffee.

"You could score but, holy fuck, she's like a white Jennifer Lopez," Stan observed.

"I think I look like Jessica Alba," I joked because I did *not.*

He looked me up and down and then nodded. "I see it but that ass, all Lopez."

"Stan, you mind not talkin' about my wife's ass to my wife or, say, *at all*?" Ty asked in a way that Stan could only give him one answer.

And he did, on a mutter, "Yeah, Ty, sorry."

Then Ty asked, "Here to see what kinda deal you can swing me on a Cruiser."

That was when I went still.

A Cruiser? As in, a *Land Cruiser*? What was he doing? We were going to the garden center to buy plants, not drop tens of thousands of dollars on an SUV.

"You know I'll take care of you, Ty."

"Yeah, I do. That's why I'm here. Get the keys to one, dark gray or black. Upgrade."

"All over it," Stan said on another maniacal grin then he ran to the building.

I curled into Ty.

"Uh, honey lumpkins," I called, his head tipped down to look at me and when it did, his mouth was twitching again. "Looking into purchasing an SUV is not exactly a quick stop."

"Okay, not-so-quick stop," he revised very belatedly.

"Right, so, can I ask why you're looking into purchasing an SUV at all?"

I asked this and his forehead wrinkled. He was perplexed. It seemed not to occur to him that he already had a car. I also had a car. He had a job as a mechanic, had sworn off poker games and he had a score to settle. I wasn't sure how an expensive SUV fit into all of that.

"Lex, we're in Colorado."

"Mm-hmm," I agreed unnecessarily.

"It snows here."

Oh. That's how it fit in.

He went on, "You don't drive the Snake in snow. You drive a Cruiser in snow. Part of the reason I sat that game in Vegas was to set myself up when I got home. I'm settin' myself up."

"Right," I whispered.

"I had a Cruiser before, had to sell it to finance my defense."

I felt my heart skip a beat at this unpleasant bit of history.

He kept talking. "Won't be summer forever and you're thinking deck plants, we need a utility vehicle."

Again, this made sense. And his sudden and far from unwelcome domesticity made my heart beat faster. And he had four hundred and fifty thousand dollars somewhere. And a job. And, clearly, a history of getting cool things in one way or another. Last, he was a grown man, he wanted an SUV, who was I to say differently?

But I needed a rewind.

"You had to sell your other Land Cruiser to finance your defense?"

"Yeah."

"Did you have to sell anything else?" I asked.

"Coupla cars I won the pinks on, few other toys. Things got cheaper when I copped a plea."

My heart skipped another beat and my body went solid.

"You copped a plea?"

"Yeah. I copped a plea."

I pressed closer to him and put a hand on his chest. "Why, when you were innocent, did you cop a plea?"

"'Cause I had no alibi, my fingerprints were found at the scene and a bunch of assholes made statements and lied about my whereabouts. They wanted second degree and were muttering about bein' aggressive and goin' for first. That nightmare ended, I had things to do and I wanted to do them so I wanted out in five, not fifteen and definitely not fuckin' twenty-five."

My sunglasses looked into his sunglasses.

And I knew.

But I asked anyway and I did it on a whisper. "This is not about justice, it's about payback."

He looked over his shoulder and then back at me, his other arm sliding around so he could hold me loosely but his head dipped close.

"This isn't where I wanna have this conversation but it has to be had. You're right. This isn't about justice. It's about payback."

I didn't have a good feeling about that so I started, "Ty—" He shook his head and gave me a light squeeze so I stopped.

"I told you who Tate is and who he was. He pulled out all the stops when that shit started goin' down. He got nowhere except on radar. I pulled him back from that so he didn't get caught in the same shit storm as me. And this goes to what I told you earlier. *You* do not get on radar. They get you in their sights, they'll chew you up, babe, spit you out and not fuckin' blink. And, sucks for you, but you got shit in your past they will use to fuck you with. And make no mistake, baby, the instant you picked me up outside the penitentiary they started lookin' into you. That means you gotta keep your mouth shut and a tight handle on it. At all times. Carnal PD is infested. The citizens of that town keep their heads down and go about their business. You do that too. You let me handle my business and I'll let you know if I need you."

"Aren't there any good cops in that department?" I asked.

"Huddle with the boys first night I was home?" he asked back. I nodded and he went on, "Update. Nothin's changed except Fuller is now chief of police rather than just the captain. Which is worse. There are three cops Tate trusts and all of them are in uniform. No rank, no power."

"Isn't there some other authority—?" I began.

"Babe, they *are* the authority."

I pressed my hand into his chest to get him to listen to me and I said, "Some *other* authority."

He shook his head but said, "Tate had hope. At the party, I heard Betty talkin' to you about Dalton, that guy who kidnapped Laurie, stabbed her and Jim-Billy?"

I nodded.

"FBI got involved in that. Agent in that case, name's Tambo, smelled somethin' funny workin' with Carnal PD. Tate thought he'd run with it. He didn't."

"Maybe you could talk to him?"

"And tell him what? I got played by pussy and dirty cops in two fuckin' states not even connected conspired against me? He'd think I was a fuckin' nut."

I slid my eyes to the side and had to admit this was true.

"Lexie, look at me."

I slid my eyes back and I got another light squeeze.

"Keep your head down and a handle on that sass. You unleash it, you do me no favors. Worse, you put yourself out there and you do, I think you get from where we met I cannot protect you."

"Can I have one exclusion? If I run into bitch-face Misty, can I unleash my sass?"

His chest started shaking and I guessed it was with laughter considering his mouth was also twitching but he said, "She's married to a police detective."

"I'll be discreet."

"You rub up against Misty, you'll be fucked."

I held his eyes thinking he was probably right about that too.

So I gave in, "Oh, all right."

That got me another light squeeze but only with one arm because his other one left me so his big hand could cup my jaw as he dipped his head so his lips were against mine when he whispered, "Thanks, baby."

Then he kissed me lightly.

My heart fluttered not only at the kiss but because his hand felt nice on my face and his arm felt nice around me.

When he lifted his head, I said, "One thing. Misty's fair game after you wreak your vengeance."

His shades held mine. Then he whispered, "I can give you that."

"Thanks," I whispered back.

"Got 'em!" We both heard Stan shout and we looked to the side to see him running to us, hand up, jingling a key fob. "Magnetic gray!"

Five minutes later, Ty and I were pulling out of the lot on a test drive.

An hour after that, I was in the Viper trailing Ty in the Cruiser on our way home.

And sitting behind the wheel of the Viper, I was having the weird feeling that Lady Luck was beginning to like me.

* * *

Ty parked under the deck. I parked the Viper in the garage. He took the outside stairs. I took the inside ones.

I met him in the kitchen, bouncing on my high-heeled wedges.

"That was *awesome*! Can we go back… *oof*!"

The "oof" was because I was so excited about driving the Viper, I didn't see his intent when he was coming at me and only saw it when his shoulder dipped when he made it to me. And his shoulder dipped so it could hit me in the stomach and he could heft me up.

My stomach got tight and I felt another tickle between my legs, this one nicer than the Viper tickle. *Way* nicer.

"Ty," I whispered to his back as he started up the stairs.

"Told you, Lex, a man released from prison's got his first day off work, he's gonna spend it fuckin' his new wife."

Another tickle. A lot nicer.

It seemed that Ty was getting around to giving me an orgasm. I wanted Ty to give me an orgasm. Therefore, I fell silent.

He took me to the top and set me on my feet by the bed.

The first thing I did was pull off my top.

His eyes went dark and he pulled off his tee.

Another tickle. A really good one.

God, he was perfect everywhere.

I reduced the area between us by half and since we were less than a foot away that made us super close. Then I undid my shorts and shimmied them down.

Ty picked me up and threw me on the bed.

No tickle that time. A spasm.

Then he hooked his fingers in my panties and tore them down my legs. He put a knee to the bed and an arm around my waist. He lifted me, dragging me further across the bed and he planted me in it. He wasted no further time. He spread my legs wide with two hands and then his mouth was there. He tossed my legs over his shoulders then his big hands came around, cupping my ass and pulling me up to him.

At the feel of his mouth and tongue and just how good it was, my entire body arched and the heels of my sandals dug into his back.

I should have known, the way he could kiss, he could use that mouth. I should have known.

Now I knew.

And he used that mouth to build it hard and he built it fast.

"Oh God, honey," I whimpered, my hips surging up, my hand going to his head to hold him close but he wasn't going anywhere. He was hungry.

Starved.

And it was so good, I was close.

But I wanted him.

"Ty, God, I need you, baby."

He kept eating, pulling me deeper into his mouth.

Oh yeah, he was good at this.

"Ty, *God*," I moaned. "I need you inside."

I said it and his mouth was gone but I was up then I was straddling him, one of his arms around my waist, the other hand between us working his jeans.

"You get it, you take it like I give it to you," he growled as I tried to focus on his face.

"Whatever you want," I breathed. I felt the tip of him, my thighs quivered in anticipation then his arm drove me down so I was full of him.

Oh yes. *Yes.*

My head fell back and I gasped.

Then I tried to move but his arm stayed tight around me, keeping me impaled.

My head righted. "I have to move," I whispered.

"You take it like I give it then *I* take," he rumbled then his hand was back between us and his thumb was at my clit.

I sucked in breath and my head fell forward, my forehead colliding with his, my arms circling his shoulders.

Oh, God. That was good. That was unbelievably fucking good.

But I had to move.

"Honey, please, I have to move," I begged, my head shifting so my mouth was on his but I couldn't kiss him. I was breathing too heavy, fighting his arm, trying to slide up.

"You wanted me inside, baby, I'm inside." His voice was thick, tight, hoarse.

He was, deep inside, so much of him, his thumb…

I made a sharp noise as I felt it starting and my body began bucking against his before it started then it happened and I arched back, crying out.

Beautiful.

Beautiful.

Like everything Ty.

Then I was on my back and Ty was driving deep, fast, hard, grunting with each stroke, oh God…phenomenal.

My orgasm washed out slowly, taking its time, my hands moved over his skin, my legs shifted around him. He caught one behind the back of the knee and yanked it high then pounded deeper.

I moaned.

He went up on his other hand in the bed, looked down at our

bodies, our connection, his thrusting cock then his eyes came to my face. He fell down to his forearm, keeping my other leg held high as he held my eyes and I breathed heavy as I listened to his grunts.

Then the power behind his thrusts magnified, I knew it was coming. He was going to give it to me. My arms around him tightened, pulling myself up, my hand went to the back of his head and I tugged it down to me and took the force of his groan in my mouth.

He kept moving inside me, kept my leg up as his climax moved through him and then his tongue slid inside my mouth. He swung my leg around his waist and gave me more of his weight as he kissed me, deep, hard and sweet.

Then he slid in to the root, his arm in the bed moved up so his fingers could sift into my hair on one side, his mouth glided down the other side and I felt his nose flick my ear.

I sighed as I squeezed him tight in my limbs.

Then I turned my head and in his ear said, "You lasted a long time, long enough to let me move."

His head came up and his beautiful eyes hit mine.

"It wasn't good for you?" he asked but not in a way where he didn't know the answer, in a way he was making a point.

"Uh...yeah."

"Then quit bitchin'," he ordered and I smiled.

Then my hand slid up to his head as I lifted my head from the mattress.

His mouth met mine halfway.

* * *

"Can I tell you something?"

It was after round two, which started approximately zero point seven five seconds after round one but lasted a whole lot longer.

Ty was on his back on top of the covers, head to the mattress. We were still perpendicular to the pillows. I was pressed to his side, my legs tangled in his, my face tucked into his throat. His clothes were all gone. My bra and shoes had been removed in fantastic ways.

I'd become acquainted with nearly every inch of his beautiful skin, I'd felt his hands and mouth on nearly every inch of mine and I'd had three orgasms.

I was sated.

And he'd been giving all day. It was time for him to take.

"Yeah," he answered.

"It's kinda embarrassing," I warned, and his arm around my waist squeezed.

"What?"

"You know…in Vegas?" I started but then couldn't continue.

He gave me a minute and when I didn't say more, he prompted, "Yeah, I know Vegas."

"I mean, when we were there."

Again I said no more.

Again he had to prompt and he did this by asking, "What?"

"That day I came in and threw sass about breakfast."

"What about it?"

I pressed closer and I sucked in breath.

Then I whispered, "I'd actually come back to the room earlier."

His body stilled beside mine.

"I saw you in the shower," I whispered.

He stayed still and silent.

Then he growled, "You're fuckin' shittin' me."

My head came up and I looked down at him to see his face was blank.

Shit. Shit, shit, *shit.*

"I'm sorry. I…" I shook my head. "I don't know. I just…" My hand at his chest drifted up to curl around his neck and I needed to instigate damage control so I whispered the truth, "It was the most beautiful thing I'd ever seen."

He blinked.

"I wanted to join you," I admitted.

His eyebrows went up as he blinked again, this time slow.

"Like... *bad*," I finished.

"Why the fuck didn't you?" he asked, voice edged with impatience then he didn't wait for an answer and went on. "Christ, woman, torture. Spendin' time with you, sleepin' beside you and hands off and you tell me, a coupla days in, you saw that and wanted to let me inside?"

"Well—"

"That why you took care of yourself in the shower later?" he asked, and it was my turn to blink.

Then I whispered, "What?"

"Babe, heard you make yourself come."

Oh God. Oh no. Oh God. Shit. Shit, shit, *shit*.

His arm gave me a shake and I focused on him. "Is that why?"

"Yes," I said softly.

His hand not around me went to his face, palm to forehead, he closed his eyes and muttered, "Fuck me."

"Ty—" I started, but he dropped his hand and his eyes locked with mine.

"That the reason behind you throwing sass?"

I bit my lip. Then I mumbled, "Yes."

"Fuck me," he repeated.

"Ty—" I began again, and he rolled me so I was on my back and he was looming over me.

"I don't even want to count the days I been usin' my hand instead of your pussy to get off."

"Ty!" I snapped.

"What? You shared the honesty but you can't take it?"

"No," I shot back, feeling my eyes narrow. "I just figured this is the start of something. We're starting something. And I didn't think I should hold anything back. Keep any secrets. That's not a good way to start. Ronnie kept shit from me all the time. Bets he made gambling. Shit Shift was into. It goes on. I know you have to keep your grand plan o' vengeance secret and I get that but other than that, if we're starting something it should be out there. So, I saw you, I liked what I saw, it made me angry I couldn't let myself have it because I couldn't be sure I could trust it and I took that anger out on you. There. Now you know."

His bizarre response was, "Think I proved a couple times real recent I got a dick."

"Yes," I hissed.

"Babe, I haven't had pussy in over five years. I walk out of the joint and there you stand. You. *All* of you. Can you get, even a little bit, how tough this has been on me? Now you're sharin' that you saw me jackin' off, which, by the way, I was doin' thinkin' of you in your bikini down by the pool, and you liked what you saw so much you had to make yourself come in the shower and you think that's good?"

I glared up at him because maybe he had a *small* point and I was using the glare as cover.

Then I mumbled, "Maybe I should have kept that to myself."

His brows shot up and he asked, "You think?"

"I was just trying to be open," I snapped.

His big hand cupped my cheek and his face got close to mine before he said, "I get it that things were fucked between you and Rodriguez but you are not lyin' naked next to him, Lexie. You're lyin' naked next to *me*. I'm a different man. You don't wanna make the same mistakes. I get that too. But you gotta get that I am not him. You're right, we're startin' somethin' here. *We* are. He does not factor in."

Okay, he had another point and maybe that one wasn't so small.

"So you're saying I should have kept it from you?"

"No, I'm sayin' you shoulda picked a better time because just then, I was feelin' good. Just then, I was lyin' there, lookin' at the ceiling, the sweetest pussy I've ever had pressed naked to my side. Just then, I was thinkin' about two weeks ago, a month ago, three months ago, four years ago, how I would lie in that fuckin' bed in that fuckin' cell and think what was done to me meant I'd never taste pussy that sweet. And, just then, I was fuckin' grateful that the life that sucked that I thought yawned before me was not the life that walkin' out of that place led me to. And then you tell me I coulda had it over a week ago and for a man who's lost five years of his life, a week is a really fuckin' long time."

My hand still at his neck squeezed and I whispered, "I didn't know any of that."

He drew in breath through his nose and looked over my head.

Then his eyes came back to mine.

"You're right, baby, you didn't. So, I'll clue you in so you never walk into somethin' like that again. It's doubtful you'll ever have done to you what was done to me so you can't know and you'll never know, hope to God. But I been out for eleven days. I still smell that place, hear the bars slammin' shut, walk everywhere with one eye over my shoulder. It's gonna take a while to shake that. And I got that for breathin'. I did nothin' but live my life. I did nothin' to be punished for, nothin' that needed reforming. Now I gotta go see a parole officer. I gotta put up with whatever shit the Carnal PD is gonna shovel. And I gotta do what I gotta do to make what was done to me right in a way that I can live with it. We're startin' somethin' and, you want it open, that's what's on my mind. That's what I'm livin' with and you're livin' with me so that's what you gotta live with. So for a while, until I settle, you need to have a care."

"I can have a care," I said softly and I also said it immediately.

And just as immediately, his eyes changed and again it was a meaningful change but this time Ty would explain it.

"Shit, what'd I do that I walked outta that nightmare straight to you?" he murmured.

"I don't know," I replied. "The same thing I did to drive out of mine straight to you."

Again, at my words, his big body stilled but this time it went completely still, immobile, like he wasn't even breathing.

"Though, I took a detour to the beach," I added.

And that was when I knew Lady Luck had started to like me.

Because three seconds later, Ty Walker threw back his head and burst out laughing.

And I got to watch.

CHAPTER TEN

I'm the Teacher

Ty was in the shower, hand pressed to the tile in front of him, head bent, water cascading on his neck, back, head, his fist was wrapped around his cock and he was stroking.

I was behind him, pressed tight to his back, alternately kissing and tasting the sleek, muscled skin, my arms around him moving on his chest, his abs, *everywhere.*

I heard the noises he was making change, they went deeper and I knew.

So I pressed my front tight to his back, my arms tight to his front and I tipped my chin back and whispered over the spray, "Finish in me."

He didn't need to be asked twice. Before I could blink the water out of my eyes, he'd turned, grasped me under my pits, hauled me up and shifted me so my back was to the side wall. My legs circled his hips, my arms his shoulders and he stepped in. My back hit tile, his hands moved to my ass and he filled me with his cock.

Beautiful.

He drove in, pulled out, in again, and again, hands at my ass, mouth on mine alternately kissing me deep and almost brutal then soft and sweet then leaving his lips at mine, our heavy breaths mingling. If he was kissing me, we closed our eyes. If we were breathing, his eyes locked with mine, they were hot, fevered, staring deep, giving and taking.

I kept my legs tight around his hips, an arm tight around his shoulders, but I pushed a hand between us to assist his driving cock in taking me there.

Feeling him, seeing him, hearing him, pressed against him and touching him while he stroked himself, living a fantasy I played in my head with my fingers between my legs and no Ty, one that was way better in real life with him right there as close as he could get was so beautiful, so hot, I was primed. Way primed. My finger had to move on my clit for about half a minute before the noises I made went desperate.

He heard them and one hand left my ass to curl around the back of my head, which was good seeing as a second after it did, my legs spasmed around him, my arm got super tight, my back and neck arched and my head slammed his hand into the tile.

A little while later, my mouth was at his throat when his cock thrust deep and his head jerked back with his orgasm.

A little while later, we finished our shower.

* * *

I was in a pair of panties and Ty's tee, my hair wet, standing at the coffeemaker pouring him a travel mug.

Ty was standing beside me, body turned to me, jeans-clad hip leaning against the counter, bowl of raspberries, blackberries, banana and yogurt mixed with some of his protein powder cupped in his huge hand held high and he was spooning it into his mouth.

It was Wednesday, two days after we became us. Two *magnificent* days after we became us. Asshole Ty was long gone. Taciturn Ty was a memory. He didn't share much verbally but he shared.

Oh yeah, he shared.

And mostly he did this through sex. *Lots* of it.

He was making up for lost time, so was I, this was true. But it was mostly that it was just that good. We managed to eat and he went to work. Monday night, he worked out after work. Other than that, we were in bed (and once we were on the couch). We'd talk in between times, before we drifted off to sleep. Or I would talk, he didn't say much and I would talk mostly in whispers. This didn't last long before he turned into me with intent. It wasn't that he didn't want to hear what I had to say. It was just that we had better things to do.

I shouldn't compare Ty with Ronnie and wouldn't tell Ty that, in my mind, I did.

But I did.

I couldn't help it. I'd had two lovers and they were night and day.

Ronnie, hit and miss. He tried but sometimes he failed and I didn't have the heart to tell him he did or where he went wrong. It upset him when I did. He'd go into himself or get mildly pissed so I learned to stop doing that.

Ty hit, every time.

This would have freaked me out, how good he was at it, but thinking on it, it didn't.

First, he had a great body and he was in command of it. Not just during sex but all the time. Second, he was strong as in *very* strong. Ronnie was no weakling and took care of his body as a matter of habit and survival. But the strength of his lean muscle was nothing in comparison to the power behind the bulk of Ty. And Ty used his strength during sex in a dizzying variety of delicious ways. Third, Ty was seriously hot and, prior to his incarceration, he had to have had his fair share of practice and then some. And last, Ty had already proved he was generous and sex was no different. He saw to me, sometimes twice (once three times) before he took care of himself. He never left me hanging or took care of me after. Not once.

It was phenomenal. So phenomenal, I didn't mind that there was no further heart-to-heart sharing from Ty. What he was giving me, *all* of it, was just fine. Better. It was perfect.

I moved to him, set his travel mug on the counter by his hip, got as close as his bowl would let me, leaned a hip into the counter and instantly started bitching.

"Seven o'clock is a ridiculous time to have to be at work."

His beautiful eyes on me, he chewed, swallowed and replied, "Told you, you don't have to get up with me."

Yeah, right, like I'd miss taking a shower with him. Not gonna happen.

I communicated this with my eyes and a tilt of my head. He read it loud and clear and his lips tipped up at the sides.

Then he spoke again. "Seven o'clock means gettin' off at four unless they need me to do overtime. I could do nine thirty to six thirty but I like the evenings clear. Don't sleep late, that time in the morning would be a waste."

"Mm," I mumbled, and his lips twitched.

"Mama, fuckin' you in the shower, doable. We *really* start to play, I won't wanna go and how are you gonna get deck furniture if I don't have a paycheck?"

He had a point.

And he called me "mama" in his soft voice. That was a new one. I liked it.

Not to mention, I was discovering we *seriously* needed deck furniture.

"Whatever you wanna do, honey," I muttered.

"Yeah," he muttered back, shoved the last spoonful in his mouth, chewed, swallowed then dipped his head to touch his lips to mine and moved around me to get to the sink, saying, "Gonna hit the gym before I come home. Be back at around six."

I turned with him so I was facing him when I replied as he put his bowl in the sink and walked back to me, "Right. Anything you want for dinner or are you gonna do a shake?"

"Food," he said, making it to me, putting a hand light on my hip and leaning his face close. "Whatever you make, I'll eat." He again touched his mouth to mine then said against it, "Later, Lex."

"Later, honey," I whispered against his.

He bent his head forward an inch, which touched his forehead to mine, and he did this for half a second before his forehead and his hand went away because he'd tagged his travel mug and was sauntering to the stairs.

I watched him until he disappeared then I warmed up my coffee, took it out to the sunny deck and sipped it at the railing, taking in a view I knew I'd never get used to.

I saw the view, I loved the view but mostly I loved that standing at that railing, this time, I felt full. Sated. Replete.

And I hadn't had breakfast.

Once I hit the bottom of the mug, I wandered into the house, refreshed my coffee and wandered up the steps. I went to my lingerie drawer, dug under my stuff and pulled out the glossy violet and ice blue folder. I opened it, pulled out an eight-by-ten then replaced the folder in the drawer.

I wandered back down the steps to the pantry. I pulled out a thick, brown paper bag that had a red stamp on the side with some lasso-style ropes around Old West–style words that said "Carnal Country Store." I took it to the island, set the picture and my mug down and dug stuff out of the bag that I bought in town yesterday after I had my job interview.

Carnal Country Store was a gift slash souvenir shop. They had a multi-theme going. Old West slash Colorado Mountains slash Bikers slash Country. It was wild but it worked. There was a lot of wood. A lot of antlers. A lot of feathers. A lot of buffalo. Being Carnal, which was definitely a biker haven and not the pedal kind, it also had a bunch of biker stuff. This was intermingled with an abundance of full-on country wares that were mostly really cute but not my style (or Ty's) and some local artisan stuff which included some seriously kick-ass pottery. And, luckily, for those with a discerning eye and because it was the only gift shop in Carnal (except the florist who had a few frames, vases and knickknacks—not having a job and with time on my hands I'd definitely spent time perusing what Carnal had to offer, so much I had it down pat), they had some nicer stuff too.

And I said this was "luckily" because, although Ty was born in that county, he was not a feathers, antlers, buffalo, biker or country wares kind of guy.

So I got the stuff I got and it was pricey but since Ty paid for nearly everything, I had most of the wad of cash Shift gave me to finance my journey. So I went a little crazy thinking some Shift in an alternate universe would want to give Ty and me a wedding present (or, as it turned out, several). I also went a little crazy because it was "nice shit" so it would fit.

I pulled out a beautiful, wide-edged, beveled silver frame, took off the back and then put our wedding picture in it. I turned it around after I secured the back and there we were. My dress. My bouquet. Ty in his suit. Me smiling bright and big. Ty looking hot.

I studied it thinking, at the time that photo was taken, I would never have guessed two weeks later I'd spend that much money on the perfect frame for that picture because that picture needed the perfect frame.

But I did because that picture needed the perfect frame.

I smiled at it then I walked it to the living room and put it on the sleek, polished wood mantel set into the stone hearth above the fireplace. It was the only thing there.

Still, it looked good.

I went back to the bag and yanked out the thick folder that held the photos I processed at the kiosk in the grocery store. I also pulled another frame out of the bag, this one six-by-eight with a simple but thick matte black edge.

I flipped through the photos I developed to find the one I knew I wanted. Ty and me and Moab, shot from waist up, my cheek to his chest, my arms around his middle, his arm around my shoulders, our shades directed at the lens, an infinitesimal section of Moab our stunning backdrop. I framed it and put it in the deep sill at the window over the kitchen sink.

I went back to the island, sipped more coffee then again hit the pantry, pulling out the two bigger bags. I took them to the island

and unearthed from bunches of tissue the three charcoal gray matte pitchers with their spindly handles in black gloss, rim, lip and inside that same gloss. Three of them, one huge. One not as huge. One a little less than not as huge. I arranged them in a circle in the middle of the island.

Out next came the wide, flat bowl of the same. I grabbed the bananas and dug in the fridge for the apples and oranges, assembled them in the bowl and put them on the short side counter between the stove and the fridge. I cleared away the bags and tissue and set the pictures on a side counter to show Ty later.

Then I went to the cupboard, found the sugar bowl and creamer and set those at an angle opposite the frame in the windowsill. I looked from bowl and creamer to pitchers to big-ass, kickass fruit bowl and was relieved to find I was right. They complemented each other perfectly.

I grabbed my mug and took a sip, my head moving in a slow swivel to take in the entirety of my handiwork.

Something was missing.

I knew what it was, put my mug down and dashed up the stairs, digging in the back of my lingerie drawer. I pulled it out and jogged back down the stairs.

I set the Treasure Island snow globe in the middle of the deep sill over the kitchen sink where the picture was angled in a corner and the sugar and creamer in the other. I'd see it every time I did the dishes. And I liked that.

I moved to my mug, picked it up, backed up until my hips hit counter and surveyed the scene.

It wasn't much of a stamp but it was something.

And every bit was perfect.

Even the snow globe.

I grinned to myself and walked my coffee upstairs to get dressed.

I had a house to clean, groceries to buy and then I had to find a craft shop.

* * *

That afternoon, I drove into the mechanics where Ty worked, my eyes moving between the three large bays at the same time searching for a parking space.

I'd driven by the garage many times since I hit Carnal but had never been there. The tarmac outside was huge. A little office up some concrete steps to the side of the bays. A plethora of bikes and cars all around. Garage sounds coming at me through my open windows.

I found my spot at the very end in front of the office, parked, shut her down, got out and rounded the trunk, eyes to the bays.

Then he came out, light gray-blue coveralls unbuttoned to the waist, the top of them hanging down, making it look like he had an upside-down shirt hanging from his hips. He had on a white wife-beater that must have been in his workout bag because he left in jeans and a tee. He looked hot even in that getup, what with the muscles and tats on display, but he could probably wear a pink polo shirt with the collar turned up and look hot (though I hoped he never did).

He had black grease stains on his wife-beater, all over his hands and up his forearms.

And I didn't care.

I also didn't care that I had on strappy, super-high platform wedges. I still ran flat out across the wide expanse toward him and didn't stop even as I noticed he saw I wasn't going to. So he did and he braced right before I took a flying leap into his arms.

Those arms closed around me, mine closed around his neck and I was suspended several inches off the ground as my hand curled over his short-cropped hair and I pulled his mouth to mine.

Then I laid a hot, wet one on him.

After I did that, I tore my mouth from his, kept my arms tight and asked excitedly, "Guess what?"

"Lex, got grease all over me. What the fuck?" was his taking all the fun out of it response.

My arms gave him a squeeze and I repeated, "Ty! Guess what?"

His lips twitched and he asked, "What?"

"Dominic at Carnal Spa gave me the job!" I cried loudly.

At that news, his arms gave me a squeeze and he muttered, "Good news."

"Uh...*yeah*!" I exclaimed, and he set me on my feet but didn't release me, just bent his neck deep so his face could remain close (ish) and his eyes could hold mine. "I just got the call. No way did I expect that he'd hire me because I'm not really local...*yet*. But he *did*! He said I have the flair and comportment—his words—that screamed '*Carnal Spa*'—also his words—and the minute he saw me he wouldn't have chosen anyone else. I start next Tuesday."

"Happy for you, babe," he said softly, his eyes warm, his lips tipped up at the ends.

"Me too," I replied. "I mean, it's ten to four with half an hour lunch break so it isn't full time and it's about two cents over minimum wage since I'm a glorified receptionist, but still. He said that he might hire another stylist and is definitely hiring someone to do facials and with the extra business they may need another hour or more. Isn't that cool?"

He didn't respond verbally but he did give me a full grin so I took that as agreement he thought it was cool.

"Let's celebrate," I declared, pressing closer to him. "Tell me what your favorite meal is and I'll make it for dinner tonight. Get a bottle of sparkling wine or something."

"Celebration doesn't say you cookin' my favorite meal and wine from a grocery store. Celebration says me callin' The Rooster and gettin' us a table."

I tipped my head to the side and asked, "The Rooster?"

"Steak place up the mountain. Fuckin' great food. Top notch."

I smiled because that did, indeed, say celebration.

"Excellent. Can I dress up?"

His arms gave me another squeeze, his face dipped closer and his voice was low and super rumbly when he said, "You can do whatever you want."

"Awesome," I whispered, his eyes smiled into mine and I liked that so much, I leaned up and pressed my lips to his.

When I moved back, his eyes went over my shoulder and started to come back to me but then they shot back over my shoulder and I felt the entirety of his frame freeze solid.

I didn't like that or the expression on his face... no, I *really* didn't like the expression on his face, which almost looked like he was in pain. So I pressed closer but looked over my shoulder to see a dark red SUV driving up to the office.

"Who's that?" I asked.

"The Keatons," he rumbled low, and that was when I froze so I was stuck in position as the SUV parked and out of each side came a body.

Driver's side was the man. Tall, straight, lean, dark blond hair. Good-looking if you didn't happen to be married to Ty Walker and Ty Walker didn't happen to have friends the likes of Tate and Wood. Jeans, heavy silver Western-style belt buckle, cowboy boots, nice sports coat, chambray shirt.

Passenger side was the woman.

Misty.

Bitch-face *Misty*.

My eyes narrowed on her as I vaguely noticed Wood and a couple of other guys moving out of the bays and Stella coming out of the office. If I hadn't vaguely noticed this I would have realized they did it because they knew cowboy guy and Misty. They knew they'd fucked over Ty and they were positioning, should something happen, to take Ty's back.

But I only had eyes for and a mind to bitch-face Misty.

She had lots of everything. Lots of leg. Lots of tits. Lots of ass. Lots of hair.

Ty's type, definitely.

She was wearing much what I was wearing. Platform sandals (though not wedges). Short skirt. Three steps up from a normal t-shirt.

But mine was better.

I wasn't wearing a skirt but cream-colored, tailored, low-rider, cuffed short shorts. My tee was blousy, a soft orchid color and one side hung off my shoulder. I'd sleeked out my hair, my belt was awesome, my jewelry understated and even more awesome than the belt. And, at that moment, I was really fucking glad I spent extra time on my hair after cleaning the house and before going into town.

Her stuff was good quality. What could I say? I was a buyer. I could see it even from far away.

But her skirt was just on the wrong side of too short. Her top just on the wrong side of too clingy and *way* the wrong side of too much cleavage. Her hair was massive. And her sandals leaped over the boundary of acceptable straight into the land of slut shoes.

Looking at her, she didn't work with Ty, no way. And she also didn't work with the fake straight arrow (seeing as he was a dirty cop) Colorado cowboy guy with his precise haircut, jeans that weren't faded even a little bit and, clearly visible even through his clothes, a body fat count that stated he spent almost as much time at the gym as Ty. And I felt I could say this coming from Texas. I knew cowboys and I knew their women.

She was just a skanky white 'ho trying to be something else.

This made me feel *way* better. Of course, I still hated her and wanted to rush across the tarmac and rip her hair out. But Ty said I was class and beauty and now I knew why. Because, in comparison to Misty Keaton, I fucking was, top to toe.

I turned back to Ty, pressed deep and when I did, I got his eyes.

"Dude, I am *way* more that than her," I informed him.

He blinked then I felt his body start shaking.

"Think I already told you that, mama," he replied in his soft voice that was better than his normal soft voice considering it was soft *and* amused.

Must be said, I was liking this mama thing.

I held his eyes and asked quietly, "You okay?"

He gave me a shallow chin dip of affirmative before answering,

"Pullin' out my .38 and gunnin' 'em down in broad daylight with witnesses kinda fucks with my grand plan o' vengeance."

I started giggling and slid my arms from around his neck to rest them on the wide wall of his chest.

"Yeah, being present at the incident, I probably wouldn't be very convincing as an alibi."

His lips tipped up. "Probably not."

I allowed myself to enjoy his small grin. Then I sighed.

Then I asked, "This the first time you've seen them?"

"Yep."

"Sorry, honey," I whispered.

"Gonna happen."

"Right," I muttered, my eyes sliding to his throat.

His arms gave me a squeeze and my eyes slid back.

"Got work to do. I'll call The Rooster, text you with a time. You good with that?"

I smiled at him. "Way good, hubby."

He shook his head once before he dropped it to touch his mouth to mine.

Then he murmured, "Go. See you later."

"Later," I agreed then I slid my hand up to his neck and curled my fingers around, holding his eyes and giving him something I hoped would carry him through having those two even close to his space. "You're far and away the most beautiful man I've met and it isn't just that you have the looks and the body, but it's a whole lot more, Ty Walker."

After laying that on him, I got up on tiptoe, kissed his jaw and avoided his eyes as I pulled out of his arms by turning and moving away.

As I strolled to my car, I smiled at the two gray-blue coverall-covered men, my eyes moved to Wood and I called, "Hey, Wood."

"Lexie," he said, jerked his chin up and smiled at me.

I walked by him and to the car, my eyes on Stella to see her head turned to the Keatons but her eyes slid to the side more than once.

Detective Chace Keaton was talking to her. Misty Keaton's head was shifting quickly back and forth and back again between Ty and me. She had sunglasses on so I couldn't see her eyes but the rest of her face I didn't get. Surprise, maybe. Hesitation, definitely. But also I detected fear.

I hoped I detected right. I wanted the bitch afraid. She deserved fear and lots of it.

I got to the driver's side of the Charger and Stella's head turned my way so I smiled and waved.

"Hey, Stella!" I called.

"Hey, Lexie. How's it goin'?"

"Awesome! Life is sweet," I replied, and she grinned.

"Good to hear, babe."

My eyes moved to the Keatons who were both now looking at me and I gave them a friendly wave and a "Hey!"

Chace Keaton's eyes did a head to toe. Misty didn't move a muscle. Neither of them gave me a "hey" back.

Whatever. So they were dirty, skanky *and* rude. Not a surprise.

I turned around, opened my door, looked over the hood of the Charger and saw Ty disappearing into a bay. I got in, fired my baby up, backed out and resisted the urge to run down the Keatons. I might hit Stella and she was cool so that would be uncool.

I drove to the entrance of the garage, looked right then left then right again then something made me look left and I saw Bubba's, the bar Tate and Krystal owned a few blocks down. I stared at it a second that slid to three. Then I turned right and headed home. I had groceries in the car I needed to unpack and put away because some of them needed the fridge.

But for some reason all I could think of was Bubba's, Tate, the Keatons and my man forced to endure painful, bitter history delivering a sucker punch whenever Lady Luck was feeling sassy.

I drove home, parked in the garage, lugged up the groceries and put them away and still couldn't quit thinking of Bubba's. So I looked at the clock on the microwave over the stove and considered my wardrobe options, made a selection, calculated the time I'd need to gussy up and made a decision.

It might be stupid. It might be smart. It might piss off Lady Luck who'd make me pay the hard way.

But I had to try.

So I got in the car and drove back into town straight to Bubba's. I parked out front and saw a line of bikes, about six of them, and several other cars including a supremely beat-up pickup truck. It was after three in the afternoon, not prime-time drinking hours, but Bubba's looked relatively busy.

Good news for Tate and Krystal. Not so good for me. If Tate was there I didn't want him to be busy and if I got an opening to do what I needed to do, I didn't want anyone to hear.

I walked through the door to Bubba's for the first time, seeing immediately it was a biker bar. I knew this not because I was intimately acquainted with biker bars. In fact, this was the first one I'd ever been in. I knew this was because there was a bevy of biker-looking dudes in it. There were also wood floors, a long bar at the back surrounded by stools, tables and chairs in front and two big rooms off either side with two pool tables each. And I was correct, it was relatively busy.

Krystal was behind the bar, down at one end, gabbing with some patrons. Tate was also behind the bar, down at the other end, leaned into his hands on the bar and talking to Jim-Billy, who looked surgically attached to his stool and was sitting at a corner, and Deke, who was standing at the opposite corner to Jim-Billy.

All eyes came to me when I came in.

"Hey, y'all," I called, and got a bunch of greetings back.

I moved to Tate's side of the bar and slid on the stool next to Jim-Billy, putting my purse on the stool beside me.

"Good to see you, Lexie," Tate said, and I smiled at him.

"Yeah, you too," I replied then slid my eyes around taking in Deke and Jim-Billy. "You guys been good?"

"Can't complain," Jim-Billy answered.

"Yeah, babe, things are good," Tate answered.

Deke just stared at me. Deke was a communicator of the Taciturn Ty variety so I didn't take offense.

"You drinkin'?" Tate asked.

"Yeah, though I'll be doing it tonight at the celebration dinner Ty and I are having at The Rooster. I got a job at Carnal Spa today."

"Good news, darlin'." Jim-Billy grinned at me.

"Thanks," I said to him then looked at Tate. "So, how about a celebratory Diet Coke with cherries in and I'll buy the boys a round?"

"How about you let me cover your diet as a congratulatory gesture?" Tate returned.

"How about you let me buy a round considering you've already made a big gesture?" I suggested then pointed out, "It's my turn."

"'Preciate that, Lexie, but I got a bar that does a fuckload of turnover and this is a world where idiots jump bond frequently. You and Ty are gettin' your feet under you so I'll cover the round," Tate rejected my suggestion, and I knew this could go on and on and in the end one person was going to get their way and that would not be me.

"Do you guys take nice pills in the morning or is this natural?" I asked at the same time giving in.

He knew I was giving in so he grabbed a glass, dunked it in the ice, put it on the bar, aimed the soda gun at it and let fly while saying, "It's a pop, babe, not givin' you the deed to my house."

"And a beer," Jim-Billy put in.

"And a whiskey," Deke added.

Tate's eyes went to them in turn as they spoke then came to me when he said, "And a beer and a whiskey."

I grinned at him.

He tossed three cherries in my drink, shoved in a thin red straw, threw a bar mat in front of me and set the drink on it. Then he opened a bottle of brew for Jim-Billy and poured a measure of bourbon for Deke and himself.

When Deke got his drink, I lifted my glass and toasted, "To me, the new receptionist at Carnal Spa."

I got grins, a couple of glasses and a bottle pointed my way then we all sucked back some beverage.

I put my glass down.

And, pleasantries and bullshit excuses for showing at his bar over, fortunately, Tate took me off the hook and went straight to it.

"How're you settlin' in?"

This had two meanings and I knew it. He and Ty were tight and he was concerned about his friend. And he had beautiful eyes but they were also intelligent. He knew I didn't mosey into his bar to share good news when I hadn't seen any of them since the party. He knew I had a reason to be there.

I took another sip and tried to suck up courage.

Then my eyes locked with his and I told him, "I love it here."

"Good," he muttered, his gaze not leaving mine and him not missing I talked about me but didn't mention my husband then, "Ty?"

"He's good," I said slowly, took another sip of drink to suck up more courage then went on, "Adjusting."

"How's that goin'?" Jim-Billy asked quietly, and I looked to him.

"He's a very strong man," I said softly. "If he wasn't..." I let that hang and looked to my glass. I tipped my head back, looked right into Tate's eyes and asked straight out, "You know how I can get in touch with a guy named Tambo?"

The air around me went wired.

Tate leaned in. Jim-Billy leaned in. Deke's body went alert. And Krystal, maybe feeling the vibe, started to drift down the bar.

But it was Tate who spoke. "Lexie—"

I cut him off by whispering, "I'm worried about him."

"Why?" Tate asked quietly, sharply and swiftly.

"I can't say." And I couldn't.

"He thinkin' of doin' somethin' stupid?" This was Krystal who either had super-powered ears or the gift of mind reading.

My eyes moved to hers. "He's not stupid. But he's angry."

"Would be too," Deke grunted.

"Deke," Jim-Billy muttered.

Deke's eyes sliced to Jim-Billy. "You would be too."

Jim-Billy looked at his beer. He would be too. Anyone would be.

"You two tight?" Tate asked, and I looked to him. He'd seen the way Ty was at the party, there and holding me close but at the same time not there. He'd clocked it and wondered about it. I knew this. He hadn't seen us together since. He couldn't know how it was before Ty shut down and after Ty let me in.

"Yes," I told him, and hoped that he'd trust that.

"How much sway you got?" Tate asked.

"Not enough." I shook my head. "Not enough for this."

"Let the man do what he's gotta do," Deke advised, and my eyes went to him.

"He had five years stolen from him."

"Yeah," Deke agreed on a grunt. "So let the man do what he's gotta do."

I held Deke's eyes. Then I said firmly, "He couldn't take more." I looked to Tate and stated, "He shouldn't *have* to take more." My gaze went to Krystal. "They've taken enough."

I felt all their eyes then I saw Tate's head turn and tip down to look at Krystal. She looked up at him. Then she looked at Jim-Billy and Tate looked at Deke.

"I have to do something," I whispered into their eye-communication exchange. I looked all around them then declared, "*Someone* has to do *something*. I've been living in Carnal eight days and even I know enough's enough." I leaned into the bar and whispered, "What's happening has to be stopped. Not just for Ty but for whoever else is getting railroaded by these assholes." I leaned back and kept talking. "Someone has to do something and that someone is going to be me. And the only thing I have to start with is this Tambo guy."

Tate's gaze cut back to me. "I'll talk to Tambo."

My heart leaped. "You will?"

He jerked his chin up. "I will. I'll also talk to the boys I trust in the department. Feel them out. See if one of 'em's a whistleblower or might be willin' to nose around."

My heart started racing then it stuttered when Krystal hissed quietly, "Tate, you could get jacked just like Ty."

"I could also clear his name, get him restitution at the same time this town learns how to live with a force that they can count on rather than question and fear," Tate returned and, not done making his point, continued. "You got tits, you get pulled over for speeding, you don't gotta get on your knees to give a blowjob to get outta some jacked-up charge just so a man in a uniform with a little authority can get his rocks off. You got problems with kids stealin' shit from your shelves, you don't have to pass an envelope of cash over the counter to pay for protection you're already payin' for with your taxes. Your husband's beatin' the shit outta you, you don't have to put up with it 'cause he's got a badge and you got no one clean you can turn to. You make food for a living, you serve a plate to a man with a badge, you don't gotta look the other way when he walks out without payin' the bill. A uniform is shitfaced in his cruiser on duty, he crashes that cruiser, totals it and it needs to be replaced and his hospital bills need to be paid and they are, on the citizens' dime, he gets stripped of his badge, not a fuckin' commendation."

Wow, seemed like things were worse than I thought and they were already really fucking bad.

And I made a mental note not to have a heavy foot in the Charger like I had a tendency to have.

And last, it was apparent Tate had been burying this for a while and it was equally apparent he was very done doing that.

"You tried that shit before," Krystal fired back.

"And Ty pulled me back," Tate reminded her.

"He pulled you back because it was getting hot," she reminded him right back, and Tate turned his body to her and the way he did made me shrink back a bit because I didn't know him all that well but I knew he was serious and his serious was a bit scary.

"Yeah, Krys, and it was gettin' hot because I was gettin' close."

I felt my eyes get big. So hopeful I was no longer scared of big, handsome, well-built, serious Tate Jackson, I leaned in and whispered, "To what?"

Tate turned to me and answered, "Don't know. Somethin'. Victim was shot but the murder weapon never found, more than one source told me the victim was known to Gene Fuller, and Eugene Fuller makes Arnie Fuller look like a fuckin' Boy Scout."

"How was the victim known to Fuller?" I asked.

"Dealer and, word is, Fuller likes his blow," Tate answered.

I sucked in breath and sat back, muttering, "Cokehead?"

Tate nodded.

I looked to the side, feeling overwhelmed by this. It was safe to say I was already overwhelmed by the enormity of what Ty lost but the fact that he lost it to dirty cops and cokeheads, people who were the dregs and Ty was no dreg, made something that was already unimaginably unfair something that was crushingly unfair. He'd had the most precious thing anyone possessed stolen from him: a chunk of his life. And the people who stole it from him did shit to deserve worse than he got. Way worse.

"Lexie?" Krystal called.

I pulled in breath through my nose and looked to her.

Then I shared, "I was at the garage telling him my news and Chace and Misty Keaton rolled up in an SUV. He had to stand there and watch them roll up to a garage, free and easy, not having parole officers and still hearing the clang of barred doors closing them into a cell. He had to stand there and watch those fucking two roll right on up. And he says I get her, she's fair game after he does whatever it is he's going to do. But I don't know if I can wait. And I don't know what he's going to do or how long it's going to take. So something has to give because there's a bitch in this town who needs a lesson and I'm the teacher."

This got me stares all around.

Then Jim-Billy muttered, "Shit, darlin', remind me not to get on your bad side."

To which I turned my head to him immediately and said, "Don't fuck over my husband, you'll be fine."

He grinned at me then his eyes slid to Tate. Mine did too and they went through a lips-twitching Deke and a grinning Krystal to find a smiling-so-big-he-looked-in-danger-of-roaring-with-laughter Tate.

"I don't know what there is to smile about," I declared.

"Then, woman, you don't got the same picture in your head as I do," Deke stated then looked at Krystal. "Lexie here takes down Misty, you make sure it happens in the bar. Sell tickets. I don't give a fuck. I'll pay whatever you charge. But I get a front-row seat."

I rolled my eyes at Krystal. She shook her head, still grinning.

"All right, Lexie, back to business," Tate said, and I looked at him. "You say you don't got enough sway. You got it in you to cause a delay in whatever Ty's schemin' to do?"

I thought about it. And what I thought were good thoughts. So I smiled.

"I might be able to arrange that," I told Tate, and he smiled back.

"Shit, boy born to bad luck, turns it around, gets smacked down then turns it right the fuck back around again. Shit," Deke muttered, and my eyes went to him to see his on Tate. "I'm in with whatever you're gonna do. I'm in for Ty but my payback is knowin' where he found her." Then he jerked his head to me.

"Boy, wake up and look around. Good women everywhere. You just gotta stake your claim," Jim-Billy informed him.

"You been outta the game a while, old-timer," Deke returned. "Tits and ass and great hair usually come attached to headaches, not loyalty and the good kinda attitude that makes your dick get hard."

This was an unusual compliment but it *was* a compliment, a compliment coming from Deke no less so I felt the need to throw out a share. "Ty and I met through a drug dealer slash pimp so maybe you should expand your search area."

Deke blinked at me. Krystal audibly stifled a laugh. Jim-Billy guffawed. Tate chuckled.

"No shit?" Deke asked.

"I'm not a prostitute or junkie or anything, past or present. Just had baggage from another relationship and that baggage hooked me up with Ty. He was a pain in my ass but, obviously, now, if I saw him again, I'd kiss him. That is before I shot him. Though Ty really dislikes him so I don't think I'll see him again which is good because I dislike him more than Ty, except of course for the fact he hooked me up with Ty."

"You put honest juice in her diet?" Jim-Billy asked Tate.

"You known Ty since his momma shot him out?" Tate asked back.

"Yup," Jim-Billy answered.

"You've known him that long, you figure he'd put a rock on the finger of anyone not the likes of Lexie?" Tate continued his mini-interrogation but I felt my heart squeeze.

"Nope," Jim-Billy replied on a toothy grin.

"Then honest juice my ass," Tate muttered and Jim-Billy guffawed again.

But I was feeling warm all over because they approved of me. I'd laid out some vague but possibly damning information and they still approved of me. And they were Ty's friends so this meant a lot.

My purse chimed. I shoved my hand in it, pulled out my phone, flipped it open and saw I had a text from Ty that read, "Rooster seven. Ready six thirty."

Apparently he was still Taciturn Ty by text.

I grinned at the phone. Then I looked at my watch. I grabbed my diet, sucked down a huge swallow, fished out the cherries, plucked them off their stems, ate them and sucked down another swallow.

Then I jumped off my stool and announced, "Gotta go gussy up for the celebration. I'll see you all later?"

"Yeah, Lexie, congratulations," Tate said.

"Later," Deke said.

"Have fun tonight, darlin'," Jim-Billy said.

"I'll walk you to your car," Krystal scarily said while rounding the end of the bar.

I couldn't see a way to avoid a somewhat frightening and I-still-wasn't-certain-what-to-think-about-her Krystal walking me to my car so I said my final farewells and headed out with Krystal at my side. She didn't speak and I didn't either. But I did stop at the driver's side of the Charger and looked down at her.

She was inspecting my car.

"Sweet ride," she approved.

Well, that was a good start.

"Thanks."

Her eyes came up to me and her voice was soft when she spoke. "I see you intend to take care of our boy. Makes me feel better. Way things were at your party, couldn't tell and didn't like that."

Maybe she had honest juice before I arrived. Or maybe she was just the kind of person who put it out there.

"We had a . . . thing," I told her quietly.

"Yeah, you'll have more what he went through. Don't give up on him. There's about two men I'd say this about. Tate is one. Ty is the other. I'm married to Bubba, love him to death, he's pulled his shit together and I'm glad but I wouldn't say this even about him. But Ty's worth not givin' up. You get him to the other side, you won't regret it."

"I won't give up on him," I whispered, deciding I liked Krystal.

She nodded and held my eyes.

Then she said softly, "Be smart. You stick your neck out, the bunch you're goin' up against, they'll whack your head clean off."

I sucked in breath but she didn't quit talking.

"You know that, what they did to your man. A man's gotta do what he's gotta do. Tate and Deke wadin' into that shit, don't got a good feelin'. Ty bein' pissed and wantin' to do somethin' about it, I get. I definitely get that. Don't got a good feelin' about that either. But men gotta do what they gotta do and we women got two things we can do: stand by their side or be smart enough to do what you just did and find men who know what they're doin' to take their man's back. Now, you set that ball rollin'." She jerked her head back to the bar. "You see to your man and keep your head down. Ty feels about you like you feel about him, he didn't survive that nightmare to come out the other side and watch his woman enduring her own. Keep yourself safe, if not for you, then for him. Get me?"

I nodded. I got her.

She nodded back, muttered, "Make him happy," then turned and walked back to the bar. She stopped at the door and called, "By the way, you got grease stains on the back of your shirt."

She shot me a knowing grin, turned, threw open the door and entered the bar.

I stared at the door long after she disappeared behind it.

Then I got in my Charger and drove home.

Ty

You're far and away the most beautiful man I've met…

The words played in his head once again as he hit the garage door opener. They'd been playing in his head since Lexie said them. Over and over. So often, they were all that was on his mind. So often, Keaton and Misty were long gone before he thought of them again. He'd forgotten those two were even there.

You're far and away the most beautiful man I've met…

Fuck him but he liked that she thought that.

He rolled the Snake in, shut her down, grabbed his workout bag from the passenger seat and hauled his ass out. He dumped the bag in the utility room as he moved through it. She'd sort his shit and he wouldn't have to ask. He knew it. He gave her diamonds and expensive shoes. She gave him everything else and she gave it in a way that he knew he didn't have to give her diamonds and expensive shoes to get it.

He walked up the stairs, rounded the railing and stopped dead.

"In the middle of something, baby," she muttered. "Kiss you in a minute."

She was sitting at a stool at the island, legs crossed, one heel to the bar on the stool, both legs shoved to the side, torso hunched over, head bent. Even though he had her back, he knew she was concentrating on what she was doing and he understood this not just because of her distracted words but also her posture.

She was wearing a pair of white slacks, wide leg, riding low, a wide slash of skin exposed below her top and above the waistband of her pants. A wide slash that was an invitation that, knowing Lexie, she had no idea she was giving. A wide slash that invited her man to shove his hand down her pants and cup her sweet ass. An invitation he decided he was going to find time that night to accept.

Her top was a light gray, satin camisole, loose-fitting and gathered at her waist, tied at the side in a big droopy satin bow. Her hair was in a sleek fall down her back. A pair of black, high spike-heeled sandals had been tossed on the floor by the side of the island. A small black purse was resting on the counter on top of it.

Also on the counter were a bunch of gray and black pitchers that, even as a man, he had to admit were the shit. They looked good on the black granite countertop.

His eyes moved from them and around taking things in.

Shit on the windowsill over the sink that wasn't there when he left that morning, her snow globe, a photo. His eyes scanned. A wide bowl that matched the pitchers filled with fruit by the fridge. His eyes kept moving and he saw their wedding photo in a silver frame on the mantel.

Seeing that photo, he felt that sharp thing pierce through the left side of his chest again and, at the exquisite pain, that area tensed and stayed that way.

His mother didn't frame photos. She didn't set out souvenirs to remind them of good times had during family vacations or outings. Their family didn't take vacations. They didn't have outings. And they didn't have happy memories to display.

But it was more than that. His mother spent her energy bitching and pissed at the world. She did not spend it making a home, definitely not for a husband she hated but stayed with for the sole purpose, Ty figured, of torturing him. But also not even for her children who she frequently forgot she had.

Therefore, Ty Walker never had a home. Even the house he bought and started to fill with shit he liked he didn't try to make a home firstly because he was a man and secondly because, never having one, it didn't cross his mind.

Pitchers, a bowl, a snow globe and some frames and Lexie did it. She needed nothing else. No flowers for the deck. No other touches. He'd be good with what she'd already done. But he also knew, what they started kept going, she'd fill his house with shit that made it a home.

He moved toward her, got close to her back, pulled her soft hair off her shoulder and bent low to kiss the point of her shoulder then moved his mouth to her ear.

"My mama's been busy," he muttered there then his eyes moved to the counter where he was going to toss his keys and he froze solid.

"Yeah," she mumbled distractedly but he barely heard her.

That was because on the counter was a scattering of dissected roses, and he knew by their color they were from her wedding bouquet.

She had a square piece of glass in one hand. In the other she had a weird gun that she was using to edge the glass with some melted metal the color of silver. He noticed that it wasn't one piece of glass but two and between them she'd pressed petals from the roses in the shape of a heart. They were overlapping thickly, both colors used, the pattern random, pieces of petal arranged in other places in the glass that looked arbitrary but somehow pointed to and highlighted the heart. He wasn't a hearts-and-flowers guy but he'd seen shit like that sold in stores and the way she made what she'd made was far from amateur.

"There," she declared, setting the gun aside on a ragged dishtowel. She held the glass up cautiously between thumb and forefinger, her torso straightening, and she asked, "What do you think?"

Walker had no response, he just stared at it.

"Is it too cutesy?" she asked, and he noted out of the corner of his eyes her head had turned and he felt her gaze on him but he couldn't tear his eyes from the heart. "I mean a heart...that isn't me. It also isn't you. But I was thinking I could etch some squiggles and shit in the glass at the corners and on the inside of the heart I could write, 'Ty and Lexie, Las Vegas,' and maybe the date of our wedding. I'll solder a hanger on top. I got a blush-colored ribbon and a sucker thing for the window and I'll hang it in the window over the kitchen sink." She stopped talking and when he still made no reply, she muttered, "Maybe that's too much. Not sure a heart made of rose petals goes with the black counters and cream cabinets of your kitchen..."

She was talking but he wasn't hearing her.

He was thinking, *Ty and Lexie.*

That sharp thing again pierced the left side of his chest.

"Your kitchen," he found his mouth saying.

"What?" she asked quietly, and his eyes moved from her hand to hers.

"Your kitchen, babe. It's your kitchen. You made that so it works."

He watched surprise flare in her eyes then he watched her beautiful face grow soft and he liked both but he liked the second better.

"Those are from your bouquet," he noted quietly, and she nodded.

Then she admitted, "I was pissed at you but not pissed enough not to keep a few of the roses." She paused then, "As in, eight."

He felt the tightness in the left side of his chest ease.

Then he wrapped his fingers around the side of her neck and slid them up and back so they were in her hair, hair he'd felt gliding over his skin, hair he felt all around while she'd worked his cock. Hair that felt better during those times than he imagined it would and he imagined it would feel really fucking good.

Fuck, but he loved her hair.

He didn't tell her that. He also didn't tell her that the thing she made was beautiful and not just because of what it was, what it said and that she'd made it with flowers from her bouquet.

Instead, he bent and gave her a light kiss.

Then he muttered, "Gotta get a shower and change and then we'll go."

He let her go and walked to the stairs, thinking, *As in, eight.*

She'd given up on him when he was an asshole but she'd never let him go.

She'd never let him go.

He made it to the top floor feeling that squeeze return in the left side of his chest.

But taking a shower knowing Lexie was in her kitchen downstairs, ready to go out with him for dinner, he let it go.

* * *

Walker was on his back, head to the pillows, his wife's naked body using his as her mattress.

Her finger was gliding along the thick swirls and slashes of the design of the tat that inked his left arm from the top of his forearm up his upper arm around his shoulder partially up his neck and across his left upper chest and pectoral. The position of her body did not allow her fingers to roam down along the part that inked across the left side of his abs and middle, curving around his side to move across his back, meeting the ink that coiled over his shoulder, the design continuing down nearly to his groin at the front, on the top of his hip at the side and along the small of his back.

"This is a lot of ink," she whispered, her eyes on her finger.

"Yeah," he agreed because it was. It took five visits to get that work done and cost a fuckload of cash.

She looked to his face. "What is it?"

"Maori," he told her, and she blinked.

"What?"

"Maori," he repeated. "Indigenous people of New Zealand," he explained.

"I know who they are but why do you have Maori ink? Do you have Maori in you?"

He shook his head. "Not by blood."

When he said no more, Lexie asked, "What does that mean?"

He had an arm wrapped low at her waist, his fingers trailing aimlessly on the soft skin of her hip.

When he spoke, he stopped trailing and curled them around.

"When I was growin' up, there was a Maori mountain man, lived a fifteen-minute bike ride away in a cabin in the middle of nowhere. He was an old fucker, bad attitude but mostly he had a bad attitude 'cause the kids in town knew he lived up there, alone, didn't come into town often, wasn't social and those kids thought it was a kick to fuck with him. I was one of those kids. Was up there doin' shit to fuck with him when he caught me, dragged me to his cabin and laid me out. I was eight. He looked about eight hundred. He still laid me out, no hesitation, smacked me down."

"Oh my God," she whispered, her finger stopping its trailing too so all of them could curl into his shoulder.

"No, Lex, once he got done layin' me out, he talked to me. Never had that. Did have a dad who didn't hesitate smackin' me down but didn't take the time to talk to me after about the shit I was doin' wrong and how to pull it together. Had the time to take his hand to me but not the time to teach me lessons. Tuku was not like that."

"Tuku?"

"Yeah, Tuku. That was his name. After that, found myself pedaling my bike up there not to fuck with him but because he demonstrated he gave a shit and I didn't have that. I wasn't wrong. He gave a shit. Didn't make a big deal about it but the next time I came he gave me his time, he gave me his company and when I kept coming he gave me his wisdom. So I pedaled up there a lot. He was in this country because he married a white woman, an American, came here to be with her so she could be with her people. Got here, she lived long enough to get pregnant and die havin' their baby. Baby died too. He loved her. That fucked with his head, he checked out, stayed in his cabin, lived and breathed and ate and worked but other than that, life yanked away the only good thing he had in it at the same time takin' the beauty they created together. He couldn't deal so he didn't."

"That's awful," she said softly.

"Yeah," Walker agreed because it was and knowing Tuku for fourteen years, it was worse because he was a man who didn't deserve that. Not even close.

"So he took you under his wing?"

Walker nodded.

"I went up there a lot, any time I could. I did my homework up there because, when he knew I was gonna keep coming, he made me bring it with me. He taught me how to hold a hammer. He taught me how to use a drill. He taught me how to change oil, fix brakes and switch out a clutch. He taught me that any man worth anything works hard and he does it usin' his hands. He creates shit. He fixes it. Although the folks who could afford his stuff were lawyers, stockbrokers, he had no respect for them. That was just his way, his opinion and he taught me a man should form opinions, do it for a reason, stick by them but keep an open mind. He was an artist both in New Zealand and here. That's how he made his living. He gave me a pen-and-ink. This," he lifted his left arm then dropped it back to the bed, "after he died, I had it inked on me. Took what he gave me to a tattoo parlor right after the funeral and got it started."

Her voice held a tone of light dawning as she whispered, "So he was your Ella."

Her light dawned clear for her *and* for Walker because she was right.

"Yeah, he was my Ella."

"So it was Tuku who brought out my Ty."

My Ty.

My Ty.

Christ. Fuck.

Christ.

Two words. Just two words. Walker had no clue until that moment that two words could mean so fucking much. He'd never belonged to anyone. He'd never belonged anywhere. Never thought he wanted to.

Until he heard those two words.

He couldn't keep the thick out of his voice when he confirmed, "Yeah, it was him."

Her hand slid from his shoulder to curl around his neck when she said gently, "I'm sorry I couldn't meet him."

"I'm sorry too. He'd like you."

She tipped her head to the side. "He would?"

"Yeah."

"How do you know? If he wasn't social—"

His arm gave her a squeeze and he cut her off. "Because you are who you are, Lex, no bullshit. Tuku was not a fan of bullshit. And he was old as fuck but he was still a man and, the way you look, not a lotta men wouldn't like that."

She grinned at him.

Then she asked, "Where's the pen-and-ink?"

"In a scroll in a closet in one of the rooms downstairs. Had it framed but when the movers moved me in here, they dropped it, glass shattered, frame cracked. Wanted it reframed but wanted it done right. Didn't get to it before I went down."

She studied him then suddenly she lifted her torso and moved her legs so she was straddling his lower gut. He felt that gut tighten when she unexpectedly exposed the lush beauty of her body to his eyes and he was concentrating on that so he didn't resist when she wrapped her fingers around his right wrist and pulled his arm up between them. Then she ran her fingers down the black marks that wound a line up his forearm starting on the inside of his wrist and ending just under the outside of his elbow.

"What does this say?" she whispered.

"Got that inside. Artist in there, tools primitive, work first rate."

"Yeah, it's cool," she agreed, still whispering. "But what does it say?"

His eyes held hers.

Then he answered, "'Vengeance is mine.'"

Her fingers convulsed on his wrist but she didn't move her eyes from him.

She dipped her head and he watched as she watched her fingertips trailing back up the marks. Then she bent slightly forward, lifted his arm and pressed his hand flat to her chest. Her eyes moved back to his as she slowly slid his hand down, between her breasts, down her midriff, down over her stomach and *down*.

All the while he felt her skin under the path of his hand, he watched her face change, get hungry. She did shit like that all the time. Hot. Fuck, he'd never had so hot. They'd just finished fifteen minutes ago and she wanted it again. She got hungry a lot and, to get what she wanted, she was a wildcat.

He fucking loved that about her too.

When she used her hand to curve his between her legs, he curled his torso up, his left arm sliced tight around her waist and her mouth instantly moved so her lips were on his. Her breathing was already labored.

He took over and slid a finger inside and watched her eyes drift half closed.

He felt his cock start to get hard.

"What you want, baby?" he murmured against her mouth.

"Can I suck you?" she asked, hot, hungry, wanting it but still hesitant.

Like he'd fucking say no.

He answered by sliding his arm up her back and his finger out, pressing in as it glided over her clit, going for and getting that sexy-as-fuck noise she made at the back of her throat, doing all of this while he lay back down, taking her with him.

Once he was settled, he whispered, "Yeah, mama, you can suck me."

She smiled then she moved, taking her time, drifting down, using her mouth, her tongue, her teeth, her hands, her hair sliding all over him as she did, so by the time she reached his cock it was hard and pulsing.

She licked and played and stroked awhile before she got serious. He let her, her hair all around, he liked it and so did she. Then she took him inside and fuck, he liked that better because she was always eager, hungry. She could take him deep and she could suck hard and she did both really fucking well.

When he was close, he pulled her up, rolled her to her back and gave back as good as he got, taking his time moving down, working her tits until she was squirming and making low noises, tasting her, touching her then he got between her legs and he ate her, hard and hungrier than she did him.

He loved the taste of her pussy. So much, sometimes he could be working or working out and he'd sense her on his tongue.

He loved that too.

He made her come and moved over her, driving deep inside before she was finished, thrusting fast and hard, watching her face settle then he moved a hand in between them and built it again. She lifted her knees high, pressed them tight to his sides, locking his arm between them, her hands moving on him fevered. He took her there again then he let himself go.

He buried himself inside her, gave her enough weight to keep her warm and worked the skin of her neck with his mouth while her hands drifted light on him.

He didn't talk during sex and didn't like his pussy to do it either. Lexie talked but infrequently and when she did it meant something. She loved his cock in her mouth and in her cunt and she let him know it. She loved his body. She loved his mouth. She loved his hands. She let him know this too. She liked him giving it to her however he wanted. He'd been creative. She never made a noise of protest, just offered her pussy however he wanted to take it, as often as he wanted it, and she got off, did it hard and didn't mind him knowing she did that either.

He loved that about her too.

He pulled out and moved down. Brushing his mouth across her chest, he rolled off.

She rolled the other way and moved to the bathroom to clean up. He lay on his back staring at the ceiling when she did but turned his head to the side to watch her walk back in the room. She tagged her panties from the floor, tugged them on, turned out the light on her side then put a knee to the bed and moved into him. She settled, pressed to his side, cheek to his pec, leg tangling with his.

He reached out, turned out his light then pulled the covers over them, curled his arm around her and tucked her closer.

"Thanks for dinner," she murmured against his chest, her arm draped around his gut giving him a light squeeze.

He didn't answer. He'd buy her an expensive dinner to celebrate her getting a job and he'd buy her an expensive dinner to celebrate the fact that he woke up next to her. In time, she'd come to know that without him saying it and she'd come to know that because that was what he intended to give her.

Instead of speaking, he stared at the ceiling he could see in the moonlight. Wood planks and beams. And he felt the soft bed underneath him, Lexie's softness at his side. Not concrete and industrial paint overhead. Hard, thin mattress under him. Narrow bed that didn't fit his frame and allowed no room to move. And no chance in hell of pussy tucked to his side. Definitely not sweet, classy pussy who dressed nice, laughed often and didn't give a fuck who saw her run across the forecourt of a garage on high heels and launch herself into his grease-stained arms just because she found herself a part-time job as a receptionist in a fucking salon.

He stared at the ceiling and waited for it.

Then it happened, her weight settled. She'd found sleep.

Then he waited again.

She detached in her sleep and rolled away.

When she did Walker did what he always did. He moved out of bed and across the room to one of three thermostats in the house. He jacked the AC up then turned to move back to the bed but stopped when he saw her purse on the dresser. It was open, the stuff inside spilling out.

Instead of going back to bed, he moved there and tagged the digital camera. He turned it on and moved his thumb over the buttons on the side, the screen displaying the pictures. Three she made their waitress at The Rooster take of them cuddled in one side of a booth. But he stopped on one.

Lexie's head turned and tipped back, facing him, but even in profile you could see her smiling big, her nose pressed to the underside of his jaw, filled champagne glasses on the table in front of them. Her arm was wrapped around his middle, his arm around her shoulders, his head was partially turned to her, dipped down. His eyes were closed and he remembered what he was thinking with his eyes closed. Lexie pressed into his side, feeling her tits, smelling her hair and perfume, knowing she was smiling because she'd just been laughing. He was thinking something whacked, so whacked it was fucking insane.

He was thinking he didn't mind doing that time because he walked out and found all that.

Standing there, staring at the camera display, Walker remembered her sitting in the booth after the waitress gave back the camera, head bent, looking at the photos on the display and muttering, "Need another frame. The mantel is looking naked."

Her muttering had proved him right. She was making him a home, *them* a home because she'd never had one either, and she intended to keep doing it.

He turned off the camera and set it on the dresser. Then he joined her in bed, curling into her back, his arm going around her pulling her close. He did this every night since he took a shot at trusting her and made them a *them*. And like every night, in her sleep, she snuggled closer before settling and he knew she wouldn't detach because every morning since they became them he woke up with his wife tucked right there.

And like every night since they became them, he fell asleep smelling her hair, not a correctional institute filled with men, feeling her body tight against his, not rough covers, the air cool, not hot as fuck, and moonlight shining through huge-ass windows, not small ones covered by bars.

But that night, he fell asleep thinking it was whacked, fucking insane but it was true.

He didn't mind doing that time when doing it meant he would walk out to Lexie.

CHAPTER ELEVEN

Filled with Brightness

"Babe."

I looked up at Ty's call to see he was standing in the opened, wood-framed glass door to the front deck, hand still on the handle, a funny look on his face.

It was Sunday, a week and a half after I got my job and we'd celebrated, and it had been a week and a half where I'd spent a good amount of effort at keeping him distracted from his grand plan o' vengeance.

And, as far as I knew, I'd been successful.

Mostly, I did this with sex.

But we couldn't have sex every minute we weren't working or eating (alas) so I'd had to get creative.

And that creativity was helped by Laurie, who came into the salon to have her hair cut and highlighted. While she was waiting for Dominic to finish with a client, I'd shared with her my deck plant vision but lack of experience seeing as I'd lived in an apartment the entirety of my adult life. But I had managed to keep a houseplant alive for a few years so I had hope if not knowledge.

In return, she'd shared that Betty of Ned and Betty owned the Carnal Hotel and the healthy, abundant flowers outside were her doing. Then she'd phoned Betty while sitting in Dominic's chair and about seven seconds later Betty had walked through the doors of

Carnal Spa to give me a very long but friendly lecture about keeping outdoor plants alive in the Colorado Mountains.

I took notes.

Three pages of them.

Dominic's "spa," by the way, was really just a hairstylist that did manis and pedis. But Dominic's gay partner, Daniel, was building a couple of rooms at the back where he was hoping to expand into facials and massages.

"*If* the biker babes in this freaking town do facials and massages," he'd said. "Color me *stunned* when I found out the bitches got manis and pedis. Been living among them for *years*, still do not understand them. I get you wanna dip your toe into rough and tumble but attach your ball and chain to it? Uh… *no.* When your man doesn't bother to shave or get a haircut, my guess would be you wouldn't want a French pedicure. But I started that trade and those biker bitches were *all over it.* There you go. I may be fucked with facials, that might be taking it a shade too far, but you can't know unless you try."

By the way, my pay stunk but Dominic was hysterical, the work was entirely stress free, I got paid enough to cover the gas to drive down and then some, it was something to do with my days, it was doing something where I met half the town (the female half) and it came with free manis and pedis and half off Dominic doing your hair. And since he was a master and I liked my manis and pedis, I thought it was awesome.

So, since I had Betty's tutelage, the minute Ty got home on Saturday afternoon, I pounced.

And I did this by announcing, "Garden center is open on Saturday until eight."

To this he'd replied distractedly, head bent to his phone, thumb moving over the keypad, texting someone, "Go on, mama. I got somethin' I need to do."

Alarm bells sounded since he didn't share that something he needed to do. It wasn't like we were attached at the hip but unless he was working out, there weren't many somethings he had to do that took him away from me and I suspected the something he had to do was vengeance related.

I thought fast then called his name softly.

His head came up and turned to me.

"I've been, um…thinking about the, uh…money you owe me," I started.

That was when I watched his body get tight.

So I quickly went on, "I've decided to, uh…donate it to the cause."

This was a lie, of course, since I was fired up to derail the cause, but I thought it was a worthy lie to tell.

I felt guilt when he blinked then his eyes flared, his body turned to me and it started coming to me with intent, the look on his face sweet *and* hot so I lifted a hand and he stopped.

"Minus deck plants and furniture," I added. "I like to have coffee in the morning with the view and I'd prefer not to stand at the railing while doing it."

His reply was all Ty. Instantaneous and generous.

"Get what you want, Lex. Before you go I'll give you the money."

This was *not* falling into my plan.

So I scrambled.

"I want you to help me pick the furniture. It's going to be yours too and you also should have what you want. I donate the leftover if you come with me. Do we have a deal?"

He held my eyes for a long moment while I endeavored to look innocent.

Then he said, "Deal."

I smiled big at him. He grinned at me. Then his head dropped to his phone and his thumb moved over the keypad. He went with me and he didn't touch his phone, not the rest of that day or the next.

This was because I went nuts at the garden center, which also had kickass patio furniture. Kickass enough that even Ty got into the selection process and it was him who went overboard.

So in the Cruiser on our way home, we had trays and trays of plants, bags of soil, coils of hoses and ten enormous pots, four terra-cotta (front deck), four turquoise (deck off the kitchen as well as top and bottom of the outside steps) and two purplish gray (our deck off the bedroom) as well as a window box for outside the kitchen window.

We also bought a round gunmetal table with four wide-seated chairs with turquoise pads and matching umbrella to put on the deck off the kitchen.

With this we bought the coolest, most awesome furniture for the front deck. A curvy, rounded, flowing huge loveseat made in weatherproof resin the color of straw with a long swirly footstool that fit into the loveseat making it a big kind of shell-like oval. Both of which had thick sand-colored pads and big square toss pillows for the back of the loveseat. This was going to sit at one end with two matching curving, high-backed lounges sharing a low, bubble-like, glass-topped table that would sit at the other end.

For our balcony, we got one large oval resin lounger that was big enough to fit two even with one of those two being Ty. But it was really a chair and ottoman shoved together. This had dark gray thick pads and a matching, oval ceramic-topped table. Making awesome even more awesome, it had a light gray canvas canopy attached that you could swing up or down depending on the kind of sun or privacy you wanted.

As usual, Ty did not fuck around. It was the nicest, most stylish stuff they had, by far. Statement furniture, classy, unusual that was beautiful to look at and comfortable.

I freaking loved it.

They did Sunday deliveries, which I also freaking loved.

The next day, I commandeered Ty to lug pots around, fill them with soil and attach the window box. While he did this, I started planting and occupied his mind by asking him (frequently) what he thought of my gardening efforts (in other words, every time I got one of the pots planted).

He approved and was very patient with me distracting him every twenty minutes to drag him wherever I was working so he could look at a planter filled with flowers, spiked and trailing greenery which I could tell he gave not one shit about. Still, it kept him home, occupied and off his phone.

Then the furniture arrived and we became occupied with setting it out and assembling what needed to be assembled. When we were done, we took a shower together and I occupied him by guiding him out to the lounger on our deck and breaking it in. It was good tall pine trees hid us from view on either side and at the front there was nothing but hill and forest. But Ty pulled the canopy up just in case. It hid the wrong part of us but it was something.

The salon was closed Sunday and Monday and Ty's days off were Sunday and Thursday so I could keep him occupied most of the time but with me at work on Thursday and him not, this presented a problem.

I solved it by calling Laurie and asking for Tate's number then calling Tate and dragging him into Distract Ty Duties. He said he'd do what he could, and I knew he did when I got home to no Ty. Ty arrived an hour and a half later and when he did he told me he was at Tate's helping him "with shit."

Success.

Yesterday evening, another Saturday, he was again at his phone and I'd run a new play, mildly bitching about not being in the mood to cook. I bitched for about two point five minutes before he told me to get my shoes on, we were going out. We went into town and had Italian. Then we went to Bubba's and drank with Ty's friends. We didn't get home until late.

Another success.

And that day, Sunday, I had my play sorted out. I told him we needed to hit the home wares store and he'd instantly balked. Garden furniture, he could do. Home wares, his reaction to the concept stated clearly were not his thing. I'd had to get creative with incentive for him to go with me. I did. He liked it. I liked it. And he went. Liking my incentive so much, I talked him into taking the Charger.

And I talked him into the Charger because I'd put something in the trunk.

I directed him to make a pit stop at a place I'd previously scoped out in Chantelle on the way to the mall. He knew why the instant we parked on the street outside the shop. I saw his face change when he looked at the sign but I got out of the car before he could say anything. I was standing at the trunk by the time he folded out and his eyes came to me but he didn't speak.

"Pop the trunk, honey, will you?"

He held my eyes but said not a word.

"Pop the trunk, Ty," I semi-repeated.

He popped the trunk. I reached in and took out the long, hard-sided cardboard tube in the back that I'd found in a closet in one of the middle-floor bedrooms. I slammed the trunk and headed to his side, taking his hand in mine and tugging him to the frame shop. It took a mighty tug but I got him to come unstuck, slam his door and follow me in.

He picked the frame for Tuku's pen-and-ink. We left the tube and then we went out to the Charger. We didn't go to the home wares store but then again, that was a ruse so we didn't need to. We went straight home so Ty could express his gratitude by fucking me on the couch, fast, rough and brilliant.

I was on a roll and hoping I was succeeding, making Ty's time with me as good as it could be, something I'd want to do anyway, but something I was determined to do so he'd want to be where I was instead of where he needed to be so vengeance would be his.

Krystal advised me not to stick my neck out. I was doing everything in my power to stop Ty from sticking out his. I liked his neck and head where it was. And I was hoping, the more I played this game, the less important his grand plan o' vengeance would be and Tate could do his work. Or, if Tate couldn't, Ty would give up and just live his life and for him to do it, I had to demonstrate it was going to be a good one, worth giving up his grand plan o' vengeance.

And so far so good. He texted but if he wasn't at work, working out or running, which he did in the mornings of his days off, he was with me or Tate.

And he seemed content, happy even, grinning more often, chuckling a few times and, twice, I'd made him burst out laughing. I was hoping these were indications that his nightmare was fading. I was hoping these were indications that he was healing. I was hoping I was helping him to get to the other side.

So now it was early evening and I was out on the front deck watering as Betty taught me to do. Sometimes, if the day was really hot, I had to water in the mornings *and* evenings after the heat went off the day. I was also feeding the plants on her schedule. They were looking good, filling out, blooming, and I was a stickler for pinching off the deadheads so every bit was healthy.

And I was also studying the funny look on Ty's face. We'd been together almost a month and some of that time he'd been closed off. I knew he still held his cards close to his chest. He didn't let his thoughts or feelings show often but he did it and I was becoming attuned to his moods.

But that look was a new one I did not get.

Until I heard shrieked, "*Alexa Anne Berry! Where you at, girl?*"

My heart skittered to a halt, my mouth dropped open then I closed it only to open it again in order to whisper to Ty, "Holy fuck. That's Ella."

"Movin' truck just pulled in the drive, mama," he told me.

"*Aaaaaahhhlehhhhhxsaaaaaah!*"

That wasn't Ella.

That was Bessie.

My heart started hammering. I smiled bright and dazzling at Ty, dropped the hose where I stood and raced by him, around the side of the house and down the walkway. I made it to the railing to see a short white moving truck in the driveway, Ella, Bessie and Honey standing outside and to the side of it looking up at the deck off the kitchen.

"*Ohmigod!*" I screeched. "What are you doing here?"

Three heads swiveled to me and three faces split into huge smiles.

"*Ahhhyeeeee!*" Bessie squealed then disappeared under the deck and I knew she was going to the stairs.

"*Girl! Look at you!*" Honey shrieked then she disappeared.

"*There's my baby!*" Ella cried then she disappeared.

I raced down the deck and hit Bessie on the fly as she got to the top of the stairs, arms tight, bodies swaying. Honey hit us and burrowed in so our arms moved to accommodate her. Ella came next and we effected a group hug, giggling and swaying.

Then we disengaged but Ella kept me close with an arm around me as I looked at her.

"What are you doing here?" I asked again.

"Well, you needed your stuff. So we rented a truck and brought your stuff," she answered.

"Got us one of those GPS's," Bessie added, grinning at me. "Took us right to your door."

"Ace crib, sistah," Honey put in. "I am no mountain girl but this place is *the shit.*"

"This is true but I need a cocktail. You cannot imagine what bein' in a big truck with these two for two full days does to a woman," Ella told me. "They weren't my flesh and blood, I'd be facin' time."

I grinned at her total lie. She'd spawned Bessie and Honey, she adored them and she put up with a lot from them and me *and* Ronnie. She did not do this without losing her ever-lovin' mind on a relatively frequent occasion that often included threats of murder but she would no sooner carry them out, or lift a hand, than she'd voluntarily be boiled in acid.

Caught up in the moment, the surprise, I totally forgot where I was and why I was there until I heard Honey whisper a low, stunned, supremely appreciative, "*Muthafuckah.*"

Bessie, Ella and my eyes went to her then went to where her eyes were aimed to see Ty was standing, arms crossed on his massive chest, just outside the open kitchen door.

"Yo." His deep voice rumbled and I sensed rather than felt the group quiver.

Everyone was silent and still for a moment, taking in all that was Ty. Since there was a lot of him and all of it was really good, this moment lasted a while.

Ella broke it by saying, "I see in the mountains they make mountains of brother. I wish I'd known this forty years ago."

Ty grinned. This caused another group quiver to glide through his female audience.

I experienced my quiver right along with my family then I realized what was happening and that it was brilliant, having them there but it could be explosive, depending on their reaction to the news of why *I* was there.

But this was family and always would be family and Ty was my husband.

So they had to know.

And they had to accept him.

Because he was family now too.

Therefore, I decided against stealth tactics and instead to launch an all-of-it-out-there-in-the-open offensive and take my chances.

So I disengaged from Ella, moved to Ty and reengaged with him, sliding my arms around his middle. He reciprocated by sliding his arm around my shoulders.

My family watched silent and every last one of them had their mouth open. Honey, wide open. Bessie, partially open. Ella, lips parted.

Then I said, "Ella, Bessie, Honey, this is my husband, Ty Walker. Ty," I tipped my head back to catch his eyes, "I've told you about my family."

My gaze went back to the girls as the reactions started.

"The fuck you say." That was Bessie.

"Uh...say what?" That was Honey.

Ella didn't say anything but her eyes had narrowed.

My body tensed. When it did, Ty gave me a squeeze.

Then he spoke and I looked back up to him. "Get these sisters inside. Give them a drink. And give them an explanation. I'll call the boys and get them over to help unload the truck." I stared at him and didn't move so he gave me another squeeze and murmured, "Now, Lex."

I nodded.

He looked to the women on his deck. "Who's got the keys?"

Bessie lifted a hand with the keys dangling from it. Ty let me go, walked to her, grabbed them with a muttered, "Thanks," and walked around them to and down the stairs, pulling his phone out of his back pocket.

My eyes went from where he disappeared to my girls to see they were all looking at me. This boded bad things. Not many women on this earth would miss watching Ty move, even if it was just to walk down some stairs.

"Um…" I mumbled.

"Get that white booty o' yours in the house," Ella snapped. "*Now.*"

I knew her tone. I was in trouble.

Therefore, I didn't hesitate because I'd learned it was better when you were in trouble with Ella to face it fast, get it over with, accept your penance and move on. I walked into the open door and they followed.

I headed to the fridge while declaring with more hope than certainty I'd get away with the stall, "We'll start with drinks."

"We…will…*not*," Ella countered, and I turned around to see them all in, the door closed and they were huddled at the island opposite me. Honey had her hands on it. Bessie had her hands on her hips. Ella had her arms crossed on her ample bosom. All their eyes were on me.

"Explain," Ella ordered.

"It's cocktail hour and you guys just got—" I began but stopped when Ella's arm snaked out and she slapped the counter of the island with her open hand.

"*Explain!*" she shouted.

"Ella," I whispered but said no more, words clogging in my

throat as they always did when she got that kind of pissed at me, be I thirteen or thirty-four.

"How on sweet God's earth are you married to a brother I've never met?" she asked.

"It's a long story," I told her.

"Well, lucky you, your three girls got the next two weeks off so you got *plenty* of time," Ella shot back but my heart skipped happily.

"You guys are here for two weeks?" I asked.

"Alexa Anne," Ella said, warning low.

I sucked in breath and took in their angry eyes. Well, Honey looked curious, not angry, but Bessie and Ella were ticked. And this was because they knew why I might keep a secret from Honey but I had no good reason to keep a secret from them. Or lie to them. And doing either would draw the wrath of hellfire down on me. We were tight, Ella the only mother I knew, Bessie closer than a sister. They had my back and I had their love and I returned both.

So I had a lot of explaining to do and the only hope I had of doing it without hurting feelings was giving it to them straight.

I walked to the island and put my hands on it.

Then I said, "About two days after I left, I picked up Ty from a correctional facility in southern California. He'd just got done doing a nickel for manslaughter."

Bessie closed her eyes and looked away. Honey's eyes got huge. Ella's head dropped to look at her hand on the island.

I kept talking.

"It was an errand for Shift." Bessie and Ella's eyes snapped back to me. "He wasn't forthcoming about this errand. I thought he wanted me to pick up Ty and take him somewhere but he didn't. He was presenting me to Ty as payback he owed. Ty needed a wife and that was me."

"Girl," Ella said low.

"No, listen to me," I whispered. "He didn't do it."

"That's what they all say," Bessie hissed, and my back shot straight.

"Well, he didn't," I fired back, and she blinked at my fierce tone.

"You're here two weeks, you'll see. He'll show you and his friends will show you. He got framed. I'll explain that to you when we have cocktails but right now, that's a part you need to know. By the time you leave to go home, you'll feel it tearing at your heart like I do, that he got targeted because he's got color and got in the sights of a dirty cop to go down for a crime he didn't commit. But you'll also leave knowing he's a good man and I'm in good hands."

"You met him a month ago," Ella reminded me, and my eyes slid to hers.

Then I replied gently and cautiously, "Spent a lot of time with bad, Ella, I know the feel of good."

I watched her clench her teeth. It wasn't a low blow. It was the truth and sometimes the truth hurt.

I pulled in another breath. "It started fake, a deal, me being his wife and he was going to get me free from Shift. Something happened and now it is *far* from fake. Now we're starting a life. It's good. I'm happy. I have a job and he has a boatload of friends who care a lot about him and brought me into the fold the second I stepped foot in that door." I swung an arm out to the door behind them. "No joke, *the second* we walked in they gave him a welcome home bash and mingled it with a wedding party. They didn't know we were fake and by then, it had only been a few days, but we weren't anymore. They don't know what you know and I'd appreciate you didn't tell them when you meet them. But what you need to know is I care about him. A lot. I'm trying to help him adjust to being out, which isn't easy most especially because of why he was in. And we're starting something, something good. Something I never expected I'd have and I'm going to do everything in my power to keep it and keep it good. Everything in my power."

I pulled in yet another breath, slid my eyes through a trio of women I loved and finished softly but with emphasis.

"*Everything.*"

They looked at me and I let them.

Then Ella asked, "He got targeted because of his color?"

"He's half black and the local police chief is not a big fan of color and when he needed a fall guy and he lost big to Ty in poker, he chose him to take the fall," I answered.

"Local? I thought he did time in California?" Bessie asked.

"It's a long story that requires alcohol but the cop business is a family business and he's got a cokehead brother in California who needed a problem solved. Against his will, Ty solved it and he lost five years of his life doing it," I replied.

"That's just terrible," Honey whispered.

"Yeah, it is," I stated firmly. "Unimaginably terrible. *Crushingly* terrible."

"You're in love with him," Ella said quietly, and I looked to her and held her eyes.

Then I whispered, "Yes. Falling in love, yes, I am, Ella. Fast. He bought me diamonds. He bought me a wedding bouquet. He bought me a Treasure Island snow globe." I pointed to the sill, her eyes followed my finger then I dropped my hand and her eyes came back. "He took me to Moab. He brought me to this house. He gave me his friends. He gave me his protection, dragging me out from under Shift. He gave me freedom from that. The air I breathe now is clean. Fresh and clean. And its air I share with Ty. He gave me all that and it took over a week for me to make him laugh." I leaned forward. "*Over a week.*"

Ella closed her eyes slowly and opened them. She knew what this meant. I was funny and I was funny because she taught me how to be. The Rodriguez family might never have had much but they always had a lot of laughter.

I kept going.

"I've been with him nearly a month and he's laughed full out three times. Only three. He gave me all that and I've managed to make him laugh three times. This is what I'm dealing with. He's generous. He's gentle. When he talks to me soft it's like a gift. When he calls me 'baby' or 'mama,' I feel it in my heart, my belly. So yes, I'm falling in love with him. And you give him a shot, you will too."

"I'll give him a shot," Honey said instantly, because that was Honey. She wasn't bright but she was loving, she was open and she'd give anyone a shot, sometimes when they didn't deserve it.

But Ty did so I looked to her and smiled a grateful smile.

My smile wobbled when I looked at Bessie. "Bess?"

"I got your back whatever," she muttered, but her eyes locked with mine. "That said, I do not like bullshit phone calls. I get this was serious shit for you and your head was probably all over the place. But I do not like bullshit phone calls. I'll make that point now, expect you to let that shit sink in and we'll move on long's I got your word that shit has sunk in."

"It's sunk in. You have my word and I'm sorry for the bullshit," I replied quietly.

She held my eyes. Then she jerked up her chin.

And that was Bessie. She *was* a bright bulb, always had been. She'd learned early to withhold her trust until it was earned and to say it like it was so no one could mistake where she was coming from. But once you had her trust, her loyalty and devotion were worth every effort it took to earn it. Except, of course, as it was with many girls, when it came to her love life. With that, as it was with many girls, she was *all* screwed up.

I looked to Ella.

"Ella?" I whispered.

She looked away and licked her lips.

"Ella?" I called, still whispering.

She kept her eyes averted and leaned heavily into her hand in the island.

"Ella, please," I begged.

She looked back at me.

"Moved on. My baby's moved on," she said quietly, her voice trembling. "And the last thing my son gave to you before you moved on was the need to take flight and do somethin' flat-out crazy to get out from under the garbage he left you. Last thing you had from Ronnie was all you ever got from him. Garbage."

She pulled in breath and wet glistened at the edge of her eyes.

"That stings, precious," she whispered.

"I know," I whispered back. "But it isn't true the only thing he gave me was garbage. He gave me more and there was a lot of it that was good. And in the end, the garbage he gave me also led me to Ty and as you can tell, I'm not complaining."

"Yeah, that's the reason I'm not blubberin'. 'Cause you look like I've never seen you look, standin' in your fancy-ass clothes that are fancy even bein' shorts and a tee, in a kitchen nicer than many I've seen that's in a house a whole lot better than many I've seen lookin' like you belong here. And you always looked like you belonged to the likes of the man I saw outside. And last you look happy, which is somethin' I've *never* seen, not happy like you got right now, the quiet kind which is the best kind. So that's why I'm still standin'. 'Cause I know my son taught you bad but I know you're *my* girl so I trust you to move onto good."

She got fuzzy because my eyes filled with tears. I felt my way around the island and I was in her arms. Then Honey's arms came around us. Then Bessie's. We held on tight without laughter and swaying but with some hitches of breath and a couple of quiet sobs.

We got it under control and let each other go.

Ella strolled to a stool, hiked her ass up on one and announced, "Now I'll take a cocktail."

All-out offensive a success, I felt relief so I moved a grin through my girls then I moved my body to where we kept our booze. I took the bottles down and something caught my eye. My head turned left and I saw my heart of petals hanging in the kitchen window.

I hadn't etched "Ty and Lexie, Las Vegas" in it because I thought that was cheesy but I had etched some curlicues and I thought it looked good. Out of place but I knew what it was, Ty did too so it was in the exact right place for us and that was all that mattered.

I felt the still-warm early evening sun beating on my skin through the glass. It was bright. Colorado was bright. I'd never experienced so much sunshine in my life.

And that's when I knew. It had happened. What just happened was only placing a stamp on it, making it official.

That warm sun shining on my skin, its brightness filling my days—the shadow of Ronnie was gone. Even with Ty's business in the background, nothing encroached, not even to throw a little shade.

My life was filled with brightness.

And thinking that, I left the bottles where they were, muttered vaguely to my girls, "Just a sec," then walked to the back door, put one foot out of it and yelled in no particular direction, "Honey! If you're avoiding the house, drama over. It's safe to come inside. It's all about cocktails and camaraderie, not tempers and tantrums!"

I stepped back in, shut the door and hit the liquor bottles, ignoring Honey's audible snicker.

I got them their drinks. I got myself a beer and they were all lined up on the stools, me at the side of the island, my hip leaning against it when Ty came up the stairs from the garage. He jerked up his chin to my family, hit the fridge and got himself a beer.

He settled, hips against the counter at the side wall, reached out a long arm, tagged my hand and yanked. I scuttled toward him, falling into his body where his arm wrapped around my waist and my head tipped back.

"Wood, Tate, Jonas and Deke are on their way. You're gonna have to direct traffic and provide payback in the form of pizza and beer," he told me.

I smiled up at him. "I can do that. Pizza place in town deliver?"

"Yep," he answered. "Heads up. Reconcile of Maggie and Wood means they're attached at the hip unless he's under a car. Tate says that you told Laurie we got good patio furniture so he warned me she's itchin' for a look and will probably find her way in his truck. So you order, order big 'cause Tate says Jonas alone can eat a large all to himself."

"He's a growing boy," I explained.

"He's a growing Jackson," Ty returned. "Tate ain't exactly small and Jonas is the spittin' image of his dad."

I looked to my girls who were all observing us. Honey with a happy smile. Bessie with an assessing stare. Ella with her head tipped to the side but her expression shuttered.

I ignored all this and told them, "Wait until you meet Ty's friends. They're all white but they're all seriously hot."

"Heard word of women, they hot *and* taken?" Bessie asked.

"Except Deke," I answered.

"Then what do I care they're hot?" she shot back.

"They're taken but they're still fun to look at."

"Girl, I got an eyeful right in front of me. More might make my head explode," she returned.

She wasn't wrong about that so I had no reply. Luckily, Honey giggling covered it.

Ty's reaction to this compliment was to take a tug on his beer then set it on the counter beside him. I watched his hand do that then I watched it come toward me and I watched it until I couldn't anymore because it cupped my jaw and tipped my face up to his while he curled his body slightly enough to give us a hint of privacy, not enough to be rude.

When my eyes caught his, he whispered, "You good?"

There it was. That was why he didn't react to Bessie's compliment. His mind was on me.

I grinned. Then I nodded.

His gaze roamed my face.

Then he nodded back, his hand dropped, he curled away and grabbed his beer.

I looked to my girls. Honey was smiling her happy smile. Bessie was looking away, blinking, and I knew this was to hide it while she fought tears, and Ella's expression wasn't shuttered anymore. Her face was soft, her eyes were lit with her sweet momma light and they were on me.

"I love you guys," I blurted.

This caused Bessie to hop off her stool and mutter, "Bathroom."

"Your right, door by the livin' room," Ty said quietly, and Bessie hustled away.

Honey smiled happily.

Ella took a sip of her cocktail.

Ty

Laurie and Jonas were loading into Tate's SUV, Tate was moving across the asphalt with Walker.

The truck unload descended into a party. Not surprising. The women cackled on the deck furniture while the men lugged boxes up two flights of steps, Ty and Wood putting together Lexie's bed in one of the middle-floor bedrooms so one of the sisters could have a bed tonight. Their surprise arrival meant Walker and Lexie had company. They were Lexie's family so this wasn't surprising either. It was good his couch was big and had two sides.

After the men did the work, Lexie expended the energy of dialing the phone to order pizzas. Fortunately, but surprisingly, she didn't have much stuff to haul up the steps. Also fortunately, since they both drank beer, she had an ample supply.

Now Wood, Maggie, their kids and Deke were gone and Tate and his family were preparing to leave. But he'd said he wanted a word. So Walker was giving him a word.

"What's up?" he asked when Tate led him to a position not in hearing distance of his truck or Walker's house. Something Walker noted. Also something Walker didn't like.

"You got a night this week you can come by my house for a talk?"

Fuck.

"About what?" Walker asked.

"You got a night, Ty," Jackson said quietly.

"This about Peña?" Walker asked.

"Ty, you got a night?"

Walker remained silent for a moment.

Then he replied, "Might have several, I know why."

"You trust me?"

Fuck.

"Yeah."

"You got a night?"

Fuck!

"Let me talk to Lex. Her family's here for two weeks and knowin' Lex, she'll wanna pack everything in so it'll be busy. I'll let you know," Walker told him.

"Right," Tate murmured.

Walker changed the subject. "Thanks for droppin' everything and comin' over to help out."

"Payback, you did the same for me this week and I didn't give you pizza and beer or feed your family."

This was true.

"Speakin' about family—" Jackson started.

"Yeah," Walker interrupted, mistaking Tate's comment. "They adopted her. They're Rodriguez's family."

Tate shook his head. "No, I meant when are you and Lexie gonna start yours?"

He'd breathed easy for a while. A week and a half to be exact. But at Tate's question, that piercing feeling again went through the left side of his chest.

Through the pain, he forced out, "Come again?"

"Know you're new. Know you're both gettin' on your feet after a lotta rough years. Know you probably got a lotta shit in your head, reckon she does too. But 'spect, what I can tell of Lexie, she's helpin' you work through that. What I know of you, you're doin' the same for her. What you probably don't know is, got somethin' good, makin' it better'll give your mind good things to think of rather than shit things to chew on. And I promise you, brother, a kid is a good thing. Your kid with Lexie, even better." He paused while Walker stared at him through the gathering dusk then continued, "Though, not if you get yourself a daughter who looks like her. Then you're fucked."

A daughter who looks like her.

Christ.

Christ.

He'd never thought of it. Not in his entire life. Never thought of making babies. Never met a woman in whom he wanted his seed to take root.

Now it was in his head and he knew it was in there in a way where it'd be near impossible to shake it out.

Christ.

"Ty?" Tate called.

"We need time to settle," Walker told him.

"Sure, I can see that. Though, you settling only to shake things up with a kid, might as well settle knowin' you got one on the way."

"Man, we've been married less than a month," Walker reminded him.

"So?"

Walker stared at him.

Then he muttered, "Fuck me, Tatum Jackson, family man and advocate for domestic bliss."

"You been busy with your woman, not around. You been around me, Laurie and Jonas, you'd see I got it goin' on," Tate told him through a grin.

"Fuck me," Walker muttered again.

Jackson kept grinning at him.

Then the grin faded and he whispered, "Think about it. And call me with a night you can come over."

"Right," Walker murmured.

Tate gave him a chin lift and moved to his SUV. Walker moved toward his condo and looked to Jackson's truck. Laurie gave him a wave through the windshield. He jerked his chin up and stopped close to the condo to watch Tate swing in, switch on the ignition and then he shifted his body to watch them drive away until they were out of sight.

He turned around and was moving to the stairs but stopped at the foot of them when he saw the shadowed body of Ella Rodriguez sitting on a step in the middle.

He tipped his head back the inch he needed to catch her eyes.

She started.

"Got good friends."

"Yep," he agreed because she was right.

Ella fell silent. Walker didn't break it but he waited because he knew she had something to say.

Then she spoke again.

"Later, when you got quiet time with her tonight, my girl's honest, she'll tell you straight she laid it out for us."

This was also not surprising.

"Got nothin' to hide," he replied, but this was only mostly true.

She said nothing, just held his eyes.

Finally, she murmured, "'Spect that's true."

She said no more and didn't move.

Walker waited.

She spoke again and she did it gently and with feeling.

"I'm sorry that was done to you, boy."

Fuck him, why did that coming from a woman he barely knew feel as good as it felt?

He didn't ask this.

He lifted his chin and said, "I am too."

"Got no doubts you've felt it. But I'm older than you, as bad as you've felt it before this happened to you, I've felt it worse. And as bad as I felt it, what I know my parents felt was worse. So I know, the like that's done to you, it leaves demons."

She was not wrong about that.

Walker didn't respond.

"What you don't know is that you got yourself a girl who's not afraid of demons. She'll take them on. You don't shut her out, lock her down when that time comes when they threaten to overwhelm you, she'll help you beat them back."

He responded to that. "I know what I got in Lexie."

"No," she said instantly and shook her head. "You might think you know but you have no idea."

"Ella—"

"My boy had demons," she whispered, and Walker's body got tight. "He shut her out, locked her down. He told himself he didn't but he did. Started before he left for Indiana, strugglin' to keep his nose clean, stay outta trouble, not get sucked into that life. But all he saw was struggle. All he felt was responsibility. All he thought of was makin' that right. His entire focus was bein' certain he was in the position to change that, not for him, for us, for Lexie. He had no daddy. He had no man in his life to teach him how to be strong and he ignored my lessons to do right, so determined to take care of us, no matter how he had to do that. And when he was growin' up, they were like a swarm of bees buzzin' around, constant, showin' him a different path, teachin' him bad lessons. They went at him hard and they went at him dirty and one night they got to him and Duane stepped in and saw him through. The only thing that boy ever did that was good in his life, I figure. I don't know all that happened, just know it happened. He saw my Ronnie through and Ronnie never forgot it. But that left him with demons and messed with his head and caught him a debt he repaid by takin' seven bullets. Instead, he shoulda taken Lexie's hand and let her lead him to the good life. And I'm tellin' you this now so you don't make that same mistake."

She stopped talking and Walker didn't reply.

So she kept talking.

"What was done to you was no good. The worst. See you with her, see you reachin' for happy. But no matter how strong a man is, you take a hit like that, it's hard to bounce back. You'll hit a wall and struggle to get through. You're a strong man and your first thought won't be to take a woman's hand. But I'm older than you. I watched a lot of boys fail 'cause they made that same decision, thinkin' wrongly that that decision is weak. Be stronger than that and know when to take your woman's hand so she can help you break through."

Again she stopped speaking and again Walker didn't reply.

She didn't start again.

So Walker drew a line under it. "'Preciate the wisdom, Ella."

She looked at him through the growing darkness. "Hope you take it to heart, Ty."

He again lifted his chin.

She stood, turned and slowly walked up the steps. Timing it perfectly, she was close to the top before she stopped, looked down at him and dealt the killer blow.

"You don't take it to heart, love she feels for you, the kind of love she was smart enough not to give my boy, you'll break her. That's *my* girl and *I* know. I see it the way she looks at you, talks about you. You don't grasp hold and let her give as good as she gets, you'll destroy her. So when I say I hope you take it to heart, Ty, I *really* do."

Then Ella Rodriguez walked up the last two steps, turned and disappeared.

And for a long time Ty Walker couldn't move because that thing piercing his chest twisted viciously.

When he got it under control he walked up his steps toward a house full of women.

CHAPTER TWELVE

Where She Parks Her Charger

Ty

"I'M TELLIN' YOU, brother, it's hot."

Walker was standing in the locker room of his gym, side to the door so he could see if someone came in. Dewey was hidden by the lockers. At the best of times, he wouldn't be seen with Dewey. They were tight, or as tight as anyone could be with Dewey. But the kind of stink Dewey produced had a tendency to make anyone reek.

Considering they were both ex-cons, he definitely shouldn't be seen with Dewey.

But he had to meet Dewey and Dewey had just two minutes ago shoved himself through the window so he was with Dewey. Even though, at this moment, he did not want to be because two seconds after he shoved himself through the window, he'd launched into his bullshit excuses.

"Haven't heard from you in weeks, Dew, no return texts, no return calls and now your cell says disconnected. Don't like that shit. Don't like finally hearin' from you only for you to spout shit. And don't like givin' you twenty-five K for six weeks of nothin'," Walker told him.

"Had to ditch that phone, Ty."

Jesus. Nothing had changed. Dewey changed phones like he changed underwear.

"Why?" Walker asked.

"They read it and hear it. I know it."

Fuck. There it was. The reason why Dewey changed phones like underwear. Paranoia. The brother thought cops had superhuman powers. This was because he got caught, sent down and he wasn't smart enough to admit he got caught and sent down because he was a dumb fuck, not because the cops had superhuman powers.

Dewey went on, "You know and I know that *they* know, you want somethin', you'll come to me and I'll get it for you. They know we're tight. They were all over me. I had to lay low."

With waning patience, Walker reminded him, "Like I explained, Dew, *you* don't do shit. *You* connect with brothers who will."

"They see that shit too."

"Bullshit," Walker bit out. "You want it, you're a fuckin' shadow and none of your connections live in the light."

Dewey pressed his lips together because Walker was not lying and he knew it.

Walker took a step toward him, not too far he couldn't see the door but enough to make a point. "I need dirt," he said low. "And there's so much dirt on these guys, I should be up to my neck in it by now. This was not a hard assignment. This shoulda taken you a fuckin' week, not six."

"They aren't exactly out in the open with their shit," Dewey returned.

"And your connections aren't gonna win citizen of the year either," Walker shot back.

Dewey stared at him.

Then he said softly, "Ty, this really the way you wanna go? You push, they'll push back."

What the fuck?

"We've had this conversation, Dew."

"But—"

"Don't like repeatin' myself."

"Ty," he took a step forward, "thinkin' on this awhile, I don't think it's good. I didn't then. I don't now."

"Right, then give me back my twenty-five K and I'll find someone who doesn't have a fuckin' opinion."

Dewey took two steps back and Walker stared him in the eyes.

Then he whispered, "Right."

The fuckwad didn't have the money. Six weeks, he'd pissed away twenty-five K. Walker half expected it, it was a risk he had to take because Dewey lived with his belly to the ground and he was connected to anyone from there to Denver who lived the same. Walker couldn't shake his tail and make those connections. He needed a man to do it for him. That was Dewey. But his friend had fucked him, not altogether a surprise but that didn't mean he wasn't disappointed.

"You sat a game," he guessed.

Dewey pressed his lips together again.

Walker shook his head then said, "You owe me twenty-five large, Dew. You jacked me around for six weeks. You got half of that to get it back. You don't, I'll find you."

"Ty—"

"Make no mistake, I'll find you."

Dewey nodded and didn't say a word. He knew Walker would find him. He knew, they were tight or not, what Walker would do when he did. He also knew to avoid that. So Dewey sometime in the next three weeks would fuck over another fucking idiot to get Walker's payback. The vicious cycle of the life of a stupid man addicted to fucking cards.

"I didn't come empty, Ty. I got somethin' for you," Dewey offered.

"Yeah? What's that?"

"Your tail is gone. Bad boys of Carnal PD are convinced five years not breathin' free, hot snatch you got at home, you'll do noth—"

He didn't finish because he found his body twisted, slammed against the lockers, his feet six inches off the ground and Ty Walker's big hand wrapped tight around his throat, his face an inch away.

"You do not call my wife hot snatch," he growled into his friend's face, and Dewey instantly nodded as best he could with Ty's fingers curled around his throat, cutting off his breath.

Ty dropped him and stepped back.

Then, knowing his point was made in a way even Dewey understood it, he moved on. "Got eyes. I know I lost the tail."

And he did. Three weeks ago. Just after Keaton saw top to toe the talent Walker had in his bed and the boys assigned to tail and do the drive-bys of the condo took in planters and deck furniture. They had eyes and ears everywhere. Walker and Lexie at The Rooster, the Italian place in town, the Toyota dealership. No doubt they looked into Lexie and no matter her relationship with Rodriguez, their lives had never mixed and they couldn't do smack with speeding and parking tickets. She was clean.

Message received was that Ty Walker was cowed, moving on, keeping his head down and nose clean, not about to fuck his future. Especially since that future included Lexie, and he had no doubt they'd all had their look at Lexie.

It wasn't a play, it was real. But seeing the results, it was a play he should have thought of, though, if he did, he wouldn't have gone for it thinking they wouldn't be that dumb.

Then again, he forgot they were half idiots.

And also, he had no idea he'd walk out to the miracle that was Lexie.

"What I'm sayin' is," Dewey kept talking, "word 'round the station, they're convinced you're movin' on. They're leavin' you be."

This news was good but Walker didn't respond.

Dewey kept going. "Ty, they leave you be then you can just… *be.* Haven't seen her, hear she's somethin'. Got that, got a job, got your life back. There's only one year left on your sentence, one year you gotta live on parole. More than a month a' that is gone. Maybe signs are sayin' you should just *be.*"

"You do time?" Walker asked a question the answer to which he knew.

"Yeah," Dewey told him the answer he knew.

"Was it fun?" Walker asked.

"Ty—"

"You earned yours and it wasn't fun, Dew. I did not earn mine. Do not fuckin' stand there and counsel me about just *being.*"

His friend studied him then he repeated quietly, "Ty, you push, they'll push back."

"Can't push back if they're paralyzed."

"You think a dozen men the last twenty years have not had your same idea, half of them brothers, you're wrong. They all got smacked down."

"None of them was as motivated as me."

This was true. He knew. He knew many a biker or black man in and around Carnal had taken their hits from Arnie Fuller and the Carnal PD. Knew they tried to hit back. Knew they failed.

He also knew he was not them.

None of them was jacked near as badly.

Dewey studied him again then said, still talking quietly, "I'll keep ears and eyes open. Anything you need to know, I'll get word to you." He paused then offered, "Freebie."

"No shit?" Walker asked and Dewey, being Dewey, grinned.

Walker did not grin back.

Instead he reminded him, "Three weeks today, Dew."

Dewey's grin faded, he nodded then he replied, "Three weeks."

Walker turned away and went to his workout bag. Dewey disappeared back through the window. Summer, long days, it was early evening, still light. Even so, no one would see Dewey. He could be a shadow standing in the middle of a field at noon. With that kind of talent at hand, him still getting tagged made him all the more stupid.

Walker bent and grabbed his bag, moving out of the locker room into the gym. The instant he hit it, he did a scan. It was automatic. He clocked everyone there, knew who'd arrived since he went to the locker room, who'd moved stations or machines, in or out of rings. Years of playing poker successfully, he'd learned to notice a shift of the eyes, a twitch of the finger, the way a man would move the cards around in his hand or what it meant when he didn't considering what he would eventually turn over.

This served him well inside and he'd spent five years polishing this skill, facial expressions, the set of shoulders, the clench of fists, a man's gait, his position in a room, in the yard. Anyone sent down with half a brain used their time to hone this skill or they didn't last long. Seeing as Walker's was already amplified, he could read a man and gauge a room at a glance.

Second nature.

This freed him to set the meeting and the frustrations it caused aside. He had other contacts but considering his first choice was Dewey, he wasn't fired up to connect with his second runner-up. The other choice was, without a tail, start digging himself. Risky and time consuming, time he'd have to take away from Lexie, something he did not want to do. An elevation in risk that could conceivably *take him away from Lexie*, something he *really* did not want to do.

Thinking about Lexie made his gait quicken. Workout done. Pain-in-the-ass meet with Dewey over.

Time to get home.

A home without Ella, Bessie and Honey.

The last two weeks had been insane. When he told Tate that Lexie would want to pack it all in, he had not been wrong. But she wasn't the only one who wanted to pack it all in. All four of those women didn't want to waste a single breath.

So they didn't.

This was good. It meant he could avoid the meet with Tate. A meeting where Tate would try to take Walker's pulse, dig and see if Walker was up to something. Then expend the wasted effort to try and talk him out of it. After that, get pissed when his effort was wasted.

Walker didn't need that shit. Neither did Tate. He owed the man his time and he'd give it to him and then try to manage the meeting so feelings wouldn't turn hard.

But he couldn't say he wasn't fucking glad he'd had genuine excuses to delay.

These included Ella treating them all to her "famous Texas chili," shit so hot, Walker couldn't taste the meat or beans, just the heat. This started a contest for each of those sisters to one-up themselves, something he could have saved them doing since he hadn't enjoyed Ella's treat but he couldn't exactly say that, as much as he wanted to, so he didn't.

Honey's offering was worse. Thankfully the bitch was dim so Lexie *and* Ella were able to draw her attention away while Bessie confiscated plates and dumped vast portions of whatever the fuck it was supposed to be in the garbage so they didn't have to eat it. Walker thought he'd have to go to bed starved but Lexie had snuck down to the kitchen and made him sandwiches then came up with them to tell him she'd run into Ella and Bessie doing the same.

At this, she'd laughed herself sick. She'd laughed herself sicker when she presented him with bologna and an excuse of, "This was the best I could do, baby. Ella was distracting Honey, I didn't have time to do more."

It was the first time since he was a kid and learned better that he preferred bologna to the alternative.

Luckily, Bessie knew her way around the kitchen. Her meat pie with cornbread topping was the shit.

When they weren't cooking, Lexie had talked him into taking them to The Rooster. And she'd talked him into taking them to the Italian place then to Bubba's. Further, Maggie had thrown a barbeque in honor of their visit, which meant they had to go. The next week, not to be outdone, Laurie had invited them all to dinner. He'd barely step foot at the top of the stairs before Lexie was telling him he needed to get his ass in the shower because they were off somewhere.

And even if they weren't, the women latched on and his time was full.

One night, they seated him at the island with Lexie's photo albums, ten of those fuckers. Clearly, she hadn't just discovered taking photos. His wife had made a habit of it for two decades. They all stood around him, the best part being Lexie standing behind him, tits pressed to his back, arm reaching around to flip the pages, finger pointing to pictures, her body moving against his as she giggled, pressing closer and circling his chest with her other arm while she reminisced. Sometimes she'd drop her chin to his shoulder and go quiet as the other three shared stories. And all four of them told their tales over photo albums, and they'd done it *for hours.*

Through it, Lexie was having the time of her life and he couldn't say he wasn't interested, seeing the pages turn, seeing their lives in pictures, getting to know her family and, as the photos passed by, watching his wife grow older, mature.

He wasn't surprised to see she was a knockout from age fourteen. She'd always had beauty but also there was no way to miss the promise of what it would be when it ripened. Then the page would turn and he'd see it ripen.

It was exactly what he expected. And he expected this because Rodriguez, who in the beginning with his talent could have any pussy he wanted lie back and spread, knew, no matter the choice, nothing compared to what he had at home.

She didn't hide Rodriguez, quickly turn pages he was in or

skim over his photos, not from Walker, not from her family. That was Lex. Nothing hidden. No bullshit. Rodriguez was a part of her life, their lives and she didn't feel there was a reason to bury him. Walker guessed this was because he *was* buried, literally, and that was enough. He'd been a major component in her life, now he was gone. That was it.

Picture night happened once but if he was not dragging their asses to restaurants, the women in his house could yammer and they did, sitting around the kitchen or on the deck furniture, Lexie sipping beer, her girls sucking back cocktails and, as with the pictures, they did it for hours.

He tried to make a point by sitting in front of a game but not only Lexie but all of them would call out his name or come to the door to the deck, tell him a story, share a joke, tell him what one of them had just said. He didn't have any desire to be in their hen huddle but he couldn't say the four of them weren't fucking funny. They were. Every last one. Including Honey. And the sound of their jabbering and laughter, he had to admit, was far from annoying.

Deep in the second week, Tuku's framed pen-and-ink had been delivered. This night included him and Bessie holding the frame up in various places in the living room while Ella, Honey and Lexie studied it, fingers to faces, heads tipped to the side, uncertain and directing them to move it somewhere else.

Walker tired of this about five seconds in, knowing exactly where he wanted it. Bessie tired of it ten seconds later and started throwing sass. She put up with about fifteen minutes more then announced, "Y'all got two seconds to make up your minds. You don't, I carry this motherfucker to the deck and throw it over the side."

At that point, Walker's patience and politeness ran out. He took over and had the frame mounted over the sofa opposite the fireplace within ten minutes. Bessie approved. Ella and Lexie shared grins. Honey declared she thought it looked better over the fireplace.

On his Thursdays off, when Lexie had to work, he was pressed into sightseeing duties. Hauling those bitches to the Colorado

National Monument the first Thursday, Lexie telling them they simply *could not* return to Texas without seeing it. But when he took them, they liked the look of it and they did drag their asses out of the Cruiser to clatter on their platform heels to a location where he could take their picture with part of the monument in the background. But then they clattered right back. No hiking trail for them, no closer look. Fuck, he wasn't certain Honey could even spell "hiking trail." Then, with uncanny senses, they located a sushi restaurant in Grand Junction like they could sniff the fucker out, dragged him there and spent a whole fucking hour in Enstrom buying enough toffee and chocolate to supply most of Dallas.

His second Thursday, yesterday, was worse because he took them to Aspen. There was shopping in Aspen. This was not good, it was not fun and, as hilarious as those bitches could be, he did not find anything about that day funny.

When he told Lexie about it in bed last night, she'd again laughed herself sick.

He had to say, he loved his wife's laugh, he loved hearing it, but at that time, Walker didn't even crack a smile because he found not one second of his day funny.

He should have known, considering Ella got a wild hair on the previous Sunday, announcing that she *had* to give them a wedding gift. He'd tried to refuse attendance at this event and all four of them had leaned on him. He couldn't bear up, not under Lexie's pleading, so he'd caved and gone. He shouldn't have. For some reason, Lex was in ecstasy (though she repeated over and over, "You shouldn't. We couldn't accept," then she did) when Ella bought them a KitchenAid mixer.

Again, the two remaining sisters went straight into one-upping their mother. This led to Bessie buying them two bags of kitchen shit, more than half of it he didn't even know what the fuck it was and the half of it he did know what it was consisted mostly of bowls and spoons. He didn't think a kitchen needed that many bowls and spoons but, regardless, now they had them. Then they dragged him from the mall into Carnal where Honey added what Lexie called a "crock" to their gray pottery collection as well as a trio of tall candlesticks Lexie arranged on the hearth. He got it when the crock was set on the kitchen counter and filled with her spoons.

It all looked good.

He still didn't have to be there during their purchases.

Even though most of this was a pain in his ass, some of it a serious pain in his ass, he'd be lying if he said on a certain level he didn't enjoy it. And that level was partly about watching his wife with her family, knowing she was happy, watching her spend time with people she loved. But it was also about getting it, why she was loyal to them, why she cared so much about them. Never in his life had he experienced family like that, and it took some time but even from the first they accepted him then they softened toward him then they sucked him in. They were why Lexie was who she was, open, affectionate, touchy, honest, funny and, the longer he was with them, the more of that they treated him to.

And he liked it.

But he also liked that they trailed him and his wife downstairs to the Viper that morning when he was on his way to work in order to give him hugs. Then they wandered to the end of the garage to wave him sleepily away because in an hour they were going to climb into their rental truck and haul their asses home.

And he liked it because he wanted his wife back—selfish but he didn't give a fuck.

And he also wanted unlimited and unencumbered access to his wife's body back.

The stairs led directly to their room, no door. And seeing as this was the case, Lexie wasn't comfortable having sex in their bedroom, telling him she was worried they'd hear. This limited them to the shower, which meant that Ty decreed she'd have two, every day, just like him.

But after two very fucking long weeks, he'd used up his shower creativity and he was done with limits.

And he knew Lexie loved her family but last night, he'd learned she was done too. He'd learned this when he firmly led her to the shower and she'd firmly pulled her hand out of his and walked to the tub. Then she'd filled it. Then she'd led him to it.

He couldn't remember if he'd taken a bath since he was a kid.

He would be taking them in the future.

And his gait quickened because tonight he could fuck his wife in their bed, on the couch, on the fucking stairs if he had a mind to.

And he had a mind to do all three.

So it was time to get his ass home.

He walked out the doors to the gym, which was in Chantelle. It was a haul but it was also a boxer's gym, which meant limited use by women and the women who used it were boxers and there to train, not preen, show off their outfits or find a man who cared about his body who would get them off. He'd heard word there was a gym in Carnal with a personal trainer who could kick ass. He had not tried this because the man's boot camps were co-ed.

This was what he was thinking as he walked out the doors and automatically scanned the parking lot.

And this was what erased from his mind when he saw the pickup. Model a few years old and taken care of. Some upgrades in order to add flash, not too many not because the owner didn't like flash but because he couldn't afford it.

And Walker knew this because the owner was leaning against the driver's-side door. He was Hispanic. And the plates were from Texas.

Fuck!

They locked eyes and Walker held his gaze as he moved to the Viper. The man pushed away from his truck when Walker neared the Snake. Walker looked away to bleep the locks, open the driver's-side door and toss his bag across the driver's seat to the passenger's side. Then he slammed the door, turned and rested back against the car, arms across his chest, legs crossed at his ankles, eyes leveled at the man.

In the past two weeks, they'd had no meeting, but Walker had

had the chance to get a brief from Tate about Angel Peña, though it wasn't thorough. This was because Peña was liked and Tate couldn't dig too deep without pinging on radar. He knew he was a respected cop. He knew he'd had commendations. He knew that Peña considered his occupation a calling, not a job. He knew that Peña's tactics were controversial. And he knew this was overlooked because his close rate on cases was exceptionally high.

Now he saw he was short, Lexie's height, which meant she'd tower over him in her heels. Decent-enough-looking guy but Walker was no woman so he really had no clue. Liked his mama's cooking if the slight gut that protruded over his big belt buckle was anything to go by. Knew to take care of himself anyway because the rest of him was made like a bulldog, strong, tough and bulky. Walker also knew he was a proud Texan as well as a proud Mexican just by the pickup, but the cowboy boots, Wrangler jeans, Western-stitched sports jacket and plaid shirt with those pearl snap buttons told the rest of the story, especially considering his belt buckle had a Mexican flag on it.

He stopped three feet away.

"Tyrell Walker," he stated.

"Detective Angel Peña," Walker replied.

There it was. Neither had the upper hand. Not yet.

Peña's gaze slid to the Viper then back to Walker.

"Nice wheels," he remarked.

Walker did not reply.

Peña held his eyes, surprisingly not uncomfortable with the height difference that was near to a foot. The world did not fit Walker's height or size nor did most of the people in it. He had never had a problem with this. He'd duck his head every once in a while knowing his frame intimidated most men, his bulk made them underestimate his speed, and both (for some you could add his color) made most people, men and women, mistake his intelligence. This put him at a near-constant advantage.

It occurred to him vaguely at that point that Lexie was one of the few women who fit him. Even in bare feet, she was tall for a woman.

But she wore heels almost all the time. He didn't have to bend or stoop as much with his wife.

He liked this too.

But now, he saw that Peña was not intimidated and he also didn't underestimate Walker. He found this surprising and disquieting.

This meant Peña had spent some time digging and he'd dug deep. Walker just had no idea what he'd found.

"Figure," Peña ended their silence, "you know I got an interest in Alexa Berry."

"Walker." His correction was a low, swift, deliberate rumble, and he was shocked as shit to see his response surprised Peña so much it took two seconds for the man to hide it.

"What?" Peña asked softly.

"Walker," he repeated. "Lexie's last name is now Walker."

Peña, face now closed, studied Walker but even with his face closed off, he did it intently.

Walker let him until he was done letting him.

"Got a wife to get home to, Peña. You gonna stare at me much longer?"

Peña blinked. Then he asked quietly, "How is she?"

"She's the wife of a man who doesn't like it much when a man he doesn't know asks how she is."

"That's an interesting response, Tyrell," Peña noted.

Walker did not reply even though he wanted to tell him not to call him Tyrell. His mother called him Tyrell. When his father was pissed, which was often, he called him Tyrell. Therefore no one called him Tyrell.

But he didn't tell him this.

Peña carried on. "She's a friend."

"Now *that's* interesting considering she hasn't mentioned you."

Another score. That one hurt. He thought he factored larger in her life.

"Things she's tryin' to forget, I reckon," Peña guessed inaccurately.

And Walker didn't hesitate to inform him of this fact. "You'd reckon wrong. Lexie doesn't need to forget. She's smart enough to learn the lessons life's got for her, eyes open, no bullshit."

"That may be so but that doesn't mean there aren't things she wants to leave in the past," Peña returned.

"You got one right," Walker told him, his point hard to miss, and he was done so he decided to move them in that direction. "You come all this way for this shit?"

"She's worth the drive *and* the vacation time."

It was a true answer but it was one he didn't want to hear.

Therefore Walker moved. Pushing away from the Snake, he shifted to open the door, again making a point that was hard to miss.

Peña didn't miss it but Peña also wasn't done.

"Win those wheels at a game?" he asked, and Walker slid his eyes to him as he opened the door and started to move around it in order to fold into the car. Peña knew he didn't have a lot of time and kept going. "Know you got the talent not to fuck around. Been years but circles in Dallas still talk about you. Wouldn't sit a game without at least a twenty-five K buy-in."

Walker kept moving.

Peña kept talking. "Makes a man wonder why, you drive a Snake, you sit only high-stakes games, yet over a three-day weekend you'd haul your ass in a fuckin' car across three states to sit a game with four men who, all together, couldn't offer up five K, much less twenty-five each."

Walker stopped, straightened and turned inside the door.

And he did this because Peña had just shown how deep he'd dug.

Walker gave him his attention but nothing more.

"If just for the fuck of it, why didn't you fly?" Peña asked. "You had the cake. Here to LA and back again, sit a table and kill a man… that's a lot to fit in in three days."

Walker didn't respond.

Peña wasn't looking for a response. Peña was happy to deliver a monologue.

"Though you take a flight, they got records. You sit your ass in a car, no one knows."

He paused. Walker gave him nothing so he kept going.

"Couldn't see why it was for the fuck of it either. You don't care the company you keep at a game, that's true enough, but they at least have to bring something to the table."

Walker kept silent.

Peña pressed on. "You sit with men who got tens of thousands of cash and collateral on the line, you walk away a winner, a big winner, every time. Then you sit with men who got shit, who are not known to sit a game of cards, total amateurs, you lose huge? How's that happen?"

Walker didn't move or say a word.

Peña kept going. "Lose so huge, it pisses you off. You, a seasoned player, a seasoned player who had to walk away down from some tables somewhere along the line. You knew the score. Never an incident but you lose to some scumbag drug dealer in LA, you get so pissed, you track his ass down, shoot him four times and a part construction worker, part mechanic smart enough to get himself a Snake is dumb enough to leave his prints at the scene. How's *that* happen?"

Walker turned fully to him and crossed his arms on his chest.

Peña held his gaze.

Then he took a step forward and said quietly, "Got a source says some preliminary witness statements were buried. You know that?"

He didn't. He had no idea. That would have been big, *huge*, years ago. Now it didn't matter.

Therefore, he still didn't speak.

"Conflicting accounts on a variety of things. Your description, the amount you lost at the game, timeline. Seems the witnesses hadn't been thoroughly briefed," Peña dropped that bomb, gave a bit of it away, paused for a reaction then when he didn't get one, he pressed on. "Got their stories straight in the end, though."

Fuck him. *Fuck him.* Under six weeks and Peña got further than Tate. A lot further.

Walker made no reply.

Peña didn't need it. "Two of those men who sat that table with you were CIs to a Detective Chet Palmer, LAPD."

Walker said nothing.

Peña continued, "And Detective Chet Palmer works in a different precinct but still, he's godfather to Gene Fuller's daughter." He held Walker's eyes and kept talking quietly. "You gettin' the connection I'm givin' to you?"

Walker finally spoke. "This is not news."

"Jackson." This time Peña guessed correctly that Tate had uncovered the last part years ago.

Walker didn't confirm. He didn't need to.

"You want real news?" Peña asked.

"If you got it," Walker answered.

Peña studied him and he did this awhile.

Then he laid it out.

"Your gun, the murder weapon, was never recovered."

He ignored the tightening of Walker's jaw at the mention of "his gun," something he knew his way around but he'd never owned until Shift gave him one, and Peña kept going.

"But it didn't disappear. Know this because another dealer done in LA had a ballistics match to that gun. Took me a bit to uncover that, even my source out there balked 'cause that information was buried so deep. I'm sure it won't surprise you that another brother got fingered for that, witnesses, prints at the scene, motive, opportunity, overwhelming evidence even if the murder weapon was never recovered. He was goin' down but he'd been down before. Gang shit. Small time he didn't enjoy. Learned his lesson. Got out. Kept clean." Peña leaned in, lost it for a moment and hissed, "*Volunteered* at the local Boy's Club to keep kids outta gangs." Peña leaned back, sucked in breath to pull it together again before he finished, "Didn't like his time, knew he was facin' more, maybe knew why, definitely knew who he was up against. Wasn't gonna go down and found his way to run away from that forever and he did it hangin' from a beam in his momma's garage."

Walker sucked in breath and looked away. It wasn't the only reaction he exposed. He knew his body expanded because he knew most of his muscles had tightened reflexively.

Another brother down. Fuck.

He forcibly released his muscles and looked back.

"Been busy, Peña," he noted.

"Told you, got an interest in Alexa Berry." When Walker's eyes narrowed he corrected swiftly, "Walker."

Walker made no comment.

Peña still wasn't done. "You copped a plea. Gave you a lotta time to think, I reckon. About what, I don't know. I could guess. Five years of my life rotted away, I know what I would be thinkin'. And, gotta say, Tyrell, wouldn't normally give a fuck what you do. Problem is, what you do won't be what you do. What you do will affect others and not just those who it needs to affect. And that's where I got a problem."

"This is not your business," Walker informed him.

"That's where *you're* wrong," Peña shot back, and Walker misread him, partially.

"My garage where she parks her Charger, Peña. My bed she's sleepin' in. The bouquet of flowers I bought her before I put my ring on her finger that she tore up and pressed the petals between two squares of glass and she hung that shit in *my* window in the kitchen so she can see them when she does the dishes. This means I am not wrong."

He'd scored again. This hurt worse and Peña didn't hide it.

But he denied it. "You don't get where I'm comin' from."

"I get you want a piece of my wife. What you need to get is every inch of her is mine." He leaned in. "*Every* inch. You don't get a piece of her." He leaned back. "No one does. No one but me."

"Like I said, you don't get where I'm comin' from."

Fuck, but he wanted to be home with his fucking wife.

Therefore, to get this done, he invited, "Educate me."

"I got an interest in Alexa Berry Walker, Tyrell, but I'm also a cop. You are not my brother. I do not know you. I do not give a fuck about you. What I *do* give a fuck about is what's goin' on in your head. And I also give a fuck about brothers goin' down in two states in two ways neither of them fuckin' good for shit they did...not...do."

Now, that...*that* surprised the fuck out of him.

He didn't give it away. He did nothing but stare.

Peña put his cards on the table.

"So, the reason I'm here is for Lexie. The reason I'm here is because, I heard she was hitchin' herself to you, I got interested and what I found got me more interested and that more interested got me more but in the end led to nothin' but questions, questions without answers. So now another reason why I'm here is because I'm lookin' for answers. And last, the reason I'm here, right now in this parking lot with you, is to warn you to remember what you got in your garage and hangin' in your kitchen window and mostly in your bed. And it's also to give you a heads-up that I'm in town, why I'm in town and whatever the fuck you're plannin', so I don't screw you, you gotta know I am."

And again, that surprised the fuck out of him.

"You're doin' Lexie a favor," he said quietly.

"Yeah, it was just for Lexie until you opened, Tyrell. I still don't give a fuck about you but you made it pretty fuckin' clear you give a fuck about her, and I spent years watchin' her be with a man who didn't so, in a roundabout way, I'm also doin' it for you."

Jesus.

"Peña," he felt it necessary to warn, "you do not know what you're up against."

"Tyrell," Peña fired back, "I know exactly the filth I'm up against. You got your color. I got my own so *I* know. And I figure, with Jackson nosin' around, he's given you the heads-up so you know I ain't stupid and, I'll confirm, I ain't. I figure you aren't either but I'll still remind you not to be and I'll do it because of where her Charger is, what bed she sleeps in and those petals she stares at doin' the dishes. I like my life so I don't waste it so I won't waste it tryin' to talk you out of whatever you're gonna do. But I'll remind you to think of those three things you got that other men would kill to have and I'll advise you that someone like me can get a fuckuva lot further in this mission than someone like you."

"You're from Texas," Walker reminded him.

"A cop's a cop, Tyrell, in Texas, in California, in Colorado or on the moon," Peña returned.

Walker stared at him. This wasn't true. Those boys pissed all over their patches, did it regularly so no one could mistake the smell and, no matter you carried a badge or not, they let in only who they wanted to let in.

Then again, what Tate said about this guy's tactics, he had balls, who knew what he could do?

Finally, he said, "No one calls me Tyrell."

Peña stared at him. Then he grinned.

His grin died and he asked quietly, "How's she doin'?"

"Ella, Bess and Honey just left after spendin' two weeks with us," Walker answered.

"Jesus," Peña muttered. "So she's happy as fuck but you've been in hell."

Yeah, he made it his business to know Lexie.

"Somethin' like that," he muttered back.

Peña hesitated. Then he pushed it.

"She make a beautiful bride?"

Fuck.

And fuck him. He gave it to the bastard.

"Magnificent."

Peña nodded, but he'd asked a question the answer he already knew.

Walker was now officially done.

"They burn you, I don't know you but, more importantly, Lex doesn't."

"I told you, I ain't stupid."

"And I'm tellin' you, you stick your nose in this, it blows back on my wife, ex-con versus cop or not, you got a problem. Am I understood?"

Peña held his gaze. Then he didn't grin. He smiled.

Then he whispered, "Waited a long time to see that woman with a man who gave a fuck. I see you haven't missed I wanted to be that man. What you don't know is, the kind of interest I have in Alexa Berry Walker, I don't care who it is just as long as he does."

"Then we got somethin' in common, 'cept, of course, I'm that man," Walker replied.

Peña nodded on another smile.

No hard feelings.

"Stay sharp," Walker told him, turning and folding into the Viper.

"Same to you," Peña replied, and Walker slammed the door.

He fired up, pulled out of his spot, glanced at Peña strolling back to his pickup and hoped to Christ the man knew what he was doing.

Then he put her in first and headed the fuck home.

* * *

Walker hit the top of the steps but he heard the music before he hit the utility room. Mood music. Alicia Keys. Their wedding presents from Lexie's family were definitely more for Lexie than for Walker, but the shopping expedition had one plus for him. Lexie hit a record store and stocked up on decent music. And it wasn't just so her family would have the soundtrack to their visit they enjoyed. It was for him.

Another way she gave.

He rounded the railing and dropped his workout bag there, looking first to the kitchen.

Around this time of day, she'd be thinking about food but mostly she knew his schedule and he knew she wanted to be close when he arrived home so she could greet him, something she always did, pressing into him and tipping her head back for a kiss. This was whether he came back from the garage or the gym, sweaty or not, his woman didn't care.

And another way she gave.

She wasn't in the kitchen so he looked to the second place she usually was, thinking he liked their deck furniture, it was the shit and it looked good. But it cost a fucking whack. He didn't mind the money, never did if it was nice shit and looked good.

But he minded it even less because she used it all the time.

When her family was there, they ate out on the back deck. Before they came, his days off, he noticed she had her breakfast and coffee out there and she did it like she did it all the time so he knew she did it all the time. Other times, she'd wander out there with her Kindle to read or her iPod to listen to while she stared at the view. Colorado was new to her, she liked it. She liked their view and she gave it her time, as much as she could when she wasn't giving that time to him.

So he turned his head to look at the deck and froze solid.

This was because she was curled in the loveseat, legs bent and fallen to the side, heels tucked close to her ass, beer in hand resting on the side of her thigh, head thrown back because she was laughing.

And stretched opposite her in that loveseat was an enormous black man who was turned away from Walker, in profile but Walker could see him smiling.

Lexie righted her head, caught sight of him, her face grew bright and she aimed a shaft of her blinding light right at him as she cried, "Ty! Look who's here!"

Then, his fucking wife, total fucking goof, like an excited teenager bolted up to her feet on the loveseat, walked to the footstool and hopped down, running through the open door to him as he forced himself unstuck and walked toward her.

In her excitement, she hit him on the fly, her soft body colliding with his, her arms, even with one hand holding a beer bottle, sliding around him, her feet bare necessitating her bending her head way back to beam her smile at him.

"Julius!" she declared elatedly yet unnecessarily.

He looked down at her face then lifted his head to see Julius had angled out of the loveseat and was grinning at him as he sauntered into the house.

Such was their bond, anytime, anywhere, it was safe to say he would be happy to see Julius Champion. Happier by far to see him for the first time wearing faded jeans, a tee and breathing free.

Except *that* time.

He tipped his head back down and muttered, "Kiss, mama."

Her smile went brighter, if that could fucking be believed, and she went up on her toes. He bent low and touched his mouth to hers as her arms gave him a squeeze. When he lifted his head, she let him go, took a step away and he turned to Julius who had made it close and also had a beer in his hand. He extended his other one and Walker took it.

"Walk," he muttered as they gripped and locked eyes, no shaking, no hug, the strength of the grip and the communication through their eyes was all they needed.

"Champ," Walker muttered back.

Julius grinned. Walker grinned back.

"Oh shit, I'm gonna cry," Lexie announced, and the men let go and both looked to her to see she did look like she was going to cry.

"Get a handle on it, Lex," he murmured, still grinning.

She nodded and visibly deep breathed, whispering, "Right. Right."

Walker shook his head and looked to Julius to see Julius was now smiling at Lexie.

"Okay!" she announced on a clap, and Walker looked back at her. "Time for dinner!" Her eyes came to him. "You doing a shake, honey, or are you going to eat with me and Julius?"

"Powder and water then I'll eat with you," Walker answered.

"Excellent!" she approved, tossed a dazzling smile to both of them, turned and headed to the kitchen.

Walker looked back at Julius. "Gonna hit the shower, brother. Be right back."

Julius jerked up his chin and replied, "I'll keep your woman company while you're gone."

Walker bet he would. He had three women, each constant, each committed, each had been in his life for years but that didn't mean he wasn't still recruiting. But Walker also knew he'd try nothing with Lexie. That said, he was not a man who wouldn't take an opportunity to enjoy a beautiful woman even though he knew it was look but don't touch.

Walker headed to the stairs. Julius headed to the kitchen.

He was nearly done in the shower when she came in. He watched through the glass as she put the big plastic cup with the screw-on lid filled with protein powder mixed with water on the vanity. Her eyes came to him before she left then she took herself four feet out of the way just to press her hand flat to the glass and give him another smile.

No physical connection through that glass but a connection, the kind of shit she did all the time. The smile was brilliant. She was pleased as fuck for him his friend was there. The protein drink delivered was yet another way she gave. She did that all the time too, mix him a drink or blend him a shake, and it was sitting on the vanity by the time he got out if she wasn't in the shower with him.

She waited for it. He gave it to her, jerking up his chin then, with no words, she headed back out.

After his shower he dressed in track pants and a white tank, sucking back the drink as he headed to the stairs. Rounding the railing on the second-story landing to make it to the mouth of the stairs down to the first level, his eyes hit the office. Then, even wanting to get to his woman and Julius, his feet moved him to the office door.

Lexie didn't have a lot of shit. Most of her furniture was still in her apartment in Dallas that Honey had moved into. And she didn't unpack everything when it arrived. Clothes, shoes, jewelry, shit like that. A couple of frames of her girls on the mantel downstairs. She'd printed, framed and put the photo of them at The Rooster in their bedroom. But she'd set up her computer in the office, added a few more frames from home, mounted an unusual print that he liked at the back wall, put her stationery, address book and other shit like that in the drawers of the desk.

He wandered to the right bedroom where they put her bedroom furniture from Dallas. Queen-size bed with feminine sheets and comforter, white background with stark swirls of green stems leading to big flowers of multiple shades of blue and pink. Feminine but good taste. Pure Lexie. One nightstand with lamp. A dresser. More prints on the wall. A guest room, where Ella slept. Now Julius's black leather duffel was sitting on the floor by the closet.

He wandered to the other bedroom. She still had some boxes piled against the wall but she'd made this her room. A big table with plastic, multi-drawered organizers on top and baskets filled with craft shit. Some shelves with more craft stuff. A sewing machine with a chair in front of it. An armchair in the corner with a standing lamp beside it where she could work comfortably.

Surprised the fuck out of him but his wife was craftsy. It wasn't just the petals in the window. She got that sewing machine set up straight off and, even with her girls there, when he was at work one day, he came home and they had huge new toss pillows on the couch. He liked them, the fabric was nice, but they were comfortable as all hell and there were a shitload of them he could shove behind him when he was watching a game.

He walked out and down the stairs, seeing Tuku's pen-and-ink on the wall as he moved. The thick matte black frame was the shit. The work was huge. He'd only had a segment of it inked on his body because he'd need four bodies his size to get it all on. It was good to see it displayed again, every time his eyes caught it, and it was hard to miss, it reminded him of Tuku, good memories. He'd been stunned when Lexie took him to the frame shop, felt that thing pierce the left side of his chest, sharper, the pain passing exquisite to be something he didn't know, never experienced. But he knew he'd never forget that feeling or that moment. Not in his life.

All this had hit him when it happened, Lexie making his house their home, never knowing when he walked in what would be added, what she'd give him next but it hit him differently this time with his brother there, seeing through Julius's eyes his house, his life, the flowered sheets he'd sleep on in the guest room.

His wife.

And when it hit him then, something settled in Walker. Settled deep. Something weighty but not heavy. Something warm. Something welcome.

This was on his mind as he took a swallow of his drink, hit the bottom of the stairs and turned to see Lexie at the stove, Julius at a stool at the island, both of them talking with relaxed faces, Julius already at home because Lexie made him feel that way. A huge man. A huge black man. A huge black ex-con, at home, relaxed, welcome because Lexie made him feel that way.

Her eyes came to him then her head turned to him.

"Go, commune with your brother." She jerked her head to the front deck. "I'll finish this and we'll eat at the outside table."

"You kickin' me out, baby doll?" Julius asked, and Lexie twisted to grin at him.

"I'm giving you time with Ty so you can talk about how great my ass is," she returned.

Julius chuckled and Walker moved to his wife.

He bent to kiss her hair and muttered, "Legs, Lex. Your ass is fine but you got fuckin' great legs. So long, wrap around my back twice."

She tipped her head way back and caught his eyes then leaned around him so she could roll hers at Julius.

His friend chuckled again.

Walker turned away from his woman and looked to Julius. Then he motioned outside with his head before he moved that way, Julius shifting off the stool and following.

They settled at the railing beside one of Lexie's flourishing pots of flowers.

"Good to see you, brother," Walker whispered.

"Good to be seen," Julius whispered back.

"All good?" Walker asked.

"Yeah. My bitches, though, all over me. I'm here to get a break. Got out, all three of them fell on my dick. They nearly killed me."

This was bullshit. By Julius's reports, all three gave superior head and one of them had awesome command of her kegel muscles. He'd served a nickel too and was just as ready as Walker to get himself some, and by some Walker meant as much as Julius could get.

No, Julius was here because he was checking on things that couldn't be checked on over the phone, not to Julius's satisfaction.

Walker didn't call him on it. Instead, he finished his drink, twisted and set the cup on the railing away from him.

When he turned back, Julius was looking into the house. He felt Walker's eyes and he looked to him.

"Okay, Walk..." He paused then said slow, "Shee-it. What the fuck?"

Walker felt his lips twitch.

Then he told him, "Walked outta that hole straight to a miracle."

"You can say that again, my man, fuck me. Believe in God but only 'bout two hours ago met my first angel walkin' on earth."

"Lexie's a lot of things, all of them good, but don't think God makes angels like that."

Julius's midnight face split into a huge white smile.

"I like that," he muttered.

"So do I. Wildcat," Walker replied, and Julius's smile got bigger.

Then some of the white died before he remarked, "Good for you. Happy for you. You deserve a miracle."

Walker didn't respond.

Julius made an accurate guess. "This ain't play."

Walker shook his head.

Julius went on, "How long did it take you to maneuver that?"

"Too long, over a week."

Julius blinked. "That it?"

"Felt like fifty years."

Julius threw his head back and boomed with laughter. Walker grinned at him while he did.

Then, still chuckling, he caught Walker's eyes. "Pretty pussy, sweet pussy, classy pussy like that, ex-con, took you a week. Fuck me. I can work it, brother, but even me, it'd take at least a month."

Walker didn't reply.

Julius's gaze went intense. "How real is this?"

"Real," Walker answered firmly, and Julius tipped up his chin.

"Real for her. That bitch in there is livin' the dream. I knocked on the door, fuckin' *me*, big black man, her a white woman in a sweet crib in the middle of fuckin' nowhere in the goddamn mountains. She took one look at me when she opened the door, knew exactly who I was and the bitch flipped. Acted like I just got home from bein' at war. She refused to call you, wanted me to be a surprise. Even made me go out and move my ride so you wouldn't see it when you got home."

No surprise. That was Lexie.

Julius carried on, "Spent two hours drinkin' beer with her and listenin' about all the shit you been doin'. She made it sound like, you got home from the gym, you'd do it flyin' through the air."

No surprise with that either. That was also Lexie. But it didn't mean hearing that from Julius didn't feel really fucking good.

Julius studied him. Then he asked softly, "It that real for you?"

"Look around, Champ, everything you see is solid. How much more real can it get?"

Julius again studied him. Then he shook his head.

Then he muttered, "Jesus, brother," he looked to the view and swallowed before he repeated a whispered, "Jesus."

This was not a surprise either. His friend felt relief, overwhelmed by it. Julius had been worried. Walker's state of mind the day he left prison, anyone who gave a shit would be. Julius walked out to three women, two children and a big family, all of whom gave a shit. They did it before he went down and they stuck by him while he did his time.

Walker walked in in chains for a crime he didn't commit and walked out to none of that and he walked out with vengeance on his mind.

"I'm good, Champ," Walker said quietly and got his friend's eyes.

"You let her in?"

Walker nodded.

"How far in?" Julius went on.

"She's in," Walker replied.

"How far?" Julius pushed.

"She's in," he repeated.

"How far?" Julius repeated too.

Walker didn't speak.

"You know what I'm askin' you, Walk," Julius told him, and he did know.

"Her life has not been a fairy tale either. You've spent time with her, I told you, you'd be shocked as shit what she's been through. We've both got our demons. We've both shared."

"That woman takes one look at you, brother, she'll know you can wrestle her demons. You give her the opportunity to do the same for you?"

Fuck. Not this shit again.

"It hasn't been two months," he evaded.

"You of all brothers know there is no fuckin' time like the present."

This was true but he was done so he shared because, as he knew, if he didn't, Julius wouldn't let up.

"She's in," he said low. "She knows what was done to me. She was waitin' for me outside of prison and we started on a deal. She had bad shit in her life, under a piece of shit's thumb. I get her outta that, she gives me what I need. A week later, I gave it all to her and gave her the choice to walk out the door. She didn't take it. She took my back. Her decision. Thirty K in diamonds, fifty K in cash I was offerin' her for the time she spent with me, and that time was just over a week. She didn't take that shot. She stayed then made a new deal. Deck furniture out of her fifty K, the rest she donates to the cause. Is that in enough for you?"

Instantly, Julius grinned.

Then he replied, "Yeah."

"Thrilled, Champ," Walker muttered, looking to the view and suddenly needing a beer.

Julius chuckled.

Then he spoke again and Walker looked back to him. "Now, a brief."

"Only got so much good luck," Walker replied, saying it all in six words. Julius got it and Julius nodded.

"Your brother fucked you," he guessed accurately, knowing the entirety of Walker's plan, knowing his first move was Dewey, having heard all about Dewey.

"Just found out tonight," Walker confirmed.

"Not unexpected," Julius muttered, turning his head to the view.

"Still fuckin' frustrating," Walker replied, also looking at the view but shifting his body to it, bending and resting on his crossed forearms on the railing.

"You know, got no contacts in Colorado," Julius stated, also shifting and assuming Walker's position at the railing. "That don't mean I didn't ask around when I got out."

"You connect?" Walker asked quietly.

"Fuck yeah."

"You mobilize?"

"Why you think I'm here?" Julius asked back. "Had no idea the pretty face who'd keep me company and sure as fuck didn't haul my ass across three states to see your face."

That was bullshit. So much of it, Walker had to fight back a smile.

Then he nodded and asked, “How long you stayin’?”

“Long enough to network and get my ass back before my parole officer knows I’m in Colorado.”

Walker nodded again and whispered, “Grateful, man. Dewey fuckin’ me, need a new avenue.”

“Well, you got it.”

Walker drew in breath, held it and let it go. He didn’t say anything and Julius didn’t expect him to say anything. Julius wasn’t doing anything that Walker would not do for Julius if he needed it. It was just that Walker needed it.

Still, that didn’t mean he wasn’t grateful. He just didn’t have to say it.

Julius knew.

Time passed as they studied the landscape.

Then Walker remarked, “Had an interesting development tonight.”

“Yeah?”

He straightened and turned, hip to the railing, eyes sliding into the house. Lexie was heading out to the back deck carrying plates on top of which was cutlery. They were close to dinner.

So he talked, low and swift as Julius listened, eyes to the view, forearms to the railing, telling his friend about Detective Angel Peña.

When he was done, he looked back into the house to see Lexie filling serving plates. Family style. As big of an event as she could make it without time to prepare. None of that business of the men filling their plates from pots and skillets. They were going to sit down and spend a while, telling Julius, as best she could, he was welcome company, his visit an event to celebrate.

Pure Lexie.

Walker looked down at his leaning friend noting the silence had lingered.

Then Julius ended it.

“That *is* an interesting development.”

“Yep.”

"You trust this guy?" Julius asked.

"Known him ten minutes, know he wants in my wife's pants and he wants that bad. Those two things are not conducive to me trusting him." He paused then went on, "Still, I do."

"Different," Julius muttered. "Name clear. Restitution."

"Don't give a shit about that."

Julius turned his head and looked up at Walker. "You should."

"Doesn't bring back five years."

"No," Julius agreed. "But the real you got that's solid and races to you practically the minute you get home, presses close even though you're still wet with sweat from the gym like she don't even notice, your name clear, restitution is a gift for her. Gives back a little of what she's givin' you."

"She didn't do five years," Walker replied.

"No," Julius again agreed and looked back to the view.

"She's with me on this, brother," Walker stated quietly.

"So am I," Julius returned just as quietly. "Whatever you do, I'm with you. You don't wanna sit back and hope this brown boy from Texas can make another miracle for you, I don't blame you. I'm just sayin'."

"I hear you," Walker whispered.

He'd just said the last word when they heard, "All right boys, soup's on," and they both turned to see Lexie standing in the opened door. "Give me drink orders and head out to the back deck. Serve it up. It's waiting."

Walker pushed away from the railing, feeling Julius follow him.

"Beer, babe," he said, moving to her.

She nodded on a grin up at him then her eyes moved beyond him to Julius. "You need a refresh?"

"Yeah, woman," Julius replied.

She grinned at him, turned and lifted her face when Walker got close. He gave her what she didn't verbally ask for but he knew she wanted, bent and touched his mouth to hers.

Then he moved beyond her into the house.

Julius followed.

When he hit kitchen, he looked back to see she was returning to the house after collecting his cup and Julius's empty.

And seeing that, Julius's words hit his brain.

Gives back a little of what she's givin' you.

Fuck.

He set it aside and walked out to the back deck to see she'd put out placemats, cloth napkins, plates, cutlery and she'd lit little, squat candles around the base of the umbrella. Some of these were recent additions she'd bought when she was with her girls, getting it in order to make a nicer table.

And there was also the food, fried pork chops, mashed potatoes, gravy, greens and rolls.

A celebration for Julius, the best she could do with no notice and it was obviously still really fucking good.

Gives back a little of what she's givin' you.

Fuck.

He again put that aside and sat, Julius sat opposite and Lexie came out with three beers, announcing, "Apple pie and ice cream after dinner. It's a frozen one but it's a good one." Her eyes came to Walker and she gave him a smile. "Luckily, went to the store on my way home from the salon before Julius showed." She sat between them and her eyes went to Julius. "He works out loads but my man has got a sweet tooth. Can't keep stocked."

"Not big on desserts inside," Julius told her as a joke but saw his mistake immediately when the shadow crossed Lexie's face. Therefore he instantly muttered, "Sorry, baby doll."

She pushed through it, declaring, "That's why I keep stocked."

Julius studied her a moment before he grinned.

Walker let him have her return smile before he shot his hand out, caught his wife behind the neck and pulled her to him. Her head turned as he moved her and he caught her mouth just in time. No touch, he wanted a taste and the minute he started opening his lips, she felt it, opened hers and gave him one. He touched the tip of his tongue to hers and let her go.

Her smile for him was a fuckuva lot better.

Then he grabbed the platter of pork chops and handed it across to his brother.

* * *

Walker slid his hand from his wife's hip, over her ass, down her spine to the middle of her back and pressed in. He didn't have to press hard. She gave him what he wanted instantly, her back arched, her arms slid out in front of her, her torso pressed into the bed and her ass tipped higher toward the ceiling, allowing him deeper access.

Yeah, she offered her pussy any way he wanted, not even a noise of protest.

Lexie was on her knees, those knees at the edge of the bed. He was on his feet beside it, powering inside her, rough, hard, nearly brutal. He hadn't had this for two weeks, he was taking it and there she was in front of him, his wildcat, so fucking wet she was drenched, so tight, so sweet, loving every second of it.

He knew this to be true when the sweet, sexy noises she was making changed, went from pleasure to desperation. She was close, it was almost on her.

He pulled out and instantly her head flew back, her neck twisting at the same time.

"Don't stop, baby," she whispered, that same desperation in her tone.

He bent forward, his hand in her back slid around her ribs to the front. He pulled her up and turned her to face him, his arm around her back now going down over her ass. He lifted her up and her arms circled his shoulders, her head tipped down, her mouth finding his, her tongue sliding inside.

He put a knee to the bed, her legs circled his hips, the other knee went in and once he was in, he fell forward, taking her to her back. Then, their mouths still connected, their tongues tangled, he surged back inside.

He lost her mouth when her neck arched.

Fuck, but his wife liked his cock.

He got up on a forearm in the bed, tipped his body slightly to the side and kept thrusting deep and hard, his eyes on her, his other hand gliding up her body to wrap around the side of her neck. Her head righted and her eyes found his.

No words, he didn't like them when he had his cock buried deep in wet pussy, she didn't need them. During sex or not, her eyes spoke for her.

And he liked what they were saying.

So his fingers dug gently into her neck as he tilted his hips and powered back in, finding her sweet spot, giving it to her and she took it. Her back arching, her arm behind his back flexing, her legs circling his hips tightening, her other hand flying to his wrist at her neck and holding on tight, she gasped first, deep, audible. Then came the loud moan and then the whimper.

He dropped to her, gave her his weight and grasped her hips, yanking her down on his cock as he drove up inside her, near savage. He was heavy. He knew it, felt and heard her breath stay labored and not just with sex. But she'd give him this. She'd done it before. She'd hold her breath until she passed out, take his cock no matter how hard he gave it to her, hold him tight like she was just then, all of this to tell him he could have what he wanted how he wanted it.

But he never did it unless he was close.

And he was close.

Then he was there. Ramming so hard and deep, she cried out, he planted himself to the root and came.

The instant he could, he took away his weight but stayed rooted and covering her.

He gave it a minute before he lifted his head to look down at her. When he did, one of her arms went from around his shoulders so she could cup his cheek, her hand shifting, her thumb sliding over the scar at his eyebrow and down to the smaller one under his eye. She did this often too, ever since he'd whispered to her one night in the dark that his mother gave him that scar by throwing a glass at him when he was nine. A glass he'd left in the living room, something she didn't like, a glass that broke on his face. A miracle it didn't do worse damage, he'd told her.

Lexie didn't agree. She saw no miracle at work in that scar, and she touched it like she could make it go away then, when her thumb moved and it hadn't disappeared, the specter of disappointment that she hadn't succeeded in erasing the physical manifestation of this memory shadowed her face before she fought it back.

He watched that specter glide through and disappear.

Gives back a little of what she's givin' you.

She was on her back in their bed for him. No less uncomfortable that it was Julius a stairway away and not Ella, he told her he was done with bathroom sex and she objected no further. Though he promised her he'd asked Julius to make certain he closed his door, he couldn't know if Julius had complied. She still gave it to him like he wanted it.

Gives back a little of what she's givin' you.

Fuck.

He should tell her about Peña, open that option to her, discuss their future and how he should play it. He knew it. Lying on top of her, still inside her, her hand still at his face, her eyes sweet on him through the moonlight, he knew it.

But he wasn't going to.

Instead, he whispered, "You took my cock hard, baby. I hurt you?"

Her lips tipped up at the ends and she shook her head.

Yeah, she got off on it.

He grinned at her.

"Missed our bed," she whispered back.

He knew that. She'd been creative, creative enough he knew she was storing that shit up. It had built so high, she couldn't contain it and unleashed it all at once. That was why he gave it to her so hard, because she spent some time and effort working him up.

"Yeah," he replied.

Her hand left his face so her arm could circle his shoulders and both arms gave him a squeeze.

"I like Julius," she murmured.

"Good," he murmured back.

Her eyes went soft and they did that often but not that way. That was new. And it settled in the way he'd felt earlier. It was weighty but not heavy. Warm. Welcome. Deep.

"What's on your mind, mama?"

"That I like it when you call me 'mama,'" she lied instantly.

He shook his head.

"Just called you that, Lex, so that wasn't on your mind," he replied softly.

She sucked in breath. Then, always putting herself out there for him, even at the beginning, she didn't do anything different now and said, "Lived under a shadow one way or another all my life. Now it's bright. Even at night. Not used to it and sometimes it hits me. That's what was on my mind."

There it was again. That thing settling, welcome, warm and deep.

He bent his head and touched his forehead to hers briefly before lifting it up and pulling out.

"Get cleaned up, baby," he muttered, and rolled off her.

She rolled with him, shoved her face in his neck a moment, kissing him there then scooted off the bed.

He got in it.

She did her business in the bathroom, came out and joined him. They'd fucked without the lights on for once but the moonlight still shone through the windows. Still, he didn't see that she got in bed without tagging her panties and tugging them on, he heard it.

That meant Walker was grinning at the ceiling as she slid across the bed and curled around him.

His wildcat was far from done.

Moments passed and he waited for it.

She gave it to him.

"Honey?" she called.

"Yeah."

Her arm around his gut gave him a squeeze. "You tired?"

"Mama, just fucked you hard."

Her body slumped into his side and she whispered, "Oh."

He grinned at the ceiling again.

Then he said, "Doesn't take a lotta energy to eat you, though."

She shifted restlessly against him.

She liked that. Wanted it. Fucking wildcat.

Walker turned into her and found her mouth in the dark. It wasn't hard to find. She'd tipped her head back to offer it to him.

He didn't kiss her. He spoke. "On your back, Lexie, and spread for me."

"Okay," she whispered against his lips.

She got to her back and spread for him.

Then Walker ate his wife and then he fucked her again.

After they were done, she got back to bed from the bathroom and again didn't tug up her panties before she did it but this time not because she wanted another round. This time, because she was out the minute her cheek hit his shoulder.

Five minutes later, she rolled, he rolled with her and he was out the minute her body settled into the curve of his.

And from her leaving him to go to the bathroom to Walker falling asleep, not once did he think of the bars, of the smells or of the feel of the institution. All that shit was gone in a way he didn't even notice that it was.

And it was unfortunate he didn't notice because, if he did, he'd have realized Lexie gave that to him too.

And if he'd realized this, the next day he wouldn't have done what he would do.

CHAPTER THIRTEEN

An Hour

"What do you think?" I asked Dominic as I showed him the flyer I'd painstakingly crafted on software I'd never used before, considering my skills with computers were limited to e-mail, Internet shopping, Facebook, downloading e-books on my reader and looking up weather and movie times.

In other words, working on it between taking phone calls, ringing up services and purchases, dusting and restocking shelves, assuring every exiting customer that they looked *fabulous*, the flyer took me five days.

And the flyer was important. It announced the soon-to-be new services Dominic's spa was offering, making his spa that was really a salon into an actual spa.

Therefore I wanted it to be right but knew it wasn't.

"I *love* it!" he cried, snatching the flyer out of my hand to examine it closer.

Perhaps I was wrong.

"You do?" I asked, thinking it looked what it was, like a blind six-year-old with learning difficulties designed it.

"It's *brilliant*!" Dominic exclaimed then shoved it back in my hand and looked at me. "Print out fifty. I'll send Daniel out with Blu-Tack, a stapler and a mission."

I grinned at him. He grinned back then his eyes slid over my shoulder to the front window and narrowed.

"Shit! Shit! On a Saturday," he snapped then hissed, "Figures."

I turned my head to see what he was looking at but couldn't see anything but a figure moving at the window behind the blinds that were partially closed against the heat of the sun.

He went on, "Never calls for an appointment. Thinks she owns the town, I swear. She always waltzes in here and thinks I can do her walk-in. Do I *look* like a stylist who accepts walk-ins? Uh… *no*."

The door opened. The figure that was obscured by the blinds moved through the door and Misty Keaton walked in.

I froze.

Shit. Shit. Fucking *shit*.

"Misty!" Dominic cried as if she was his bestest best high school friend who he hadn't seen since they got shitfaced at their graduation party and they'd just locked eyes at their twenty-five-year reunion and he had not been bitching about her five seconds earlier.

But Misty was frozen too, her eyes on me. Clearly, she had no idea I worked there.

I came unlocked first and moved to the reception desk, not taking my eyes off her, my mind filled with options on how to play this. So many of them, I couldn't get a lock on a single one and all the while I moved I felt Dominic follow.

"Long time, no see, darling. What brings you to Dominic's House of Eternal Beauty?" Dominic asked Misty. (This wasn't actually the name of the salon, it was called Carnal Spa, but Dominic referred to it by different, inventive, hilarious names all the time.)

Her body jerked and she hesitantly moved to the high front of the receptionist desk.

"Uh, here to see if you can fit me in, Dominic," she said softly, her eyes shifting back and forth between Dominic and me. She stopped in front of the desk and locked on Dominic. Sucking in breath, she gave him a shaky smile and finished, "Emergency procedure."

She was nervous. And she was nervous because of me.

She should be. She knew I knew what she did. She knew I was standing there wanting to tear her hair out, scratch her eyes out and take her to the ground, kick her in the stomach and spit on her when she was down (amongst other things).

Unfortunately, for Ty, I could not do that.

Fortunately, she didn't know that.

My eyes narrowed on her. Like she felt it, her eyes slid to me and I was pleased to see her face pale. Then they shot back to Dominic when he spoke.

"Girl, you *know* I love to have my hands in your hair. But I got a one o'clock half highlight and cut and while she's cookin', one of my sweet little blue hairs is comin' in for a set. My afternoon is *all decked out.* Kayeleen's on lunch but, she gets back, her afternoon is full too. We can't help you out. Make an appointment. I think I got an opening late the week after next."

"But the thing I need my touch-up for is Tuesday night," she told him.

"Sorry, precious, no can do," Dominic replied, shaking his head. Her eyes slid to me and back to Dominic, her mouth working with indecision and I'd know why when she spoke again.

"Dominic, this is a big deal for Chace. He told me a while ago and I clean forgot about it. And you know he's not a man who likes roots," she admitted softly.

Good. Chace was going to get pissed at his wife for being a moron.

Good again. It was clear by the way she said it, she was a moron often and Chace didn't like it. The worried look in her eyes said he also didn't mind telling her.

And good yet again. It was clearly not all fun and games in the Keaton household.

And one last, big, fucking good. She *did* have roots. That blonde was *way* fake. I liked that.

All this made me feel better. *Tons* better.

My eyes unnarrowed and I felt my lips tip up.

"Sorry, darling. It's impossible today," Dominic told her.

"Well, can you squeeze me in sometime Tuesday?" she asked Dominic and, now feeling helpful, I moved to the schedule book, flipping it open and turning pages.

"Let me see…" I entered the conversation, scanning the scribbles on Dominic's columns as well as Kayeleen's. Then I looked at Misty. "Sorry, babe. Nothing open. All booked up." I flipped the page then another then another and kept going until I was two weeks out and told her, "Got an opening two weeks Thursday. Two o'clock. That good for you?"

She stared at me. Then she whispered cautiously, "I need it Tuesday. Can you move someone around?"

"Nope," Dominic answered for me, and her eyes went to him. "Tell you what, my lovely, couple places in Chantelle, they do decent work. Maybe they can fit you in. Lexie here will book you now, though, so if they can't, I can take you in a couple of weeks. You just call, you get in in Chantelle."

"Everyone in Carnal gets their hair done by you or Kayeleen. I can't go to Chantelle," she told him.

"Precious, listen," Dominic returned, his voice getting tight. He was losing patience. "I'd love to help you but I've said I can't and I can't. Sorry your man isn't gonna be happy but, Misty, I told you before, you need me, you call two, three weeks in advance. I got a bunch of biker bitches who have standing appointments. They do *not* change. And you do *not* ask those bitches to change. Now, you work with Lexie here, get yourself a standing appointment so you can avoid *dis*appointment. You can't get in at Chantelle, go to the drugstore, buy a bottle and I'll sort out the damage when you get in."

The bell over the door went, my eyes moved to it and Dominic kept talking.

"There she is, my one o'clock. Hello you!" he called, then back to Misty he said, "Lexie will set you up. Enjoy Chace's thing, darling." Then to his customer, "Get over here, gorgeous. Let's touch up that beauty."

And he bustled away as his biker babe client moved toward him while eyeing Misty with unconcealed disdain at the same time eyeing me with unconcealed curiosity.

I ignored this, settled in my roller chair and grabbed a gel pen with a fine tip and flowers printed on the sides of it that wrote in purple ink, the only thing in Dominic's pen holder, which also happened to be purple. As was much of the interior of the salon not to mention the sign outside. But the pen holder also had glittered white butterflies on it (as did the outside sign).

I pulled off the cap and positioned the tip on the schedule book.

"So," I said, smiling brightly up at bitch-face Misty. "Two weeks Thursday? Two o'clock?"

Her eyes slid down to me. "Uh…"

"Then standing appointment every six weeks?" I asked.

"Um…" she mumbled.

I tipped my head to the side.

She bit her lip.

"Thursday? Two weeks? Two o'clock?" I prompted.

"I, uh…okay," she said.

"Excellent." I bent my head and wrote her name in, missing out the "bitch-face" part (for obvious reasons). Once done, I looked back at her, still smiling and asked, "Does Dominic have your number?"

"Yes, um…I think so."

"Okay then, you need an appointment card?"

"Uh, no, I'll remember."

She wouldn't, the idiot. She didn't remember Chace's big thing on Tuesday night, no way she'd remember an appointment with Dominic.

However, this could also mean that she had no intention of taking the appointment. Seeing as I worked there, she was probably thinking she'd make her standing appointment in Chantelle, no matter that everyone in Carnal took advantage of a talent that should be in New York or LA but was in a small town in the Colorado Mountains because his gay partner happened to be a mountain man.

I didn't care whether she missed it or moved stylists. Either way worked for me. Though I hoped for the latter as that would mean I'd have less chance of seeing her again.

"All righty," I said. "Then we'll see you in a couple of weeks."

She stared at me and she bit her lip. Then, for some totally insane reason, she went for it.

"You're Ty's new wife, aren't you?"

Bitch, bitch, *bitch*.

How fucking *dare* she mention Ty to me.

Bitch!

"Yep," I replied on another dazzling smile.

"I, uh..." Her eyes slid beyond me to where Dominic was whispering under his breath with his client then back to me where she said softly, "Do you know who I am?"

"You mean do I know you were the one who was fucking Ty's brains out when someone in LA was committing murder?" I asked back and watched her blanch. "Oh yeah, I know who you are."

She lifted a hand and I saw it was trembling before she tucked hair behind her ear and dropped it.

"He told you that?"

"Yeah," I replied. "He told me. But that was then. This is now. New life. New wife. It's all good," I lied, and I knew she bought it because she blinked.

"Really?" she asked.

I shrugged. "Sure. We're happy. It's all good."

"So he's not mad at me?"

It was my turn to blink. I couldn't help it. I couldn't believe it.

Was she that dumb?

I mean, *seriously?*

"Now, why would he be mad at you, Misty?" I asked softly. "Are you saying you lied to the police and he *was* fucking your brains out in Carnal while someone was committing murder in LA?"

Her torso rocked back an inch and she answered quickly, "No, no. I didn't do that."

"'Course you didn't." I said it like I didn't believe it because I didn't believe it because the fucking bitch was lying.

She studied me and I could swear her lips were quivering.

Then she quickly pulled her shades out of her black-rooted, blonde hair and shoved them on her face.

"Well, uh... nice to meet you and, um... see you in a few weeks."

"Can't wait," I forced out with a bright smile.

She nodded, looked over my shoulder, turned and hurried out.

I watched the doors close behind her then clenched my fists. Then I deep-breathed. I watched her through the half-closed slats as she got in her car and pulled out of the space in front of the salon.

I immediately got up and turned to Dominic.

"I'm sorry, can I have a break? I need to run to the garage. I won't be long. There's something I need to talk to my husband about."

"Bet you do," the woman in the chair, a client I'd never met, stated instantly. Her mouth was tight, her eyes glittering and shrewd, her overall look screaming biker babe. "Know Ty. Know who you are too. Know that bitch fucked him one way, got her shit off then fucked him another way that got *his* shit totally fucked. And I also know you just gave a performance good enough to win a fuckin' award. I could trust myself to move and not do it to take that bitch down, I would have clapped."

I blinked though I didn't know why she surprised me. I'd been learning through on-the-job training that biker babes didn't really beat around the bush and I'd long since learned that Ty was a man who was well liked.

"Yes, precious," Dominic answered my request softly.

My body jerked out of its surprise, I looked to him, saw his eyes warm and understanding on me and realized then that he knew too. This was probably what they'd been whispering about because I also knew Dominic had been in town just under four years and he'd never said boo to me about Ty and unless gossip was shared while Ty was doing time and he was just too polite to mention it (which wasn't Dominic's way), he didn't know until now.

"Take all the time you need," Dominic finished.

I nodded, grabbed my shades off the desk and started to the door.

"When you see Ty, tell him Avril says hi," the biker babe called after me. I waved behind me, shot a smile over my shoulder then went out.

The salon was about six blocks away from the garage on the same side of the road. We worked close but I hadn't yet hoofed it down there. Ty and I spent a lot of time together and I pushed the time we spent together to distract him from other things. I didn't want to seem clingy so I gave him space during the day.

But I also liked my time with Dominic, Kayeleen and the clients at the salon. I didn't get but half an hour for lunch and I used that to continue my perusal of Carnal and acquaint myself with local lunchtime takeaway eateries.

But Ty needed to know what just went down and the way I played it. I was hoping he wasn't doing what he wanted to be doing but if he was, he'd need to know. Even if he wasn't, seeing as Avril knew all about it, it would get back to him eventually so, again, he needed to know.

And it needed to be me who told him.

I didn't hurry. Anyone seeing me would think I just felt like a visit and by "anyone," I was worried that Misty was still around and watching. I got to the end of Main Street, turned the corner on my high-heeled platform sandals and walked as casually as I could across the forecourt.

"Yo, Ty!" I heard shouted from the shadows of the bay and I knew I'd been spotted but not by who. Not visiting him at work meant I did not know his workmates, except Pop and Wood.

Then I saw Ty, no coveralls this time, jeans and tee. Tee greasy, jeans too, this meaning I was again going to be at the stain remover in the utility room. Something I was getting to be a dab hand at. A black-mark-covered rag was in his hands. He'd come to the opening of the bay where he stopped and leveled his eyes on me.

I got close, those eyes narrowed and he started moving again, his long legs eating the distance right to me.

Apparently, even my shades didn't hide my mood. Definitely should never play poker.

He met me in the forecourt, got close, toe to toe, and bent his neck so he could lock his beautiful, light brown eyes with my shades.

"What happened?" he asked.

I sucked in breath then shook my head. "Nothing…nothing big." I took in another breath. "I'm just shaken up. Shaken and pissed. And, well, you should know, so I'm here to tell you. Misty came into the salon to get her hair done."

Ty's eyes didn't leave me, not even to blink, and he asked, "And how did that go?"

"I smiled. I made her appointment. I was nice."

"And?" Ty prompted when I said no more.

"And she asked if I knew who she was. I told her I did. I laid it out what I knew but also told her we were happy and moving on."

I watched Ty's jaw clench.

"I'm sorry," I whispered. "Was that wrong?"

"She ain't stupid pussy, she's just toxic pussy. She's gotta know I'm gonna tell my wife that shit so, no, it wasn't wrong."

I took in a deep breath and relaxed, not even realizing I was as wound up as I was with worry that I'd fucked up.

Then it hit me so I asked, "She's not stupid pussy?"

"Fuck no."

I felt my brows draw together. "Really?"

"Uh...yeah, babe. Really. Outta her deal she got Chace Keaton's ring. He didn't mind dippin' into that twat but he didn't wanna put a ring on it. He's a cop but his daddy is not. Aspen money. Moved out from under his father's thumb to be his own man. Doesn't mean he's not gonna accept his inheritance when Daddy dies, seein' as he's an only child."

I shook my head. "If he's got money, he's got connections. Are you saying they leaned on him, *made* him marry Misty? Are you saying *that's* what she got out of the deal?"

"She spread for me but she was a girl who'd *never* take black home to Daddy. Never. She spread for Keaton with her sights set. So, yeah. That's what she got out of the deal."

"You know this for sure?"

"Only word I got on that is Tate's so, again, yeah, I know this for sure. Don't know how he got it but I know whatever his source, he wouldn't repeat it unless it was solid."

"Why would Keaton do that?" I asked.

Ty's face dipped closer. "Because, baby, he wanted to be his own man, he became his own man and when he did, he made a dirty bed.

That doesn't mean Daddy doesn't loom. That motherfucker is dirty and they know just exactly *how* he's dirty. And they would not give one shit about settin' one of their own blowin' in the wind, they needed to do that. He does not want Daddy to know that shit. He does not want to take that hit from Daddy. And he does not want Daddy to find a nice charity to give his cake after he dies because he'd rather save some fuckin' near-extinct bird than give his dirty cop son who shit all over the family name his money. So Keaton either took one for the team or they let him blow. He took one for the team and bought a lifetime of toxic cunt."

"Wow," I whispered.

"Yeah," his lips twitched then, "wow."

Well, there you go. That explained why things at home for Misty weren't so hot. He might have taken one for the team but he hadn't promised he'd spend his lifetime pretending he liked it.

"Just FYI, hubby, Misty gave some things away at the salon and I'm not sure it's all hearts and flowers in chez Keaton," I shared.

That got me a grin. "Good news, mama. 'Specially since things are exactly hearts and flowers at chez Walker."

My heart flipped and it felt good because his words felt good and I whispered, "Ty."

His hand came up and curled around my neck just as his head dipped closer. "You made my day, baby," he whispered then finished, "and not just because I got to watch you struttin' your sweet ass through the forecourt in those shoes and shorts."

I grinned at my husband then I whispered back, "Good."

His hand gave me a squeeze. "That all you got?"

I shook my head. "Not exactly she, uh . . . well, Ty, no joke, after I told her we were happy and it was all good, bitch-face Misty asked if you were mad at her."

Just like me, he blinked.

Then he asked, "No shit?"

I shook my head. "No shit."

He kept his hand where it was but lifted his head and looked over mine, muttering, "Fuck me."

"I'm thinking, the last five years, a bleached blonde with an unhappy home life is rethinking the deal she made and which man she left blowing in the wind," I noted.

His eyes tipped down to me and I noticed instantly he was no longer feeling in a warm and squishy mood.

His growled, "Don't give a fuck," confirmed it.

"Me either, except I hope every day she wakes up to a man who doesn't want her and every night she goes to bed beside him, that bitch-face chokes on her decision until the bile she forces down grows so much it cuts off her air forever and leaves doctors stumped at her untimely but deserved demise."

After I was done, Ty blinked again. Then his fingers at my neck got super tight as he threw back his head and roared with laughter.

I smiled but didn't laugh since I was watching him.

He looked back at me but again dipped his face close. "Shit, mama, remind me not to piss you off."

"Okay, don't piss me off."

He grinned and I returned it because I was pleased I'd brought back his good mood.

Then I said, "I gotta get back to work, honey."

His hand at my neck brought me closer while he muttered, "Yeah."

Then his mouth was on mine, he kissed me short but it was wet and it was hot. Then his mouth broke from mine and he whispered, "Later, mama."

"Later, Ty," I whispered back and he smiled at me, straight out. No lips turned up. No grin. A big, beautiful one, and I loved that. I loved that those were coming more often, more relaxed, more natural.

I loved it.

Then he gave my neck one last squeeze, let me go and turned away.

If I'd have known what was going to happen that night, I would have taken my chance to watch him go. I would have made him kiss me longer. I would have tried to make him laugh one more time.

But I didn't know.

And since I didn't know, I, too, turned and walked away.

* * *

I was on my way home from work after popping to the store to pick up some stuff for dinner and the elaborate dessert I had planned (whipped cream and chocolate pudding parfaits *with* chocolate sprinkles) and just in case Julius needed snacks while we were at work.

And I was just outside of Carnal when I saw the police lights flash and heard the short, warning whir of the siren before it was shut off.

I looked to my rearview mirror, felt the adrenaline rush then my eyes instantly went to my speedometer.

After what Tate said at Bubba's, I'd memorized the speed limits in and around Carnal. Thirty in town. Forty on the stretch I was on between town, the turnoff to our condo and beyond for another half mile. Then fifty-five all the way to Chantelle.

I was careful, super careful, always.

As I was now. I was going just under forty.

Shit.

I pulled to the side and the cruiser pulled to the side behind me.

Then I watched in my mirror as Officer Rowdy Crabtree sat in his cruiser for a couple of minutes talking on the radio. My rapidly beating heart slid up into my throat when he opened his door and folded out of the vehicle.

My window was already rolled down so I didn't take my eyes off the mirror until I lost sight of him at the side of the car. It was then I turned my head to the window.

I got him when he arrived at my window where he immediately bent at the waist, his shades hit mine and I smiled.

"Hi, Officer," I said.

"Miz Walker," he did a mini-dip of his chin, "license and registration."

"Can you tell me why you stopped me? I was a mile under the speed limit," I replied.

"License and registration."

Shit. Shit. Fucking *shit*!

I turned to my purse, grabbed my license then bent to the glove compartment and found the registration. I turned back to him and handed both out of the window.

He studied them, as cops do. Then he looked down his nose at me while I peered out my window up at him.

"My understanding, Miz Walker, is that you are now a resident of the state of Colorado."

"Um…I am."

"Plates on your car say Texas."

Shit. Shit. Fucking *shit*!

Was that bad? Could I get a ticket for that? A fine? Didn't I have a window to get that shit done?

I didn't know. I wished I knew.

"Driver's license is from Texas too," he went on.

"Uh…well, I just moved here not too long ago—" I started but he cut me off.

"I do know that, Miz Walker, but vehicle registration, plates and driver's license should declare the proper information, including address. You live in Colorado, these should state Colorado."

"Okay," I told him. "I'll see to that on Monday. I have the day off. Won't be a problem."

"Monday isn't now, Miz Walker," he replied.

Dick.

He was fucking with me. I knew it. Just because I was married to who I was married to.

The thing I didn't know was just how much he intended to fuck with me, and from what happened to Ty and what Tate said, the how much could be a whole lot and none of it I would enjoy.

And worse, Ty would lose his mind.

I opened my mouth to speak but saw another cruiser heading our way and I didn't like that. Carnal wasn't a big town when it came to it but the town was one thing and the city limits another. The police department had a big area they covered that went beyond the town proper, out across the valley and up into the hills where there were quite a number of developments, homes, ranches and even some businesses.

This meant the department didn't just have Andy and Barney keeping an eye on things. They had manpower and seeing as they'd played Ty the way they'd played him, I'd paid attention to this manpower and noticed there seemed to be a lot of it. Not just cruisers but also plainclothesmen with badges on their belts I saw in the grocery, at La-La Land Coffee, in the bakery, in the sandwich place.

They were all over and they seemed to make a suffocating point of being very visible.

Like now.

It made matters worse when the second cruiser slowed and swung a wide u-ey to come to a halt behind Crabtree's.

This did not bode well. One Carnal uniform and that uniform being Crabtree was bad enough, I didn't want to have to deal with two.

My heart started racing harder as the adrenaline surge spiked and my hand inched toward my purse with my mind on my phone as I kept my eyes out the window. I looked up to see Crabtree had his head turned to the cruiser and his jaw was hard.

Hmm. That was interesting.

I looked to my side mirror and saw a uniform get out, one I'd seen but didn't know.

"Got this, Frank," Crabtree called but I kept my eyes to the mirror and watched the second officer continue to approach.

"Need a quick word, Rowdy," he stated when he got closer.

"In the middle of somethin', man," Crabtree replied.

"Need a quick word," the one called Frank repeated.

"I said, in the middle of somethin'." Crabtree was getting impatient.

Frank came to a halt a couple of feet from Crabtree and I turned my head to look at him.

"And I said, need a quick word," Frank returned, his voice low and tight.

Crabtree made an irritated noise and Frank's shades dipped down at me then he gave me a chin lift.

"Ma'am," he said.

"Officer," I replied.

"We'll have you on your way in a minute," he informed me, and I hoped that meant good things.

At that, Crabtree stalked angrily back to the cruiser and Frank followed him.

I turned forward and waited, eyes glued to the mirror because they were nose to nose and it didn't take a behavior specialist to see the conversation wasn't about who was going to bring the beer to the department picnic that weekend.

This lasted awhile. Long enough for Crabtree's face to get red and my heart, already hammering, hammered harder and my skin, already tingling, tingled faster because he was already a dick, I didn't need to be dealing with an *angry* dick.

Then Crabtree stepped back and thrust my stuff at Frank. Frank took it and Crabtree stomped to his cruiser. He was in and had it fired up, reversing and nearly clipping Frank who was walking to me as he squealed out and my head turned to watch as he drove thirty yards then did a hair-raising u-ey and sped back into town.

By this time, Frank was at my door and I stopped craning my neck out the window to stare after Crabtree. I tipped my head back to him.

He was offering my license and registration to me.

"There you go, Lexie," he said quietly, and I blinked behind my shades at his use of my name but my hand drifted up and I took the documents. "May wanna see to gettin' to the DMV soon's you can." He was still talking quietly.

I nodded and whispered, "Okay."

"On top a' that is my card. You get..." he paused then finished "...any further attention, I'm askin' you to call me. Not Ty. Not Tate. Me."

What the hell?

"Uh..." I mumbled.

"Smart way to play it." He kept talking quietly. "Not to rile your man or the ones got his back." I stared at him, stunned he had this info as he paused then finished, "I think you get me."

I didn't.

"I can't keep things from my husband," I told him.

"They play with him, he'll deal. They branch out to you, what's he gonna do, Lexie?" he asked, gave me a second and then advised, "Think about that."

What I thought was, if Ty knew they were playing with me and I didn't tell him, he'd lose his mind. He would, of course, lose his mind that they were playing with me, but he'd lose his mind more if he knew I'd endured it, didn't tell him and contacted Officer Frank, a man in a Carnal PD uniform I did not know but I did know I couldn't trust.

Ty knew I could take care of myself, he knew I knew the score and he knew I had his back. He wouldn't like it if this continued happening but he'd deal. If I kept something from him, he might not.

This, I wouldn't know until hours later and events that led to heartbreak, was a very bad decision.

At the time, I just nodded because I was beginning to shake and I needed to get home.

"I have perishables in the car," I told him softly.

He nodded. Then he said, "Sorry, Lexie. Really sorry." He tapped both hands on the edge of my window and finished, "Drive safe."

He lifted his hands in front of him, stepped back and moved away from my car.

I tossed the stuff in my hand to the passenger seat, put my car in gear and carefully checked all my mirrors before I pulled out, terrified, in my state, that I'd not pay attention and get hurt or hurt my baby so I paid acute attention to my every move. And I did this until my baby was in the garage and the garage door was falling behind her.

Home. Safe.

I sucked in breath.

Then I grabbed my purse, got out and flew up the steps.

"Yo, baby doll," Julius greeted from his place camped out in front of the television.

"Uh...hey, Julius," I muttered distractedly, moving directly to the island, putting my purse on it and, with trembling hands, digging for my phone.

"Hey, Lexie, you okay?" Julius asked, and I had my phone in my hand and my thumb was finding Ty.

"Uh...uh..." I put my phone to my ear because I'd dialed Ty and my eyes went to him to see he'd made it to the kitchen. When he saw my face he stopped dead. "Kinda...no."

"Mama," Ty said in my ear, and I dropped my head and looked at my hand holding onto the edge of the island.

"Uh, hey, honey."

Silence then, "What?"

God, he could hear it in my voice.

"I got...um," I swallowed. "I got pulled over on the way home."

Now I got total silence on the phone.

Silence on the phone but in the kitchen a big, angry man rumbled, "Fuckin' shit."

When what I got over the phone lengthened, I whispered, "Ty?"

"Please tell me you were speeding."

"No." I was still whispering.

"Fuckin' with you?"

"Crabtree," I confirmed. "Until another cop stopped, named Frank and he—"

Ty didn't let me finish. He bit off, "Right."

"Honey, I—"

"Later, babe."

"Ty, I—"

"*Later*, babe."

Then he was gone.

Shit.

Shit, shit, *fucking shit*!

I dropped my phone hand and looked at Julius.

Then I whispered, "I shouldn't have told him."

Julius shook his head. "My woman got pulled over by some

dirty cracker cop who was fuckin' with her, makin' her look like you do right now, which means you're feelin' exactly what you look like you're feelin' right now, or worse, just so he could fuck with me, she didn't tell me, I'd lose my fuckin' mind."

I nodded. This was good.

Then I asked, "Is he gonna lose his mind anyway?"

Julius held my eyes. Then he said, "Don't know, baby doll. But do know, he does, he won't lose it at you."

"He's got a lot to lose if he loses it with someone else," I reminded him quietly, my voice trembling.

"He does, Lexie. But he's a man and it's his decision to lose it to make a point about someone fuckin' with his woman. You just gotta let him make his decision then you gotta roll with it."

It was then my whole body was trembling and it wasn't the only thing. There was wet trembling at my eyes.

I was engulfed in a bear hug, Julius's arms tight around me, Julius's answers weighing on me.

I still didn't know if I did the right thing.

I would find out later, after I pulled myself together, after Julius helped me bring up the groceries and put them away and after I'd calmed down over a beer that I didn't.

Not at all.

* * *

Ty hit the back door and my eyes were already there because I'd heard the Cruiser pull in under the house.

I felt hope. He was home. Not in a jail cell with some dirty cop calling his parole officer to tell him to start the paperwork to send my man back to California.

I thought this was good.

The expression on his face said I was wrong.

I felt my face pale then I felt my breath stick in my throat when his eyes found me and his powerful arm slammed the door so hard the glass shook and it was a miracle it didn't shatter.

Instantly, Julius saw it, felt it or both and he stepped toward Ty and whispered, "Walk."

Ty didn't take his eyes off me. His long legs took him to the island opposite me. He stopped and put his hands on top of it in a way that stated clearly he wanted to use his hands for something else.

The minute his hands hit counter, he announced, "Went to Tate."

I nodded because I thought that was good. Tate was better than losing his mind on Rowdy Crabtree.

Even so, I was confused because he looked beyond pissed. He looked enraged.

"Went to Tate," he repeated.

"Okay," I replied.

Suddenly he leaned forward in a way that made me lean back even though the island was between us and he barked, "*Went to Tate, Lexie!*"

"Okay," I whispered.

"Told me," he went on and I shook my head, still confused.

"Told you what?"

"Told me you played me."

My breath stuck in my throat.

Oh God.

Oh God.

"What?" I pushed through the breath clogging my throat.

"Couldn't believe it, not you," he replied.

"Ty—"

"Not you," he repeated.

"Ty," I whispered. I'd started trembling again, knowing this was bad, very bad, the worst, and he moved, his long legs taking him to the stairs and I watched, still confused but also terrified. So terrified all I could do was stare at the stairs and not move.

Something was wrong. Very wrong. Cataclysmically wrong.

And I knew what that wrong was.

And I wanted my feet to take me to the stairs so I could sort it out with Ty in private but I was so terrified of what I'd done and his reaction to it I couldn't get my feet to move.

"I'll talk to him," Julius muttered, but I still didn't move though I saw him at the stairs because I was still staring at them.

And I stared at them feeling my breath stick in my throat, my heart beat hard and fast in my chest, my palms itch and my blood race, hot and frantic in my veins.

Then I saw legs and heard Ty rumble, "Not your gig, brother."

"Walk, listen to me—"

"Not your fuckin' gig," Ty cut him off, rounded the stairs and came straight to the island.

On it he slammed down rolls of cash.

"Fifty K. Your pay. I'm outta here. You got an hour to get your sweet ass outta my house."

Yes. Yes. Something was wrong. Very wrong. *Cataclysmically* wrong.

And I knew what it was. And I knew by his face he meant every word.

Still, I whispered a shaky, "What?"

"You played me, Lexie, *you...fuckin'...played me*," he growled, leaning into me. "Goin' to Tate and Deke behind my fuckin' back. Spreadin' for me to keep me distracted. Your pussy's got no chain?" he asked, his words pummeling me, then he leaned back and clipped, "Bullshit. Just as heavy as all the fuckin' rest."

Each word hit me like a blow.

"Ty, I—"

"Played me," he finished for me then lifted a big hand and jabbed a long finger at me on every "you." "*You* did not rot in that *fuckin'* place for five years. *You* do not got a skin tone that makes you a mark. *You* like black cock but takin' black cock, babe, does not make you black. *You* do not get to call the plays with this shit." He jerked his hand back and his thumb to himself. "*I* do."

"Listen to me."

"Time to listen to you, Lexie, was fuckin' weeks ago before you spread your fuckin' legs, just like fuckin' Misty, and fuckin' played me."

His words hammering me, the blows so vicious it felt in places my skin had split open, I still found the strength to shake my head and take a step toward him saying, "Please, lis—"

"Do not get near me, bitch," he growled and I froze, my eyes locked to his, the blood going so fast through my veins it felt like I was burning alive. "An hour," he bit off. "I come back, you are *out.* You aren't, Lexie, I'll put you out."

Then he turned, rounded the island and prowled to the door.

Then he was gone.

An hour later, so was I.

CHAPTER FOURTEEN

Shattered

Ty

Ty Walker opened the back door to his house and walked in to a big, seriously pissed off black man with tree trunk legs planted apart and beefy arms crossed on his chest.

He knew he'd get that when he got home.

He also didn't give a fuck.

He closed the door and looked Julius right in the eye.

"She gone?" he asked.

"You are one serious dumb fuck."

"She gone?"

"Oh yeah, brother, she's gone."

Ty Walker's jaw clenched so hard he was lucky it didn't freeze shut.

He jerked up his chin and headed to the stairs.

He was nearly there when Julius spoke.

"She loved you."

That was bullshit. She didn't.

She did, she wouldn't have played him. She knew what playing him would do. She knew, he found out, she'd be right where she was now. Wherever the fuck that was. But wherever it was, he did not fucking care.

Walker kept moving to the stairs.

Julius kept speaking.

"You broke her."

Ty rounded the railing and tried to shut him out.

Julius kept at him.

"Never seen a woman break like that."

Fuck, the man needed to shut *the fuck* up.

His foot hit the first stair.

"Shattered," Julius called after him.

Walker kept moving.

He hit his room and stopped dead.

Right in the middle of the bed was fifty thousand dollars in cash and four jewelry boxes.

Four.

She'd even left her wedding rings.

He stared at them then he closed his eyes tight and dropped his head.

He opened his eyes, moved to the safe in the closet, opened it and went back to the bed. He stowed the shit, closed the safe and kicked himself that he didn't come upstairs with the fucking bourbon.

* * *

Two days later…

"Yo, Ty!" Wood called him.

He looked from the belly of the car he was working on and across the garage to Wood who was turned, looking out a bay.

Walker's eyes moved that way and he moved out from under the car when he saw Tate stalking his way.

Fuck.

Tate stopped five feet away.

"Lexie needs a couple of hours to get the rest of her shit outta your house. For reasons I'm guessin' you get, she does not want to ask you herself and she does not want you there," he stated.

"Tell her to name the time and I'm gone," Walker replied instantly.

Tate stared at him like Julius stared at him for an entire day any time he saw him until he'd connected with his man and went back to California—like he thought Walker was one serious dumb fuck.

Then Tate jerked up his chin and started to go.

"Jackson," Walker called, and Tate stopped. "Tell her the safe will be open. She'll know why. And tell her she's plain stupid she doesn't take what's hers."

"Great, I'll continue this junior high bullshit and tell her that, Ty. You got anything else I should whisper to her at recess?" Tate asked, pissed as all hell. Not at his errand, not doing this for Lexie but because he was pissed at Walker. And he was not hiding it.

"Nope," Walker answered.

"Terrific," Tate muttered, turned and stalked away.

Walker moved back under the car.

* * *

Three days later…

Walker worked out hard and he worked out long then he returned home late, giving Lexie plenty of time to do her thing.

He parked the Cruiser by the Snake in the garage. Then he took the stairs, braced for what he would find.

But when he got to the top of the stairs, it was all there. The pitchers, the snow globe, the frames, the crock with the spoons in, the fruit bowl, the KitchenAid, the toss pillows.

Fuck, she didn't show.

Fuck!

He needed her shit *out.*

Now he had to call a still seriously pissed off Tate.

Or stop acting like a fucking idiot and continue perpetrating exactly the junior high school bullshit Tate called it and phone his soon-to-be ex-wife.

He dropped his workout bag by the stairs, reminding himself to sort it. There was no Lexie to take it away and deal with it. Not anymore.

He headed upstairs and hit their room then something made him stop dead.

His head turned and he saw the frame that held the picture of them at The Rooster was gone. He felt his chest compress and his gut tighten as he walked to the closet.

Her clothes were gone.

He retraced his steps down the stairs and went right, to the guest bedroom.

Cleaned out.

He moved to the office.

Her computer gone. The frames gone. Her print gone.

He moved to the other bedroom.

Void of everything.

He walked back up the stairs and to the closet. Looking down, he saw the safe was closed. He moved to it, crouched in front of it and opened it.

Money and jewelry still there.

"Fuck," he whispered to the safe. Then he slammed the door shut using all his strength. It flew back open, hit the back of its hinges and swung shut again.

He surged to his feet and barked, "*Fuck!*"

He prowled back downstairs to his workout bag, bent to it, dug through it and found his phone. He straightened as his thumb moved on the keys, taking him to her number.

He clenched his teeth as it rang.

He got voicemail. No surprise.

"This is Lexie. Busy right now, leave a message."

He clenched his teeth harder at the sound of her voice.

Then he heard the beep. "Don't be stupid. Come back, get your cash and diamonds. You need me gone, I'll be gone. Just get them."

He flipped his phone shut.

Then he stood by his bag and stared at the snow globe in the kitchen windowsill and his eyes lifted.

The petal heart was still there.

Except that picture of them at The Rooster, she left everything that was them.

Everything.

He turned his head away.

Then he sucked in breath through his nose and walked into the kitchen to blend a shake.

* * *

Five days later…

His cell ringing woke him up.

He rolled, tagged it off the nightstand, looked at the display and it said, "Unknown caller."

Considering his business and the ball Julius got rolling, it could be anyone.

His eyes slid to his alarm clock.

Anyone, even at one thirty in the fucking morning.

He sat up, flipped his phone open, put it to his ear and growled, "What?"

"She's with Shift right now." He heard a woman say and he knew that woman.

It was Bessie.

But he couldn't think of Bessie because he'd stopped breathing.

Bessie kept talking.

"Motherfucker finds out shit, found out she was home, was all over her. And now, way she is, no job, no money, no schoolin', no fight left in her, no nothin', that asshole is gonna be *all over her*. But you knew that, didn't you? You just didn't fuckin' care."

She didn't wait for him to respond. She got finished saying what she had to say and gave him dead air.

But Walker was still fighting for breath.

When he got enough in, he shifted to sitting on the side of the bed and stared at his display in the dark as his thumb moved over the keypad, finding Lexie's number.

He hit go and put it to his ear.

Two rings then, "We're sorry. This number is no longer in service..."

"*Fuck!*" Walker snarled as he shot out of bed.

He flipped the phone closed then back open as he turned on the light and prowled to the closet. He found the number he needed and put the phone to his ear as he turned on the closet light and headed to his bag.

Three rings then Tate saying, "Ty, this better be good."

"I need you to fire up your computer right now. I need addresses for Ella Rodriguez, Bessie Rodriguez and Duane Martinez."

Silence then, "What?"

He tagged his bag and started back to the bedroom. "Bess called. Shift's got Lexie."

"Shift?"

"Martinez."

He dropped his bag on the bed and moved to the dresser.

"Fuck," Tate whispered.

"Tate, don't got a lot of time."

"Ty, you are not allowed to leave the state."

"That's why I don't got a lot of time. I need you to give me those addresses so I can get there, get shit done and get home without anyone knowin'."

"Ty, you fuck up—"

Walker stopped dead and barked into the phone, "*Quit wastin' my fuckin' time!* You gonna get me those addresses or you gonna fuck me?"

"Let me go after her."

"No."

"Ty, I'll get the addresses, leave tonight."

"No."

"Why no?"

"She isn't your wife, Tate, she's mine."

Silence.

"You're wastin' my time," Walker warned.

"You bringin' her back?" Jackson sounded disbelieving.

"Yeah," Walker replied instantly.

"Brother—" Tate started.

"Did you not fuckin' hear me? Martinez has got her." Walker's voice was low and tight with anger and impatience.

"I get you. I get what you're feelin' but you gotta listen to me a second, Ty. You did not see her. She stayed with Dominic but I saw her, Laurie saw her. The state you left her in, you cannot waltz into Dallas and bring that woman home."

That thing pierced his chest again but the feeling was different. Savage. Brutal. Inflicting damage.

He powered through it.

"I'll deal when I get there."

"Let me go and talk to her. I'll leave Jonas with Pop, take Laurie with me."

"This isn't junior high, Tate."

"You do not know what you're dealin' with, Ty."

"This is wastin' my fuckin' time," he said low.

Silence then, "I'll get the addresses, I'll come over and I'll go with you."

"Suit yourself. But be here soon. You got half an hour. You aren't here, brother, I'll head to Dallas and find her myself."

"Fuck, Ty, it takes twenty minutes just to drive to your place."

"Then you better drive fast."

Then Ty flipped his phone shut, tossed it on the bed and turned back to the dresser.

Tate Jackson drove fast.

* * *

Seventeen hours later…

"Do you get me?" Walker asked, and Shift, prone on the floor in front of him, spit out a mouthful of blood.

"Yeah," he grunted.

"Just to be sure," Walker went on. "You lose her number, you lose her fuckin' *memory*, you don't, your next visit will be from Julius Champion. Now, let's confirm. Do you get me?"

"Yeah!" Shift snapped, sliding angry eyes up high to Walker.

"Good," Walker muttered, his eyes moved to Tate who was staring with distaste at the floor.

Tate felt his gaze. He looked to Walker, tipped up his chin and followed Walker out, both of them stepping over one of the two prone enforcers Walker had laid out before he turned to Shift.

* * *

An hour later…

The door to the tidy but tiny house opened the minute Walker and Jackson hit the end of the front walk. The screen door opened after it. The house door closed instantly and the screen door banged behind Ella Rodriguez who stood on her front stoop, arms crossed on her chest, eyes glaring down at the advancing men.

"You are not here," she announced when they were four feet away.

Walker kept moving and stopped at the bottom of the two steps of her stoop.

"She's in there, Ella, I advise you let me by," Walker said quietly.

"She's gone."

"She was with Shift not twenty-four hours ago," Walker returned.

"She was. Bessie got her. They're gone."

"Where?"

Her eyebrows shot to her hairline and her voice pitched four octaves higher when she asked, "Boy, you think I'm gonna tell you that?"

"I need to talk to her."

"Yeah," she nodded her head once. "I see that. But what you *really* needed to do was take her momma's advice those weeks ago when she laid it all out for you."

"Ella—"

Her eyes narrowed, her face twisted, she leaned forward and the shutters flew up on her eyes, exposing her pain.

"Told you," she said quietly, her voice trembling. "You had her in your hands and *I told you*, you weren't careful, you'd destroy her. I'm not wrong often and again, I... was... *not*... wrong."

There it was again. That thing piercing his chest. More pain. More damage.

Ty Walker stood at the bottom of a stoop of a tiny, tidy house in a not-great, not-bad area of Dallas and engaged in a stare down with a protective, loyal, loving black woman. A stare down he had no hope in fuck of winning.

"Ty, let's go," Jackson said quietly from his side.

"You do her no favors, keepin' me from her," Walker said softly.

"Way I see it, ain't no single body on this earth ever did Alexa Berry no favors," Ella returned.

"Walker," Walker corrected and Ella's back shot straight.

"Not anymore," she aimed and fired her kill shot, it penetrated its target, leaving devastation in its wake, then she turned and slammed into her house without looking back.

Walker turned on his boot and prowled down the walk to Tate's SUV. Tate bleeped the locks before he made it and he didn't hesitate to swing in.

Tate swung behind the wheel. Then he turned to Walker.

"What now?" he asked.

"We find a place to sleep, we sleep, we go home," Walker answered the windshield.

"Home?" The word was low, angry and unbelieving and, slowly, Walker turned his eyes to his friend.

"Home. Where your computer is. Where your database is. Where you start to do what you do. They'll leave a trail or they'll surface. You'll find them. You'll tell me where the fuck they are and then I'll fucking go get my fucking *wife*."

Tate stared at him a second.

Then he grinned.

Then he turned to face forward, switched the ignition and guided the SUV to the nearest hotel.

Lexie

Two weeks later…

Panama City Beach, Florida

I liked this time of night at the beach. Dinnertime. When most everyone was eating, a breeze came off the gulf, the air was still warm but cool and the beach was nearly deserted.

There were a couple of kids playing Frisbee some ways away. A man running with his yellow lab at the water's edge, this taking a while because the dog kept bouncing into the waves. He'd have to turn around, jog backward, call. The dog would ignore him, he'd run forward, the dog would leap out of the water in great bounds then the guy would turn back around and run some more only for the dog to bounce right back into the surf. A bit down the beach there were combers walking with heads bowed, toeing things in the sand, bending sometimes to pick them up, getting close to the water's edge to wait for a wave to clean the sand off what they found so they could get a better look.

But that was it. Mostly just me sitting on my ass, the sand and the waves, all I could see, all I could hear.

It didn't make me feel at peace but, these days, it was the best I got.

I sighed and dropped my chin to my jeans-clad knees that were bent to my chest, my arms around them and I watched the waves.

I could do this for hours and I did.

I heard the footsteps in the sand behind me but didn't turn. Someone coming from our motel. Definitely a motel. The Beacon. I suspected it was built during the late fifties, early sixties and since then they'd changed not one thing. Not even the curtains or the bedspreads.

It was clean, it was seriously freaking cheap, they gave you a discount if you bought a week in advance and it was right on the beach. But those were all it had going for it.

It was certainly nowhere near what Ty gave me in Vegas.

Not even close.

But it was on the beach so people stayed there. Like Bessie and me.

And whoever was making their way to the water.

I put the footsteps out of my mind and stared at the sea.

Then it hit me the footsteps stopped.

I felt him behind me.

And I tensed as I felt him move.

Then I closed my eyes tight when all that was him, and damn, there was a lot of him, surrounded me.

He sat behind me, right at my back, his long legs on either side, knees bent, insides pressed to the outsides of mine. His long arms circling me. His massive front pressing into my back. His jaw pressing into the side of my hair.

And there he whispered, "Mama."

That one word tore through me like a blade.

I opened my eyes and saw sea.

"How did you find me?" I asked the waves, and the minute I started speaking, his arms convulsed.

"Tate," he answered.

Right. Of course. His bounty hunter friend.

Scratch Tate off my Christmas list.

"We gotta talk," he said gently.

"Nothing to talk about," I replied.

"You know there is, baby." He was still talking gently. It was nice. I'd heard him be gentle. I'd heard him be soft. I'd heard him be sweet. I'd heard him be quiet. But none of them was as gentle, soft, sweet and quiet as the way he was now.

But it didn't matter.

Nothing mattered anymore. When shit mattered, it could hurt you.

So nothing mattered anymore and I was determined to keep it that way.

"No, there isn't," I told him.

His arms gave me another squeeze, "Lexie—"

I cut him off. "Unless you brought the divorce papers. You said you'd deal and all I had to do is sign. Is that why you're here?"

His arms tightened on the words "divorce papers" but they didn't loosen even after I was done speaking.

And his answer was instantaneous.

"No it fuckin' is not."

"Then you wasted a trip."

"Lexie, baby, listen to me."

"Think you said enough."

His tight arms gave me a gentle shake. "I was pissed—"

"Yeah, I got that."

"Babe," another gentle shake, "listen to me."

I fell silent. The sooner he did what he had to do the better. Then he would be gone and it would just be me and the sea.

He waited a second then he went on, "You know why I was pissed."

I didn't reply.

"Five years of my life, Lexie."

I still didn't reply.

"I lost it. Pissed and powerless. The Carnal PD wanted to play with my woman, I had no play of my own. Been powerless a long time too, Lex, man like me, *any* man, fuck, baby, any *woman* loses their power, it does not fuckin' feel good. And there I was, they were fuckin' with you, I could hear your fear on the goddamned phone and I had not one…single…fuckin' play. I went to Tate to calm my ass down so I didn't do somethin' stupid and *really* lose you and he decides to lay it out for me, what he's been doin', how you instigated that shit. I lost my mind. It wasn't smart, it wasn't right, too much comin' at me at once, I acted out, fucked up and hurt you again. But all that, you gotta know from all you *do* know, was understandable."

"You're right," I told him.

A hesitation filled with surprise then, "Come again?"

"You're right. I figured that all out right away and you're right. It's understandable."

Ty was silent.

I decided I was done.

"The thing you don't understand is, I'm used up, Ty. I am *so* done. And that, well, that used up the last I had."

His arms tightened again and his legs pressed in, pulling me deeper into him all around.

"Lexie—"

I interrupted him.

"My parents were crackheads. I was born addicted. Did you know that?" I asked and didn't wait for an answer. "No. You didn't. I don't talk about it. I didn't do it but still, it's embarrassing. Baby born in a crackhouse addicted to crack. That was me. I made the papers just being born. Bad luck right off the bat. Luck so bad, it hit the papers day one I was on this earth. And Lady Luck wasn't done. I told you my mom OD'd. And I told you she never held me. They took me away from her and she didn't even notice, never came back to take a shot, never came back to see her baby, never came just to hold me. She probably held a million crack pipes to her mouth but she never held her baby. Not once. I also told you my dad got killed by a loan shark, owed so many people for the dope he was smoking, he went to a loan shark and then couldn't pay him. My grandfather hated him so much, he'd never let my dad see me and he never *did* see me, my dad didn't. Then again, he never even tried. Then there was Granddad, you know all about him being a dick. My first boyfriend a pimp. His drug dealer best friend used me as an errand girl."

I shook my head, took a deep breath and finished it.

"I'm done. So fucking done. I have no more to give. And you. You need to find a woman who's got a lot to give, see you through, whatever fucked-up shit you decide to do, find a woman who's got what it takes to stand by you."

"I'm playin' it Tate's way," he told me and my heart leaped.

But I didn't let on.

Three-week crash course in poker face and I found I was a natural.

"Good," I replied immediately but emotionlessly. "I'm glad for you. That's smart."

He responded to my tone or, more accurately, his body did and I knew this when I felt it go still all around me.

Then he whispered, "Lexie—" but I cut him off again.

"Ty, just go. This is done. It's done. It was done the first time you told me my pussy came with a chain but that used to be me, thinking Lady Luck would eventually smile at me. She doesn't. She hasn't. She never will. I'm her favorite toy. Keep sticking my hand out hoping to grasp onto something good and she keeps slapping it. That shit stings. Not gonna stick my hand out there."

His body again moved, drew me deeper and he started, "Mama—" but I didn't let him continue.

"Tate found me, he can find Ella. You get the divorce papers to her. She'll get them to me. I'll give you one last thing, Ty, my signature, but that's the last thing you, or anyone, gets out of me."

His head moved, his chin pulling my hair back then his mouth found my ear and he whispered, "Baby, please, God, just please fuckin' listen to me."

And that's when I lost it. I couldn't take much more. Not without breaking and I couldn't break again. The last one left too many scars, too many wounds that didn't heal in a way I knew they never would. I couldn't be torn apart again. There was no way in hell I'd survive it.

So I lost it.

But a different way.

"*Just go,*" I hissed. "Fuck, Ty, if I make the decision that I want to just be, can't I just fucking *be* without all this fucking *bullshit?* My grandfather controlled my life and with that, I had no choice. Then Ronnie did and with that, I did but did I make the right choice? No. Then Shift controlled it and my choices were limited but I still didn't make the right ones. Can you give me one fucking thing in this nightmare and let me make my own fucking choice?"

When I was done speaking I felt his body had gone still again, stone still.

And silent.

Then he asked quietly, "Nightmare?"

"Nightmare," I replied firmly.

Ty didn't move.

By a miracle, I held it together.

Then he moved but it was to rest his chin on my shoulder and I closed my eyes because I needed him to go, go, *go* so I could fall apart again on my own.

Then he said, "Your nightmare, mama, was my dream."

My heart clenched.

He kept going. "Never had a home until you gave me one."

My breath started sticking.

"Never had anyone give to me the way you gave to me."

My breath stopped sticking and clogged.

"Never thought of findin' a woman who I wanted to have my baby."

Oh *God.*

"Never had light in my life, never, not once. I lived wild but I didn't burn bright until you shined your light on me."

Oh God.

"Whacked, fuckin' insane, but, at night, you curled in front of me, didn't mind I did that time that wasn't mine 'cause it meant I walked out to you."

He had to stop. He *had* to.

He didn't.

"Your nightmare," he whispered, turned his head and against my neck he finished, "my dream."

Then he kissed my neck, gave me one last squeeze of his long, strong, powerful arms, then he let me go, shifted back, got to his feet and I heard his footsteps walking away.

When I couldn't hear them anymore I opened my eyes and saw sea.

I didn't move for a long time and anyone studying me from the huge cement patio with rusted lounge chairs would think I was lost in my thoughts, not sitting in the sand with rivers of salt flowing down my face.

When the tears were spent, I let the breeze dry my cheeks until they felt scratchy and tight.

Then I got up and wandered up the beach, up the stairs to the patio and to my room. I needed to call Bessie in hers and talk about dinner. I didn't eat much but she'd wait even if I picked at my food while she ate hers and I knew this because that's what she'd been doing for weeks.

I dug my key out of my back pocket, put it in the lock, twisted it and walked into my room. The sun was setting but it was still light. When the door closed behind me, I couldn't see anything because the drapes were pulled.

I flipped the switch, took two steps into the room then froze and stared at the bed.

A pile of rolled bills of cash sat in the center of my bed next to four distinctive-colored boxes.

My eyes darted around the room, half expecting Ty to walk out of the bathroom, pop out from behind a curtain.

The other half, fuck me, fuck me, *fuck me*, was hoping.

He didn't walk out of the bathroom and he certainly didn't pop out from behind a curtain.

And because he didn't, my legs gave out from under me, I sank again to my ass, shoved my face between my knees and cried fucking more fucking rivers of fucking salt.

CHAPTER FIFTEEN

Eleven Hours

Three weeks later…

My cell ringing woke me up.

I rolled, grabbed it from the nightstand, looked at the display and it said, "Ella calling."

I blinked, groggy, confused, it had to be the middle of the night.

Why was Ella calling?

Shit. This couldn't be good.

I flipped it open and put it to my ear. "Ella, honey, what's up? Is everything okay?"

Silence then, soft, gentle, trembling, "Oh baby."

My heart skipped then stuttered to a halt. I shot up to sitting in the bed, the phone pressed tight to my ear.

"Ella?" I called when she said no more.

Now *my* voice was trembling.

"Lexie, precious…" she trailed off and again said no more.

"Ella," now my body was trembling, "what's happened? Is it Honey?"

Silence then, so soft it was near a coo, "No, baby. It's Ty."

My body stopped trembling because it had started shaking.

"What's Ty?" I whispered.

I heard her draw in a deep breath then, "Got a call from a man named Julius."

Oh God. Oh no. Oh God no.

"Told me Ty was out in that fancy car of his, goin' too fast…"

Oh *God*. Oh *no*. Oh God *no*!

"Lost control, wasn't wearin' a seat belt."

He didn't. Ty didn't. I'd nag him and he'd do it but I had to nag him.

Live wild, mama.

I closed my eyes.

Oh God.

Oh no.

Oh fucking God, no.

"Lexie, baby, you there?"

No. No. I wasn't. I wasn't anywhere. I was lost. Totally lost. More lost even than the lost I'd been for a month and a half.

Lost forever.

"Yes," I lied, opening my eyes.

"He…he…" Another audible breath. "He's alive, precious, but they say he's not gonna last long. This Julius man said that maybe you'd wanna see him before he…he…" Another audible breath while my body shook the bed and my throat burned so bad I knew it would never feel normal again. "Passes. But he said there isn't a lot of time."

Suddenly full of energy, I threw back the covers and jumped out of bed. "Where is he?"

"County hospital outside Carnal."

"I'll get the first flight," I announced, glad for the first time I had fifty thousand dollars of my husband's money.

My husband's money.

My husband.

My throat constricted, cutting off my air.

I forced saliva down it and doing it fucking hurt. But it worked. I could again breathe though I was doing it shallowly.

"Did he give you a number?" I asked.

"Yes, baby," she answered.

"Can you…" I grabbed my suitcase and tossed it on the bed. "Can you…will you, when I get my flight, will you talk to him for me?"

I couldn't talk to Julius. I couldn't connect, even over the phone, with anything that belonged to Ty.

I couldn't.

"Anything, Lexie," Ella whispered.

"Thank you, honey," I whispered back then stopped dead, froze and I couldn't stop it. It hit me, no controlling it. It was too strong, the feeling overwhelmed me and the sob tore out of my throat, the sound so loud, it filled the room, reverberating, bouncing back and beating into me like fists.

"Baby," Ella cooed in my ear. "Get your suitcase, get your clothes," she guided me. "Pack. I'll call Bessie. She'll call for tickets. Just get yourself packed. That's all you have to do. Bessie'll take care of you."

Bessie would. She'd been doing it awhile. She would do it forever.

Three good things in my whole, fucking, entire life—Bessie, Honey and Ella.

And the fourth was dying in Colorado.

"I'll get packed," I whispered.

"That's my baby," she whispered back. "Now I'm gonna let you go and call our Bess, yes?"

"Yes," I replied quietly.

"Pack, baby."

"Okay, Ella."

I heard her disconnect. Then I felt it slice through me leaving nothing but raw in its wake.

Then I pulled my shit together and started packing.

* * *

One hour later…

"I saw him," Bessie said.

We were in her car on the way to the airport.

"What?" I asked, my mind on other things, my head so full it was aching, about to explode.

"With you on the beach," she went on.

I sucked in breath and stared out the windshield.

Then I whispered, "Bess—"

She kept going. "Watched," she whispered. "Watched him with

you. Didn't go to you, the way he was…" She cleared her throat. "The way he was with you. I liked it, Lexie."

I closed my eyes, clenched my teeth then opened them and begged, "Stop."

She was silent.

Then she wasn't.

"Thought you took so long to call me for dinner, he was gettin' through to you. You called, I was surprised. All these weeks, kept thinkin' how I could tell you, how I could talk you into—"

"Stop."

She stopped.

Then she started again.

"Shoulda talked you into givin' him another shot."

She should have. She should have done that.

But even if she did, I wouldn't have listened.

"Doesn't matter now," I whispered.

"No," she said gently. "Doesn't matter now, Lexie."

It didn't matter now.

Nothing mattered now.

She fell silent and kept driving.

* * *

Ten hours later…

I'd run the gamut, convincing myself my voice would be the miracle healing elixir that would wake Ty up the minute I whispered in his ear in his hospital bed and set him to healing to knowing by the time my plane touched down at Denver International Airport that he'd be dead by the time I arrived.

I struggled through the stupid, insane, trying process of hauling my ass down a concourse and into a fucking *subway* to get to the terminal. Whoever heard of such ridiculousness. You had to get somewhere, you got there, you didn't need then to get on a fucking *train* in the fucking *ground*. Hours in the air then you're underground? Insane!

Then that fucking train expelled me and what had to be seven thousand other people. I jockeyed for position with them to get to the fucking escalators. I finally got to the terminal and there was Julius and a very beautiful, slim, elegant but highly accessorized (and all of her accessories were pure gold) black woman.

He enfolded me in a hug and informed me gently that Ty was holding on. Then she (her name was Anana) enfolded me in a hug and we waited what felt like a year for my big bag, the only one I had so the one I had to use, to come out at baggage claim. Then they led me out to Ty's Cruiser.

I nearly lost it the minute I saw Ty's car. A car we bought together. A car that, upon seeing, irrationally I had the thought I could not set my ass in because it wasn't his, somehow it was *ours* and I couldn't deal with a reminder of what used to be the beauty of *us*. An us I threw away. I had to get away from it, run, find a way to go back in time and make the right decision. Turn in Ty's arms on the beach, put mine around him and accept back into my life the us he came all the way to Florida to give back to me.

But both of them saw me losing it and took control, getting me in, getting me buckled and getting us on our way.

Shortly after, I hit a fog then shortly after that, I hit understanding—pure and undiluted.

What the fuck was I doing?

If Ty lived for me to see him die, he was still going to fucking die.

My tall, beautiful Ty with his amazing curly thick lashed, light brown eyes and his fantastic tattoos and his defined muscles and his deep voice calling me "baby" and "mama" was going to die.

What did it matter if I saw him breathe again before he did it?

What did anything matter?

God, why couldn't I have done it even when I tried? Why couldn't I have found my way to nothing mattering before Lady Luck, the stupid fucking *bitch*, took my fucking Ty?

So I shut down because it didn't matter. Nothing mattered.

Not anymore.

Except I'd be there for the funeral.

So, shut down, I didn't notice it until Julius had already hit the garage door opener to the condo, the door was up and he was pulling in.

Seeing the Snake hit my eyes as we slid in beside her, a new slice traced through the ragged edges of raw leaving agony in its wake and my head, resting on the window, came up.

And I was so out of it, my mind so saturated with sorrow nothing penetrated, it didn't occur to me that there was the Viper, right there, shining, in one piece, without even a scratch.

"What are we doing here?" I asked.

"Need to get somethin'," Julius mumbled.

I looked around, confused.

All this rush, me flying three quarters of a continent to get to Ty's bedside in order to perform my wifely death vigil and we were making a pit stop at Ty's house?

"Julius, I don't mean to sound..." I paused, "...but...I..." I hesitated then pulled it together when he turned and looked through the seats at me. "I'd really like to get to Ty," I finished on a whisper.

His eyes went out the side window and he looked at something. Then he looked at Anana. Then he looked at me.

Then, "I won't be a second," was his totally fucking *unhinged* reply.

I gawked at him.

He threw open his door and folded out of the car.

Anana spoke. "Honey, why don't you go on up with Julius? You gotta use the bathroom?"

Actually, I did.

So, since we were making this fucking ridiculous stop to do whatever the fuck Julius had to do while my husband was dying somewhere close, I'd use this time to visit the bathroom. And during that time, I'd convince myself, after I watched my husband die. The husband I let go. The husband who tracked me down in order to try to win me back. The husband I told to go away. The husband who, the last thing he heard from me was me calling us a nightmare. After I watched *that* husband die, while I was taking a bathroom break before that happened, I'd convince myself I wouldn't fucking kill Julius.

"Yeah, be back," I muttered, threw open the door, got out and hustled to the door to the utility room, hoping to all that was holy Julius was hustling his tall, massive ass too.

Through the door to the stairs and up them, I saw Julius was standing a few feet from the opening at the top of the stairs and my eyes narrowed on his back as I climbed the stairs and they did this because he was *not* hustling.

And I heard him say, "Later, you'll get this was the only play I had to make."

I hit the top of the stairs, took three steps in, my eyes unnarrowed and my body froze solid when my eyes hit Ty standing five feet in front of Julius.

Vaguely, I noticed he was frozen solid too, his eyes on me like my eyes were on him.

Well, maybe not the same because I was sure my eyes communicated total, complete, body-rocking, earth-shattering shock that he was standing, breathing, in one piece, wearing faded jeans, a skintight white tee, looking as gorgeous as always and very, very, *very* healthy.

Healthy.

Alive.

Standing.

Gorgeous.

In one piece.

Breathing.

Ty.

"And, baby doll," I heard Julius say but didn't tear my eyes from Ty. "You give it time, beautiful, you'll get it too that this was the only play I had to make."

I watched, stunned, motionless, as Ty's eyes sliced from me to Julius.

"What fuckin' play?" his voice rumbled, so deep, so low, it reverberated against my chest.

Healthy.

Alive.

Standing.

Gorgeous.

In one piece.

Breathing.

Talking (or rumbling).

Ty.

"I told Lexie you got in a car wreck and were dyin' and she needed to come home and say good-bye. She dropped everything, Walk, and here she is. I may be fucked in the head but, to me, that fuckin' says it all." Pause while I continued to stare at my husband then, "Oh yeah, brother, I see you're pissed but it was the only play you two gave me."

I didn't move, didn't speak, just kept staring at Ty even after his angry eyes cut to me and changed from angry to something else altogether.

"Lexie?" he called but I didn't move, didn't speak, just kept staring. "Lex," he said.

I stared at Ty and counted them down.

Eleven.

Eleven hours.

Eleven hours I thought the man standing in front of me, the man I loved was as good as dead and then... then... he just *would* be.

Dead.

But he wasn't.

He started moving toward me and I came unstuck, backing up, and he stopped and growled, "Julius, she's headin' toward the stairs."

I stopped.

I stared.

Healthy.

Alive.

Standing.

Gorgeous.

In one piece.

Breathing.

Ty.

I crumbled to the floor at the same time I dissolved into tears.

"Fuck." I heard Ty clip then I was up, strong arms around me, and I heard as well as felt the rumble of the words, "Get outta my fuckin' house."

"Brother—"

"*Now!*"

That was barked.

Then I was going down, ass in his lap, his arms around me. I shoved my face in his neck, my arms went tight around his shoulders, so tight, holding on. I was never, not ever, not fucking *ever* going to let go and I sobbed into his skin.

His mouth at my ear, he whispered, "Baby, calm down."

I didn't calm down.

Eleven hours I lived with the knowledge of his loss.

It was too much.

I couldn't calm down.

One of his arms got tight and the other hand stroked my back.

"Lexie, baby," he murmured, lips still at my ear. "Calm down."

"Ee-ee-eleven hours," I gulped into his neck.

"Come again?"

"Thought you were lost for eleven hours."

His hand stopped stroking and both arms closed tight around me.

"The l-l-last thing I told you wa...was that we were a nightmare."

"Mama, breathe," he whispered.

I sucked in breath and it hitched so many times, the sound was as painful as the hitches actually were, my body bucking violently with each, and Ty growled in my ear.

Then he snarled, "I'm gonna fuckin' *kill* Julius."

My body bucked again as my breath snagged audibly and I pressed closer.

Ty fell to the side and I was holding so tight, I went with him. Then I was on my back on the couch and I felt Ty's long body stretch out beside mine. His heavy leg tangling with mine the instant I straightened them and when I felt his torso press deep to my side and partially over mine, I loosened my arms enough for him to pull back. I let my head fall to the couch and I looked at him through watery eyes.

Then my breath hitched and my body bucked again.

"Fuck," he bit off, his hand coming to my face, pulling hair away, wet hair that was sticking to my wet cheeks. "Lexie, baby, you got played. I'm right here."

I nodded. "I know."

Hair gone from both sides of my face, his big, warm hand cupped the right side, his thumb moving over my cheek, sweeping through the wetness as his face got close and I looked into his eyes, still the most beautiful feature I'd seen on any face in my life.

"So," he whispered. "Get a handle on it."

And I did.

Two handles actually. Both hands went right to his head and pulled it down to me.

Then I was kissing him.

Then he was kissing me.

Oh yes. That was better.

Then I was pulling off his tee. Then he was tugging off mine.

Then I was yanking at his belt. His hips knifed away but only so he could undo and haul off my jeans and my flip-flops went flying as he did. Then went my panties.

He rolled over me. I opened my legs. His hips slid between, his hand was working between us to finish the job I started while his mouth was working mine, his tongue inside. I was tasting him again, God, *God*, brilliant, *beautiful.*

Mine.

His hips moved back then surged forward and he was inside me.

My mouth tore from his as my neck arched.

God, *God.* Brilliant. *Beautiful.*

Mine.

He rode me fast, hard and I welcomed him, circling his hips with my legs, my hands hungry, roaming, my mouth hungrier, latched to his, drinking. Suddenly, I couldn't drink anymore and our lips brushed close as our heavy breath mingled and there it was. There it always was. So close. So huge. He rolled his hips and hit the spot and all four of my limbs clutched him to me as I cried out when I came.

It took Ty two minutes longer. One minute I was in no state to watch. The next one I did with avid, devoted concentration.

After, his head dropped forward and his face disappeared in my neck.

His cock was buried deep. My limbs were still holding him tight.

Healthy.

Alive.

Gorgeous.

Breathing.

In one piece.

Deep in me.

Ty.

I closed my eyes and sighed.

"One way to get you to calm the fuck down and stop crying," he said against the skin of my neck and my body went still. His head came up, he looked down at me and grinned. "Divorce papers are on the counter, mama. You want me to get up and go get 'em so you can sign 'em?"

I decided I'd get pissed later at the belated but highly inappropriate show that he had a very good sense of humor.

Instead I declared, "You get up and go anywhere, I'm tackling you."

His body shook as his grin spread to a smile. Then he asked, "You honestly think you can tackle me?"

"I didn't say it would be a successful tackle."

And then my husband burst out laughing.

And I watched.

He didn't give this to me often but I always watched. This time it was way better because he was doing it while still inside me.

His laughter died to a chuckle, he dropped his forehead to mine and his hand came up and curled around the side of my neck.

And when he did the last, the laughter died, his eyes held mine and he whispered, "Is my mama home?"

I swallowed but I still knew my eyes got bright and my voice was husky when I whispered back, "Yes."

He closed his eyes, shifted the lower half of his face and touched his mouth to mine. Then he lifted his head away, opened his eyes and I felt his thumb stroke my jaw.

His gaze again locked with mine, he told me gently, "Missed you, baby."

I swallowed again and my arms and legs tightened around him. "Me too."

"Do not ever leave me like that again," he ordered.

I decided not to remind him he told me to.

Instead, I said softly, "Okay."

He stared at me. Then he said softly back, "Okay."

He bent his head, touched his mouth to mine, pulled gently out and reached out a long arm. He tagged my underwear, shifted his lower half and pulled my panties up my legs.

He rolled off me and got to his feet, righting his jeans as he moved.

I lifted up, my torso turning and twisting to keep him in my sights as he walked to the kitchen.

Then I watched, my chin on my arm resting on the back of the couch, as he tagged a manila envelope from the counter, walked to the junk drawer at the side, dug through it and found what he wanted. I watched him walk to the kitchen sink. He dug out a bunch of dishes and put them on the counter. (At a glance, it was very clear Ty was not tidy, so I kept it solely at a glance.)

My breath stopped as I watched him strike a match and light the envelope on fire. He twisted and turned it until it was a sheet of flame in his hand.

He dropped it in the sink and watched it burn out. He tossed the matches on the counter and started directly back to me.

"Divorce papers," he stated.

I stared at him in shock.

Then I watched my man and his big, beautiful body with its equally beautiful tats walking back to me.

I grinned.

He grinned back.

Then I couldn't help it, I burst out laughing.

Ty

"All's well that ends well, my man," Julius said in his ear.

"All's well that ends well, my ass, Champ. Jesus fuckin' Christ, are you insane?" Walker shot back, and he felt his wife's body shift.

He looked down at her.

He had a fuckload of her toss pillows shoved behind his back on the armrest of the couch so he was only partially reclined. She had one hip in the back of the couch, the rest of her soft body was on his, his arm curled around her back, hand up his tee she was wearing, his fingers trailing the bare skin of her rounded ass.

He was talking on the phone.

She was watching her finger tracing his tat and she was doing this like she was committing it to memory.

She was wearing his tee and nothing else. He was wearing his jeans and nothing else. He hadn't even bothered to button but two of the buttons mainly because he wasn't done with her.

"She there?" Julius asked in his ear.

"Yeah," Walker replied.

"She stayin'?" Julius went on, and Walker's pulse spiked.

"Yeah," Walker repeated.

"She naked?" Julius kept going, and Walker clamped his mouth shut.

Julius chuckled, assuming mostly wrongly. Lexie was in his tee but still, by no means was access hindered.

Then Julius spoke again.

"You give this time, you'll stop bein' pissed and thank me. Now, seein' as you two are reuniting and I ain't sleepin' on no couch, Anana and me have checked into Carnal Hotel. My woman, for some fuckin' reason, right now is sittin' in reception playin' fuckin' Harry Potter fuckin' Clue with the proprietors. I'm gonna leave her to that shit 'cause, you know me, brother, I got no interest in fuckin' Clue. Colonel Mustard did it, *however* the motherfucker did it, his ass is in the hole. Don't need a reminder a' that shit. So I'm gonna get my trunks on and take a dip. We'll all go out and celebrate tomorrow 'cause the next day, Anana and me gotta get our asses home. You're buyin'. That Rooster place. And you're buyin' 'cause, no matter how pissed you are right now, you know you owe me."

Before Walker could reply, Julius gave him dead air.

He flipped his phone shut, tossed it on Lexie's jeans on the floor and scowled at it.

"We need a coffee table," she noted quietly, and his eyes moved from his phone to his woman.

She'd stopped tracing his tat and her eyes were on him. They were still slightly swollen from crying but they were also still beautiful.

The most beautiful thing he'd ever seen.

We need a coffee table.

Fuck.

Fuck!

His mama was home.

She was home and those fucking divorce papers were ashes in his sink.

That something inside him, that thing she gave him, that thing that had been gone since she was, making him feel hollow, empty, came back, filling him up. It shifted and again started settling.

She'd been there now for hours. After he burned the papers, he went back to her and took his time welcoming her home and he didn't do it with words. The first time was urgent, desperate, the same feelings for both of them but for different reasons.

The second time was not.

When he was done with her, she got on her phone. She got on her phone because, no matter he'd fucked up and hurt her, people who cared about him were worried.

First up was Honey. The easy one. Walker listened to Lexie dealing with surprised relief and then tears.

That done, next up was Ella. Same drill at first, surprised relief then tears. Then, this surprising Walker, guilt. Guilt that Ella didn't give it up to Lexie that Ty had come looking for her. Guilt that she'd kept information from Ty about where Lexie was. Guilt that her protective instinct was less protective and more misguided and stubborn mingled with sadness that she'd cost them time that didn't end in tragedy but she'd lived with that possibility for over eleven hours so the ghost of that was there all the same. Then more tears.

Lexie handled that, next up was Bess. Again, surprising Walker because Bess could be one hard bitch and she'd taken on taking care of Lexie so he figured she'd hold one serious fucking grudge, it was the same drill at first, surprised relief then tears. Then what he expected came, but the angry emotion was not directed at him and he knew this because he listened to Lexie dealing with Bess threatening murderous intent to Julius.

Lexie handled that, tossed her phone to the floor and turned to him.

That was when he learned that Bess had rescued her from Shift. In fact, Bessie had called him while on her way to rescue Lexie from Shift.

And Lex told him what Shift wanted, or, more accurately, intended to take but he blocked that shit out. He had to. He already took their future in his hands once, leaving the state in order to perpetrate a felony against that piece of shit. He didn't need a real manslaughter charge on his hands.

The minute Bess got her, they went to Ella, made plans and took off.

The beach, where Lexie thought she could find some peace.

Bess went because, another surprise to Walker because she might be a hard bitch but she also seemed one who had it going on, she didn't have it going on. She was screwing her boss who was married, stringing her along and had been for years. She was also between apartments and staying with a friend who had a cat she did not like and a tendency to play whale song for relaxation purposes, something else Bessie did not like. And she was between apartments because she kept thinking her married boss was going to stop stringing her along.

Watching Lexie's drama, Bess got her head out of her ass and realized it was time to quit pissing away her life and make a change.

So they took off to start new lives.

And they had the money to take off because, a couple of days before, without anything else of value to get her what she needed, his wife sold her fucking Charger.

He didn't say it when she admitted it but he'd be rectifying that fucking situation the next fucking day. That ride was sweet and his wife loved it, doted on that fucking thing, called it "her baby."

So she'd be getting a new one.

And, lastly, Walker learned that by the time Julius made his entirely fucked up but inarguably successful play, she was still in that fleabag motel, spending her days in her head at the beach and the proof of this was the very sweet, honeyed tan that kissed nearly every inch of her skin. Bess was working in a kid's arcade in order that they didn't piss away all their money while Lexie pulled herself together and they figured out their next move.

After she got done giving, Walker had called Julius.

And now she was there, eyes on him, body on him.

"You gave, mama, now you take," he whispered, and felt her hand flatten on his chest.

"What are you gonna give me?" she asked when he said no more.

"Everything," he answered immediately, watched her lips part and more fucking tears fill her eyes. His arm tightened around her back and he slid her up his body so they were face to face. "But first," he went on quietly, "you give me one more thing."

"What?" she whispered.

"Tell me where your rings are so I can go get 'em and put 'em back on your fuckin' finger."

She stared at him and he watched one tear slide over and glide down her cheek. He lifted a hand and, with his thumb, he swept it away. When he did, she got a handle on it.

Then she said, "They're in my purse."

"Where's your purse?"

She looked adorably confused for a moment, like she forgot what a purse was. Then she focused and said, "In your Cruiser."

He nodded, slid out from under her and moved to the stairs to the garage, buttoning enough buttons on his jeans to keep them on his hips.

Julius had played him too, saying he was in town to deal with something that came up with Walker's shit. An angle Julius kept working even though Walker told him that angle was dead and he was working with Tate and hoping Peña was out there seeing to shit. That said, Walker didn't try too hard to discourage his friend from this mission, mainly because Julius's angle was giving them shit they could use.

Julius brought Anana because Julius said Anana wanted to meet him. He'd given them the Cruiser to deal with their business because Julius had lied again and said they were having trouble with their car, a two-seater, when that was bullshit and they needed a backseat to put Lexie in.

He didn't like his brother's tactics. Julius's play was extreme and he could not imagine thinking for eleven hours that his wife was on the verge of dying. But when he went to the Cruiser and saw then grabbed her purse from the backseat then saw and grabbed her bag from the back, he couldn't help but think that regardless of how extreme the play, Julius was right. All's well that ends well. And Julius's play had ended spectacularly well and Walker's errand was conclusive evidence of that fact.

He carried them both upstairs, left her bag by the railing, took her purse to the island, dug through and found she had all the boxes in her purse. She didn't check them, had them close all the time. Definitely a smart decision. Probably also an emotional one.

He found the one he was looking for, opened it, pulled out the jewelry box inside, flipped it open and saw both rings embedded there. He tagged them and moved directly back to his wife, resuming the exact same position but with her torso more on his so her left arm was not caught between his body and the couch.

He positioned the rings and slid them on her finger.

Lexie didn't give him the chance to do what he intended to do and that was put his lips to them. She did a face plant in his chest and he felt her body rear and her breath catch on more tears.

He let her hand go and wrapped both of his arms around her as she slid her face up and pressed it into his neck.

Then he waited. This jag didn't last as long, she got a handle on it and he listened to her pull in steadying breaths. She lifted a hand, swiped at her face and settled cheek to his shoulder. That was when he lifted a hand and slid her hair away from her face and off her neck, feeling its softness fall and glide down his shoulder and arm.

He missed that. He knew he missed it but having it back he realized he *missed it.*

He wrapped his arm around her again.

"Now, baby, tell me what you wanna take," he said gently, and heard her pull in another breath.

Then she asked, "Are you okay?"

His answer was immediate and he tightened his arms on her when he gave it. "Fuck yeah."

He felt her smile against his skin before she lifted up and gave the smile to him visibly.

It faded slowly and she said, "I don't mean now, honey. I mean with everything that's going on."

His head tilted slightly on the pillows. "Everything that's going on?"

She bit her lip, hesitant, unsure and, fuck him, scared.

Fuck.

He gave her another squeeze and asked, "Baby, what the fuck?"

"With Tate," she stated quickly, and he got it. She was bringing up what bought her his anger and caused him to act like one serious dumb fuck, breaking her and nearly destroying them.

"Do not hesitate with that shit, mama," he told her. "With me, do not hesitate with *any* shit."

"Ty—" she said quietly, still unsure.

"Lex, do you think, six weeks without you, I didn't learn my fuckin' lesson?"

She blinked.

He kept going. "I learned, baby. Lived raw for six fuckin' weeks, wasting my own goddamned life *and* yours. Downloading on-line divorce papers…" He shook his head, not going back there. Not fucking there. Doing that shit cost him too much, he couldn't go back there. So he finished, "Fuck yeah, I learned."

"Lived raw?" she whispered, and he felt his brows draw together.

"Yeah, lived raw. The way a man lives when he fucks up his own life and does it by hurting the woman he loves in a way he cannot fix. A man like that lives raw and I was a man like that."

When he was done speaking he saw her lips were parted again but she just stared at him, silent.

"What?" he asked.

Lexie kept staring at him so he gave her a gentle shake.

"What?" he prompted.

"The woman he loves?" she breathed, and it was his turn to blink.

Then he confirmed, "Yeah."

"You love me?" she asked like it was a concept she'd never believe, and her response shocked the shit out of him.

"Uh…yeah," he answered. "Babe, a man like me who got fucked

like me doesn't share, at all, unless he trusts who he's sharin' with, unless their opinion matters, unless *they* matter and the way I got fucked, no way a man got fucked that way would share with pussy, *any* pussy and you know that. But with you, I shared. You played me to distract me but I wasn't hard to distract because I *wanted* your distraction. Spent five years with ninety-nine percent of my headspace taken up with my grand plan o' vengeance. I get out, ready to take that on, and a few days later I'm tourin' fucking Vegas then headin' to Moab and then at the fuckin' garden center."

His wife kept staring at him, lips parted, not making a noise, which was good because he wasn't done.

"I fuck up and lose you, I risk it all to go to Dallas to track you down and see to the errand of makin' sure Shift gets where I'm at, will always be, and I do it in a way he won't forget and I do that by further breaking my parole, committing a crime and beatin' the shit outta him *and* two of his crew."

At that, her eyes got big but he still wasn't done so he kept talking.

"Two weeks later, I find out where you are and I pick up a phone and call a man who does not like me because, years ago, I took a fuckload of his money at a table. But I know he's got more money, lots of it. I also know he lives two hours away in Aspen and I know he's got a private jet, the only hope I got of flyin' cross country without getting tagged and sent back to California. Luck shines because this man may not like me but I lay it out for him, *all* of it, mama, and I find this fuckin' guy is a fuckin' romantic. He fuels up his jet, lies on flight logs sayin' Tate Jackson is his passenger and flies me to fuckin' Florida. This guy is so much of a fuckin' romantic, I come back to the airstrip without you, swear to fuckin' God, he looks near as devastated as me. Now, no man does all that for a woman he doesn't love and definitely not a man like me."

He stopped speaking and saw her lips were not parted, her eyes not wide.

Her mouth was hanging open and her eyes were huge.

She snapped her mouth shut.

Then she asked, "You beat up Shift?"

"Bessie called me, told me he was dickin' with you, got outta bed, hauled my ass to Dallas and, yeah, the one word he spoke he had to spit out a mouthful of blood to speak it."

"You beat up Shift." This time it was a statement so Walker didn't respond. Then she asked, "You arranged a ride in a private jet to get to me?"

"Mama, you were in fuckin' Florida. First, I cannot take that time to drive it, too much of a risk someone findin' out I'm gone and where I went. I did not want to bring you back only to be sent away. Second, I take that time to drive it and find you've moved on, I lose that time. I had to catch a flight and that was the only option open for me."

Lexie didn't speak, she just stared at him.

So he started, "Lex—" but got no further.

And he got no further because she whispered, "You know, I love you too."

That thing, that thing she gave him that started to settle again, shifted and warmed, digging deep, taking root.

"Lexie—" he whispered back, his arms convulsing around her but he again got no further.

"Fell in love with you when I opened my eyes in Vegas, turned in bed and saw you put my bouquet in a vase."

Fuck him.

Fuck... *him.*

"Shut it, mama." He was still whispering.

"At the pool, when you showed, my day started."

His arms now gave her a warning squeeze.

"Shut it," he growled.

"Sitting at the breakfast table, seeing your wedding ring, being able to really look at it on your finger up close for the first time, I had to touch it so I could remind myself I was the one who got to put it there."

Fuck.

Him.

"Shut it." This time, it was a rumble.

"The next morning, when you *didn't* show at the pool, I had to find you so I could start my day."

He rolled and shifted until he was on top of her and he repeated, "Shut it."

"Six weeks without you, I'd wake up and hours later go to sleep and not once did my day dawn."

"Baby, shut... *it*."

"You took the shadow off my world."

All right, his woman wasn't going to shut it, he was going to shut it for her.

So he set about doing that.

And when she was reduced to making nothing but those sexy-as-hell noises in the back of her throat each time he slowly slid his cock in and filled her then whimpered when he slowly slid it out, he was again ready to talk.

But he was going to be doing the talking.

"Look at me," he ordered after filling his wife with him, his voice thick and her closed eyes instantly opened, the small arch she had in her neck righting and he had her attention. "I don't give a fuck we're both still raw. I don't give a fuck, even without that, we're still new. I don't give a fuck we got shit out there pressing in. I wanna plant my baby in you."

One of her feet was in the couch, the other leg wrapped around the back of his thigh, both arms were around him, hands roaming. But at his words, both legs curved around his hips and both arms went tight.

And he had his answer.

"Ty," she breathed.

"We both know we got no time to waste."

One of her hands slid up to wrap around the back of his head.

Then, pure Lexie, no bullshit, no hesitation, she gave even though he already knew he had what he wanted. But even if she said no, he was lying on top of the only thing in the world he ever truly wanted and she was filled with his cock.

"Okay," she whispered.

"You go off the Pill tomorrow," he ordered, and she instantly nodded.

Pure Lexie, no bullshit, no hesitation, she gave.

Instantly.

He grinned at her. His woman grinned back.

Then he slowly pulled out and slid back in again as he watched her eyes drift closed.

He dropped his head and kept going slow, but, lips to her ear, he asked, "How many you want?"

"Four," she answered immediately, and he quit moving, luckily on an inward glide and his head came up.

"Four?" he asked.

"Four," Lexie answered.

"Four kids?" he added detail in order to confirm.

She grinned again. "Four kids."

"Shit, mama, good thing we're gettin' started tomorrow."

She giggled.

Walker didn't watch. He dropped his head so he could feel her laughter on his tongue.

Then he felt her laughter on his tongue.

Then her laughter stopped because he again got busy.

CHAPTER SIXTEEN

Official Steel Magnolia's Rulebook

Ty

Ty was still brushing his teeth when Lexie finished, spit, rinsed, reached and shoved her toothbrush back in the holder affixed to the wall between their two basins. She took a side step closer to him, and he watched in the mirror as her head bent and she dug into some flowered bag that was sitting on the counter between their sinks. She pulled out a pale pink round case, turned and walked into the little room with the toilet. He heard something small splash into the toilet and again and again and again, and this went on awhile. She walked out of that little room, dropped the case in the small trash bin and her eyes slid to his in the mirror.

She grinned.

Then she reached into the shower stall and turned on the water, tugged off his tee she wore to bed and shimmied out of her panties. She stepped in.

He bent his neck, spit, rinsed, reached and shoved his toothbrush opposite Lexie's in the holder.

Then he moved to the shower.

* * *

Ty was standing with a hip against the counter, bowl of sliced bananas, cut strawberries and yogurt held up in front of him, spoon in his other hand, shoveling the food into his mouth.

His eyes were on his woman who was back in his tee and a clean pair of panties, hair wet, combed back but drying fast and wavy in the Colorado air. She was filling a travel mug of coffee for him at the same time eyeing the dirty dishes, the stains and crumbs on the countertops and the piles of mail all the while looking like she wished she could stop eyeing them.

Before she left, there was a time or two when he came home when their bed wasn't made but this was rare. A time or two when she'd done a half-assed job of it, yanking up the covers, fluffing pillows and tossing them wherever they'd land, but this last was more than he'd ever do. A couple of days would go by where their clothes would remain on the floor where they'd discarded them or tossed them in the preliminaries to fucking. A week might go by where she'd let mail stack up on the side kitchen counter. A few times she'd leave the dishes in the sink and do them the next morning.

But under all that was always clean and eventually she'd get to tidying.

Clearly, six weeks of buildup was about five and a half weeks too much.

He chewed, he swallowed then he spoke. "Fill the dishwasher, mama, and I'll empty it. I'll take out the trash. I will not vacuum. I will not clean a fuckin' toilet. And, on the inside, I had enough of sweepin' and moppin' for a lifetime. So, I will kick in in the ways I just said. Other than that, it's up to you to decide if you can hack it or if we gotta find a cleaning lady."

The first words he spoke, her eyes came to him.

When he was done she asked, "You'll fill the dishwasher and empty it. Did you actually *do* that while I was away?"

Even though he sensed she was teasing him, his gut tightened at her tone.

He'd just got finished fucking her in the shower. Before that, she made a show that she was taking them forward, with him all the way to their next step of building a family. And after she did that, she'd grinned at him.

But, since their shower, he got that tone and that tone matched the set of her frame. Quiet, pensive, borderline uncertain.

He'd bought that, being a dumb fuck, treating her like a dick, saying shit to her he shouldn't have said, comparing her to Misty, a woman he hated *and* she hated. And, it was arguable, but he got the sense his wife hated Misty at least as much as he did. On some level, it could be worse, seeing as Misty was a sister and Misty strapped the sisterhood with the shit he piled on Lexie, shit she didn't deserve. Misty perpetrated a betrayal to that sisterhood, an unforgiveable one.

But Lexie was treading cautiously, probably not even knowing she was doing it. Twice he fucked up, twice he was a dick, twice he lashed out and mouthed off. The first time, she didn't do shit to deserve it. The second time, she did but his response was way the fuck over the line.

Now, he could see, she was going to do everything she could so she didn't buy a third time.

Ty would take that tone over the one she spoke to him with when she was on the beach, her voice void, dead, remote. He never wanted to hear her talk like that again, feel the darkness that shrouded her, experience her being so far gone, he knew he could run flat out every day for the rest of his life and never reach her. He never wanted that back, for him or for her. That was so agonizing, he'd take anything else from her, even this.

That said, he still didn't like it.

So he put his spoon in the bowl, set it aside and ordered gently, "Mama, come here."

Lexie, being Lexie, came direct to him.

He wound an arm around her waist, pulling her body to his and her hands came up, flat on his chest, not to hold him back, just to rest them there as her head tipped way back to look at him and his other hand wrapped around her neck, his thumb moving on her jaw.

"It's gonna take time for you to trust me again—" he started but she cut him off swiftly.

"I trust you."

His thumb stopped stroking and his fingers gave her a light squeeze as he dipped his face closer. "Baby, you don't."

"I do."

He shook his head and asked quietly, "Can you shut up a minute so I can talk?"

She pressed her lips together but her eyes flared.

Now *that*, he liked.

He beat back a grin and talked.

"Drama over, we're back to us and I didn't just fuck up, I did it huge. I said nasty shit that shouldn't have been said and I can't take that back. The wounds I inflicted went deep and I can only hope to Christ one day they heal over. Until that day, mama, all I can promise you is that I'll do all I can do to beat that shit back and never do that to you again."

She nodded, her face getting soft and Ty kept going.

"But we got a rocky road ahead of us and I don't know where it's gonna lead before we get to the other side. The only thing I can give you is, that shit comes outta my mouth and cuts you, you gotta understand that shit was planted in me and I gotta get it out. I'll try to do it in a way that doesn't harm you but I obviously am not battin' a thousand with that so I can make no promises except I'll try. What you need to give me is to know it is not about you, it's about me. You gotta suck it up and stand by me. You gotta know, in the end, I'll work my ass off to make it all worth it to you, and you gotta always remember I love you and I have never, not once, said those words to any breathing soul so you also gotta know what that means."

She blinked.

Then she asked, "You've never told anyone you love them?"

He shook his head and answered, "Loved one person in my life, Tuku. He died without me sayin' those words to him. And, to this day, even though he was not a man prone to that kind of shit, I wished I'd said it and I wished he'd died knowin' what he gave me and all he meant to me."

She nodded, her face understanding in a way that made the wound he had from what they went through, a wound still raw, a gaping wound torn open in the left side of his chest, pulsate because he knew from her look she'd learned that lesson the day before.

He didn't do that to her but what he did forced Julius's hand so he had that to make up for too.

"I can give you that, Ty," she whispered, her hands pressing into his chest.

"Thanks, baby," he whispered back then still spoke soft but firm when he ordered, "Now, I took that shadow out of your life but this mornin', I see it's over you. Get rid of it. This is you and me, people live through this shit and if they manage to do it together, it makes them stronger. Power through, mama, and get to that other side with me."

She stared into his eyes and kept whispering when she asked, "How did you know?"

He dipped his face even closer, gliding his hand from her neck up into her hair and his arm around her got tight. "*My* Lexie beams bright and she can do that shit even in her sleep. The Lexie shuffling around this kitchen is doin' it under a cloud."

She held his eyes. Then she pressed closer. Finally, her lips tipped up at the ends.

Then she said, "Okay, honey, I'll turn on the light."

He felt his lips tip up at the ends too before he replied, "Okay."

She got up on her toes and kissed his throat. He closed his eyes when he felt her lips and the brush of her soft hair on his jaw. He opened them when she dropped back to her feet.

When he had her gaze again, he reminded her, "We got busy and you didn't get your take last night. Lotta shit goin' down and I'm skippin' my workout tonight to come straight home and take you to the Dodge dealership outside Gnaw Bone before we gotta be home to get ready to take Julius and Anana to The Rooster."

Her brows drew together. "The Dodge—?"

"Gettin' you another Charger."

Light dawned then right on its heels denial started. "Ty—"

He shook his head and his fingers in her hair fisted and tugged gently. "Gettin' you another Charger."

"But…I don't…you can't…" She paused then finished, "The money."

"The angle Tate's workin' doesn't cost a fuckload of cash to grease the palms of scumbags who won't do something for nothing. You need a car that I can trust. The Snake would do in the summer, a Charger's better for the winter. You loved that car. What I did meant you lost it. I got the cash, you're gettin' another one." He paused then finished, "Tonight."

"But—"

He cut her off. "And, this weekend, fuck me, we're goin' shoppin' for a coffee table."

She blinked. Then tried again, "But—"

"And I gotta send more money to Ella to get your shit back."

"My shit is at Dominic and Daniel's. They have an old ranch house with a barn so they could store it for me. They were waiting for me to settle somewhere so they could send it to me."

Well, thank fuck. One problem that wouldn't cost a fucking fortune or take weeks.

"Good. I'll talk to the boys, get your shit home."

She grinned. Then she told him, "We don't need a coffee table."

"You said last night we do," he reminded her.

She pressed closer. "Ty, honey," she said softly, "I get what you're trying to do but it's going to be okay. *I'm* going to be okay. You don't have to give me my every heart's desire to prove to me you love me."

"Mama, every other time I wanna turn on the fuckin' TV, gotta first locate the remotes and this usually involves diggin' them outta the cushions. That shit's a pain in the ass. Last week, got up and kicked over a nearly full beer I put on the floor. That shit's *also* a pain in the ass. We need a fuckin' coffee table."

She giggled. He heard it, saw it, felt it and liked it.

Then she said, "All right, baby, we'll buy a coffee table." Pause then, "And a rug."

Pushing it.

Whatever.

"And a rug," he agreed.

She smiled at him.

He brought them back to the matter at hand.

"So, what I was sayin', we gotta get you your ride, we gotta take Julius and Anana out so we can pay them back for causin' you fear, heartbreak and the need to make a mad dash across the United States in order to watch me die, but you also gotta be briefed. I don't know what you got planned today but I want you in town, at the garage, twelve thirty. We'll go to lunch at the diner and I'll fill you in."

"I'm going to be unpacking, cleaning the house and finding out if Dominic replaced me," she informed him then smiled again. "So lunch with my husband fits right in."

His arm gave her another squeeze and he smiled back.

Then she asked, "*Did* Dominic replace me? He hadn't when I talked to him a couple of weeks ago but—"

"Mama, I'm not hip on the goings-on at the local salon. Think, to be a Steel Magnolia, you gotta have a pussy."

After he said that, his wife burst out laughing, so hard, she couldn't hold her head up. She dropped it to his chest, her hands clenched in fists in his tee and her shoulders shook with it. And as he listened to and felt her humor, he wondered why he didn't give her more of it.

He had to make up for that too.

Her head shot back and, still laughing, she informed him, "I'm not sure there's an official Steel Magnolia's rulebook but I think you're right, that particular requirement goes without saying."

He grinned at her.

Then he changed the subject to another important one he had to touch on before he went to work and as he did it, his fist slid out of her hair and his arm moved down to wrap around her shoulders.

"All right, Lex, you got a busy schedule but take some time, call Bess and talk to her about drivin' out here. She wants to put Dallas in her past, we got an extra room while she gives Colorado a try."

The laughter fled her face but warmth suffused it. Her body, already pressed close, melted into his and she whispered, "Ty."

"But, she takes that room, she sleeps with the fuckin' door closed."

The warmth stayed in her expression but her eyes lit with more humor as she said quietly, "All right, honey, I'll make that clear."

He grinned at his wife. Then he muttered, "Gotta get to work, baby."

She nodded. He dropped his forehead to touch it to hers, dipped his chin so he could brush his mouth to hers then he let her go, walked around her, nabbed his travel mug and slid the backs of his fingers along her hip as he moved back by her, saying, "Later, mama."

He felt her eyes on him as he walked through the kitchen to the stairs and heard her saying, "Later, honey."

And having that back, all of it, from waking up with his wife to fucking her in the shower to being with her in the kitchen to feeling her eyes on him while he walked to the stairs to hearing her soft, sweet, "Later…" he knew he missed it when it was gone but it being back he knew he actually *missed it.*

But it was back and as he moved down the stairs, he prayed to God that this time he kept his shit together and took care of it.

* * *

Two and a half hours later, Ty was under the hood of a car when his phone rang. He swung out, straightened, nabbed a rag, used it to do a half-assed swipe to get the grease off his hands, pulled his phone out of his back pocket and saw a number he didn't recognize but an area code he did.

Dallas.

He flipped it open and put it to his ear.

"Yo."

"Ty." He heard a man say.

"Yeah?"

"Angel."

Fuck him.

Peña.

"Peña," he greeted.

"Just so you know, Duane Martinez came in two days ago to make a belated report that he was assaulted by one Tyrell Walker."

Fuck.

"You're shittin' me," Ty rumbled.

"No, a fuckin' drug dealer pimp walks into the fuckin' police station lookin' like the weasel he is but a healthy one and he does it to report a fuckin' assault."

Then Ty heard a deep chuckle.

Ty was not amused.

Peña kept talking. "Seein' as I got an interest in Martinez and all his dirty deeds, he was flagged and sent to me. So, he made this report to me. Now, make no mistake, Ty, I take my work seriously, but

I gotta admit, he gave this report, I lost my pen. Swear to God, don't know where I put that fucker."

And at that, Ty was amused. Therefore he dropped his head and grinned at his boots.

"Sucks, man," he murmured into his phone.

"I know. Don't worry, I found it since. I also called up to Carnal and found out you were down with the twenty-four-hour flu so no way you could be violatin' parole, drivin' your ass into the Lone Star state to deliver a message with your fists. Got a statement from a Tatum Jackson confirming the state of your health and Jackson would know because his wife brought you chicken soup. Heard that did the trick and was glad to hear it, *esé*."

Ty lifted his head and looked out of one of the bays, still grinning. "It was a quick recovery."

"Good news," Peña muttered then went on. "So, I've reported this to Mr. Martinez, asking him if he wants to amend his statement. To say he was shocked as shit would be an understatement. He had neglected to include the information that there was a man with you that apparently you referred to as 'Tate' but he included this information when I spoke to him again. I asked if Mr. Jackson's wife was also in attendance during his recent ass-kicking, considering she stands as both your and Mr. Jackson's alibi, but he said no."

Ty was close to laughter but he didn't give in to it because Peña kept going.

"I then reminded him that it was an unlawful act to make false statements to the police, that he had no evidence of said ass-kicking as he nor his esteemed colleagues who also got their asses kicked had any medical attention where there were actually records made. And last, the only three witnesses were the three who allegedly got their asses kicked and I explained, since their three rap sheets could be used as a set of encyclopedias detailing the wide array of crimes available to commit, not one of them was a reliable witness."

Ty listened to Peña take a deep breath before he continued.

"I further informed them that the man they were accusing

of being accessory to a crime was an ex-cop and current highly respected fugitive apprehension agent, something else that I could tell shocked the shit outta him. I then reminded Mr. Martinez that it is 'hood lore that a Tyrell Walker wiped his ass at poker some years back and Mr. Martinez was not exactly quiet when he crowed about Mr. Walker being sent down for manslaughter seein' as he still owed him a whack. I suggested that perhaps he was using the police force to extricate him from this debt and that such an endeavor would be frowned upon. He saw the wisdom of retracting his statement, which was lucky for me because I had no record of it and my cap is not big on that shit."

Jesus, Shift wasn't only a piece-of-shit motherfucker, he was also seriously fucking stupid.

And Ty was *still* grinning when he noted, "What you're sayin' is I owe you."

"No." Peña's voice got low. "What I'm sayin' is, don't know what shit brought Lexie back Dallas way, but thank you for provin' me not wrong you give a fuck about your wife. Martinez spread wide he was recruitin' Rodriguez's pussy for his stable and was already takin' orders. You took care a' that so I didn't have to. And also what I'm sayin' is, the message you sent was not received. He may leave Lexie alone but he is one pissed-off black man, and that rage is directed at you. You got some experience, I bet, watchin' your back. Use it and stay diligent."

Ty's grin died and he muttered, "Fuck, what I do not need is another fuckin' problem."

"Well, now you're makin' me feel like Santa Claus," Peña replied, and Ty turned and walked deeper into the garage.

Then he asked, "You gonna share?"

"Well, I wasn't seein' as I want your nose clean with all that I'm doin' though I may be in Dallas but my karma must be in Carnal since I got a message for you this morning from one of your neighbors."

Shit.

Peña kept talking.

"First, I'll tell you that, when I was up there, I walked into the Carnal Police Department and flashed my badge. The officer on duty at the desk, not a very bright bulb, took one look at it, opened the doors wide *and* gave me his code to the copy machine. Considering those fuckwads have been gettin' away with murder, literally, I figured they all couldn't be as dumb as the man they got guardin' the door so I also figured I didn't have much time. But I did use my time at the copy machine wisely before someone cottoned on to my activities and I was cordially and collegially ousted."

Shit.

Peña was not done.

"I will not share with you what I found. I will also not share with you what some of Carnal's citizens I spoke with in a variety of establishments readily shared with me. What I *will* share with you is that, after spending some time since leaving the beautiful state of Colorado acting on some of the things I learned during my vacation, my activities have been noted. And this morning, an Officer Frank Dolinski phoned me wanting to have a cop-to-cop chat."

Holy *shit.*

Ty felt his gut get tight but Peña was still not done.

"Now, Officer Dolinski told me that he heard word some time ago that you were being paroled and, seeing as he's either one smart motherfucker or clairvoyant, he knew your release could mean good or bad things. But, good or bad, he told me you got a lotta friends in that burg, all of 'em been nursin' not a small amount of antagonism for over five years, so it was gonna mean *something.* Further, Officer Dolinski's father was a cop, as was his grandfather, and he actually likes his job, wanted to follow the family tradition since he could remember and earned his badge to protect and serve and not doin' both to cover his own ass. So, he's been payin' a lot of attention and when I say that I mean *a lot* and when I say a lot I mean for a *fuckin' long time.*"

Ty was listening, his gut tight and his chest squeezing, and when Peña didn't continue, he prompted, "Yeah?"

"Yeah," Peña replied. "So, Dolinski set the ball rolling *prior* to your release but shit like this goes slow and you were out before things could get sorted."

"What shit goes slow and what things are gettin' sorted?" Ty asked.

"Dolinski's deep-cover mission for an internal investigation into pretty much the entirety of the Carnal Police Department with specific interest in Police Chief Arnold Fuller," Peña answered.

Ty's body went solid.

Holy fuck.

Peña continued.

"This investigation centers around a variety of things including Fuller's mishandling of a case when a serial killer was hunting his patch after which a complaint was lodged by a Special Agent Tambo of the FBI. This complaint was not only about Fuller's department fumbling the case but also Fuller's manner and professional approach, questioning his suitability to be in his job. Tambo's complaint was added to complaints from Carnal's citizens that were piling up, and IA started sniffing around but could get nowhere seein' as tracks were covered and nearly every cop in the department was dirty so they needed an inside man and, mud's so deep at Carnal PD, they couldn't see clear of it and find one."

Peña took in another deep breath, Ty did it with him and Peña kept on.

"Dolinski's coming forward as a whistleblower and willing undercover agent set the ball in motion for an intense investigation into the entire department but centering on the aforementioned fuckup with the serial killer. This as well as the possible collaboration of local law enforcement officers in the cover-up of the murder of a drug dealer in Los Angeles and the extradition of a Carnal citizen to stand trial for that crime. IA in *LA*, who are working joint with your local IA on that particular concern, apparently has some information that the dealer murdered was allegedly dealing blow to one Detective

Gene Fuller, who happens to be Police Chief Arnie Fuller's brother. And ole Gene reportedly likes his blow, enough to get in deep with a dealer and, on a cop's salary, the only way to cover that debt was for the dealer to go away."

Holy *fuck*.

Peña kept talking.

"As you know, two dealers dead in California by the same gun, a .38. What you *don't* know is that Detective Chet Palmer has a .38 registered for personal use. But, when questions were asked, Detective Palmer was requested to produce this gun and couldn't do so saying, when he went to get it, he noticed it was missing. He then belatedly reported it stolen *and* says that it's been years since he's touched that gun so it could have been years ago it was stolen. Two and two began to make four and the person making four in Carnal for IA is Officer Frank Dolinski."

Holy fuck.

Peña *still* wasn't done.

"See, the problem Dolinski has now is that there is a very clever Carnal ex-cop whose friend went down for a crime he didn't commit and, if you don't mind me sayin', a very clever current cop in Dallas who's got an interest in that man's wife who are both nosin' around. Makin' matters worse, for some reason I'm sure you know nothin' about, although some time has gone by, Special Agent Tambo *and* his superiors have suddenly started asking questions about the complaint Tambo lodged, and they haven't been real thrilled with the answers they've been receivin'."

Ty closed his eyes, his lips twitching, and opened them when Peña went on.

"Instead of shruggin' their shoulders and movin' on, they've decided to start leaning and they got a lot of weight. All this and Dolinski's already got his ass swinging *way the fuck* out there. It is not lost on all concerned that two black men in two states framed for murders they didn't commit, one taking his life, one losing five years of his, if uncovered, will make national news. Dolinski says because of this things are *in*tense at the Carnal Police Station, and he wants me to be aware that if these outside factions keep up their activities, some twitchy people may get seriously fuckin' twitchy and Officer Dolinski says he's *this close* to askin' his girl to take his hand in marriage. He'd actually like to get the chance to ask her, not to mention marry her and make a family with her, and not get his head blown off and some random black guy who's unlucky enough to look at one of these assholes funny servin' time for that crime."

Ty was silent and he was silenced by surprise.

Then he asked, "You backin' off?"

To that, Peña was also silent for long moments before he said quietly, "Been chewin' on that."

He paused a long pause then continued.

"And, see, I wanna help Officer Dolinski out. Only got a very long phone call to get to know this guy but I got the feelin' he's a good man. Know, doin' what he's doin', he's a moral man and a brave one. Problem is, he shared with me that someone got the idea that all this started with you gettin' out. It was all quiet before you came home so they felt the best course of action was to make a statement and *get you back in*. And seein' as you weren't helpin' with that, not barrelin' into Carnal, guns ablaze, metin' out retribution, but instead enjoying your newlywed status, they felt it was necessary to draw you out. And they felt the best way to do that was to fuck with your wife. So, Officer Dolinski told me they put that plan into action, and he promised me he'd do what he could for Lexie."

The reason why Frank intervened when Rowdy pulled Lexie over. He heard it over the radio and hightailed his ass to take her back.

Ty drew in a deep breath.

Peña kept right on going.

"But I'm not feelin' good about that promise or how long it'll take for this shit to get done and if shit's so buried that wrongs will never be righted. I'm not big on wrongs not bein' righted. Wrongs bein' righted are kinda why I got in the cop business in the first fuckin' place. So I still feel I gotta do what I can do to make that happen."

Ty made no response.

So Peña asked, "You gonna talk to Mr. Jackson?"

To that, Ty answered, "Yeah, but we're not backin' down either. Frank's a good man and I feel for him. He's already taken Lexie's back. The thing is, I don't wanna go back in and Lexie and I wanna start a family. I want my kids to have a father who doesn't have that kinda shadow hangin' over his head. The mission is to stay free and clear my name. I trust Frank but one man against many isn't gonna do shit. I cannot say I'm not smilin' inside that these guys are feelin' the heat enough to get twitchy so not sure I wanna turn down that heat. We'll do what we can to have Frank's back but it's not only his future that's ridin' on this."

Silence, then Peña exposed he'd honed in on one thing in all that Ty said. "You and Lexie tryin'?"

Fuck.

Ty didn't want to answer but he did. "Yeah."

Then a surprised, "Already?"

"Angel, I lost five years. You think I'm big on pissin' away any more?"

"Got a point," Peña muttered.

"Anyway, Lex wants four kids. She's thirty-four, she wants that, we gotta get started."

He listened to Peña roar with laughter before, "*Madre de Dios, esé*, you just cured me. *Tu esposa es muy linda*, but four kids? That's about three headaches and definitely three college tuitions I'm glad I'm gonna miss."

Shit. That wasn't something he'd thought about. He was rethinking his vow never to sit a game of poker again, and definitely the coffee table shopping expedition when Peña finished it.

"All right, Ty, don't expect an invitation to the baby shower but you got my number now. You need me, *she* needs me, I'm a phone call away. I'll keep an eye on Martinez and give you a heads-up, I hear anything."

"Thanks, Angel, and a little payback, not for you but just in case Frank calls you, we haven't been sittin' on our hands. He needs to lean on someone to flip, he leans on Crabtree."

"Crabtree?"

"As in Officer Rowdy Crabtree."

"What you got for him to use on Officer Crabtree?"

"What I got is that Officer Crabtree visits Denver every other weekend and he does this because there's a certain service he can get in Denver he can't get out here in the mountains. And this service is provided by men who look like boys and it's provided for a fee."

A low whistle then, "How solid is this?"

"*Very.*"

"Ole Frank gave me his number," Peña told him.

"'Spect you'll find time to call."

"He's not on your speed dial?"

"Frank's givin' me *and* Tate a wide berth these days."

"Probably smart," Peña muttered.

It probably was and now Ty knew why. Before, he thought Frank had gone to the dark side, which meant his stepping in for Lexie didn't make sense. Now it made sense.

"One thing," Ty added. "Frank's gonna use this, he needs to do it soon. If he doesn't, Crabtree is gonna have a talk with someone else. He sits a cruiser, he's not gonna be pullin' my wife over for bullshit, and he was involved in my shit so I got a desire to watch him squirm. This info is new, we've not been sittin' on it long and we won't sit on it much longer. He flips for Frank or he flips for me but he's gonna flip."

"Right," Peña whispered.

"Right," Ty confirmed.

"You got more?" Peña asked.

"We do but what we got is shit I'm gonna keep. Crabtree isn't the only one needs to squirm."

Silence then, "Right. Okay then, Ty, again, stay sharp."

"Same to you."

"Keep her happy."

Jesus.

"That's another mission, Angel."

This got a chuckle then, "I'll bet. Later, *amigo*."

"Later."

He flipped his phone shut.

Then he flipped it open and called Tate.

He flipped it shut again and got back to work.

* * *

At twelve thirty, Ty was standing with Wood just outside a bay when the Viper turned into the garage and growled down the forecourt.

Ty and Wood stopped talking in order to watch. So did every single man on Wood's payroll and Ty didn't even have to turn to confirm. Lexie had visited him in the forecourt of the garage twice and once was incentive enough for any man to stop what he was doing and pay attention.

But watching her park the Viper, throw out a long, tanned leg and fold out of his car wearing a pair of black short shorts, the tight, berry-colored, halter-topped tee she was wearing that day by the pool in Vegas, high-heeled black sandals on her feet, a pair of classy, black-framed shades covering her eyes and her long, soft, shining hair falling over her shoulders could cause even Rowdy Crabtree, with his closeted tendencies, to have one motherfucker of a wet dream.

Ty grinned.

Wood muttered, "Shit."

Ty's grin got bigger.

Lexie shouted excitedly across the forecourt, "You left me the Snake!" and then she did it.

Racing across the forecourt, he braced and she launched herself in his arms. This time, she wrapped her long legs around his hips and when he caught her, he did it with hands to her ass.

She gave him a hard kiss, pulled away and gave him a huge smile, her light beaming bright and blinding.

Good.

She'd flipped on the switch.

And she liked the Viper. A lot.

"Babe, I'm at work," he reminded her but didn't even twitch in an effort to put her on her feet.

To this, she turned her head to Wood and greeted, "Hey, Wood."

"Hey, Lexie. Welcome back."

"Thanks," she replied. "Happy to be back."

Wood's eyes did a sweep of them while his lips twitched and he noted, "That actually wasn't lost on me."

She shot him a smile then asked, "Do you mind your mechanics engaging in public displays of affection?"

Ty shook his head. Not in denial, because he found it amusing his wife was a goof.

He'd missed that too, as in *missed it.*

Wood answered, "Just as long as you keep your clothes on."

"Can do," she muttered then looked back at Ty. "Soooo," she drew this out then went on, "the bad news is, Dominic hired someone."

She didn't look too broken up about it but, still, he knew she liked that job so he murmured, "Sorry, mama."

Her smile flashed and she continued, "The good news is, he caught her with her fingers in the cash register only *two days* after she started and fired her ass so…" Her arms that were curled around his shoulders disappeared as she threw them in the air and Ty had to lean back so his wife wouldn't topple the other direction as she shouted, "I'm back in!"

Ty turned his head to Wood and explained, "My wife's a goof."

Wood chuckled.

"I'm not a goof," Lexie protested, winding her tanned arms around his shoulders again.

"Baby, you're a goof. Total goof," Wood declared. "But you stick with that, you work it."

Wood was not wrong about that.

"Okay," she said quietly, turned to Ty, lifted her shades to her forehead and gave him big eyes that told him without words to stop telling people she was a goof.

That was when Ty chuckled.

He squeezed her ass, gave her a small heft to communicate his intentions, her legs loosened from his hips and he dropped her to her heels.

She moved her shades back to her eyes and leaned her body into Ty as Ty said to Wood, "Lunch."

"Right." Wood jerked up his chin. "Take your time. You been doin' so much overtime, actually saves me money you take a long lunch."

"Thanks, man," Ty muttered.

"Later, Wood," she gave her farewell.

"Later, Lexie," Wood returned.

Ty moved, Lexie grabbed his hand and laced her fingers through his.

When she did, his tightened.

They were halfway down the forecourt when she asked, "Overtime?"

"Wood and Pop are always busy and gettin' busier, especially in the summer," Ty answered. "They got a good reputation for their work and got enough work that they can keep the cost of parts low and pass that on to customers so folks from Chantelle and even Gnaw Bone go outta their way to use us for regular maintenance and repairs. But Pop's been workin' on Harleys for goin' on fifty years. He's good at it, passed that shit down to all his boys so men with bikes from as far away as Aspen, Grand Junction, Glenwood Springs even Denver bring 'em to Pop. They were two mechanics down when they took me on and they held off hirin' in order to cover me when I got out. Their desire to continue tradition of good work, they don't hire just anyone and still haven't found another guy. Seein' as I had to take a few unexpected days off, so Wood wouldn't eat that, I started workin' late to make up the time. Then he needed me, I kept that shit up and started workin' Thursdays. Gym stays open late, could go after the garage was closed and did 'cause I had no reason to get home."

It was more than that. It was all the evidence of the them he fucked up all around that he told himself to get shot of and never could bring himself to do it that made him not want to go home. Now he was glad he didn't get rid of it. But just a day ago, walking down the stairs in the morning and up them at night was a form of torture.

Not to mention, considering he was an experienced mechanic therefore his salary was far from shit and Pop and Wood paid time and a half overtime, he'd made a fuckload of cake.

"Are you going to keep doing that, the overtime, I mean?" she asked, and his hand gave hers a squeeze.

"Depends," he answered then joked, "I gotta save for four college tuitions, I probably should start now."

He felt her shades on him as they turned the corner to the sidewalk and he looked down at her.

"Is money an issue?"

She clearly didn't take it as a joke.

"Babe, we stick together, *nothin'* is an issue."

"What?"

He stopped, stopping her with a tug on her hand then he drew her close, letting her hand go and winding both arms around her. When her shades hit his, he spoke.

"This is it, Team Walker, you and me. We want somethin', we find a way to get it. We hit a rough patch, we find a way to get over it. We face a challenge, we find a way to beat it. It's good, we savor it. What I'm sayin' is, this team is a winner. We never forget to celebrate the victories and we get a lotta those because we never admit defeat."

She stared up at him, unmoving, silent and with the dark lenses on her shades, he couldn't see her eyes.

So his arms gave her a squeeze and he called, "Lexie?"

"Team Walker," she whispered.

"Team Walker," he repeated firmly.

Her hands slid up his arms, his shoulders so both could curl around the sides of his neck where she squeezed as she got up on her toes and said softly, "I like that."

"That's good because the position you play on this team lasts a lifetime."

She grinned then smiled then giggled.

Then she put pressure on his neck, he bent and took her mouth.

He let her go, took her hand and guided her down three blocks and across the street to the diner.

They were seated in a booth at the back, a booth he requested because no one was sitting around it so no one could overhear. His back was to the wall. His woman was across from him.

They'd ordered, got their drinks and Ty started sharing, including Detective Angel Peña's involvement, which got him a loud gasp then a sweet smile that was not for him but for Peña, who she might not think about a lot but she clearly liked. It was a smile Peña would have liked to have seen. It was a smile Ty was glad he never would.

Their food was served and he was in the middle of telling her about Crabtree when his phone rang. He leaned forward, pulled it out, looked at the display and it said, "Tate calling."

"Eat, mama, gotta take this. It's Tate," he muttered. She nodded and continued to devour her curly fries and cheeseburger as he flipped his phone open and put it to his ear. "Yo."

"Brother, you sittin' down?"

Fuck.

"What?"

"Misty Keaton is dead."

Ty froze. Then his blood turned to ice because he guessed their play.

"Do not tell me they're gonna try to pin that shit on me."

"Hard to do since she was done with Rowdy Crabtree's service revolver."

Holy fuck.

Two birds, one stone.

His eyes went to his wife who did not miss his words, tone and vibe and was staring at him with one ketchup-soaked fry halfway to her mouth, eyes big, face pale. Ty gave her a short head shake in hopes of calming her fears. She nodded once but he knew by the look in her eyes he hadn't succeeded in calming her fears.

As he did this, he asked Tate, "No shit?"

"From your brief this mornin', seems like momma is smothering the weak cubs," Tate remarked.

Ty sat back and looked to the side. "Means neither of them can flip."

"Exactly what it means," Tate confirmed.

"You think they know Julius's connection got shit on both of 'em?" Ty asked.

"They do, Chace Keaton is up next."

"Crabtree sittin' in a cell?" Ty asked.

"Crabtree is in the wind."

Hope.

"How'd Crabtree find wind?" Ty asked.

"No clue. Keaton reported his wife missin' day before yesterday. Yesterday mornin' they found her body dumped at the side of the access road that leads up to Miracle Ranch. Yesterday afternoon they caught one fuckuva break, happening on the kill sight deep in Harker's Wood in a way that you'd think they knew just where to look. Lotsa blood, all Misty's, found the murder weapon tossed 'bout two hundred yards from the scene. Ballistics match came in this mornin'. Crabtree did not report to work yesterday or today. My guess, he woke up, found his revolver gone, knows the way they play and wasted no time packing his bag."

Ty gave five seconds headspace to Misty Keaton taking bullets and her body dumped at the side of an access road. His grand plan o' vengeance included all involved living a long fucking time with the bitter taste of Ty's retribution on their tongues. He hated the bitch and he wanted her to pay. But not that way. Not that he felt bad for her. The world was not a poorer place without that toxic pussy in it. Just that that punishment wasn't near enough.

Then he let that bitch go and noted, "Hard for them to hand Crabtree his shoelaces, he's in the wind."

"Yep," Tate agreed.

"You think we got a problem with Julius's boy?"

"I think it would be worth it to have a conversation with him but, no. Sources say CPD is runnin' scared and not just your man in Dallas. I think these are desperate acts, not strategic maneuvering based on covert intel," Tate replied.

"Then it's good news Julius is in town, he can have a word."

"Julius is in town?" Tate asked, and Ty's eyes went to Lexie.

"Yeah," Ty answered. "Seemed he was gettin' impatient with me and Lex takin' our time reuniting so he decided to get Lex's ass home. To do that, he phoned Ella and to get Ella to phone Lex, he told her I'd been in a car crash, was dyin' and if she didn't haul her ass from Florida, she'd lose her chance to say good-bye to me on my deathbed."

Loaded silence then a low, "You are fuckin' shittin' me."

"No."

Cautious silence then, "She haul her ass from Florida?"

"We're at the diner havin' lunch."

Total silence then, "Brother..." Pause then, "Fuck, it good?"

He smiled at his wife. Then he told Tate quietly, "Yeah, brother, all good."

Ty watched as her face lost some of her concern and got soft.

Yeah, all good.

"Good," Tate said quietly back.

Unfortunately, Ty had to bring the conversation back around. "Seems we gotta step shit up before everyone who can prove I didn't do it gets dead."

At that, Lexie's eyes got big again. He gave her an it's-all-good chin lift even though it wasn't. This time, she trusted him and popped the fry in her mouth.

"Seems we do. I'll talk to Deke," Tate replied.

"I'll talk to Julius."

"Right." Then, "Happy for you, Ty, Lexie's back."

"Not as much as me."

A smile in his voice with, "I bet." Then, "I'll tell Laurie."

"Good. I'll tell Lex you're tellin' Laurie."

A chuckle in Tate's voice with, "Good."

"Junior high," Ty muttered.

"Yeah, but not the shit part of it," Tate returned.

He had that right.

"We done?" Ty asked.

"For now," Tate answered.

"Then later."

"Later."

He flipped his phone shut and caught Lexie's eyes as she was taking a big bite of burger. It wasn't hard to catch her eyes. She was staring at him.

She put the burger down, chewed twice and with mouth full, prompted, "Well?"

"Misty's dead."

Her entire torso jerked forward and back as she did a slow blink and stopped with eyes wide.

Then, mouth still full, she asked loudly, "*What?*"

"The wicked bitch is dead, mama."

She stared, chewed, swallowed, grabbed her soda, sucked deep on her straw, slammed the cup down and instantly commenced throwing sass. "Well, shit! If she's dead, how can I have a bitch smackdown with her?"

Ty felt his body shake with laughter as he said, "Sorry, baby, gonna have to give up on that dream."

"Fuck," she whispered, glaring down at her plate.

Ty studied his wife, grinning.

The woman was dead and Lexie was pissed that she didn't get her chance to engage in a catfight before Misty bought it.

And, there it was. Lexie hated Misty more than he did.

Seeing that, he suddenly understood it and knew that emotion was for him, not that Misty had betrayed the sisterhood. Misty was his wife's focus because, no matter what authority and power was around her, Misty was the one person in his nightmare who could end it. And she didn't. And she didn't just to get a ring on her finger and a shot at a big inheritance.

That was not what Alexa Walker was about.

And Alexa Walker loved him and that love ran deep.

Ty had endured the consequences of Misty's greed and he hated her because of it. But Lexie paid the price of Misty's actions and that price was expensive. But she paid it twice and she'd do it again.

Knowing this, that gaping wound in his chest tightened and started to close.

Misty Keaton took five years of Ty's life and six weeks of his wife's.

And now the bitch was dead.

"Babe," he called quietly, and her angry eyes shot to his. "That toxic pussy was found dumped by an access road, shot dead. It's done for you, for me. Team Walker is movin' on."

He watched the anger seep out of her eyes but they grew thoughtful.

Then she asked, "Are *both* members of Team Walker moving on?"

At her question, his hand moved across the table to tag hers, his fingers curling around and holding tight and he leaned in.

"Vengeance is mine," he whispered, and her fingers convulsed in his then he went on. "And the way I'm seein' to that is that my woman and the babies she gives me are gonna have a man and a daddy who does not have this shit hangin' over his head, whose name is clear so they are free to live wild *and* burn bright without this shit draggin' them down. To do that, Team Walker celebrates each victory by livin' wild and burnin' bright without this shit draggin' them down. Misty Keaton is dead. We... are... movin'... *on*."

She held his eyes and asked, "After all this, Ty, is it that easy for you to let it go?"

"I'm not lettin' shit go. I'm focused on clearin' my name. But Misty's gone, she cannot help with that. So I'm movin' on from that part of it and I'm takin' you with me."

His woman stared at him. Then she squeezed his hand. Then her head dropped and her hand moved in his so his eyes went to their hands where he saw and felt her thumbing his wedding band.

When he did, two memories came back, strong and fierce. Her fingering his wedding band at the breakfast table in Vegas and her explanation last night as to why she'd done it. In the weeks that passed he'd not forgotten that she did that in Vegas, and he often wondered about why she did it. Now he knew. And watching her touch their symbol that he wore, he felt the gape of his wound grow even smaller.

"You ever take this off?" she softly asked their hands.

"Never," he answered just as soft.

"Never," she repeated, this time a whisper. Then he watched her draw in a deep breath.

"Mama," he called, not because he wanted to. She could study his ring while touching him for as long as she wanted, but they had shit to talk about and he had four college tuitions to worry about so he eventually had to get back to work.

Her head came up and her eyes met his but her thumb kept moving on his wedding band.

"You with me?" he asked.

"Team Walker is a winner," she said softly. He grinned at her and she stopped thumbing his ring, her hand gave his a squeeze, then she let it go and went back to her food saying, "Now, you mentioned Crabtree when you were talking to Tate. What's up with him?"

She nabbed a fry, pushed it deep into her enormous mound of

ketchup and tossed it into her mouth. She looked at him and he told her about Crabtree.

Then he told her about Frank.

Then he told her about Chace Keaton.

Then he told her about their plan.

After all that, he paid the bill, walked her back to the garage, made out with her standing by the Viper, let her go knowing she was heading to the grocery store and he watched her drive the Snake away.

* * *

Ty waited, hip against the side counter in the kitchen, for Julius to get back from delivering his wife's cosmopolitan. They'd had dinner at The Rooster and were back at the condo for drinks and continued conversation.

Ty was now an eyewitness as to why Julius had three women who'd each put up with two other women having a claim to their man. It was not the gold that Anana was dripping. It was the cosmo she was sipping.

Julius Champion doted on his bitches with every look, touch, move, word and breath. Ty Walker was no woman but he had one who doted on him like that so he knew it felt good.

His eyes moved to his wife, who was wearing a white sundress, another halter top, dress skimming her body to her hips then flaring out in a wide skirt that went down to just above her ankles. The silver, high-heeled sandals he bought her in Vegas on her feet, his diamonds at her ears, neck and wrist, her hair up in a mess at her back crown, tendrils escaping but the arrangement highlighted the bling. With her tan, the not-minimal cleavage she was showing, most of the skin of her back on display and the fabric skintight to her hips, she was, as usual, all that but a fuckuva lot more all that than normal.

Julius sauntered back, got close, grabbed his vodka rocks from where it was sitting on the island and leaned his hip on the island opposite Ty.

"I'm guessin', since you didn't find time to give me a brief before we went to dinner, that all is good with your boy," Ty said quietly.

He'd phoned Julius that afternoon after having lunch with Lexie and they'd had a very long conversation.

"We had a chat," Julius replied. "He said there is no fuckin' way they got wind he's makin' moves. I reminded him his job description does not include any of his movements blowing back on you and that you gave him a fuckload of cake to perform these duties to your satisfaction. He reminded me he is not a fan of any cop but that he's had his own run-in with the local boys, knows what was done to you, has got a skin tone where he gives a shit and he appreciates the pay but likes the work and would in no way fuck this for you. I don't know him but for this job but the man who gave me his name is solid. I trust him. He knows why I need this and it would shock the piss outta me he steered me wrong."

Ty looked to his friend and summed it up. "So we're good."

Julius caught Ty's eyes, smiled and nodded. "We're good."

This meant CPD were scrambling.

This was good and it was bad. He liked that they were scared. He liked that they were so scared the plays they were making were huge and stupid and he couldn't say, after thinking on it, that he didn't get something out of watching them turn on their own.

But he didn't like to think of where that scared would take them if they set their sights outside the inner circle.

Ty looked back at the two women who had been standing at the railing, drinking, talking and looking at the view. Now they were folding their long bodies into the loveseat to focus on drinking and talking.

As he watched, suddenly they both burst out laughing.

Ty smiled then, without taking his eyes off the women, said to Julius, "And the phone call that took you away at dinner?"

Julius replied immediately.

"I say this and I say this so you know I do not mind it. Colorado ain't a hard place to be, Anana's lovin' this trip and I'd go down for you. But I cannot risk a trip to Dallas after haulin' my ass out here twice."

"Understandable," Ty muttered.

"Not done," Julius said.

Hearing his tone, Ty looked to him then Ty read him. He'd seen that look before, not often, but he'd seen it and when he'd seen it was any time Julius spoke about the man he killed. A man who he did not pray to God for forgiveness for killing. A man he was not only glad was dead but glad he got to make him that way and he felt this because he loved his sister. And what he said next was because he loved Ty.

"Made a couple of calls. Lexie is not unknown after her time with Rodriguez. What she was known as was untouchable. The minute her foot stepped over the Dallas city limits, Shift got word, thought you got shot of her and she was fair game. He was dickin' with her and bidin' his time. Since Rodriguez hit the cement without his face, Shift knew what he was gonna do with Lexie and he figured at her return the time was right." Julius's eyes started to burn when he said low, "So, no. You mistake me, Walk. I am done with him, which means *he* is done."

Ty pushed away from the counter, turned to his brother and murmured, "Champ—"

Julius shook his head. "Got a man on it already."

"He ordered the hit on Rodriguez." Ty told him something he had not shared and Julius blinked.

"They were brothers," Julius whispered, shocked and now even more pissed because Julius had a number of rules he lived by and the one at the top, right under taking care of your family, was never turning on a brother.

"You been gone from Dallas awhile but that's what Peña says is on the street. Shift has already mentioned my name to a cop. I do not need his dead body found. What I need is for that motherfucker to be incapacitated. And I figure, as payback for his efforts, Peña should get whatever cops get when they take down a drug-dealing pimp who'd order a hit on his brother. You got connections in Dallas. You rally them not to make Shift stop breathin' but to make him stop breathin' free."

Julius's eyes were wide and he replied, "You tellin' me you want me to get word to my boys to ask them to work with pigs?"

Ty leaned toward him. "He killed his brother and he moved to pimp my fuckin' *wife*. I already kicked his ass and that didn't make me feel any better. If I got a choice to dispense punishment, I do not choose for him to buy a bullet. I choose for him to keep breathin' while…he…*rots*."

Julius held his eyes and Ty knew that his now were burning because Julius replied quietly, "I get you."

"He goes down, they give Peña enough to make him stay down. He manages to live a long life without gettin' shanked, he lives it never fuckin' breathin' free. They do this, they do it for me, they do it for Lexie, they do it for Rodriguez and if that isn't enough, they can have every bill left in my safe and they can do it for that."

"Keep your cash, Walk. I'll state your case."

Ty held his friend's eyes.

Then he whispered, "All you're doin', all you've done and all you're gonna do, no way I can pay you."

"I ask for compensation?"

He hadn't. He wouldn't.

And knowing that in that moment, Ty Walker was overwhelmed.

"No way I can pay you," he repeated on a whisper.

"You're my brother and family don't pay shit."

Ty didn't respond.

Julius kept talking. "Though, just so you know, you just dropped a shitload of cash on a car for your wife I coulda boosted for you and had delivered in a week."

At that, Ty burst out laughing. When he quit, he felt eyes, looked to the deck and saw his woman grinning at him. He smiled back. Then he looked at Julius.

"Heat is on in Carnal, Champ. Not sure I should have a hot ride in my garage and *definitely* unsure I want my wife's sweet ass *in* that hot ride."

"Probably a good decision," Julius muttered through a grin.

Ty grinned back.

Then his grin faded and words he'd said earlier that day came back to him.

And he was not about to make the same mistake twice.

Therefore he asked quietly, "Remember I told you about Tuku?"

Julius nodded.

Ty went on, "Got good friends, a lot of them, feel deep for them all. Only three people in my life got more from me, one of 'em's in the ground, one of 'em's sittin' on the deck and the last is standin' right in front of me."

Julius said not a word but held his eyes.

Then Ty whispered, "Gratitude, brother."

Julius kept his eyes locked with Ty's and whispered back, "Debt paid."

* * *

Lexie's lips brushed his neck as her hips moved up and he lost the hot, wet silk of her pussy as she pulled off his cock. She moved down and her lips brushed the inside of his left pectoral over his heart. She moved further down and they brushed across his abs. She fell to a hip in the bed, swung her leg from around him and rolled off the bed.

Ty watched her move to the bathroom. Then he rolled to turn off his light and shifted to pull the covers from under him to over him. He flipped Lexie's side of the covers back. His eyes went back toward the door to the bathroom as the light went out and she wandered out. She stopped and tagged her panties from the floor. An indication she was done and she would be. He'd made her sit on his face until she came then he'd fingered her cunt and clit until she came again then he let her suck him until he almost came and last, she rode him until they both came.

It was a long and energetic night.

Time to sleep.

She turned out the light and put a knee to the bed, shifted to him and curled into him.

He wrapped an arm around her and trailed his fingertips over the panties covering the cheek of her ass.

"Love our bed," she mumbled into his chest, voice sleepy.

He did too, now that she was back in it, but he didn't articulate this.

She didn't mind and he knew that when she whispered, "'Night, honey," giving his gut a squeeze with her arm.

"'Night, mama."

He felt a slight smile as her mouth moved her cheek.

Then she was out.

Five minutes later, she rolled.

He went to jack up the AC and rejoined his wife, his eyes passing the shadow of the picture frame that was back in its place on the dresser.

She'd carried it with her.

Seeing that frame, knowing he'd always been with her, that wound closed tight.

He joined his wife in bed and curved into her body. She snuggled closer.

And it was not lost on Ty Walker that for over six weeks, sleep did not come easy. Memories invaded, not good ones. Demons. Demons of prison and demons of living a dream he never thought he'd have then losing that dream.

Only last night did they retreat.

And that was because, his wife being there, she was there to beat them back.

So he let her do it again and fell asleep thinking of nothing but her warmth, her softness, the scent of her hair and fucking her in the shower the next morning.

CHAPTER SEVENTEEN

The Home Stretch

"Alexa Walker?"

"That's me." I smiled at the delivery man standing on our back deck. He smiled back, offered me his pen-like doohickey, I signed the screen on his other doohickey, gave it back to him and he handed me the big, soft-sided envelope.

I took it, gave him a wave and shut the door on him. I hoped he didn't take offense when I also flipped the lock (these days in Carnal, couldn't be too careful) then I took the package to the island and ripped it open.

Two plastic-wrapped tees fell out and I didn't hesitate to rip the plastic off, pleased to feel the cotton of the tee was soft and supple, not scratchy and stiff. I shook the first one out, Ty's size, and held it out in front of me.

Then I smiled huge.

I flipped it around and looked at the back.

My smile got bigger.

I ripped open the next one, girl-fit, my size but same color, same words on the front, different words on the back.

I cleared all the packaging away, shoved it in the garbage bin and laid the tees side by side on the counter, smoothed them out flat, stepped back and stared at them.

I'd found the site on-line, design your own tees and pay practically nothing to get them express.

So I bought Ty and me black tees that said on the front "Team Walker" in big white letters and in smaller-lettered italics with quotes under it, "We never admit defeat." On the back of Ty's it said, "Mr. Humongo" and on the back of mine it said, "Mr. Humongo's Mama."

I freaking *loved* them.

Ty would take one look at them and think I was a total goof.

I didn't care. And if he only wore his at home while watching games, I didn't care about that either.

But I was wearing mine in town.

After, of course, all the bad guys went away. Had to keep my head down. Too much happening, I didn't need to be in their face.

It was Monday about a week and a half after I got home and all that time had been busy.

I got home on a Thursday. Ty had to work both Friday and Saturday. Friday was taken up with me getting the house in order, catching up, sorting shit out, getting my car and then dinner with Julius and Anana.

Saturday, Ty arranged for Tate, Deke, Jonas and Bubba to go get my shit from Dominic and Daniel's and me unpacking it.

Sunday was shopping where we bought a square coffee table and a big rug for the living room that was a beautiful light cream with a black edge that went perfect with the black couch and Tuku's pen-and-ink. Ty again slid straight into shopping mode with no pressure from me and he also bought a big, oval, art deco, black dining room table with six matching chairs, their seats and backs upholstered in cream. We moved the sectional and TV from the side wall all the way across so it formed a cozy seating area in front of the fireplace and left a huge expanse of space behind it where we put the dining room table when it was delivered.

I, of course, on a lunch break bought the big, round, glass vase I had my eye on at the Carnal Country Store, and the proprietress thanked me profusely for buying it saying, "Sugar, that thing has been on my shelf for a year and a half. Ranchers and bikers do not have an eye for glass vases. But I thought it was pretty. I gotta learn, if it don't have an antler or a skull on it, I'm screwed."

I was happy to take it off her hands and happier that she'd marked it down fifty percent.

The vase looked perfect in the middle of the table.

The next Thursday, Ty's day off but I was back at work, I came home and it had two dozen blush and cream roses in it.

That was my husband. He did bling of all kinds, some of it didn't shine as bright but that didn't mean it wasn't awesome.

Outside of the time I spent with Ty, reacquainting myself with friends, getting back to work, unpacking and sorting our home, I spent my time getting my shit sorted. I went to the DMV and got a Colorado driver's license and plates for my new (red with wide black racing stripes running up the hood, roof and down the back, 2012, fucking gorgeous) Charger. I'd already had my mail forwarded from Dallas but I put another forward on it when I left, sending it to Ella. I again changed that. I also got on-line and changed all my information with anyone who carried it. I'd closed my bank account in Dallas when I was there but opened one in Carnal. And Ty put money in it so I could pay off my credit cards, which I did.

I did all this because I would do all this (eventually) but I did this as a matter of priority because Ty asked me to make certain that "those assclowns got no shit to fuck with you with."

I saw the wisdom of this advice and didn't delay.

Bessie had politely declined our offer but did not decline keeping the cash I earned from my Charger, cash I left behind with her. She promised me, once she got on her feet, she'd pay me back. I let her promise me that and when she tried to pay me back, I would decline. I knew she'd take care of me for free, I knew she'd take care of me no matter what but I needed to give her that. It didn't cover what I owed her for pulling me together after I fell apart but then again, nothing would. But it would be something.

She left Panama City Beach and headed to Miami. She'd never been there but she heard it was a fun place to be and was going to check it out. The last word I had from her (which was yesterday) was that she liked it, wanted to give it a shot and was currently looking for a job.

I had mixed feelings about this. Dallas was a one-day, very long haul from Carnal. Miami was a lot fucking further. But she'd been in a shit situation and unhappy almost as long as I had been with Ronnie.

It was good she was making this change and if she liked Miami then I would like Miami for her.

And anyway, it would be fun when Ty and I could visit her there.

Things had changed for Ty and me and when I say that I mean for the better. There was nothing between us now, it was out there, open, talked about. He shared more. I got to listen more. Day to day, he relaxed more, he smiled more, he laughed more and my man was fucking funny so I laughed more too. We'd weathered one hell of a storm but we did not come out with nicks and dents. We came out tougher, stronger, closer.

But even though home life was good, great, *the best*, the sun shining all the time not only because it was August in Colorado but because there were no clouds over our life, Carnal was different.

There were clouds over Carnal, big, black, threatening thunderclouds. Everyone felt them. Everyone was being cautious, quiet, braced and waiting for that first crack of thunder and bolt of lightning, hoping they weren't too close when it struck.

Although the news traveled slow, the murder of Misty Keaton, allegedly by Officer Rowdy Crabtree, sent low, buzzing shockwaves through the town.

I thought Ty would at least receive suspicious glances but this did not happen. Ty had been gone awhile but Ty was well-known. Well-known enough that folks knew that was not his style.

But the town was humming with gossip and at the salon, as it had a tendency to be at salons, that hum was fast, furious and *prolific*.

Therefore I learned, not surprisingly, that Misty was not well liked. No one had much against her five plus years ago, though she was known as a gold digger intent on making a good marriage. But public opinion of her plummeted when she lied about Ty's alibi, then took another significant drop when she married Chace Keaton.

This was because many guessed the connection, and, to my surprise, I learned that many liked Chace and didn't like him saddled with the likes of Misty. When she married a town cop who happened to be in line for a large inheritance, she instantly decided her shit didn't stink and let everyone know she felt that way and they should too.

This behavior was further frowned upon. After that, what was left of her popularity took a nosedive but she didn't care much seeing as she had a hot guy in her bed, his ring on her finger and his daddy's fortune on the way, all she had to do was wait for the old man to die.

Through salon gossip, I also learned that this didn't work out for her as she had planned. From the beginning, Chace made it blindingly and *publicly* apparent that he was not blissfully married. He put up with her. He went through the motions. But he didn't like either. And because he could barely stomach the sight of his wife, when he needed to get him a little somethin' somethin', he went elsewhere and did this openly.

By the time Misty Keaton had walked into Carnal Spa that day I met her, she'd spent five years living with a man who could barely stand the sight of her, didn't hide that and cheated on her repeatedly and blatantly. Salon buzz said that, as year slid into year and Chace didn't come to heel, Misty became more and more beaten. Salon buzz said that, even though she was what she was and did what she did, she actually loved her husband, and his continued hatred of her was wearing her down. Salon buzz also said that even before Ty was released, Misty was rethinking her actions. Salon buzz further said that Misty was coming to the conclusion that Chace's daddy's millions weren't worth that. And salon buzz said that Misty bought it because the authority knew this and needed to ensure she didn't do something they wouldn't like much.

And last, salon buzz said that Rowdy was set up to take the fall mostly because he was an asshole. In a long line of local cops that people did not like or trust, Rowdy stood out prominent because he was not only the dick I knew him to be but a *serious* dick. He used the authority his position provided him as a weapon, his badge and uniform as a shield. He regularly and randomly fucked with citizens of Carnal and he did this for shits and giggles.

Although no one believed Rowdy took Misty Keaton to Harker's Wood, shot her and left his weapon—primarily because he had no motive to do this and wasn't stupid enough to leave that kind of evidence seeing as he *was* a cop, just a dirty one—still, no one really cared if he went down for it.

"What comes around goes around," Avril stated, smiling gleefully and leaning against the high front of my reception desk, in for a mani/pedi and also gossip.

But underneath all this gossip and speculation, there was fear. A woman was dead. No one liked her much, but that was pretty extreme. Whoever was spooked was seriously spooked, and the citizens of Carnal were worried about what was next.

As for me, it was difficult to admit, but I felt a sense of calm settle over me as all this gossip filtered into my brain.

While my husband was serving a sentence for a crime he didn't commit (and, to that day, after I went to sleep, he got up and jacked up the AC so high I woke up with a frozen nose every morning and he did this because the heat, stench and feel of that place had beat into his bones and he needed that cool, clean air to beat it back), I liked knowing that Misty wasn't living the dream she'd lied her way into.

Sure, I couldn't say I wanted her dead. But I could say I felt that maybe there was justice at work out there in the universe knowing she'd lived her own version of five years of hell.

And it made me feel better that, if she'd lived, she wouldn't have what Ty and I had.

So she'd betrayed him and used him and when he was down, she stepped right on him to haul herself up to what she thought was the next level of life and bought herself misery, heartbreak and, eventually, being dragged to the woods in the middle of the night and shot to death.

She definitely deserved misery and heartbreak, if not being murdered, so I felt that yes, maybe there was justice at work out there.

And I just hoped it kept working so my man could eventually *really* breathe free and live with a clear name.

I left the tees where they lay and headed out to the mailbox thinking about what I was going to do the rest of my day. It was late morning and considering I got up at an ungodly hour to shower with Ty, after he left, I'd cleaned the house and done the laundry.

Then I'd gussied up to go into town. We needed some groceries. I wanted to stop by La-La Land to get a latte and maybe something for dessert because Shambles made the best of everything sweet, Ty had a sweet tooth and he'd told me the day before that he'd been home now for months but had yet to wander into La-La Land. So I felt it a moral imperative to introduce him to their goods, which were *good.* I was also thinking of going to the mall and getting some fabric to make curtains for the guest bedroom. There were horizontal blinds in there but the room needed color. The walls were an eggshell white but it was utilitarian. Maybe I'd head to the hardware store and get some paint chips. In fact, Ty's and my room could use some work. I'd get some paint chips for that room too.

I was thinking all this as I got the mail and brought it back. When I started sifting through and opening mail, my head was filled with possible colors, color combos, maybe a new comforter cover and sheets for Ty's and my bed, not to mention, looking into filling our room a bit by setting up a reading area because winter would be on the mountains soon and I'd need it when I lost my deck.

So I wasn't paying attention to what I was doing until I slid my finger into the side of an envelope, tore it open, pulled out and unfolded a trifolded sheet of paper, turned it over, saw it was handwritten, looked at the salutation then the closing signature and went still.

I realized my error right away. I'd opened Ty's mail accidentally.

But I couldn't stop myself from reading it.

Ty,

I did wrong, I did bad and I know I'm going to pay.

But before I do, I have to do right.

I sent this to a girlfriend of mine in Maryland. I told her, if anything happens to me, to put it in the mail to you. I also sent her some other things. They'll go to other people.

And they say that I lied about not being with you that weekend. They explain that Arnie came to me asking for a favor and that I'd be compensated. I won't say how and the other stuff won't say how either. That doesn't matter and it would hurt another good man who got caught in the net.

I've done enough of that.

But in that stuff I said straight out that I lied and Arnie Fuller asked me to do it and compensated me for doing it. I was with you that weekend, all weekend. You didn't attend a poker game and you didn't kill a man because that whole time you were with me.

I would say I'm sorry but I expect you don't care if I am. I would explain why I did what I did but I expect you don't care why either.

But I will say that I'm glad you're happy. I met your wife and saw her with you at the garage so I know that to be true. I talked to Stella and she said you're doing great and moving on. You were always a strong guy and I guess I figured you'd make it and I wasn't wrong.

I still wish I didn't do what I did to you and not just because I have to write this letter and what it means that you're reading it. I've been thinking about it for years, five years, and I thought it would be worth it but it wasn't.

I hope what I've done will be enough to clear your name and right the wrongs done to you.

And that's it, I guess. There isn't much more to say.

I made a lot of mistakes in my life, you were always a good guy and the biggest mistake I ever made was doing what I did to you.

I hope you live free and happy.

Misty

By the time I was done reading it, I didn't know how I managed it because my hand was shaking so hard.

But I managed it and when I was done I managed to move across the kitchen to the side counter by the stairs to get to my purse and grab my phone. Then I managed to find Ty's number, hit go and put it to my ear.

Three rings then, “Mama.”

“Ty,” I breathed, moving back to the letter and then I couldn’t figure out what to say.

“*What?*” he barked in my ear. I jumped at his harsh tone and realized he’d mistaken mine.

“No, no, it’s not bad, baby, it’s not…” I sucked in breath. “Okay, now, listen. I was thinking about paint chips and curtains and going to La-La Land to get you some dessert for tonight and so I wasn’t—”

“Babe,” he bit off, clipped and impatient.

“Right,” I whispered, sucked in more breath then went on. “I accidentally opened your mail and what I accidentally opened was a handwritten letter from Misty Keaton that lays it out that she lied about not being your alibi.”

Silence. A very long silence. A very long, very *heavy* silence.

So I called, “Ty?”

“You’re shittin’ me.” That was a whisper.

“No,” I whispered back.

“You’re shittin’ me,” he repeated.

“No, honey.” I kept whispering. “Do you want me to read it to you?”

“Yeah.”

I picked it up, my hand still slightly shaking, and I read it to him.

My hand dropped to the counter when I was done and he murmured, “Shit.”

“You okay?” I asked.

“Fuck,” he murmured in answer.

“That’s not an answer, honey,” I said gently.

Silence.

“Ty? Honey, talk to me.”

“Right now, Lexie, take that upstairs and put it in the safe.”

I grabbed the envelope with the letter and immediately started walking to the stairs saying, “I don’t know the combination.”

“Twenty-four, fourteen, thirty-three, sixty-seven.”

“Um…is there a bunch of right and left rolling with that?”

"Mama, it's a keypad."

"Oh," I whispered.

"Twenty-four, as in, two then four, then hit the enter key, one then four, enter key and three then three, enter then six then seven, enter and open. You with me?"

"I think I can negotiate a keypad, honey lumpkins, but my locker at school you had to do all this winding around, back and forth, and eventually I had to learn how to pop it because I could never get the fucking thing open."

"This isn't your locker at school. It's a fucking expensive fireproof safe with a keypad."

"Whatever," I muttered then said, "I'm here, hang on." I squatted, punched in the numbers then turned the handle and it opened. I put the letter in on top of Ty's wads of cash, his gun, clips, ammo, the envelope with our marriage certificate and my boxes of diamonds. Then I closed the safe. "It's there."

"Good, baby. Gonna call Tate and see how to play this. Obviously, I can't waltz into the Carnal Police Station so it needs to be safe until I know what to do with it."

"She said she sent other stuff."

"Well, I'm not feelin' like waitin' while that shit processes its way to someone who's gonna pull their thumb outta their ass and turn the wheels of justice so my name is cleared. I'm a priority to me. She sent that shit in the mail, who knows what the fuck's gonna happen to it, but whoever reads it isn't gonna know who the fuck I am and since they don't know, they aren't gonna care as much as me."

I grinned into the phone and muttered, "I see your point." I listened to his soft laughter then asked, "Do you think this will do it?"

"Don't know."

"I think we should send a copy to Angel," I suggested.

"Definitely one of the plays we need to make. But I wanna talk to Tate and I want him to have a look at it. Sit tight, mama, I'll call you."

"I was going to go to the grocery store and, um...other stuff." I didn't elaborate because I was thinking Ty was not in the mood for a paint chip and new curtain discussion. "Do you need me to stay at home or close to town, just in case?"

"Close to town but you don't gotta stay home. Do what you gotta do in town. The other stuff can hold. Yeah?"

"Yeah."

He didn't say anything and he also didn't disconnect.

So I sat on my ass in the closet and asked quietly, "You okay?"

"This could be it."

"Yeah, baby, this could be it," I whispered.

"Toxic pussy knew her number was up, spurred her finally to do right. Took that to finally make that bitch do right. Still, she did right. So I guess I can lose that sour taste in my mouth every time I remember I slid my cock inside her."

"Another bonus," I muttered and heard him chuckle.

"And she's dead and I'm alive and breathin' and able to slide my cock inside you."

That got a couple of tingles but I ignored them and on another mutter said, "A bigger bonus."

"Got that right, mama."

I smiled at the phone.

Then I ordered, "Go, call Tate, let's get the wheels of justice turning to clear my man's name."

"Right. Later, babe."

"Later, honey."

I heard him disconnect and I stared at the safe.

Then I got off my ass and hustled out of the closet, the bedroom and the house. I had groceries to buy, dessert to procure and then I had to get home so I could be available to get the wheels of justice turning to clear my man's name.

* * *

The Charger growled through the development and I was riding high on a day that included the delivery of kickass Team Walker tees, a letter from beyond the grave from bitch-face Misty that exonerated my husband, the discovery and purchase of two bottles of not-cheap champagne I found at the liquor store and the fact that Shambles had an entire lemon poppy seed cake with drizzle icing and a thick layer of lemon cream frosting in the middle that I could buy to end the fucking fantastic celebration dinner I had planned.

So I did, I bought the whole cake.

But as I neared our house, I saw a beat-up, rusted, old-model SUV in our drive and leaning against the side sucking on a cigarette was a petite, older, white woman with shoulder-length hair that had a lot of frizz. At the end of the SUV and out in the street, for some reason staring up the hill into the wood, his back to me, was a very large, very tall black man.

Hearing my approach, he turned to face the Charger and I noticed he was older too, though he only had a hint of white in his hair to indicate this and didn't look near as old as the woman.

He also looked a lot like Ty.

Shit.

I pulled in beside them in the drive, feeling their eyes on me the entire time I parked, switched off my new baby, pulled out the keys and folded out of the car.

"Hey," I greeted as I rounded the trunk, seeing they were still where they were when I drove up, woman against the SUV, man at the end. Firm distance between them.

He was still handsome, very. She was not. The skin on her face was hanging down in a weird way, lots of wrinkles and they looked like ripples of sags. The bottom lids of her eyes drooped a bit, exposing some pink. She needed an emergency visit to Dominic's spa and not just for a facial. Her hair had a bad dye job and she'd chosen a weird shade of light brown that wasn't all that attractive.

As I came to a stop on their side of my car, they were still staring at me but neither of them spoke.

I broke the silence. "Um, I'm guessing you're Ty's parents?"

The woman didn't take her eyes off me when she sneered, "She's guessin' we're Tyrell's parents."

Hmm. Seemed Ty's mom hadn't softened with age.

She went on, "Two white girls hitched to black men in this county. Me with him," she jerked her head to the man who was still hanging out at the end of the SUV, "and you and the black half of my son."

The black half of my son.

I wasn't really sure I liked how she put that.

"Well, um… I'm glad to meet you," I said quietly.

"Well, um…" she parroted sarcastically then she leaned in, "you were glad to meet me, you wouldn't a' been in town with my boy for months without meetin' me."

I didn't know what to do with this. Ty talked about them but all in the past. I let him talk and my questions were few as they always were, allowing him to share at his pace and not pushing. I didn't actually know they still lived close.

Of course I couldn't tell her that.

"We've been kinda busy." And that wasn't a lie.

Her eyebrows shot up. "Too busy to meet your man's parents?"

"Well—" I started but she cut me off.

Looking me up and down, she said, "'Spect he hasn't met *your* parents either and 'spect it's not for the same reason we haven't met you."

I read her inference and this was because it was hard to miss.

"Actually, my parents are both deceased so it would be difficult for Ty to meet them but if they weren't and *I'd* actually met them before they died, which I didn't, then he would have."

Okay, so I was getting mad. I could feel the sass rising in me and I was trying hard not to throw it but unfortunately not succeeding.

At this point, Ty's father moved forward.

"I'm Irving Walker. Irv," he told me as he got close, his hand extended.

I tipped my head back to look at him and saw he wore an expression that held some curiosity, some uncertainty and not a small amount of cautious warmth.

Therefore I took his hand, squeezed it and introduced myself, "Alexa. Alexa Walker. Everyone calls me Lexie."

He smiled and his smile was near as beautiful as his son's.

He released my hand and jerked his head down and to the side to indicate the woman.

"This is Ty's ma, Reece."

I looked to her, decided to make an attempt at civility and extended my hand. "Hello, Reece."

She held my eyes then hers dropped to my hand before they came back to mine. She lifted her cigarette to her mouth, wrapped her lips around it in a weird way where it looked like half the tip was between her lips, she sucked deep and all her sags contracted in a highly unattractive way. She let the cigarette go on a sucking noise and blew out an enormous plume of smoke. It was so enormous I dropped my hand and took a step away so as not to get caught in its fog. Surprisingly, so did Irv.

"Reece," he muttered, sounding pissed then, "Jesus."

Her eyes shot up to him and she snapped, "What? Look at this shit." She swung an arm out indicating me but that arm flew wide indicating, I guessed, everything in our local vicinity. She dropped her arm, leaned toward Irv and hissed, "*Look at this shit.*"

I did not like being referred to as shit or the home my husband provided for me being included in that and I felt my eyes narrow as my control on my sass slipped a hefty notch.

Reece wasn't done. "My eyes don't deceive me, those wheels are brand new. Though, my eyes *could* be deceivin' me since I'm blinded by the fuckin' *rocks* she's wearin' on her fuckin' *finger.* Now tell me, how does my idiot son go down for some bullshit crime probably some white man committed then he gets outta prison, hooks himself a class act like this bitch, puts that fuckin' *rock* on her *finger,* her ass in a brand-new set of wheels, keeps his fancy-assed condo, gets his job back that pays him near to sixty fuckin' grand a year and, all that, he's got no time for his momma. He's got no time for his daddy. He's got all that, he don't share the love with the two people responsible for him breathin' on this earth."

There was a lot there to get pissed at, a lot that deserved some sass thrown, my control snapped and I was going to throw it.

And I opened my mouth to do that but Irv got there before me.

"Weeks, woman, I watched you work yourself up to this shit, *fuck*," he growled the last word then turned to me. "Knocked her up thirty-seven years ago. Biggest mistake in my life. Keep makin' 'em. She tells me she wants to go see her baby, time has come, here we are. She don't wanna see her baby. She's pissed like she's always pissed and like always, I got no clue *why* she's pissed. Her son is home, he's married to a beautiful woman, he's gettin' his life back and she's pissed. What the fuck?"

I had no answer to his question but even if I did, I had no shot at answering it, Reece spoke.

"What the fuck, *Irv*, is that I get here and I see all this." She again flung her arm out, multitasking by flicking the cigarette in her other hand between Irv and me into the street. "Same old shit. Same as always." Her droopy eyes came to me. "This one," she jerked her head to Irv, "served me a lifetime of a whole lotta nothin'. My boy, though, *he* knows how to get himself somethin'. Does he share? *No.* God, he gets outta prison and *still* he's got ways to get himself somethin' and *still* he does not share."

Irv probably opened his mouth to retort but I was done.

And I communicated this by locking eyes with Ty's mother and throwing some serious fucking sass.

"Go home," I ordered, and went on without giving either of them an opening. "And don't come back. I don't know you but I *do* know you taught your son to make certain he took his dirty dishes to the sink by throwing a glass at him and giving him a scar. Ty's lucky, he's hot and that scar, admittedly, makes him hotter but he's *not* lucky he's got a mother who'd risk blinding her son in one eye because she's a lunatic with a bad attitude who would throw a glass at a nine-year-old child. Then, years later, after he endured a nightmare, not appear at his door with open arms and a welcome-home bouquet but months later show up at his house for the sole purpose of behaving like a bitter shrew and expressing her whacked opinion that she thinks her son owes her shit. My husband does not owe you shit. He does not owe giving you what he's worked hard to earn. He does not owe you his time. He does not owe you one fucking *thing.* Now go home and do *not* come back."

She gaped at me but I turned and tipped my head back to Irv.

"You didn't give him much more but I get a sense you get what Ty endured and *why* he endured it and that shook you. You want a relationship with your son, you build it without her," I jerked my head at Reece, "in attendance. And you do *not* show uninvited and unexpected. You ask for his time and he gives it to you when and if he's ready."

Before either of them could reply, not that I'd fucking listen to another word either had to say, I stomped around my new baby, jerked open the door, sat my ass in it, punched the button on the garage door opener and turned on the car. I drove in. I hit the opener again. Then I carted up the groceries, champagne, cake and my latte, putting the ice cream directly into the freezer, the champagne in the fridge and, after that, setting Shambles's cake on a plate and putting it on the counter of the island by the tees so Ty would see it the minute he got home.

Then I called my husband. I shared the trip through the light fantastic that was my first meeting with his parents, listened to his rumbling disbelief and inadvertently calmed his anger by ranting through angry sips of my fast-cooling latte, doing this for some time and with a fair amount of curse words which, for some bizarre reason, eventually led to him cutting me off by roaring with laughter. He then told me he had four college tuitions to earn, which calmed my ass down. I let him go so he could get back to work providing for our future family, walked out to the back deck and looked down.

They were gone.

I went back into the house.

* * *

The chicken breasts were set to marinate, the salad was prepared, the homemade dressing was fermenting in the fridge and I was sitting out on a lounge chair with my Kindle, reading a romance novel and thinking sex with Ty was way better than what the chick in that novel was getting when something caught at the corner of my eye.

I looked up and across the deck to the side of the house and froze solid.

This was because a wiry black man about two inches taller than me with cornrows in his hair who I'd never seen before in my life was standing there looking jittery.

Shit! What now?

He took a step forward and I visibly braced so he stopped.

"I'm Dewey," he announced and I relaxed, slightly.

I knew Dewey. Well, I didn't *know him*, know him but Ty had told me about him. I didn't think he was a threat but his being there probably didn't herald good tidings.

I didn't get to say hi. He took four steps toward me and started talking, he did it fast and what he said made me freeze solid again.

"Don't got much time and can't be seen here. But got word that Ty's parole officer is doin' a random inspection of his house. Today. And he's got Fuller with him. They're comin', don't know when they'll get here, could be any minute. Can't be seen goin' to his place of work and someone might be listenin' in on my phone so couldn't call. So I'm here. I 'spect you'll tell him. I also 'spect, he's got somethin' in there they can't see, like, say, somethin' that shoots bullets, you'll deal."

Then, right before my eyes, he disappeared.

Since Ty did, indeed, have something in the house that shot bullets, I didn't delay in twisting in the lounge, dropping my Kindle to the table beside me and snatching up my phone.

Ty picked up on ring two, saying hilariously but I was in no mood to laugh, "Jesus, mama, the Pope there now?"

"No," I replied quickly. "I just got a five-second visit from your friend Dewey before he went up in a puff of smoke. He told me your parole officer is on the way, with Fuller, to do a random inspection of the house."

"*Fuck!*" Ty snarled.

"Baby, what do I do?" I whispered. "Can they ask me to open the safe?"

"They can do anything they fuckin' want," he answered on a growl. My heart sank and he went on, "Right now, get a bag, fill it with all the cash, the gun, clips and ammo, leave the diamonds but be sure to get Misty's letter. You put that shit into the bag and take it to the trunk of your Charger. Pull the Charger out and park it in the guest parkin' spaces down the way. Those spaces are off my property and the Charger is in your name. They see it and want to search it, you ask for a warrant. Stand firm on that, mama, 'cause they'll try to push you. I'll instigate damage control to sort that shit out but you gotta do that now, just in case."

From the minute he started speaking, I was on the move so I had a bunch of plastic grocery bags, was already dashing up the second flight of stairs and I breathed, "Okay," because I was out of breath from running and fear.

"Okay, lettin' you go now. Call back if there's somethin' you need to know."

I was dropping down on my knees in front of the safe when I said, "Right."

"Later."

He didn't wait for me to reply, he was gone.

Without delay, I did what he asked, took a deep breath and rechecked the safe just in case I missed something. I shut it, made certain it latched and raced down the stairs to get my keys then to my car. I stowed the bags in the trunk, pulled my new baby out and parked it off our property. Then I raced back up the hill. The garage door was cranking back down and I was dashing up the stairs into the kitchen when my phone in my hand rang and it said, "Ty calling."

I flipped it open and put it to my ear. "Hey," I wheezed out.

"We good?" he asked.

"We're good," I answered.

"Good," he said. "Now, Deke's on his way and, he gets there

before our company, he's gonna store that shit in the tool cabinet in his truck. Then he's gonna stay. I do not want you in that house alone with that motherfucker there."

"Okay," I replied, also not wanting to be alone in our house with that motherfucker here either. I leaned into a hand and pulled in deep breaths. "Is this…is this expected? I mean, is this normal? Are they allowed to do random inspections like this?"

"Yeah. That said, I'm surprised. My parole officer seems cool. He's a brother and when I say that, he's one of the few brother brothers a brother like me has, half and half. He did not say it flat out but gave indications he's not Fuller's biggest fan and had an understanding of why I was sittin' across from him. But I made parole for a reason and during my visits, he didn't communicate he had any concerns. But this shit happens. I shoulda been prepared, especially with the heat on."

"It's okay, it'll be okay," I assured him, but I wasn't feeling assured. I was freaked out. "Team Walker bests any challenge they face," I finished more to convince myself than Ty.

He was silent then he said with a smile in his voice, "Yeah."

"The good news is, I threw so much sass at your parents, I think I'm clean out of it. You know, just in case Fuller pisses me off."

There was soft laughter in his voice when I heard, "Yeah, that's the good news." I sucked in a calming breath then his voice came at me, soft and gentle, "You okay, baby?"

I looked at the clock on the microwave and saw it said a quarter after three. He was done with work in forty-five minutes. And I doubted, with my day, he'd do overtime or go to the gym.

"You coming home right after work?" I asked, just to confirm.

"What do you think?" he asked back, but it was confirmation.

"Then I'm okay," I answered.

"Good," he whispered then still soft he said, "Now, mama, Fuller is gonna dick with you. Team Walker is in the home stretch. Stay sharp."

"I'll stay sharp, honey," I whispered back.

"That's my Lex," he muttered. "See you soon."

"Right. Love you, Ty."

"Down to my bones, mama, right back at you."

Suddenly, I was perfectly calm.

"Later," he finished.

"Later, baby."

Then he was gone. I put my phone down on the counter, saw the tees and smiled to myself. But I jumped and whirled when I heard a knock at the door.

Standing outside was a supremely well-dressed black man. He was also supremely handsome, bald head, thick, black, well-trimmed goatee, bedroom eyes. Tall, not as tall as Ty but a lot taller than me. Great body.

I stared at him thinking that Ty's parole officer was hot.

I moved to the door, searching behind him but seeing no company. I opened it and finally really looked at him to see he looked surprised.

"Hi," I greeted, and he stared at me so I asked, "Can I help you?"

"Are you Lexie?" he asked back.

"Uh…yes." I played the game but found it weird when I confirmed my name that he smiled, big, broad and white. "Sorry, have we met?"

"I'm Samuel Sterling."

Cool name.

I smiled. "Hello, Samuel Sterling."

His smile got bigger and he noted, "You're back."

Well, that was interesting. It seemed Ty shared with his parole officer.

"Uh, yeah. Just over a week now. Would you, um…like to come in?" I invited, stepping aside so he could do so.

He didn't move. He simply studied me. Then he remarked, "You have no clue who I am."

"Uh—" I started, wondering, if I did say I had a clue who he was, if that would expose Dewey's visit when he spoke again.

"Own a jet, Lexie," he informed me quietly.

Oh my God!

I blinked. Then it was my turn to study him, and it hit me that parole officers probably didn't wear two-hundred-dollar, shiny, killer polo-necked shirts nor did they have custom-made Italian loafers.

He smiled again, took three steps into the house and I turned with him as he did and shut the door behind me. I kept staring at him as his eyes did a sweep of the place and landed on the tees. They came back to me and his smile was huge.

Then he spoke. "I was close to town on business. Thought I'd stop by, see how Ty was seeing as how Ty was the last time I saw him was not good." He dipped his head to the tees and commented, "I suspect he's doing much better."

"He is," I whispered.

"Good," he whispered back.

"Uh…thank you for, um…doing that favor for Ty and me. But back then I was just…" I threw out a hand. "Well—"

"You don't know me so you owe me no explanations, Lexie. I'm just glad you're back."

I grinned at him. "So am I."

He grinned back then his eyes cut to the door behind me and his body went alert.

I turned around to see Deke at the glass. Deke didn't knock. Deke opened the door and I jumped out of the way.

"He is?" he asked, jerking his head at Samuel Sterling.

"A friend of Ty's," I answered.

"What kind?" he shot back.

"The good kind," I replied.

He sliced his eyes to Samuel Sterling then back to me. "Keys. Now."

I still had my keys in my hand. I held them out to him. He took them and then he was gone.

I looked to Samuel Sterling who had his eyebrows raised and I shared, "We, um…have a bit of, uh…situation."

His eyebrows lowered but his look turned sharp before he asked, "Can I help?"

"If you have time, you can stay for a drink and if the afternoon progresses like I think it will and I give any indication I might be losing my temper and on the verge of what my husband calls 'throwing sass,' you can wrestle me out of the room no matter how much I fight you."

He held my eyes. Then he said quietly, "So it's *that* kind of situation."

I sighed. Then I said, "We have that kind of situation every once in a while. But we think we're in the home stretch." My eyes slid to the side and I muttered, "I hope."

"Team Walker never admits defeat," Samuel Sterling said and my eyes shot back to him.

"What?"

He moved to the counter and touched a tee. Then he looked back at me.

"Never admit defeat, Lexie. No matter the situation. And no matter what resources you have to call upon to do it."

After saying that he dipped his chin without losing contact with my eyes and I could swear he was volunteering for duty.

I smiled at him. He smiled back.

I heard the garage door start to crank open and I whispered, "Deke's back with my car."

And he was. The garage door cranked down, Deke came up the stairs, looked at me, looked at Samuel then grunted, "Beer."

I hustled to the fridge and I got Deke a beer. I gave him the bottle thinking he wouldn't take offense. After asking his beverage preference, I also got Samuel one of Ty's bottled waters but since he was obviously a millionaire or something, I poured it into a glass.

I got myself a diet and since I wasn't on the phone with a Ty who was being sweet, my calm evaporated and I tried very hard as the minutes slipped by not to start hyperventilating.

Conversation was scarce and only included Samuel and me as Deke's monosyllabic grunts made Samuel give up on him. Both men were sitting at the stools and I was at the side of the island when the air in the room started pulsating and my eyes went to the boys then to the door.

The glass showed another good-looking black man, light-skinned, close-cropped hair like Ty's, close-trimmed beard unlike Ty, as tall as Samuel Sterling, as wiry as Dewey but in a lean, attractive way, not in a jittery, felonious way and, even though I didn't know him, he had a face that said he was pretty extremely displeased.

But he was not what I was looking at. I was looking at the man in the uniform standing behind and beside him, glowering through the glass. Older, he had thin, light brown hair going gray at the temples and beyond, a serious beer gut that fell well over the belt on his uniform pants and small, mean eyes.

Arnold Fuller, Chief of Police.

And more, beyond him was not only Officer Frank but also Detective Chace Fucking Keaton.

Shit. Shit. Fuck!

I moved to the door, hoping I was schooling my features. I opened it and my eyes darted between the men, hoping I looked surprised and curious.

"Uh, hi. Can I help you?" I asked.

"Does Tyrell Walker reside here?" Ty's parole officer asked.

"Yes, this is Ty's home. I'm Ty's wife, Lexie." I looked at Fuller then Frank and back to Ty's parole officer before I whispered, "Is Ty okay?"

"Yes." I heard Samuel say from close behind me. "Is Ty all right?"

"And you are?" Ty's parole officer asked.

"Samuel Sterling, a friend of the family."

"Right," Fuller muttered, and I watched Ty's parole officer twist instantly to throw him a glare.

Then he turned back and looked at me. "Mrs. Walker, I'm Jamarr Gifford. I'm your husband's parole officer. We're here to perform a random inspection of your home. This is normal procedure for parolees, as I suspect you know."

I nodded, stepped back and hit Samuel who didn't move so I stopped but spoke. "Yes, I knew this could happen. Ty told me."

"That might be so." I heard Samuel say from behind me and I twisted my neck to look up at him. "But wouldn't such an inspection occur when Mr. Walker was in attendance?"

"We—" Jamarr Gifford started.

"Perhaps you should return when Ty is back," Samuel suggested.

"No," I cut in when I felt the vibe change, and not in a good way. I turned back to the door. "It's okay. You can do it now. But, can Samuel and Deke and I stay while you do this? We won't get in your way."

"Of course, Mrs. Walker," Jamarr Gifford said, stepping in and the men behind him came in with him, fanning out. "We'll do our best to complete this quickly." His eyes went to Fuller and he finished on what sounded like a warning, "And without disruption or disorder."

"Okay, well, go for it," I invited then said, "And you can call me Lexie."

Jamarr Gifford's eyes came to me. He did a quick top to toe then nodded, all business. He turned and nodded to Officer Frank and Keaton and he and those two men moved forward.

Fuller planted his feet apart, his arms crossed on his chest and glared at me.

I pressed my lips together.

Samuel did not. "Are you not participating in the inspection?" he asked Fuller.

"I'm the chief of police," Fuller answered.

Samuel didn't miss a beat. "Is it protocol for the chief of police to attend a random inspection such as this?"

Fuller's face twisted as he replied, "It's protocol for the chief of police to do whatever he wants, includin' makin' sure this shit ain't no farce." He paused and his eyes moved. I followed them and saw he was looking at Gifford. "Seein' that it's all in the family," he concluded, his point not even slightly vague.

"Right," Samuel whispered, his anger not even slightly hidden. Then he asked, "Can I have your name?"

"What?" Fuller bit out.

"Can I…" Samuel paused, "have…" another pause… "your *name*?"

Fuller rocked back on his heels on a stubborn, good ole boy, "Nope."

"Arnold Fuller," Deke piped in, and I swallowed back a hysterical giggle.

"Thank you," Samuel said to Deke, then his hand came to my waist lightly and he murmured, "Lexie, why don't you come back, finish your soda. Okay?"

I looked up to him, nodded then moved back to the island.

I sipped my soda as men moved about my house inspecting things.

Five minutes later, I watched Keaton come down the stairs, round the railing and stop five feet from the island.

"I'm sorry, Mrs. Walker, but there's a safe upstairs I'll need you to open."

I nodded, put my drink down and moved. Samuel started to move with me, I stopped and said softly, "It's okay, Samuel. Ty has nothing to hide."

He gave me a close look, nodded and settled back on his stool.

I led Detective Keaton back up to the safe, trying hard not to feel creeped out that this man was in our bedroom *and* in our closet and hoping he didn't paw through my underwear drawer.

I knelt down in front of the safe and opened it for him, getting back to my feet and stepping out of his way. He crouched in front of it and reached in.

Then, I didn't know why, but I spoke.

"Detective Keaton," I called, his head tipped back and his not-at-all-unattractive blue eyes locked on mine. And when they did, I knew why I spoke.

Because his eyes were haunted.

"I…" I started on a whisper then softly went on, "suspect you know that Misty wasn't my favorite person." His eyes flashed then shuttered and I hurried on, "But even so, I'm sorry. It was a shock to hear what happened to her. She didn't deserve that. No one does. I met her once and she…" I trailed off then forged on, "I'm sorry, really, really sorry for your loss."

He stared at me.

Then his neck bent and I pulled in breath wishing I kept my mouth shut.

I was about to leave him to it when he pulled out one of my jewelry boxes and asked, "You work at the salon?"

"I, uh…yes. I work at the salon."

I watched him open the cardboard box, pull out the jewelry box in it, flip it open and he fingered my earrings.

Then he said in a voice so soft, I could convince myself I didn't hear it, "Then I suspect you know that my wife was not my favorite person either."

Oh my God.

I held my breath.

He flipped my earrings closed, replaced them in the box, put the lid on and placed it back in the safe. He pulled out another one, going through the same motions as with my earrings, unveiling my necklace and as he inspected my necklace he went on in that same super-quiet voice.

"But even so, I'm sorry that happened to her." Pause then even quieter, "She didn't deserve that."

He stared at my necklace, his thumb moving over the diamonds in an absentminded way that I knew he wasn't even seeing them.

"Are you…" I whispered. "Are you okay?"

"Walker always took care of his women," he murmured instead of answering, still thumbing my necklace, and I held my breath again. Then I jumped when he snapped the lid closed. "Good that he finally has one who deserves it."

I stared, stunned silent and immobile while he replaced the box and shut the door to the safe. Then he stood, taller than me, my head tipped back and he moved so he was in the closet door. He looked across our bedroom to the staircase then he looked back at me.

When he had my eyes, he said in that super-quiet voice, "Shit will go down, Lexie, it's gotten ugly and it's gonna get uglier. But do not be alarmed. Frank and I will take care of you and Walker."

I blinked, now stunned silent, immobile and thinking I might be in the throes of a coronary but he said no more, moved through the bedroom and at the top of the stairs he shouted, "Got nothin'."

"All good here too," I heard Frank shout back as Keaton jogged down the stairs.

I ran after him.

I hit the downstairs after Keaton and Frank did, rounded the railing and stopped dead.

And I did this because Tate, Laurie, Bubba, Krystal and Jim-Billy were all in our kitchen. I was so absorbed in what was happening in the closet, I didn't hear them come in.

Jim-Billy pulled his head out of my fridge, looked at me, gave me a broken smile and said in a way like he was reminding me of something I knew but, of course, I didn't, "Thanks for the invite, girl. Like any time I can get my beer without payin' for it."

"Right, like you pay your tab," Krystal muttered loudly, crossing her arms on her ample bosom and rolling her eyes to the ceiling.

Jim-Billy closed the door on the fridge (with a beer in his hand, incidentally), and turned to Krystal.

"I do," he said.

"Yeah, once a year," she shot back.

"Well, I still do," Jim-Billy returned.

"And you expect a discount," she retorted.

"Anyone would, seein' as I order in bulk."

I giggled.

"We're done here, Mrs. Walker," Gifford called to me. Officer

Frank and Keaton were already standing with him at the back door. "We appreciate your cooperation."

"Lexie," I told him, moving toward the kitchen.

"You are not fuckin' done," Fuller snapped, and I stopped moving.

Gifford looked to him and stated, "Your boys said all's good and I didn't find anything."

"Gifford," Fuller clipped, throwing out an arm, "there's alcohol right in front of your face."

"That's not a condition of Walker's parole," Gifford returned, and Fuller's eyebrows shot up.

"What?" he bit out.

"Tyrell Walker, even after repeated tests on remand and during his incarceration, never tested positive for drugs *or* alcohol. He has no history of problems with either or evidence of use of the former. Alcohol is only prohibited for those parolees who have an addiction or past incidents where alcohol was a factor."

Fuller's lips twisted, he leaned slightly to Gifford and clipped, "That's bullshit."

"It isn't," Gifford returned with restrained patience.

"Never heard of a parolee allowed to have alcohol," Fuller retorted.

"Lucky for you this is not a highly populated county like Denver and lucky for you your patch is even smaller so you don't have a lot of experience, but it isn't unheard of for a parolee to be allowed alcohol and Tyrell Walker is one of them. He was a model prisoner. He earned benefits due to good behavior. His parole was recommended by the warden, his rehabilitation counselor *and* the guards. And I personally inspected this home for its suitability for his occupation prior to his release. All was in order then, as I told you before your visit to my office this morning, and you have two of your own boys here, as requested, and it's all in order now. So we're done and we're leaving," Gifford replied.

"Then maybe I *will* have a look around," Fuller shot back, Gifford's back shot straight and the entire room went on hyperalert.

But it was Tate who spoke and all he said was, "Arnie."

Fuller's eyes cut to him and he snapped, "What?"

Tate didn't reply, he just held Fuller's eyes. They went into stare down and I again found myself holding my breath.

Then the garage door could be heard cranking up.

My eyes flashed to the microwave clock.

Ty was home.

I didn't know whether to be relieved or pissed this wasn't done before he got home.

What I did know was that I didn't want my husband to be forced to share Arnold Fuller's air. What I also knew, unfortunately, was that I had no choice in that matter.

And that sucked.

Fuller instantly broke eye contact with Tate and turned to Officer Frank. "Walker's back, search his car."

"Arnie—" Frank started.

"What'd I say?" Fuller snapped. "Search his fuckin' car." Then he finished, "And his wife's."

Frank sighed, looked to me and said quietly, "Sorry, Mrs. Walker, can I have your keys?"

Deke went up in a half squat on the stool, pulled my keys out of his pocket and threw them across the island. Frank caught them the moment Ty made it to the top of the stairs. His eyes came to me and did a quick but thorough assessment. I tried to smile, his eyes dropped to my mouth, giving nothing away, then his body rounded the railing and he took everything in.

Fuller opened his mouth to speak but Keaton immediately moved forward while talking. "Walker, we're here to do a random inspection of your house and we need the keys to your vehicle so we can inspect it."

Without hesitation or word, Ty underhand-tossed them to him.

"He's also got an SUV. Search that," Fuller ordered sharply.

"Jeez, how long's it gonna take for these guys to go so we can get this party started?" Bubba muttered loudly.

"Careful, Jonas," Fuller whispered. "You don't want me lookin' into the permits for your wife's bar."

"Careful, Arnie, Krystal owns that bar with me," Tate put in angrily.

"Everyone just relax. We'll look at the cars then go," Gifford attempted to soothe the escalating tempers.

"Mama," Ty called and I looked to him. "Come here. Kiss."

I blinked at what I thought was an absurd request. Then I stared at my husband who seemed totally calm and was exuding complete patience like he was waiting in a not-very-long line to get popcorn at a movie.

He raised his brows, his patience waning but not with the proceedings, with the delay in my welcome-home kiss.

So I went to him, put one hand to his chest, one to his flat, tight abs, got up on my tiptoes and offered my husband my mouth. He wrapped his arm around my waist, curled his fingers around my hip and took it.

When he lifted his head, I grinned, dropped back to the soles of my feet, turned slightly to the side and leaned into his long, strong body.

Then I looked at Keaton, "Keys for the Cruiser are downstairs on the hook on the door in the utility room."

He stared at me half a beat, nodded and moved.

I looked around the people in my kitchen, thrilled but not surprised at this show of support for Ty but wondering if everyone being there meant plans for my kickass celebration dinner were ruined.

I was kind of hoping they were.

But mostly hoping they weren't.

"These tees are…the…*shit*!" Bubba shouted suddenly, lifting Ty's up and holding it out for everyone to see, turning it back to front. Ty saw it and I knew he did because his fingers at my hip dug in.

Bubba dropped his arms and looked at Krystal, "Babe, we gotta get us some of these."

Krystal replied instantly, "Long's mine's a tank."

Laurie giggled.

I was wishing I'd put them away because they wouldn't be cool if everyone had their own. They were only cool because Ty and I did. I was also wishing that I'd had the foresight to buy myself a matching tank, which would be awesome.

Since I was nursing my snit that Bubba and Krystal were going to steal my kickass idea, I didn't feel Ty move.

I only knew he did when I heard in my ear, "Mama, you are a total... fuckin'... *goof*."

I instantly lost my snit, melted deeper into my husband, tipped my head back, caught his eyes and grinned. He grinned back. Then he leaned in and kissed my temple.

When he straightened, I relaxed even deeper into him and looked back into the kitchen.

That was when I saw Samuel Sterling's eyes on us. When his caught mine, his handsome face split in a huge, beaming white smile.

Samuel Sterling was one seriously hot black man.

And Ty was not wrong.

He was also a complete romantic.

* * *

Ty had just finished, I'd come five minutes ago and I was sitting astride him, his cock still hard and filling me, his back was to the headboard, my face was in his neck, one of his hands was wrapped around the back of my neck, the other arm wrapped around my waist and his lips were at my ear.

"Took my back," he whispered, and I tried to move to lift my head but his fingers tightened on my neck and I stayed where I was. "On the move, rushin', outta breath to cover me."

"Ty—"

"I love you, Lexie."

My heart skipped and warmth flooded through me.

"Ty—"

His hand gave me a squeeze and he cut me off, whispering, "Love you, baby."

His hand moved then, sifting then fisting in my hair. I lifted my head and he guided it to his mouth where he kissed me, hard, wet and very deep.

When he released my mouth, he didn't release the hold on my hair and pressed in so my forehead touched his and I looked up close into his beautiful, curly-lashed eyes.

"You know," I whispered, my hand sliding up his chest to wrap around the side of his neck, "I love you too."

"On the move, rushin', outta breath to cover me," he repeated. "Yeah, babe, I know."

I smiled at him.

Then, still whispering, I said, "I gotta go clean up."

To that, his fist loosened in my hair but his big hand cupped the back of my head and pressed my face in his neck. I felt his jaw slide down my hair and in my ear, he murmured, "Don't like losin' your pussy."

"Honey—"

"Let me keep it a minute."

What could I do?

I did the only thing I could, not that it was a hardship, I gave in on an, "Okay."

His arm around me gave me a squeeze and I rested against his big, solid warmth for a while until his arm gave me another squeeze, lightly lifting me up and I got his message.

I kissed his neck, rolled off him and exited the bed. I went to the bathroom, cleaned up and wandered out to see Ty hadn't moved except to pull the covers over his lower half. He was still in bed, back to the headboard, lights on at both nightstands, his eyes on me.

I moved to my panties, tugged them on then tagged his Team

Walker t-shirt that I'd flung on the end of the bed with mine. I pulled it on and when I got my head and arms through and was yanking it down, I caught his eyes to see his lips twitch.

"So, will you wear it in town?" I asked.

"Mr. Humongo?" he asked back then shook his head, his lips tipping up. "No fuckin' way."

"Well, I'm wearing mine," I muttered, putting a knee to the bed then crawling to him and throwing my leg over to sit astride him again.

I rested my hands on his chest. He shoved his up the back of the tee and they roamed but his eyes caught mine and his were now serious.

"No matter what Keaton said, you don't trust him. You don't trust *anyone* but the inner sanctum. Tate, Deke, Peña, Wood, Maggie, Laurie, Krystal, Bubba, Pop, Stella and Jim-Billy. Get me?"

Obviously, I'd told him everything.

I nodded.

"Not even Frank," he went on.

I nodded again.

"Also not Dewey."

I nodded yet again.

"Nobody," he kept going.

"I get it, hubby," I said, pressing my hands into his chest. "Nobody."

"But maybe Sterling," he amended on a mutter, and I was thinking he was right.

I didn't get my kickass celebration dinner. The celebration took its usual turn when our friends were around. Deke took off and brought back two cases of beer. Laurie got on the phone and Pop brought Jonas over and both stayed. Stella came with them. Krystal got on the phone and ordered pizzas. Wood popped by for a beer but didn't stay long because Maggie was at home with the kids. Shambles's cake was decimated but part of it being laid to waste was Ty eating a huge slice with ice cream so I didn't mind. I managed to keep the champagne away from the impromptu partygoers but they weren't really champagne people. Except, possibly, Sterling, who stayed for the festivities but drank beer like all the rest.

Then, as they do, the men went out to the deck to huddle. Sterling went with them.

I would learn after they left and before Ty and I went up to bed to have the real celebration that Tate was taking the money, gun, weapon paraphernalia and Misty's letter. He had a scanner and was going to scan it and send it to Angel that night. He was also going to send it to other people. He was further going to make a shitload of copies of it, give Ty and me some but keep the original safe. And lastly, Ty had contacted his friend Max's wife Nina, who was an attorney in Gnaw Bone. Nina was also on Tate's e-mail list to receive a scanned copy. That said, she'd already been on the line to Colorado's attorney general's office to discuss Ty's case and how the letter shed new light on it and to get the ball rolling to uncover whatever else Misty had sent to whoever else she sent it to.

Although the attorney general's office assured her that they felt this was as serious as Nina Maxwell communicated to them it was and would be acting on it thus, that was as far as we got.

It would be nice to get a knock on the door in five minutes and go down to see the governor there to grant Ty a full pardon with a thousand news reporters behind him ready to receive his statement that Tyrell Walker was a wronged man and Arnold Fuller was a racist, asshole, dirty-cop dick but I doubted that would happen.

So I would take what we had since it was way better than what we had yesterday.

"Do you think Keaton is working with Frank?" I asked Ty.

"I think Keaton's wife got shot and Keaton's shook. He did not do me dirty except that he married Misty and was and is known to look the other way frequently, and clearly he did it during my gig. How dirty he is, I have no idea but I do know you jump in the mud, it's impossible to stay clean. And I know he jumped in the mud way before what went down with me. His seein' the error of his ways now does not surprise me. But I wouldn't trust him to change a light bulb."

I nodded.

Then I pointed out, "Fuller, today, was arrogant. I don't think he knows what Misty got up to or what Frank and possibly Keaton are currently up to."

"Fuller has been a big fish in a small pond for a very long time. Fuller has convinced himself he's untouchable and the long ride he's had has helped him do that. He's got shit on people, he's got people in his pocket and he's demonstrated that his retribution will be fierce if he's crossed and not just with me and Misty but often and for decades. He's not dumb as his boys but no man should suffer from hubris. Hubris is the worst thing a man can have because it makes you weak without you knowin' you're weak. Hubris has brought bigger, smarter, more powerful men to their knees. A man like him, it'll destroy."

"I hope so," I whispered.

His hands stopped roaming and his arms wrapped around the middle of my back, pulling me close so my torso was plastered to his and our faces were an inch apart.

"Seein' that man in my house I thought would rile me. Seein' how he was, though, it was the first time I felt any real hope. All this shit goin' down around him, even right in front of him, Gifford clearly hatin' his guts, citizens there in his face that they were not scared or cowed and he still stood there proud, thinkin' he had the upper hand. That isn't smart. He's blinded by his perceived power. It's the wrong way to be."

"But he . . . with Misty—"

"Misty was a speck of dust that he blew off. He cannot blow off the IA or the FBI or Tate Jackson. He's got more powerful enemies than him and he doesn't see it. Means his plays will be off."

"I hope so," I repeated on a whisper and got a strong squeeze of my man's arms.

"Team Walker is in the home stretch, mama," Ty whispered back.

I sighed, he smiled then he ordered, "Get off me, baby, we don't know what tomorrow'll bring. We need to sleep."

I nodded, touched my mouth to his and rolled off.

He turned his light off and slid into bed. I turned off mine and rolled back to curl into him.

I fell asleep tucked to his side. As usual, what seemed like moments later, I was on my other side and felt my husband leave the bed. He was never gone long and this time was no different. Then he was back and curving his long body into mine.

I snuggled back into him, doing it deep and fell back to sleep.

CHAPTER EIGHTEEN

Christmas Comes Early

Ty

Lying on his back on the couch, Ty heard his wife's heels on the floor then he heard them disappear and he moved his eyes from the game to over the back of the couch because he knew her feet hit rug.

When he saw her he didn't know whether to grin, frown or get up, grab her, throw her on the couch and fuck her hard and quick before their company came.

This was because she'd just come from being upstairs for an hour, she was tricked out and she looked good. Another sundress, this one black, clingy t-shirt material, tank in the front with straps that crossed at her back, exposing a good deal of skin and a long expanse of her legs were also on view because the skirt wasn't *short* but it was short. She had on a pair of spike-heeled, ash-colored sandals with an abundance of criss-crossed thin straps. So many they nearly covered her foot, rode up her ankle and the shoes had to zip up the back. And last, she had on big silver earrings and so many silver bracelets on one wrist, he could hear them jingle even over the commentators on television.

He hadn't seen the dress before…or the shoes. His woman had a lot of clothes and shoes so it could be she'd dug something out of the closet. Then again, one night after work that week, she'd gone with Laurie and her friend Wendy to the mall, she'd come back after Ty was home from the gym and she'd done it carrying numerous bags. He'd been on the phone so he didn't pay much attention but the next day he got home from work, he saw two more frames on the mantel. One held a photo Laurie took of Ty and Lexie with her family at Maggie's barbeque and another of Ty and Julius that Lexie took on the deck the night after they had dinner at The Rooster.

But those frames did not take numerous bags to haul home and Ty was discovering the reality of something he already knew. His wife liked to spend money and it wasn't just on frames. It was her discussion of painting rooms, making curtains, setting up a "reading area" in their bedroom and going so far as dragging his ass up to the office so she could show him a website where she picked out furniture for this "reading area" that he had to admit was the shit but he also saw the price tags so there was a reason it was the shit.

He made good money and they could have a good life even if she didn't work. He didn't just put the money he got from selling the Skyline down on the house but also earnings from a couple of games. Therefore, he bought every upgrade the new build came with and still the mortgage was low. But they had three vehicles, all of which had taxes, plates and insurance that were a bitch. Not to mention their development was a nice one that attracted a certain income bracket not only because property values were high due to its seclusion and views but also because the HOA fees were near crippling. It made for nice, well-kept landscaping and meant the roads were cleared quickly when it snowed but it also was a monthly whack.

He knew his wife was setting up house, making a home for him *and* for her, something neither of them had ever had, settling them into a nest where they'd feel safe that was theirs together. He also knew she was acutely aware that his life had been interrupted and she was running to catch up so he wouldn't walk into their home every day and be reminded of the time he lost.

And even after his outlays on informants, furniture and vehicles, he still had a fuckload of his earnings from Vegas and a healthy bank balance due to his overtime.

But his woman was off the Pill and if her parts worked and his did too, the amount of sex they had, she'd be knocked up soon and, as far as he knew, babies didn't come with government checks to cover their upkeep for the first eighteen years.

Lexie was social and she loved her job because it allowed her to be social with every bitch in town. The pay, however, was shit. She essentially made spending money, but not the way she spent.

Therefore, she had to slow down.

The problem with this was, he didn't have the heart to tell her to do it mainly because she was right that morning after his mama came home. He wanted her to have her every heart's desire, not because he had to make up to her what he'd done, just because he wanted to give her that.

So Ty had a decision to make. Suck it up and continue to work overtime so he could give his woman her every heart's desire or have a chat with his wife.

He was also uncertain how to respond to her appearance because he knew with it and the huge-ass grocery shop she did yesterday, as well as the massive bouquet of pink and ivory roses that was in the vase on the dining table and the banging around she'd been doing in the kitchen all morning that made the house smell like brownies (first) then garlic, that she was going all out for their afternoon visitor.

And Ty didn't know how to feel about that.

Because their afternoon visitor was his father.

It was Sunday after their drama-filled Monday, and Ty's phone rang on Wednesday morning at nine o'clock sharp.

Irving Walker had taken a day and a half to think about it, pull up the courage and he was on the line asking Ty hesitantly how he was doing and even more hesitantly if he wanted to meet for a drink.

Ty had flat out said no.

"If I'm gonna be around you, you're not gonna be around booze," he told his dad.

"I can do that," his father replied quickly.

Too quickly.

Ty didn't like it. Before he was sent down he had little to do with his parents and what he did have to do with them, he didn't do it. His mother frequently showed to ask for money and his father infrequently showed drunk off his ass to bitch about his mother.

While he was involved in his shit storm, however, they had completely disappeared. After he went down, a couple of years in the joint, his father started writing. Ty hadn't read his letters. He also didn't save them. After he received five in the same amount of months and returned zero, they stopped coming.

"You wanna explain the recent love you and Mom been showin'?" Ty asked.

"Ty—" Irving Walker started.

"If you can call it love," Ty cut him off to say. "Got a wife, a good one. She loves me, she's got my back. Her people show, meet me for the first time, find out my recent history, they're laughing and drinkin' cocktails in my kitchen within ten minutes. My parents show, in five minutes Lex is so pissed, she's throwin' sass and then she's on the phone with me ranting. Like I said, I got a wife, a good one who loves me, which means I love her and can't say I'm particularly thrilled about the fact that my parents piss her off and set her ranting. I try to shield her from that shit, not have it show up in my driveway."

"You know your ma," Irv told him.

"Yeah, and I know you. Lex told me you weren't smashed. A miracle."

His verbal bullet hit true and he knew it when Irv spoke.

"Ty," pause then, quietly, "son."

Ty waited. That was all he got. It was more than he ever got before but it was not enough.

So he went on, "I'll tell you, not because you deserve to know but because, you can pull your shit together to be a better fuckin' grandfather than you were a father, then I'll want my kid to have that because you're the only shot my kid'll have at a grandfather and you can take from that that Lexie and I are tryin'. But this love you and Mom are showin' does not end with me handin' cash over so she can blow it on smokes and you can drink it."

Irv was quiet a moment, and it was a long moment.

Then he said softly but with feeling that trembled in his voice, "Burned in me, what was done to you."

It was Ty then that was quiet.

Irv kept talking. "Burned in me over five years."

Ty still didn't respond.

Irv finished it and he did it on a whisper. "I can be a better grandfather."

Ty sucked in breath before he said, "All right, Dad. I'll talk to Lexie, see if she's comfortable with you bein' in our house. I know one thing though, Mom doesn't show. I'm protective of my wife, she's protective of me and I do not want Mom rilin' her up and she will just by showin' her face. Lexie's still pissed and unless Mom gets her head outta her ass, Lexie won't get unpissed. She knows what was done to me and she's sensitive to anything that might get at me. Keep Mom away."

"It'll be just me," Irv assured him quickly.

"I'll talk to Lexie, let you know."

"You...you," Irv said, still talking quickly then he paused then, "you done good with her, son. She's not hard to look at but that's not what I mean. She...she..." Another pause, then quietly, "It's good you got one with sass. Back then...years ago...Reece...your ma," another pause then, "way people were, the way they were knowin' she was with me, her folks, anyone... shit they said, way they looked at her... at us..." Ty heard him blow out a sigh. "She couldn't take it."

Ty stood still and stunned.

Christ, thirty-six fucking years and his father was sharing.

What the fuck?

Irv continued, "She got pissed at me 'cause there were too many a' them to get pissed at. Even your ma, way she is, doesn't have enough vinegar to sustain bein' pissed at the world so she focused. Shoulda let her go, let her be but felt I owed it to her since I knocked her up and fucked up her life."

"You wear a full-body coverall when you were datin' her?" Ty asked.

"What?" Irv asked back.

"Dad, she made her choice, you didn't make her make it. She couldn't live with it, that's on her. You didn't owe her shit, not puttin' up with her anger for-fuckin'-ever, not dealin' with her shit by poisoning your body, not makin' your sons put up with it."

"It was gone by the time you could process it, son, but I loved her once and she loved me. She got bitter and wears it on her face but back then... You hooked yourself a beauty, Ty, but back then your mom was nothin' to sneeze at. And, I know you won't believe it, not now, but she was funny. Shit, boy, made me laugh so damned hard, thought I'd bust a gut anytime I was with her."

Ty stared unseeing out of the door of the garage, hearing this information, shit he did not know, shit he could barely believe that was still, fuck him, shit that was good to hear and he replied, "Spent five years learnin' a lot, most especially that every breath is worth something. So, I won't piss this away and not tell you I don't appreciate, no matter how late it is, you sharin' with me. But I'll point out, it's still fuckin' late. I rotted for five years—"

Irv interrupted him with, "I wrote you—"

Ty cut right back in. "Yeah, but didn't see you in the courtroom, Dad. Didn't see you before I went down, when that shit was swirlin' around me, not once and before that, when I did, every time I did, you were shitfaced."

"And that's what I'm explaining."

Fucking shit, this was enough for now. He was done.

So he moved it that way. "Lexie wants you in our home, you can explain it more when I'm not at work."

"She said I could come if I called and didn't bring Reece," Irv said softly.

"Yeah, but I give a shit about my wife and what she's feelin' so you're just gonna have to wait until I confirm."

A pause then, "I'll wait, Ty."

"And I'll call, either way."

"'Preciate it, son."

Ty pulled in breath. Then he finished with, "She lets you in, when you come and spend time and then forever, you treat her like crystal. Her life has been shit and she's got no blood family. The family she made for herself means the world. She makes you her family, you do not fuck her. You fuck her, we're done. That's it. Done. Are you with me?"

"I'm with you, Ty."

"Right. I'll call."

"I'll be waitin'."

And, obviously, Lexie said yes and she did this about point two five seconds after he finished telling her about the phone call.

Which led them to now.

His wife, tricked out for a visit from his father who didn't give him much but a few knocks and a lot of nothing until he had a telephone conversation with him a few days before.

Their Monday had been dramatic, their week not uneventful.

Nina Maxwell, his new attorney he and Lex had gone to meet on Thursday, was a very pretty blonde with two young children, a law degree, an excessive amount of energy and more sass even than Lexie.

This meant Peña had heard from her twice. It also meant the attorney general's office had heard from her daily, and not just the one in Colorado but also the one in California. And it further meant that, along with communications they got from Samuel Sterling, the ACLU had heard from her.

She was all over it.

So, lastly, this meant that the attorney general's office had not fucked around in locating the communications Misty had sent and contacting Chace Keaton to obtain a sample of Misty's handwriting, which, Nina reported, the man had delivered to Denver himself. They also contacted Misty's friend in Maryland and obtained a sworn statement that not only did she receive the documents from Misty with instructions of what to do with them, she'd also received frequent and increasingly frantic phone calls from a firstly anxious then downright terrified Misty including one warning her she'd be receiving the documents and getting her assurance that she would follow through should something untoward happen with Misty.

And she'd followed through.

With a man with the kind of money and influence of Samuel Sterling and an increasingly interested ACLU at her back, Nina wasn't accepting any bullshit or delays. Still, she was getting them, and this likely had to do with the fact that Internal Affairs in Colorado and California were trying to hold her back while they sorted their shit.

Nina Maxwell might be the pretty blonde mother of an infant and toddler who, in person, was very sweet and fucking funny, but when she was not dealing with him but for him, she was making it clear she didn't give a fuck about IA investigations. She gave a fuck about a half-black man who had five years stolen from his life and deserved a clear name and restitution, not when they got around to getting their shit sorted but yesterday. And the woman was a pit bull.

Therefore, Ty was lying on the couch watching a game, not wound up about his future, Lexie's future and the future of their children. Peña was on it. Tate was on it. Julius's boy was on it. Fucking Chace fucking Keaton was on it. Samuel Sterling was *all over it.* The ACLU were sticking their noses in it. And Nina Maxwell was living and breathing it.

So he was lying on the couch, drinking a soda, watching a game and wondering if he had enough time to make his wife *and* himself come in the enjoyable effort of planting his seed in her womb before his father showed.

And, lying on that couch, drinking a soda and watching his woman in that dress and shoes with her tanned skin, round ass and long fucking legs on show as she nervously fluffed, arranged then rearranged toss pillows, Ty made his decision.

And that decision was, two birds, one stone.

So he put his soda on the coffee table, put one foot to the floor, did an ab curl and lunged.

He caught Lex at the waist in mid-fluff of a pillow. She cried out in surprise, dropped the pillow and hit him front to front. He fell back then rolled so he was on top.

Then he yanked her skirt up to her waist.

"Ty," she breathed, eyes big and on him.

"New dress?" he asked, his hands moving around her waist, back, down and into her panties.

"Uh...yeah," she whispered, her hands moving to his chest and resting there like she didn't know whether to push or something else.

He rolled his hips with intent and she spread her legs either because his hips were giving her no choice or because she wanted it. Either way, he felt his cock start to get hard.

"Ty." It came again, breathy and her fingers curled into his tee.

He pulled his hands out of her panties, sliding them down the backs of her thighs then, when he got to the backs of her knees, he yanked up. Hard.

And he did this while asking over her gasp, "New shoes?"

"Ty—"

He cut her off. "New shoes, baby?"

"What are you...?" He ground his hips into hers. She trailed off and whispered, "Yes. New shoes."

He dropped his face close to hers and one hand went to the side of her neck, one hand slid up to trace the edge of the leg of her underwear as he spoke.

"Mama, I want you to have everything you wanna have. *Everything.*"

He paused as his fingers made it between her legs, one slid in and pulled the gusset away and he watched her eyes heat as her lids dropped halfway and her lips parted.

"But," he went on softly, dipping his head so his mouth was a breath from hers, "you gotta slow up. We got attorney fees and, all this effort," he slid his finger lightly through her wet, "could mean a baby soon." He brushed his mouth against hers, feeling her breath had escalated and he whispered, "This dress is the shit, baby, and you look fuckin' good in it. I know what you're doin', for me, my dad comin'. But you don't gotta be you all tricked out. You just gotta be you. He's gonna like you. He *already* likes you. The thing you gotta get is the effort is his to make *you* like *him*. Not my mama goin' all out to make *him* like *her*."

"Oh…okay," she whispered, and Ty slid his finger deeper through the wet folds, her chin went up half an inch, her legs spread wider, her hips tipped up as she gasped and he grinned.

"Stick with me, baby, I'm not done," he whispered back and he watched her try to focus on him and he beat back his grin growing to a smile as his finger dipped deeper and she bit her lip. "Our house is already a home 'cause we live here. We got time, means you got time to build it, make it what you like." He brushed his mouth against hers again and said softly, "Home is you, Lex, not a place. I lost a lot but right now," he found her clit, pressed, rolled and listened to her whimper as he finished, "I got it all. You don't have to break your neck or the bank to give me anything more. Yeah?"

"Yeah," she breathed, her hips tipping up further, her fingers releasing his tee to slide around to the back, pull it up and dive in. And he knew, the look on her face, the wet at his finger, she'd say "yeah" to just about anything.

Still, she'd said yes so one bird down, one to go.

His finger rolled and his mouth brushed hers again and he whispered, "What you want, wildcat?"

She lifted her head off the couch to get his mouth but he moved it away, her eyes opened slightly and she whispered back, "Your cock, baby. Hurry."

"Already?" Ty asked, brushed her lips, she lifted her head to get more and he again pulled away. "Thought I'd finger fuck you first."

Another whimper, her hips jerked, she liked that idea.

But she said, "We need to hurry and finger fucking doesn't make babies, Ty."

He pressed harder, rolled and her neck arched. "No, but it's fun to watch."

And it fucking was.

She righted her head and whispered, "Ty, we don't have—"

He moved his finger, drove two inside and engaged his thumb.

Her mouth stayed open but only so she could moan low in her throat. Her whole body arched and her nails dug in and raked up his back.

Yeah, fuck yeah, it was fun to watch.

And feel.

His fingers moved, going deep, his thumb relentless.

"Hurry, mama, I want in there when you're done," he told her, voice thick.

"Okay," she breathed, moving her hips to ride his hand then, desperate, "Your mouth, honey."

"You come in my mouth, I watch until you do."

"Ty—"

"Hurry."

Her neck arched and her hips went desperate too. "Ty."

Fuck, his wife was beautiful. And that was the only reason he kept doing what he was doing because she was so fucking wet, he wanted his mouth down there.

But he couldn't watch and he liked watching.

So he watched.

"Reach for it, mama."

She did and he knew when the noises came fast and low, her nails stopped digging and her arms wrapped around to hold on just as her legs curved around his hips tight, heels digging in to use him for leverage to reach for it, get more out of his hand.

Then her neck arched, her back arched and he knew she was there so he growled, "Mouth."

She dipped her chin and offered her mouth. He took it and kept working her with his hand while her noises drove down his throat straight to his aching cock. He was waiting until she was done so she could keep his hand before he took her with his cock. Finally, her body melted under him, her limbs loosened but stayed around him, he knew she was done and he was about to go for his fly when his phone rang.

Not wanting surprises, he'd given certain numbers their own tones.

And that tone said Peña.

Fuck!

He cupped his woman between her legs, released her mouth and arched his back so she wouldn't take his weight when his hand at her neck moved to reach to his back pocket and he yanked out his phone.

"Peña," he muttered to his still-dazed wife and she blinked, not processing this because, just like Lexie, she'd come hard and she was riding the residual wave.

Ty flipped his phone open and put it to his ear. "Please, fuck, tell me this is worth interrupting what I'm fuckin' doin'."

There went the daze. She blinked again then one hand came out of his tee so she could slap his arm and she snapped, "Ty!" But she did it without sound, only her lips formed his name but he knew it was a snap because her eyes were narrowed and her face was pissed. He was hard, he wanted to bury his cock in his wife who was hot, wet and under him but he still couldn't stop from grinning at her.

"*Mi amigo*, that's just plain cruel," Peña said in his ear but there was a smile in his voice. Ty's words and the frustrated growl he said them with were not lost on him and therefore Ty did not get this fucking guy. If Ty was miles away and knew he was on the phone with a man who was with Lexie doing what he was doing with Lexie, there would be no smile in his voice.

Then again, Peña hadn't tasted her so he only had the dream and did not know the reality was way fucking better than the dream.

"This worth interrupting what I'm doin'?" Ty asked.

"Don't know. Is a warrant for conspiracy to commit murder, a successful raid last night that means the evidence locker bought itself a whole *fuckload* of smack and blow and twelve… I repeat, *twelve* ladies of the evening walking their Lycra-covered asses into my precinct this mornin' after a hard night at work sayin' they're happy to turn evidence *and* act as witnesses, all of this nailin' Duane 'Shift' Martinez to the wall in a way he won't come unstuck anytime soon worth interruptin' what you're doin'?"

Ty had frozen.

Then he gently moved his hand from between his woman's legs and planted his forearm in the couch beside her to hold his weight off her but otherwise kept his position as he asked, "You got any more detail?"

Peña chuckled.

Then he gave Ty detail.

"Yeah, well, the angels in heaven above swooped down on Dallas these last few weeks. Started with me walkin' out my front door, *at home*, I might add which wouldn't have made me happy except that on my welcome mat was a manila envelope *full* a' shit. Typewritten but, who gives a fuck that God's angels use computers. Suddenly, I got leads comin' out my ass. Now, the borin' stuff is that raid was a raid of Martinez's stash. Far's I know all of it, and there's a lot. Un-fuckin'-protected and all in one place. We're talkin' millions of dollars of dope here. The guy doesn't have a gun on it and he keeps it all in one place. I knew that man was light between the ears but fuck… me."

Jesus, Ty knew Shift dealt but he had no fucking idea he was in that deep.

"Millions of dollars?" Ty asked.

"Yeah, sucks to admit it, *esé*, but even I didn't know his operation had escalated to that level. But this means his suppliers are not gonna be happy he can't distribute and, shortly, it'll be destroyed without goin' up someone's nose or in someone's veins. Also means, case you didn't know, the more dope, the bigger the operation, the more shit that could hit the streets, the weightier the book gets thrown at the ones who own it. And that kinda operation is makin' the DA salivate. Now, our DA, he's pulled himself up from rough beginnings, stayed clean but had friends who chose dark paths and he watched them get lost down those paths. He's a crusader. This motherfucker is on a mission and has been since he got his ass elected. He's gonna take a dealer with that amount of product he intended to put on the street and destroy lives and he's gonna symbolically shove that product right up his ass. But I got more."

"The warrant," Ty said carefully, not wanting Lexie to catch on. Not yet. Not until he could give her his undivided attention.

"Yeah. The warrant. Got a boy in holding. This boy was caught with a gun in his possession. And this gun's got a ballistics match on it says it did Ronnie Rodriguez, amongst others. And this boy has a protective instinct so this boy made a deal. And this boy shared the hit he confessed to doin' on Rodriguez was ordered and paid for by Martinez."

There it was.

Holy fuck.

There it was.

Brother taking down his brother.

Ty remained silent. Peña didn't.

"And this boy ain't dumb like Martinez but he does have a screwy family. And when I say that, I mean, this boy does business, he does it at his momma's kitchen table, *with Momma there*. She's lookin' out for her boy, makes sure he don't get screwed providin' excellent service without gettin' paid a good wage. She negotiates the deal, she takes a cut, her boy does the job. Therefore, she's in holding too and she's also facin' time but she's also not dumb and makes her own deal. Her boy goes down, she goes down but so does Martinez. We have the shooter, we have the gun, we have his word and we have his momma as witness."

Yes, absolutely.

Duane "Shift" Martinez was a piece-of-shit motherfucker.

Peña kept going.

"And I'm not gonna get into the fact that Martinez is *not* like Rodriguez with his stable. He takes freebies, he takes 'em often and once that boy gets off, he gets chatty. Therefore, he's shared a lot with his girls. *A lot.* Too much. *Stupid* much. And another way he is not like Rodriguez, they have a light night, he don't like that and doesn't see that johns may not have a hankerin' for a 'ho with a black eye or busted lip. Therefore, they had it good so they are not big on how bad it's got the last four years and are not feelin' the love for their daddy."

Processing it all without giving it away to Lexie, Ty said nothing.

"So," Peña spoke into his silence, "don't got me a calculator handy but the minimum jail time on possession with intent to distribute, pimpin' and conspiracy to commit murder all added up means Duane Martinez is oh-fish-ah-lee fucked. And since he's an asshole who don't discriminate who he feels like bein' an asshole to, he gets sent down, there are boys in there who do *not* like him. I'm not thinkin' good thoughts about his survival rate."

Ty rolled off Lexie so his back was to the couch but his front still pressed to her side and he avoided her eyes which he felt on him and he asked, "You got him?"

"Lookin' for him now. He's got three enforcers, uses his girls in the daytime hours to cut and bag the dope and they're all in interrogation rooms as I'm speakin' to you and they're all yappin'. It shouldn't take long. Now, what I wanna know is, did these angels fly from Colorado?"

"Payback," was all Ty said, and he got silence.

Then he got a quiet, "Okay, then, I appreciate it so I hate to do you a dirty after you handed me gold but..." He hesitated. Ty braced then he went on, "It is standard procedure to inform the victim's family when the perpetrator has been caught. I'm makin' this call then escaping this office that right now looks like the Ninth Best Little Whorehouse in Texas. And I'm doin' that to get in my car and drive to Ella Rodriguez's house. I reckon about a nanosecond will elapse after the door shuts on me when she'll be on the phone. There is no love lost between the Rodriguez women and Martinez. But that doesn't mean this news is not gonna hit these women and hit hard. It's obviously up to you how you're gonna play it but you gotta know they're gonna know and soon and prepare to pick up the pieces."

"Right," Ty said quietly.

"Now I got more."

Fuck.

"Right," Ty repeated.

"As much as Dolinski can keep a line to me, he does. That Misty Keaton woman's activities have thrown a freeze on shit at the CPD. These fuckers are scared shitless and don't know which way is up. They are not scrambling. They are immobilized. They are also lookin' to their leader who is actin' business as usual."

Not a surprise.

Hubris. The fall of many a man.

Peña kept going.

"Now, they don't know if he's got an ace in the hole that's gonna shine the light of the Mother of God on them and save them at the last minute or if he just don't give a fuck and has his own exit strategy planned. My guess would be the latter. What you need to know is it might be the former. That said, the good news for you is, you and Lexie have unofficially been declared off limits."

Good news?

It was *great* motherfucking news.

Peña continued.

"This is not comin' from the top. This is the boys makin' up their own minds that they don't wanna dig a very deep hole any deeper by fuckin' with either a' you. The ACLU bein' involved. You gettin' an attorney who, apparently, locally has a reputation for being a ball-breaker and a liberal one at that. And the entrance of one Samuel Sterling into this hubbub—a man I don't know but I've done some checking and he's got weight, a fuckload of money and both he earned for himself so this is no dumb motherfucker. He also takes no shit and further takes *absolutely* no shit due to his skin color. Therefore it doesn't take a leap to figure that, if he's in the position to step in when a brother is doin' it, he will and anyone who knows him knows this. *All* this means you got so much firepower at your back, they won't say boo to you."

"Proof you are Santa Claus," Ty muttered.

"Well, no, 'cause the boys at CPD are scared shitless but Fuller has convinced himself his skin deflects bullets and he don't give a shit who he says boo to. Sayin' that, *now* I'll prove I'm Santa Claus 'cause there has been a recent occurrence which meant that, on the fly, there needed to be some sharin' and that sharin' is... now wait for it..."

Peña hesitated dramatically. Ty clenched his teeth and he gave it.

"Detective Chace Keaton has been workin' undercover for the IA for the last thirteen months."

Ty shot up to sitting and rumbled into the phone, "You are shittin' me."

"What?" Lexie whispered, also sitting up with him, rearranging her legs so they were over his thighs and putting a hand to his chest.

He looked to Lexie, shook his head then touched his forehead to hers briefly before he pulled back and gave a still-talking Peña his attention.

"Nope. No shit. This guy was deeper than Dolinski, in the inner sanctum. IA wants a clean house and they wanna make an example and considering how messy this shit is, they're pullin' out all the stops, but it is still takin' time. Now, the reason Dolinski learned this is because Keaton was in on a strategy meetin' and the play that was to be instigated was that Fuller wanted you down and out. And to do that, he was gonna light a fire under your parole officer's ass to do a random inspection of your home."

Ty closed his eyes at confirmation of this play but opened them when Peña kept at it.

"Now, they didn't know if they'd find anything so they decided to find somethin' whether it was there or not. And to make certain it was enough not only to get you in hot water but set you to boil, they were going to plant a firearm *and* dope during that inspection, which Fuller was going to make damned sure had his boys involved in it, obviously so they could plant the shit. And just because they're dickheads of mammoth proportions, they were also gonna plant dope in Lexie's car."

Ty opened his eyes but clenched his teeth.

Peña kept speaking.

"As Keaton was involved in this meeting, he informed IA of this plan. IA told him he had a comrade in arms that he didn't know he had and Keaton manipulated the situation. He made it so it was Dolinski and him who did the inspection and he leaked the information in a way you'd have a heads-up. Luckily, you had your shit together and half the town was in your kitchen. This gave Dolinski and Keaton an excuse *not* to follow through with the plan seein' as Jackson was there as was Sterling and they'd both sniff that shit out faster than snot. So, they aborted but I say aborted in quotes because they weren't gonna do it in the first place. But at least they didn't get their asses in hot water and under suspicion because they didn't."

So Ty had angels too.

And one of those angels was fucking Chace Keaton.

Fuck.

"So, Santa says, while your ball-breaker attorney does her thing, Keaton's got your back. Dolinski tells me that Keaton tells *him* that Fuller is already making noises about his next play. Keaton is in place to deflect it. I do not know this man's story and I do not have a line to him. I do know his wife recently got dead. I also know she fucked you in the sense that that is the definition of understatement. And I also know she got dead and they think he's still a loyal foot soldier so somethin' is fucked with that. So this man might have your back but you keep an eye to it."

"Always do," Ty told him.

"Good. Don't stop, Ty. And when I say that, not for a minute."

"Like I said, Angel, always do."

"Right," Peña whispered.

"You got more?"

"Just like all the little boys and girls, Santa's generous and they're turnin' their stockin' inside out hopin' for one more piece of candy."

"I'm not sayin' I'm not grateful," Ty said quietly. "I'm sayin' I got news to break to my wife and an imminent visit from my father, a drunk, an asshole the last thirty-six years but now a man who wants to get to know his son and daughter-in-law and try to be a good grandfather. So I got gratitude, Angel. I just don't have time."

Silence then, "Sorry, Ty, never stops for you."

"Not a problem, Angel. And no, it doesn't but I got hope this shit storm will end soon and all I'll have is sunshine."

"I hope so too, *esé*. Stay sharp."

"Same to you."

Then he heard the disconnect.

"What?" Lexie asked the minute he pulled the phone from his ear.

Ty clenched his teeth again, tossed his phone on the coffee table with a clatter and framed his wife's face with his hands, bringing her close as he leaned into her.

And he gave it to her quick and straight.

"They found the man who killed Rodriguez and they also found that hit was ordered by Shift."

He watched up close as her eyes got huge. Then she closed them, turned her head slightly away and pressed her lips together.

Ty slid his hands back into her hair and whispered, "Mama."

Lexie's eyes opened and came back to him.

"I don't believe this. Ronnie loved him," she whispered.

"Yeah," Ty whispered back.

"And I thought Shift loved Ronnie."

He didn't respond because he didn't need to. It was obvious Shift didn't love Rodriguez.

"They were brothers." Lexie was still whispering. "How could he do that?"

"No fuckin' clue, Lex."

She held his eyes, he couldn't read hers.

Then Ty spoke. "Angel is on his way to Ella right now."

"Shit," she said softly.

"'Spect you're gonna have to deal with that," he warned her.

"Yeah, no love lost but still, it'll be a blow."

Watching her face and, for once, unable to read it, he moved his hands forward, taking her hair with them until they were at the sides of her neck and he asked, "This a blow for you?"

Her head tipped to the side and her eyes grew unfocused like she was thinking about it and he then understood why he couldn't read her. She didn't know what to think.

Then she decided what to think and her eyes focused again on his.

"It's surprising," she said quietly. "But, I don't know. Weirdly, it's good to know what happened, who was behind it. But it doesn't breathe life into Ronnie and even if it did, it wouldn't matter. That's... it's..." She swallowed, shut her eyes tight for a second, opened them and continued, "All that is gone. All those years, all that feeling I had for him and now this is just, it's just..." She trailed off but lifted her hands to wrap her fingers around his wrists and she finished, "Ty, it's strange to feel this way but it's just... *news*."

Ty stared at his wife. She was over it. She was over Rodriguez. She'd moved on.

With him.

His fingers squeezed her neck and he bent to touch his mouth to hers. When he pulled back he dropped a hand but used the other one to wrap around the back of her neck and tuck her face in his throat. Both her arms moved to curve around his middle.

Once she settled she sighed.

Then she asked, "Does Angel have Shift?"

"They're lookin'."

She nodded.

Ty kept talking. "Dad's here, Ella calls, you take all the time you need. I'll keep him busy."

She nodded again.

"Lex, we're close," he assured his wife with a squeeze at the back of her neck. "Pretty soon, these hits'll stop comin'."

Yet again, she nodded.

A knock came at the back door. Lexie tensed and so did Ty.

His dad.

Jesus, God, he hoped his father had his shit together and this did not mean another hit.

Her arms slid from around him so she could pull down her skirt.

"You good?" he asked. "I can ask him to—"

She shook her head, pulled her face out of his neck to tip it back to give him a small grin she wasn't committed to but she was trying. It wasn't a blow. She wasn't suffering but the news was not good. Her family was going to have a past loss made fresh again. She was going to have to deal with that and she wasn't looking forward to it.

Then she whispered, "I made brownies."

Ty studied her face. Then he grinned back.

Then he set his wife aside, got up and went to go let in his father.

* * *

His father showed up sober. Nervous but sober. And his nerves didn't fade no matter that there were flowers in a vase, Lexie was tricked out, she'd made some snack where she'd baked cups of rolled-out pieces of bread she'd cut the crusts off of and then filled with some sausage, mushroom, olive, cream, garlic and cheese stuff that tasted the shit then offered up homemade brownies with a thick layer of chocolate frosting she'd served with ice cream.

She was saying plainly that Irv was welcome, this visit meant something to her, she wanted to make it nice. But Irv still didn't get it and relax. Lex went all out being Lex, smiling, joking even touching, his arm, his hand.

Irv did not loosen up.

Ty acted as normal, not overtly welcoming but not hostile either. Watchful but not tense. He wasn't going to go all out like his woman was doing.

This was Irv's penance, whatever was going on in his head that wouldn't let him relax, Ty was not going to bust his ass to let him off paying it. One visit where he's sober, one phone call where he pulled up the courage to share was not going to buy his father that.

Ty would wait and see and give it to him when he earned it.

When Lexie's phone rang, Ty took over with his father and Irv wound up tighter. It was then Ty saw that Lexie actually *was* helping his father relax, it was Ty he was worried about winning.

This didn't change his manner but when his wife wandered to the front deck for privacy, Ty explained her absence completely and honestly. Laying it all out about Lexie, her dead parents, her dick of a grandfather, her being taken in by the Rodriguez family, her relationship with Ronnie, most, if not all, of the path that led her to Ty and her recent news. He did this in an effort to make his father understand why his wife was crystal and should be treated as such.

From the look on his father's face when he was done speaking, he figured Irv got it.

She was gone awhile. When she came back, she got Irv another soda and led him onto the deck. It was then Ty decided he had business he needed to see to and he was going to let his wife get to know his father without him there as a physical reminder of just how bad Irv fucked up.

When he told her he needed a few minutes, she nodded.

He made his excuses to his dad, walked up the stairs, went to the office, closed the door, pulled his phone out of his back pocket, sat in the swivel chair and dialed Julius.

"My man," Julius greeted.

"You don't fuck around," Ty replied and heard a deep chuckle. Julius knew what Ty was talking about. Ty kept talking. "You know I appreciate it. What I need to know is if I got debts to pay."

"Welcome to the jungle," Julius stated.

"Come again?"

"You were forced to live in a zoo, Walk, a controlled jungle that has guards and bars. But outside that, you mighta skirted the real jungle but you didn't live in it. LA has a jungle, Dallas too. And in the jungle, it's survival of the fittest."

"Not sure you're answering my question, brother," Ty told him.

"Okay, then I will," Julius returned. "See, got a brother who's got a brother who had a brother and when I say that I mean they shared blood. He didn't get a cap busted in his ass. He got two to the face, five to the chest. A signature. He was not feelin' the love for Momma and the Hit Man so he laid them out."

There it was.

Julius wasn't done.

"Got another brother who's got a brother who was lookin' into expandin'. Business is boomin', my man, and he wanted more turf. Now he's got it."

There was more.

Julius continued.

"Got *another* brother who's got a brother who sells gash. Always recruitin'. Didn't mind he got himself some more when girls lost their daddy. They got a new daddy now."

And that was the rest of it.

So Julius finished.

"What I'm sayin' is, you don't owe dick. A man goes down, other men move in to stake their claim. Shift was not liked. My chats pointed out the benefits of workin' for the cops, get that asshole outta the way, divvy up the leftovers. No one's hurtin' in this scenario, everyone got what they wanted. You're good."

Ty couldn't say he felt peace deep inside his soul that the loss of Shift to the underbelly of Dallas meant Peña didn't clean the streets but instead bought himself different headaches with new names and faces. But, even so, it meant Ty lost himself a headache and he had enough of them, he could use losing some pain.

"You know it without me sayin' it," Ty said softly.

"I know it," Julius returned then noted, "Been two days since I been updated on the Life and Times of Ty Walker, 'spect there's news."

Ty had kept him briefed and he didn't delay in relaying his update.

When he was done, with a smile in his voice, Julius noted, "Soon, your free will be *free.* Means you and Lexie can haul your asses out to LA."

"Just as long as one, the other or all of your women take Lex to a beach."

"That we can do."

Ty grinned at his phone.

Then they said words of good-bye.

He flipped it shut, folded out of the chair, shoved the phone in his back pocket and walked back down to his wife and father.

CHAPTER NINETEEN

That Felt Good

Ty sucked back the last of his beer and I watched as his long arm reached out to put the empty on the coffee table.

I was tucked into the back of the couch, my front tight to my husband, my cheek to his chest, my nearly finished beer in my hand resting on his abs and we were watching a movie.

His dad was gone. The visit had not been great, it had not been shit. I'd invited him back, Ty had not protested. Irv had said he'd be delighted to come but no plans were made. There was something going down with Irv and Ty and I suspected, when plans were made, they'd be done through Ty.

I didn't pry. Ty needed to work this out without me in his face about it and he knew I was there when he needed me.

After Irv left, I made dinner and Ty told me the rest of what Angel had to say. To say I was stunned was an understatement. Then again, Chace Keaton had given it away that day in the closet. I just didn't get all of it.

We ate dinner and we hit the couch.

And I didn't like the dregs of beer. Warm beer at the bottom of the bottle was not my favorite thing so I wanted another one and I knew my husband did too.

So I pushed up on my elbow that was between the couch and Ty and looked down at him.

"I'm getting us more beer," I said when his eyes moved from TV to me.

His answer was to stretch a long arm out to tag the remote and hit pause. Then he looked back at me. I grinned, put a hand in his chest but pushed up on my hand in the couch.

Something caught at the corner of my eye. I turned, looked over the back of the couch for a scant second and at what I saw, instinct drove me to drop instantly down, all my weight hitting Ty. It came as a surprise to him and he grunted, his hands going to my hips, his lips beginning to curve up because he thought I was messing around then he saw my face and they stopped.

"Someone's doing something at the back door," I breathed, my lungs constricted, my breath sticking in my throat.

Ty went solid under me for a nanosecond then he bucked his hips to pull out his phone as he whispered, "Stay here. Do not move. I'm not back in five minutes, you dial 911 then you call Tate."

I opened my mouth to protest but didn't get a sound out before his phone was pressed into my hand, he was out from under me and he was gone.

I lay there hyperventilating, listening and clutching Ty's phone in my hand. Ty didn't have shoes on and I'd taken mine off when we hit wind-down mode on a Sunday night, which was to say, approximately five seconds after we waved his father away. I couldn't hear him move, I couldn't hear anything.

Then I heard the back door open.

Then nothing.

I kept hyperventilating, counting to thirty then counting to thirty again, trying not to think about my husband having enemies, no weapon and no shoes.

I counted to thirty again.

I got to my seventh set of thirty when I heard the back door close and the lock flip. After that, I heard the vertical blinds slapping against each other as Ty pulled them over the door then another slap as he shut them. This happened again and I knew he was at the window over the sink.

I lifted up and looked at him over the couch. I watched as he moved around the house, a manila envelope in his hand, closing all the blinds including the ones at the wall of floor-to-ceiling windows that it took three long tugs to get both sides of them across the expanse.

I'd never seen those blinds closed. It felt weird being closed in our house. We were in a development but removed. There were houses close but with the trees around, they felt far. Being the last house in the development, up an incline that grew significantly steeper after the last house before ours, our place felt separate, private. There was no need to close the blinds so I never had.

I felt a shiver trill up my spine at the need to close the blinds and another one when Ty walked to stand opposite the coffee table from me where he lifted up the envelope and started to study it, turning it back to front.

I curled my legs in an S and got up on my hand, my eyes also on the envelope.

"What's that?" I asked.

"No clue. Was sittin' at the back door." I looked up at his face to see him looking at me. "You see who put it there?"

Dusk had fallen. It wasn't dark but there wasn't a lot of light left. Our house faced west, the back was darker than the front and the outside light wasn't on.

I shook my head and answered, "It was a man. A big guy but not you, Bubba, Deke big. Short-sleeved shirt, plaid. That's all I saw."

"So you didn't recognize him?"

I shook my head.

He nodded and looked back down at the envelope.

He moved to open it and I tensed, whispering, "Honey," not wanting it to be an envelope bomb or something because I didn't want our house to explode. I loved our house, of course, but mostly I didn't want Ty and me to explode with it.

He ignored me, pushed the clasps back, flipped open the lip, turned it over and a CD in a transparent green plastic case slid into his hand.

I got off the couch and moved to him as he turned the envelope to look inside. I made it to him as he leaned forward and dropped the envelope on the coffee table and was looking at the case back to front.

"Is that it?" I asked.

"That's it," Ty answered.

"No note?" I went on, looking down at the case which was a CD, no writing, nothing.

"No note, nothin' on the envelope," he replied.

Without another word, he moved to the stairs. I hustled after him. His legs were longer than mine and he was already in the office, reaching to the computer to turn it on when I got there.

My computer was an all-in-one unit, just a big, long monitor, a wireless keyboard and mouse. Shiny black. It was awesome. I bought it because it looked good, not because I knew anything about computers. Still, the dude at the store said it was a really good one and I'd noticed it was super fast, at least compared to my old one.

Ty dropped the CD on the desk and felt around the sides of the computer. After about a second, the CD drive slid open at the side.

I kept quiet and reminded myself to breathe as the computer booted up. Ty loaded up the CD, shoved in the drawer and sat down in the swivel chair, rolling it to the desk, his big hand covering the mouse.

I leaned into the side of the chair as the computer read the disc then opened up a window listing things Ty could choose from for what he wanted to do with the disc.

He picked, double-clicked, the screen went entirely black. I held my breath, hoping that it wasn't some virus that would explode my computer because I liked my computer and my man that day asked me to slow down spending. He did it in a way that was *super* nice and we didn't need to drop a whack on a new computer when mine was only five months old.

A small, square screen popped up. My breath came back and I blinked as what I saw and heard hit my brain. Ty's hand moved the mouse, he maximized the image and it filled the big monitor.

Then I stared.

"Holy fuck," Ty whispered.

Holy fuck was right. And also a big, fat *euw*.

This was because we were watching what appeared to be a homemade porn video and it was not a good one. Not that much porn was high budget, high quality, just that this was *bad*.

And it was bad for more reasons than the director clearly had no vision.

Two women working an old guy. He was tall and lean but he was old. And he was into some seriously sick shit.

Seriously sick.

I'd never seen anything like it. I didn't know anyone was into that kind of thing. I didn't actually even know that kind of thing existed and, watching it, I wished I *still* didn't know.

I was staring in fascinated horror, wanting to pull my eyes away but for some reason not able to. I wondered why some anonymous man had dropped this at our back door. I wondered how anyone could get off on that crap.

And as I was wondering and struggling with the nauseous roil in my stomach, I heard Ty whisper, "The blonde."

I had been concentrating on the activities, not the participants, so I focused on one of the two females, the blonde not the brunette.

Then I froze.

It was Misty Keaton.

"Ohmigod," I breathed.

I felt Ty's eyes on me but mine didn't move from Misty. Thinner, younger, I couldn't guesstimate by how much but half a decade, at least.

"You ever see that man?" he asked.

My eyes moved to the guy even though I didn't want them to considering what the women were doing to him and I shook my head.

"The other woman?" Ty went on.

I looked to her and shook my head again.

"Look, Lex, at the salon? Grocery store? Anywhere?"

I kept looking and, for my man, I did it hard though it cost me. Then I shook my head.

I felt Ty's eyes move away from me and I forced mine to his hand, which was again moving on the mouse. He hovered the cursor at the bottom of the screen so the controls on the video came up and I saw the video lasted over thirty-five minutes.

Gross. I couldn't imagine sustaining that activity for one minute without hurling, much less over half an hour.

Ty clicked on the control and the action stopped when he slid the cursor across the control to take it to the end. The screen went blank. He slid it back half a centimeter and we were treated to an empty bed, covers mussed, no one in the room.

I sucked in breath when the camera caught Arnie Fuller, full face and close up, his attention focused on something then the screen went blank.

He'd made the tape.

And it was highly likely one, a couple or all the participants didn't know he'd done it.

But I was guessing they knew shortly after.

"Phone," Ty rumbled and I realized I still had his phone in my hand.

I lifted it up and he slid it out of my grip, instantly flipping it open. His thumb moved over the keypad and he put it to his ear.

Then I heard him say, "Tate? Ty. You in for the night?" He paused then, listening as well as clicking, opening up the DVD directory and the hard drive directory, then, "Just got a delivery, anonymous, DVD sex tape left at the back door. Hang on."

He looked at me and pushed the chair back, dipping his head to the machine.

"Save it but bury it, babe. At least two places."

I nodded, reached out, moved the keyboard to face me, grabbed the mouse and got to work.

Ty went back to the phone, "I'm here." Pause then, "Yeah, Lex saw the guy who left it but didn't recognize him and he was gone before I got out the back door. Misty Keaton is on the tape, younger, thinner, gotta be around the time she fucked me over or just before. I don't know the other two in the tape and Lexie hasn't seen them. But I do know Arnie Fuller made it seein' as he was on-screen after the festivities were over, camera caught him turning it off. It is not fun viewing, brother, but I'm at a loss why this was slipped to me. I need you to take a look at it and tell me if you got more."

Another pause while I created directories "Recipes" then "Cookies," then dragged the video file across windows, dropped it in and renamed it "Chocolate Chip."

Ty said, "Right, we'll be over soon's we save it. Sorry, Tate, need this info or I wouldn't fuck up your Sunday and, no way around it, you see this sick shit, it's gonna fuck up your Sunday."

He was not wrong about that. My Sunday hadn't been the greatest but we'd got to the good part. Still, that video fucked up the whole day.

I kept going, creating another directory called "Addresses" then "Christmas Card List" then saved the file under the name "Out of Town."

Ty was back to Tate. "Right, we gotta shut the computer down. Be there as soon as we can. Thanks." I heard him flip his phone shut and say to me, "Close it down, babe."

I did and he ejected the DVD. He put it back in the case while I moved out of the office and down the stairs. He followed me down and I went directly to my shoes. Ty got his boots on in no time flat and waited while I finished with my zips then we both hoofed it to the car. We took the Viper. Ty stayed within the speed limit but I knew it cost him.

When we hit Carnal, I spoke into the strained silence.

"What do you think this means?"

I looked to him and saw his eyes flash back and forth from road to rearview mirror as he answered, "I think it means Arnold Fuller's net is unraveling."

"That man in that video is important and he's blackmailing him," I guessed.

"That man in that video is important and Fuller's got him by the balls," Ty replied.

"Misty?" I whispered.

"Fuller's go-to pussy."

Hmm. This seemed to be true. After what I saw, I was actually beginning to feel sorry for Misty. She looked like she was loving every minute of it in a way she looked like she was trying really, *really* hard to pretend she was loving every minute of it, which meant she was not. Even if the guy was hot, not old enough to be her father, no girl could love every minute of *that.*

Ty kept talking. "The question is, this guy's important, how many more men like him does he have by the balls? And question two, who got hold of this and gave it to me?"

"It wasn't Keaton or Frank," I said softly.

"Crabtree?" Ty asked.

"No, it wasn't him. I'd recognize him anywhere, even in the dark."

"Then his net is unraveling," Ty muttered.

I went silent, uncertain what this meant but knowing it was only partially good and the rest could be very bad.

We arrived at Tate and Laurie's house which was on the other side of Carnal, through some winding roads up on a hill. A long two-story house, the bottom floor mostly built into the ground, a deck that ran the entire front of it and jutted off the end. It was embedded in trees and I loved our view and, even as days slid into weeks, I was not used to it. Still, I had to say that the seclusion and quiet of Tate and Laurie's house surrounded by dense Colorado forest was definitely a close runner-up in cool.

Ty parked, waiting for me to round the car, and took my hand as we walked through the bright outside lights up to the deck. Tate came out the sliding glass door that I knew led to the dining area off the kitchen and he slid the door to.

His eyes moved down to the DVD case Ty was carrying.

"Already told Jonas he's to stay upstairs but Laurie's curious. How bad is this shit?" Tate asked when we got close.

"You like gettin' some from your wife?" Ty asked back when we stopped at Tate.

Tate's lips twitched and he answered the obvious, "Yeah."

"Then keep her far away," Ty replied.

Tate's amused eyes slid to me. I cocked my head because Ty was not wrong. He was going to have to work hard to get that shit out of my brain the next time we had sex. Lucky for me, he always worked hard.

Tate opened the door and motioned us through. We went in and I'd been there before but, again, even with what was happening, I processed how cool it was and repeated what I did the other times I was there and memorized Laurie's flair with décor, intending to use it myself one day. This was essentially making everything look really, freaking good, purchasing nothing but top quality but underlying it all was comfort for her boys, and she decorated in memories. The place was full of pictures.

Laurie's ass was planted on a stool at the butcher block–topped island in their awesome kitchen like she kept vigil there, cell phone on the counter in front of her, laptop open and on, a half-full glass of what looked like iced grape Kool-Aid in a super girlie but kick-ass glass in front of her. Her eyes were riveted to us the minute we entered and they were visibly curious.

If I wasn't still seriously grossed out and totally freaked out, it would have amused me to consider super-hot, tall, great body, total man Tatum Jackson drinking from that girlie glass.

Then again, the way Laurie spoiled her boys, she probably had a whole other set they could drink from.

Jonas was flat out on the couch watching TV and he was not curious. Clearly Dad spoke, Jonas listened or, alternately, there was something he was really into on TV.

We exchanged greetings then Tate headed through the kitchen toward a back room saying, "Closed party, baby."

"Tate—" Laurie started. He stopped, turned, caught his wife's eyes and shook his head. She looked to me. "That bad?"

"My brain is still burning and if Ty wasn't holding my hand, I'd be bumping into stuff because I'm temporarily blind," I answered.

She wrinkled her nose in a "gross" look that, considering she hadn't seen it, didn't do it justice.

Tate led us down some stairs, through a room with weight equipment in it, down a hall and into a room he clearly used as an office considering the desk, filing cabinets and office equipment. He already had his computer booted up. He didn't delay in sitting in front of it and loading up the DVD. He set it to go.

Then it went.

"Fuck me," he whispered, then, not done being horrified and expressing it, "Jesus fuckin' Christ."

"Told you, brother. Sick shit," Ty muttered.

Suddenly, Tate leaned forward, the first impact of what he saw wearing off and he focused.

"Jesus fuckin' Christ." He was still whispering.

"What?" Ty asked and I got closer to him, my hand still in his tensing

"Trane," Tate said.

"Train?" I asked.

Tate's head turned slowly and he tipped it back to look up at us. "Trane. Trane Keaton. Chace's father."

My body locked right beside my husband's that was doing the same.

"Come again?" Ty asked but the words were tight, forced through his lips.

Tate looked back at his computer monitor. "That's Misty. Don't know the brunette." He looked back at us. "But that is definitely Trane Keaton of the Aspen Keatons. Chace was in uniform while I was on the force, hadn't made detective yet and his dad came around more than once. Hotshot. Shit don't stink. You didn't forget him mainly because he didn't want you to. He was in a police department with men who got more testosterone than most and *still* took his time pissin' in every corner. Jackass, huge. Dickhead, bigger. Treated Chace like shit. Chace's choice to bail on Aspen and the good life and live in a small biker town wearin' a uniform was not Daddy's favorite thing and he made that apparent."

Tate turned back to the screen, commandeered the mouse and did what Ty did to take the video to the end. He saw Fuller. Then he thankfully closed the video window and turned back to us.

"You suss it out?" he asked Ty.

Ty moved to the desk, rested his fine ass and a hard thigh on the edge of it, foot hanging. I again moved to lean into him and his arm curled around my hips.

"Heard of his perversion, set Misty on him, got 'im by the balls," Ty answered as a confirmation he had sussed it out.

Tate nodded but said, "More."

"Give it to me," Ty invited.

"I will but I'm also gonna break it down, some speculation in this shit but gotta tell you, Keaton turning to the dark side threw me. He was a straight arrow. Made Frank look crooked. That said, he was no choirboy and I mean that only in the sense that he liked to get him some and he's a good-lookin' guy, he had choice and he enjoyed it, including Misty. He didn't talk about it but I reckoned he might play as much as he liked but when it got down to bein' serious, no way the likes of Misty Keaton would have his ring on her finger. He might accept a woman who had some experience *some.* If he couldn't bag himself a virgin, though, he would not be settling with a girl of Misty's array of knowledge. He's a man who likes control and my guess is, he wouldn't mind he had to do a fuckload of training seein' as, when he was done, he'd get it just like he liked it. Just a guess but Chace wanted a quiet life, out from under Daddy's thumb, white picket fence he earned his own self fencing in a family with two point five kids and a wife who made kickass pies, was the leader of his daughter's Brownie troop but still gave world-class head," he paused, looked at me and said, "Sorry, Lexie."

"That's okay," I whispered on a grin.

Tate grinned back.

"And?" Ty prompted when Tate didn't continue speaking.

So Tate continued speaking.

"What I'm sayin' is, this man was his own man, not his father's son. He was who he wanted to be. Took balls to walk away from all that. So, him goin' under shocked the shit outta me. Everyone knows Misty got Chace outta your deal and everyone knows Chace didn't pretend to like it. Before that, he kept his head down, his nose clean, did his job. Like all the boys, he wanted to stay employed, he looked the other way with shit but he didn't participate in it. Without family to hold him close, a connection to the community, like Frank has, why he stuck around Carnal and put up with that shit, I don't know. My guess was, him movin' on or quittin' altogether would get him a big 'I told you so' from Daddy. Also could be, Fuller's network was so vast, would be hard to find a job if he left Carnal. I know I didn't go back into police work after that, bad taste in my mouth. But I had ties to the community, I grew up here, this was home, found a way to stay and earn a living. That said, if Keaton told Fuller and his boys to go fuck themselves and moved clean across the country, that would not have surprised me. What surprised me and what I never got was why a man like Chace, his own man, a straight arrow and a man who liked control, buckled regarding Misty then, directly after, entered the inner sanctum."

Ty's voice sounded distracted when he muttered, "Didn't enter it, was shoved in it."

"Bet he's seen that video," Tate muttered back and I closed my eyes.

Seeing his dad like that, I couldn't fathom it and I didn't even have a dad. But being married to the woman who did that to his dad, knowing she trapped his dad *and* him, it was no wonder he hated her and didn't hide it.

But this was worse. To keep his father from enduring untold humiliation should that video leak, a good man got pushed into the mud. He could go to the grocery store or out to have a beer anytime he wanted but he was still in prison, controlled, his life not his own nor his decisions. And, as far as I knew, he didn't do anything to deserve any of that.

And that sucked.

"Not hip on the Aspen social scene, Tate." I heard Ty say, and I opened my eyes as he went on. "What does knowin' Fuller has this guy by the balls mean to me or anyone but Keaton?"

"First, it fills in blanks about Misty and Chace. Second, Trane may not be local but Trane is Trane. He's got money, money buys him power and he wields it. He may live two hours away but there are a lot of ways to squeeze a guy like that, you got that video, and keep squeezin' him until he's dry. Wasn't invited and even if I was, wouldn't go to the wedding, but I bet Trane sat up front watchin' his son marryin' the woman who saw to his sick kink and he smiled big while adjusting his pants 'cause Arnie had his boys in a tight grip."

"Makes you wonder how many balls Fuller has his fist wrapped around," Ty noted.

"Money, power, judges, lawyers, other cops . . . if he made a habit of collecting that kinda video," Tate motioned to his computer with his head, "then he would think he's untouchable 'cause if he goes down, *they all go down*."

And there it was.

Shit, shit, *fucking shit*.

"We gotta find that girl in the video," Ty stated.

"Fuck yeah, we do," Tate agreed. "Misty's dead, who knows how many assignments he sent her on and now we'll never know. That girl was not doin' that shit because she got off on it but she got somethin' from it. One, she could have shitloads of info and two, if there's more where that came from, the shit that's happening in Carnal, there's a lot more twitchy men out there than the ones employed by Carnal PD, and this mess has already seen one woman dead."

"Maryland," I blurted, saw Tate's eyes come to me and felt Ty's.

"What?" Tate asked.

I shook my head, feeling stupid butting in on the boys but I worked in a salon and I heard it all there. Everyone went to see Dominic or Kayeleen and not just ladies from Carnal, from all around.

And none of them was friends with Misty.

"She didn't have any friends," I said then pulled in breath and went on, "and she wasn't a pro. She was in love with Chace and, yes, maybe the promise of his father's money, but the woman I met a few weeks before she was murdered was down, beaten. Ronnie had girls and I know that kind of beaten, when life forces you into that. Some of them had just given up but most of them were hard. That wasn't the same kind of beaten as Misty, and Misty wasn't hard."

I looked between the two men and kept talking.

"She'd had hope. She'd played her part willingly to get what she wanted, screwed in the head how she did it but hoping in the end she'd win Chace around. She didn't. And, after they backfired, clearly she was rethinking her actions with Chace *and* Ty. She said in her note to Ty that another good man got caught in the net and she didn't want to harm him further. If Trane is a jerk, she meant Chace. Everyone knows she loved him. So, she's not a paid whore. She's a girl who made a play for the man she loves who, if what you said was true, would never tie himself to her any other way. And, since that wasn't her vocation, doing what we saw on that video," I tipped my chin to the monitor, "she'd wanna be with a friend. She pretended she liked it and I don't want to examine it up close, but from what I saw, it was pretend. And to do something that gross, she'd want some safety, someone there who she could trust, someone there she was close to. And the only friend I know that Misty has is in Maryland."

Tate nodded and muttered, "I'm on that."

"You need to know," Ty said at this point, "Angel called today. Keaton is also working with IA. He's been with them thirteen months. We know Fuller instigated that inspection on Monday. What we didn't know was the play was to plant shit. Keaton and Frank worked together to derail that plan without losin' their cover. Frank didn't know Keaton was with IA. He knows now and so do we."

Tate stared at Ty in unconcealed surprise a moment before what appeared to be relief moved across his handsome features then he shook his head and whispered, "Jesus, this web is so fuckin' sticky, everyone is caught in it."

That was, unfortunately, true.

Ty gave me a squeeze, I looked up to him and he said, "Give Tate everything you got on the guy you saw delivering the envelope."

My eyes went back to Tate and I told him, "Not small, not huge, a man, plaid, short-sleeved shirt. It was dark, I didn't even get his hair color but—"

"Newcomb," Tate cut me off and I blinked.

"No fuckin' way," Ty replied instantly. "Loyal foot soldier for years and that motherfucker makes Fuller look like a poster boy for affirmative action. Newcomb had a white hood and robe in his closet, I would not be surprised. He wouldn't scratch an itch he had on his ass if it meant it might in some way help me."

"Newcomb's also got a wife who took off three years ago leavin' him with three kids and one of them is a daughter who has leukemia and it isn't lookin' good. Those kids need him to go down *or* disappear like they need holes drilled into their heads. He's inner sanctum, caked in mud so, they all go down, he's fucked. He's doin' what he can to divert attention to the higher-ups in hopes the buzzards will see him breathin' when they pick over the meatier carcasses and leave him be. He's also a big guy and he doesn't ever wear tees. He's not in a sports jacket and slacks on duty, he's in short sleeves, always plaid."

Ty made no reply.

Tate kept speaking. "I'll get to the girl in Maryland. You said you were savin' this on your hard drive, you do it?"

"Yeah," Ty answered.

"You got a writeable DVD?"

"Yes." That one I answered.

Tate looked at me. "Make copies. Get one to Nina, hand delivered. Express one to Peña, you give him a heads-up to look for it and you send it from the post office in Gnaw Bone. Mick Shaughnessy is the top cop in Gnaw Bone, clean as a whistle and, because of that, he hates Fuller's guts. Fuller doesn't step foot in Gnaw Bone, he did, Mick would lose his mind. You'll have no eyes on you there. You put one in your safe and then you spread them around. Krystal and Bubba, Deke, Jim-Billy, Wood. The fact you have it has to be dropped in the right ear, I'll think about which one that'll be and do it. What I'll also do is let people know that they got a lot of work to do if they think they can sweep them all up. That shit heading to Dallas, they'll figure it isn't worth it even to try."

Tate then looked at Ty.

"But this means two things. One, even the boys in the inner sanctum are turnin' on each other, which leads us to two, desperate times, desperate measures. You're close to bein' cleared but you aren't. Somethin' goes down and you got a gun, currently, you're fucked even if it means protecting yourself, Lex, your home. Still, you feel you need that insurance, I'll go get your gun."

I looked at Ty to see him shaking his head. "Not gonna trip on my own feet now."

"Smart," Tate muttered. "Fucked that you can't have that insurance, but smart."

Talk about guns and insurance, anonymous men silently wandering up our stairs to leave envelopes, Ty closing us in, I felt a full-body tremble and Ty's arm around me got tighter.

"All right, Tate, again, I owe you but right now, gotta get Lexie home. We haven't had a great day so we need it to be done."

Tate nodded and stood, his eyes coming to me.

"Stay strong, darlin'. This'll be over soon."

I nodded too. Tate's eyes moved to Ty, they exchanged a look then Tate led the way out. There was idle chitchat in the kitchen with Laurie but not much before Ty shut it down and got me out to the Viper.

We were winding our way down the hill when he asked gently, "My mama okay?"

I wasn't.

But I hoped soon I would be.

So I lied, "Yeah. Fine."

"Bullshit," he muttered but said no more and reached out a hand to mine. He squeezed firm and warm then he let it go.

As we were waiting for our garage door to open, I was thinking, doors locked, blinds pulled, no gun, anonymous men lurking in the dark with sick-ass sex tapes, I was still glad to be home.

Ty pulled in, shut the Snake down and I was ready for his tee, a beer then bed so I had my buckle off, the door open and was folding out before he hit the button to bring down the garage door.

Again, at the corner of my eye I saw movement, turned my head, froze half straightened from the car with my eyes aimed over the roof and I hissed urgently, "*Ty!*"

But he'd seen him before me and Ty was already out, standing in his opened door, turned to look in the opened door of the garage where Rowdy Crabtree was standing two feet in.

"What the fuck?" Ty rumbled, and it was his pissed rumble that, even not directed at me echoed in my chest.

"Close the garage door," Crabtree ordered.

"Fuck that, Rowdy, get the fuck outta here."

"Close the door, Walker!" Crabtree snapped, taking a step closer.

"Not one more move," Ty growled.

Crabtree stopped then his body went completely still and I noticed then he did not look good. Not dirty but his hair was a mess like his hands had been going through it. He had serious stubble that said he hadn't shaved in a good long time. His eyes were bloodshot. His body was frozen but it still communicated he was wired. And he, surprisingly but fortunately, held no weapon.

"We gotta talk." Rowdy's tone had changed, wheedling, borderline needy.

"Gonna say it one more time, get the fuck outta here," Ty warned low.

"Got somethin' for you, we need to talk deal," Rowdy told him.

"Nothin' I need from you, no deal I'd make," Ty replied.

"You'll want this."

"Rowdy—" Ty started but Rowdy cut him off, talking swiftly, urgent, the desperation coming closer to the surface.

"I didn't do Misty."

Ty scowled at him and asked, "No shit?"

Rowdy shook his head emphatically. "No way, Walker, no motive. Don't barely know the bitch."

"And you think I care about this because…?"

Rowdy shook his head again, this time communicating Ty was getting no more until he agreed to the terms. "We need to talk deal."

"I'm seein' you don't get this but I don't need shit from you. You been to ground so you don't know I don't need you. Right now *you* need *me* and I got absolutely no fuckin' love for you so you can go fuck yourself. Now get outta my garage or I make the only call to Carnal PD they want to get from me and that's me tellin' 'em you're in my garage."

"What I have is good, Walker," Rowdy rushed to say.

Ty moved to pull his phone out of his back pocket.

Still rushing, Rowdy informed Ty, "You went down for Fuller's brother in LA."

"Not tellin' me somethin' I don't know," Ty muttered, flipping open his phone then, eyes to it and not to me, he said to me, "Mama, get your ass over here, behind me. Now."

I shifted out from the door, slammed it and moved.

Rowdy spoke. "He's got a partner."

"Know that too," Ty said as he moved out of his door, slammed it and I moved close to his back. He was also hitting buttons on his phone, I could hear the beeps.

"It was about dope," Rowdy quickly put in.

"LA Fuller likes his blow, this too is not news," Ty murmured, lifting the phone to his ear.

"LA Fuller likes his blow and also doesn't like a middleman. Killed that dealer you went down for not because he owed him so much as because he took over his business," Rowdy said.

I felt Ty's body get tight and he dropped his phone hand, flipping it closed.

Oh my God!

Rowdy kept talking, taking another step in. Ty's entire body went tight making it look like it expanded and he was bigger than he was, which was already big and Rowdy wisely stopped.

But he didn't stop talking. "He owed him, he owed him a whack. But he also learned from that mistake. Distribute, you got a constant supply without havin' to pay for it, just skim it off the top. He had connections all over the place, set up a network of sellers and, as a cop, he could provide them excellent protection. Shit worked great for him, a couple years later, he and his buddy expanded the business, took over another dealer's supplier and territory, same way as you. Dealer goes down, another guy gets framed, they take over. They had it sweet. Now they got heat."

"You got any evidence of this?" Ty asked.

"I—" Rowdy started.

Ty interrupted him, "Yes or no, Rowdy, you got anything solid behind this?"

Rowdy held his eyes. Then he shook his head.

"Motherfucker, you are wanted for murder and you walk into my garage offerin' me a deal when you really got nothin' and your word is worth shit?" Ty asked.

Rowdy's shoulders went straight and he declared, "I didn't kill Misty."

"Tell someone who gives a shit," Ty returned.

"I just handed you Fuller *and* his brother *and* that brother's partner," Rowdy reminded him.

"You didn't hand me shit. Half of what you told me, I know and so do a fuckload of people who actually can do something about it. The other half you got no evidence to support."

At that, Rowdy lost it, leaned in and snapped, "I'm not goin' down for takin' out that gash."

To this, Ty was quiet for several long seconds until I put my hands to him, curling my fingers in the back waistband of his jeans and pressing close with all the rest of me.

Then he spoke and when he did, it was quiet but that quiet still rumbled. "Hurts like a bitch, doesn't it?"

My stomach flipped.

Rowdy's torso shot back and his face went pale.

"Now, you listen to me, you piece of shit," Ty whispered. "You do not breathe my air or my wife's. I don't see you until I see your picture in the paper then I can toss that shit in the trash where it fuckin' belongs. You get near me or my wife again, your shit storm magnifies to epic proportions. I know what you like, Rowdy. Five years ago, you fucked me up the ass but you did it metaphorically 'cause you like ass fuckin' but not men. Boys. The younger they look, fuck, the younger they *are*, the better."

I was peering around Ty, staring at Rowdy who was now white as a sheet but Ty wasn't done.

"I know where you do your ass fuckin'. I know who you fuck. I know how much you pay for it and I know how often you do it. My guess is, you do not want your buddies to know you like givin' it up the ass to boys. Another guess, once you go down for whatever the fuck they get you for, you do not want to be a cop in the joint who's known for gettin' off on that shit. My wife and I never see you again, that secret stays safe. We do, I spread that shit wide. I'll remind you, over five years ago, you fucked me so I would advise you don't test me because it's takin' all the control I got not to lay you out. Now, nod if you get me then get… *the fuck*… out of my… *fuckin' garage*."

Rowdy, eyes wide, face ashen, nodded once, turned and scurried out of the garage.

Ty turned to me, his burning eyes caught mine and he ordered, "You move with me. You are not outta my reach."

I nodded.

He turned again to look out the garage as he opened the door to the Viper, moved into it and turned again. His eyes came to me, he reached in, hit the button and the garage door started to crank down. He moved out of the door, slammed it and we both watched the garage door until it settled.

Then he turned back to me. "Upstairs."

I moved. Ty followed. I watched him turn the lock on the utility room door to the garage then I walked up the stairs. Ty again followed.

I took four steps into the kitchen and turned.

He stopped two steps from me and ordered, "Stay there, don't move."

I nodded again and he moved. I saw him scan the first floor then heard his feet as he moved through the two floors above us.

He came back, again stopped two steps from me and held my eyes.

"Are you okay, baby?" I whispered, doing my own scan, seeing nothing, reading nothing, he was blank.

"Two and a half weeks," he replied.

"What?" I asked.

"That piece of shit has had two and a half weeks, tastin' my nightmare."

My breath stuck in my throat.

Suddenly, he smiled his beautiful smile and whispered, "That felt good."

My breath forced through in a rush and I whispered back, "I bet it did."

Then I smiled back.

His expression changed and at what it changed to, my nipples got hard.

"My mama owes me some pussy," he said softly.

That was when wet rushed between my legs.

My husband held my eyes a second, two, three, then, I had no idea why, perhaps it was the intensity pulsing off him, I whirled and ran on my high heels to the stairs.

He caught me almost all the way up the first flight and I thought he'd lift me up and carry me to our bed but he didn't. He turned me, planted my ass on a stair, my panties were gone in a whoosh then his big body was on me, his mouth on mine, his tongue in my mouth.

I circled him with all four limbs.

Then my skirt was up to my ribs, my legs were over his shoulders and his mouth between my legs. My man was hungry. Having waited a long time for his celebration feast, he was going to enjoy it.

Lucky for me, I got to too.

And I did, it was the hardest, longest, most intense orgasm he'd ever given me, which was to say I ever had, and he'd given me some hard, long, intense, *brilliant* ones.

It was so good, he had an arm around my hips lifting me up, his other hand in the step for leverage and I was taking his cock before I'd come down and knew it was happening.

He alternately assaulted my mouth with his or his lips brushed mine as he held my eyes while he thrust deep inside me and I held on, limbs tight, lifting my hips with every drive in order to give him more.

Then, suddenly, we were up. Still connected, he moved up the last steps but planted me on the floor in the hallway, his hips moving faster, harder, his cock going deeper as I watched his eyes burn, felt our quick breaths mix, my legs locking him to me, my hands wandering under his tee on his hot skin.

I felt him, I loved every inch of him on me and in me but his eyes held me enthralled.

"Love you, Ty," I breathed, staring into his eyes. "Every inch of you, baby, everything that is you."

He didn't speak. He rarely did when he was inside me or just having sex with me. He just thrust harder, each now coming with a grunt, his eyes hotter, with desire but it was more. In those beautiful eyes, shining clear was not only the triumph he was sharing with me but also all that he felt for me.

And they were locked to mine, giving me something precious.

Then I lost them as his head jerked back when he came then almost instantly fell forward and his face disappeared in my neck.

And I knew he'd come hard too.

But that was only part of the reason I held him close and tight in all four limbs.

And we would guess though never know for sure but that was when my husband planted our daughter inside of me.

CHAPTER TWENTY

Sunshine

Two days later…

It was ten thirty when it happened.

I was in the salon and it was Tuesday. My Monday had been busy acquiring blank DVDs, burning a shitload of them and driving around distributing sick-ass sex tapes to Ty's lawyer, our friends and expressing one to Angel.

In doing this, I got to meet Nina's husband and Ty's friend, Holden "Max" Maxwell, a tall, built, seriously hot mountain man with a great smile and a weirdly protective but definitely sweet and attentively affectionate manner around his wife. Upon meeting him, being around the two of them together for ten minutes and with all my recent experience, I mentally kicked myself for not moving to Colorado years ago.

But the day had gone by without incident, which was good. We'd had enough the day before. We could use a slow day in our ongoing drama.

Tuesday was always a big day for Carnal Spa but then again, every day was now since Dominic added his new services. But that morning seemed more so.

Dominic had a lady in his chair he was doing a cut on while he had another lady in foils, her hair cooking while she was gabbing to Jazz, our nail technician who was working on a client. Kayeleen had a cut in her chair. The back rooms were full. Dominic had been right to take the risk and add actual spa treatments; biker babes and mountain women embraced them wholeheartedly. The massage therapist had a client on her table and there was another woman getting a facial. Kayeleen's next up, Stockard, was twenty minutes early and drifting. She'd been in before so I'd met her and the last time she was in, she was also twenty minutes early and she was this way because she liked to gossip, which was what she was doing.

I'd just rung up some product a woman had popped in to buy. I was dealing with her credit card receipt as she said her farewells and wandered to the door so I was looking down at my desk when I heard her surprised gasp.

I looked up at the sound and saw her standing in the opened door looking out of it and up, her mouth open. I couldn't see what she was looking at, the blinds at the windows were fully closed, it was late August but the heat was already on the day, burning intense in preparation for Indian summer. Whoever or whatever she was looking at was out on the sidewalk standing by the window.

Suddenly, her body jerked, she nodded, muttered, "Sorry, excuse me," and scuttled out the door.

Approximately point two five seconds later, Ty filled it.

I stared and vaguely felt the buzz change in the room considering it was filled with women and a gay guy. Ty naturally had that affect on women and gay guys, of course, but everyone knew what was going down with him. He had never visited me in the salon. He was *all* man in coveralls half hanging down and a wife beater streaked with black marks in a purple beauty salon that had zero masculinity in it. His mood invaded the room the instant he appeared in the door, and that mood controlled it.

The whole room.

I just stared at him because I didn't understand his mood. I'd never felt it before. Since I came back after our thing, he played his cards faceup on the table. I knew what he was thinking because he shared it in a multitude of ways, on his face, with words. He didn't hide from me anymore. He might hide from the world but not from his wife.

And he wasn't hiding now, though his eyes were intense but his face was blank. It was his aura that was speaking for him.

I just had no idea what it was saying.

And I had little time to figure it out. His long legs ate the distance from the door into the salon, rounding my receptionist desk and I kept my eyes on him the whole way, swiveling my chair as he moved to me.

I sat in it when he was in my space, my head bent way back, my back pressed deep into the chair to keep my eyes locked with his.

Then he bent and I was up. I heard gasps at the movement but could only feel surprise. One of his arms wrapped around my ass, the other one slanted across my back, his fingers driving into my hair, cupping my head then he slammed my mouth down on his and he kissed me.

Automatically, my legs circled his hips, my arms his shoulders and for two seconds I contemplated the fact that out of the blue my husband walked into my place of work, lifted me into his arms and was giving me an intense kiss that spoke volumes and in that two seconds I heard a woman whisper, "Ohmigod," and Dominic mutter, "Now, *that* is *hot*."

But that was all that filtered in before Ty's kiss swept me away, deep, hot, tongues tangling, his arms holding me so tight they were crushing me to him, the kiss so intense the world melted away.

Then his hand fisted in my hair, gently tugged back and I lost his mouth but gained his eyes when I opened mine.

And it was then he whispered, "Just got a call from Nina. The California attorney general overturned my conviction. The governor himself is issuing a public apology today and opening discussion about restitution. IA in LA last night arrested Eugene Fuller and Chet Palmer at the same time LAPD did a sweep of their dealers and raids of their storage facilities."

He stopped speaking and I did nothing but stare.

So he went on to whisper, "It's done, mama. I'm clear."

I still did nothing but stare and I did this even as my throat closed and my vision decreased because my eyes were watery.

"Baby," Ty whispered, his arms giving me a squeeze. "It's done and there's no going back. The gun used to commit the crime I went down for surfaced two weeks ago when a gangbanger got arrested while carrying that gun. Its ownership was traced back to Palmer who had it in his possession when that murder was committed. This from a witness who owns a gun shop and regularly rents him an alley where he said, when Palmer went in for target practice until six months ago, he always used that gun. A solid alibi and no access to the murder weapon. It's done. I'm clear."

I continued to stare then it happened.

The sob tore through me making my body jerk violently and filling the room which, upon hearing it, went completely silent.

Then I shoved my face deep in my husband's neck, tightened my arms and legs around him and burst out crying.

I felt his head turn and heard, "Mama," murmured in my ear and then I reared back, eyes fuzzy, cheeks wet, my head shot up and jerked from side to side.

Then I shouted, "The California governor is issuing a public apology for wrongly convicting my man!"

Another sob tore out of my throat and I shoved my face back in Ty's neck as his arms tensed around me, his body shook with what had to be silent laughter and the salon filled with cheers and whoops.

I didn't cheer or whoop. I held tight to my husband, my body convulsing with my emotion, my husband holding me tight right back.

I felt his head turn again and in my ear I heard, "Mama, get a handle on it."

I reared back, tried and failed to focus on his face and snapped, "No! No fucking way! This feels too good. I'm never getting a handle on this!"

I shoved my face back in his neck and kept right on crying.

"Ohmigod! We need champagne! We need champagne right now!" Dominic was shouting and I heard movement around me including the cash register opening. "Stockard, girl, get your booty over here. Take this. Go down to the liquor store. Get champagne, not the California kind, the French kind. From the chill cabinet. Stop by the grocery store to get cups. I don't care if they're Dixie cups, just get lots of them. Jazz, finish her off later and run down to the garage, get those boys in their coveralls down here. We gotta celebrate!"

Through this, I kept crying.

Then I heard Ty whisper, "Not sure how I feel about celebratin' with a gay guy and a bunch of pussy in a salon and, babe, equally unsure how Wood's boys are gonna feel about it."

To that, I again jerked back and informed him, "They're gonna have to suck it up."

He stared in my eyes as I blinked the wetness out.

And when I finally (kinda) focused on him, I saw he was smiling, white, huge, beautiful and right there for the world to see.

And seeing that smile, I burst back into tears.

* * *

Forty-five minutes later…

The party had begun in earnest in Dominic's spa.

Someone bought pre-prepared deli trays from the grocery store. More champagne was carted in with the addition of beers. Shambles hoofed it down to the salon and added a tray of just-out-of-the-oven chocolate and butterscotch chip cookies.

Jim-Billy was there as were Krystal and Laurie. The boys from the garage were there and this included Pop and Wood, Stella hanging back to hold down the fort in the office. Maggie showed about five minutes after Wood got there. Ned and Betty arrived ten minutes after Maggie.

Dominic, Kayeleen and Jazz were working and socializing, which meant they were working slowly.

No one cared. If they had to wait an extra half an hour to sit in a chair, they could do it with a Dixie cup of champagne in their hand and a kickass cookie.

The rough-guy mechanics, by the way, gave not one shit they were drinking champagne *or* they were doing it with a bunch of pussy and a gay guy. I had a feeling this partly had to do with deli trays, cookies and the fact that it was one of them who brought the beer. Though I had a feeling it was mostly to do with Ty.

I was sitting in Ty's lap in my chair behind the receptionist desk, sipping champagne, a perma-smile on my face, talking to Jim-Billy, Betty and Krystal who were all hanging over the high counter of my desk at the same time I was wondering at the state of my mascara when Tate and Deke walked in.

I felt my heart skip then stutter when I saw their faces. I also felt Ty's body tense under mine.

They only had eyes for Ty and, like Ty when he walked in, I couldn't read their faces but I felt their vibe and I didn't get it.

I didn't get it until they walked straight up to the counter at my desk, Betty, Jim-Billy and Krystal peeling back to give them space, and Tate started speaking.

"At nine o'clock this morning, a tri-county police task force marched into the Carnal Police Department, seized all records and arrested all the officers on duty excepting Frank Dolinski and Chace Keaton. Mick Shaughnessy and his boys from Gnaw Bone were tasked with rounding up those not on duty, and it's been reported that Mick himself took Arnie Fuller into custody fifteen minutes ago."

I stared at Tate, my mouth hanging open.

Ty said nothing and since I was staring at Tate I could only assume he was too (though his mouth was probably not hanging open).

Then I heard Dominic shout, "We need more champagne!"

And it was at that, I watched Tatum Jackson grin.

Ty

Eleven and a half hours later...

Ty stood leaning against the Snake, which was parked on the lookout off the mountain road that was a winding seven miles up from Tate Jackson's house.

His eyes were on Carnal sitting below in the valley, lit up in the dark night, the flickering lights sending a hazy glow into the velvet of the midnight sky and the dark, near-black blue of the mountains.

He'd never, not once, spent time reflecting on his place of birth. It was what it was, as good a base as any.

With five years of very little to do but think, it was not lost on him that he'd spent a great deal of his life aimless, breathing, moving, earning and winning money to acquire things and partaking in all the pussy that caught his liking that was thrown his way. He fucked who he fucked when he felt like it, treated them well enough but when he was done, he always walked away and didn't think about them. He was where he was when he was there doing whatever he was doing at the time.

He had no plan. He had no passion.

Tuku would be pissed.

And he had always been alone. It had never bothered him, he'd never thought of that either. Like everything else in his life, it was what it was.

But after today, experiencing the euphoria of a town released from subjugation and the righting of the wrong done to one of their own, he realized that when he felt he was at his most alone, he was not. He belonged to Carnal. They'd never turned their back on him.

They'd just been powerless, less than Ty but powerless all the same. He'd simply been so absorbed in his shit storm, he didn't recognize it.

And that day, Carnal had stopped being the place he'd been born and where he stayed just because he stayed. It became home and he realized it always was.

But amongst those who made their home there along with Ty, there were some who not only didn't turn their back but did more.

And he heard the Harley pipes of one of them as the bike approached.

Tate rolled the bike to a halt six feet away, shut it down, threw his leg over and walked to Ty, stopping three feet away. Ty could see his eyes on him but he could also feel them.

"Brother, it's nearly eleven. Why the fuck do you want to meet me up here alone? Where's Lexie?"

"My wife is passed out and she ain't gonna move for about ten hours," Ty replied low and quiet. "Maybe twelve. She doesn't even know I'm gone."

Ty watched Tate grin slowly as he accurately deduced the meaning of Ty's words.

Ty didn't grin. He looked around his friend to the town.

Reading the mood, Tate fell silent for some time, shifting his body, turning his eyes to the town then he spoke softly, "Asked Laurie to marry me right here."

"Good spot for that," Ty said to the view.

"Her last birthday, I brought her up here last thing just like that night," Tate went on then, "asked her to marry me on her birthday, decided last year this was where she'd end every one of them from now on."

Ty didn't respond. Tate being a romantic was surprising but not that surprising. He was married to a good-looking, kindhearted woman. You didn't win that kind of woman and keep her as happy as Laurie obviously was without treating her right.

Tate fell silent for another length of time and when he was done with silence, he turned back to face Ty and started, "Ty—"

Ty cut him off by slicing his eyes to him.

"Years ago, you weren't ready to give up. I was buried under shit, couldn't see my way clear of it. So deep under, couldn't even hear you. Even if I could, I wouldn't listen. My power was stripped. I was pissed, in pain and both made me stupid." He held Tate's eyes and whispered, "Shoulda listened."

Tate shook his head. "Don't go there, brother. You're free, look forward and rejoice, do not look back and despair."

"That isn't what this is about, Tate. I feel no pain. Not anymore. That doesn't mean the journey wasn't torture but it led me to Lexie so I can live with that. What I need you to get is that you were right, I was wrong and you deserve to know that."

"You don't have to tell me this, Ty," Tate said softly.

"Yes, I do, Tate," Ty replied softly.

"Okay, then, you do," Tate returned. "But, you will remember, I was in that pit of snakes and I shoulda done something about that years ago. I didn't and you went down."

"You hold no responsibility for what happened to me."

"I don't see it that way."

"Brother, you had a son you needed to look after and pain-in-the-ass pussy who was making your life a misery," Ty reminded him. "You had things you needed to see to and they were priorities. When you got out, they'd never done anything as bad as they did to me. You couldn't foresee how bad it would get. But you tried to deal with it then and I pulled you back. That is what this is about."

Tate fell silent.

Ty didn't.

"Since the day I was released, you knocked yourself out. You had my back, you took care of Lexie when we had our thing then you did what you could to help me sort that. It's important to me that you know I'm grateful. I've been tryin' to figure out how I can show how much but, keep thinkin' on it, nothin' comes to mind and I know why. I get it. You're a man who has everything so there is no way to show that appreciation because there is nothing I can hand you that you want or need. And I get that because I am now that same man.

So the only thing I can give you are words and, my guess is, that'll be enough. If it isn't, you name it and it's yours."

"Friends do what I did for friends," Tate returned.

"No they don't, Tate. *You* did what you did for me because you're you. That's what I'm talkin' about."

Tate was silent a moment then he said, "Well then, you guessed right. Words are enough."

Ty nodded.

Tate tipped his head to the side and asked jokingly, "We done with the near-midnight, in-the-middle-of-fuckin'-nowhere heart-to-heart?"

Ty didn't feel like joking and answered, "No."

"Then what—?"

"Love you, man," Ty interrupted quietly. "Learned the hard way not to delay in expressing that sentiment so I'm not gonna delay. You call me brother and I got one who's blood who don't mean shit to me and today, all this shit done, rejoicing and reflecting, it hit me that I got two who aren't blood but who do mean something. And you're one of those two."

"Ty—" Tate murmured.

"I will never forget, until I die, what you did for me and my wife and until that day I will never stop bein' grateful."

"Fuck, man," Tate whispered.

"Now, do those words work so you get what what you did means to me?"

Silence then, "Yeah, they work."

"Good, then now we're done with our near-midnight, middle-of-fuckin'-nowhere heart-to-heart," Ty declared, turned, opened the door to the Viper and started folding in.

He stopped with his ass nearly to the seat and looked up over the door when Tate called his name.

"I don't have a blood brother," Tate said. "But you should know there's a reason I call you that."

Ty nodded.

But Tate didn't need to tell him that. He already knew. His actions said it all.

Then he sat his ass in the car.

Then he got that ass home to his wife.

Lexie

Half an hour later…

I woke when I felt my man slide in behind me, his arm curled around me and pulled me close.

I snuggled closer.

I wanted to ask where he went but I figured he'd tell me if he wanted me to know.

Then I fell back asleep.

And I was so exhausted by a day of celebration and an evening of more energetic celebration with my husband and me alone, I didn't notice the AC wasn't jacked up.

* * *

The next day…

4:15 p.m.

I drove through our development with Ty following me and my teeth clenched when I saw them hanging out, some cars but mostly vans with big aerials and dishes on top parked everywhere but in our drive. I hit the garage door opener with the timing I'd perfected from experience, knowing right when the signal caught so that I could roll up and not have to wait for the door to open and glide right in.

I usually glided right in. My journey right then was slowed by the reporters and cameramen converging on my baby just outside our drive and if one of them put a scratch on her, I was going to have to break my promise to Ty and lose my mind.

I kept my eyes straight and my car moved at a crawl. I hit driveway and they fell back but I couldn't exactly gun it and screech in, as much as I wanted to.

Nina had warned that, regardless of the fact that she had made a statement to reporters outside her office in Gnaw Bone yesterday afternoon after the governor of California issued his apology and pardoned Ty—and she also made another one late this morning after Ty and I woke up to a media maelstrom right outside our house—they wouldn't listen to her when she ended both saying, first, "This will be the only statement made on behalf of Mr. Tyrell Walker. Mr. Walker and his wife are relieved justice has finally been served and would now like to put this revolting episode behind them. They ask that you respect their wishes to move forward with their life in peace." And at the end of the second statement, "As I said yesterday, Mr. Walker and his wife do not wish to speak to the media. I ask again on their behalf that you please allow them to put this grueling event behind so they can carry on with their rightful but delayed freedom to enjoy their future unimpeded by further upheaval."

Obviously, they didn't listen to her.

It was okay when we were at work and when I say that, I mean it was okay for Ty. Wood, Pop and three mechanics made it clear that the forecourt was private property and unless they were getting work done on their cars, they were not to leave the sidewalk. The garage was set back a whack from the street and had some outbuildings in front of it. So Ty worked in peace.

I didn't even though Dominic called Daniel and Daniel, who had four inches and sixty pounds on his boyfriend and was also a serious mountain man, just a gay one, informed the reporters they were not invited in the spa. Luckily, the clients coming in that day found walking through a river of reporters shouting questions very exciting.

I did not. The constant buzz from outside and the shouted questions anytime a client came through the door were nerve-wracking and a total letdown from the jubilation of the day before. I was high on relief and belated justice and they were cutting into my happy trip, which was super uncool.

Nina assured us this would go away. It would take a while but it would and we just needed to stay quiet and be patient.

Ty informed me that we were doing what Nina said we were doing, exercising the freedom to enjoy our future unimpeded by further upheaval, and that included me not losing control on my sass and throwing any at annoying reporters.

I was thinking that to do this, I needed to evacuate the state of Colorado. I figured both Wood and Dominic would not balk at Ty and me taking a vacation. However, I was only back at work for a few weeks and I couldn't do that to Dominic after taking off on him once. Not even doing it to celebrate something as miraculous (albeit deserved) as what had happened to Ty or to escape the media onslaught.

So, it was put a clamp on my sass, something I promised my husband I would do.

Which was hard normally but now it was taking superhuman powers.

Ty glided the Snake in beside me and hit the garage door opener before he'd switched her off. I waited in my car and watched in the rearview mirror as the door fell, not getting out in order that they wouldn't get a shot of me coming out of my car like they did when I walked into and out of the salon that day. Both times I was escorted by my husband who left work that morning in order to drive up and trail me down then walk me into the salon. He also showed at the salon when we were both off in order to escort me out to the Charger and trail me home. We should have taken one car but he wanted to go to the gym after work, a plan thwarted when the news people didn't go away all day.

As the door went down and settled, the shouts and cries of questions and requests for statements were drowned but not gone.

I got out, stood in my door and glared over the roof of the Charger at Ty as he folded out. He caught the look on my face, stopped dead and burst out laughing.

I didn't find anything funny, therefore I slammed my door and stomped out of the garage, into the utility room and up the steps.

I'd crashed my purse down on the side counter and was listening to Ty coming up the stairs when something caught my eye and I froze, staring out the back door.

"No fucking way!" I shouted.

"What?" Ty asked.

I lifted an arm, pointed at a wide but flattish cardboard box leaning against the glass at the back door, turned to my husband and proclaimed, "If that's a box full of sick-ass sex tapes, I don't wanna know."

Ty's eyes were glued to the box. He moved through the kitchen, opened the door, tagged it, closed the door, locked it, swung the blinds closed, wound them shut and walked the box to the island all the while I stood there and glared.

His head turned to me and he muttered, "Peña."

I blinked, not prepared for that word to come out of his mouth. Then I asked, "What?"

The fingers of Ty's big, strong hands were already shoving through an opening at the side as he answered, "Express from Peña."

Great. This could mean anything, and that included more sick-ass sex tapes.

I stomped to Ty as he tore the box open with his Mr. Humongo strength. He set it down, pulling out something inside that was wrapped in layers of bubble wrap. He tore that free and my breath stuck in my throat at what he unveiled.

It was a shining sun with wavy rays expanding out made of chips of Mexican tile artfully arranged and embedded in terra-cotta. It was unusual and extraordinary. I'd never seen anything like it.

It was magnificent.

Ty set it back on the pile of bubble wrap he'd shoved in the box and pulled out an envelope, slit it open with a finger and yanked out a card.

Then he whispered, "Fuck."

I got close and read the card held in his fingers.

On it, it said simply, "Welcome to sunshine, *esé*."

What should have been a happy day destroyed by annoying reporters melted instantly.

Just as instantly as I melted into tears.

And an instant later, I was in my husband's arms.

* * *

The sunshine Angel sent us was made to decorate the outside of a house.

Without me asking him to, Ty mounted it in the kitchen so we were sure to see it every day.

* * *

One day later…

We came home to another box. This was a bottle of champagne from Samuel Sterling. Nothing on the note except a scrawled, black "SS," which was super cool.

I looked up the label on the Internet and found that bottle of champagne cost four hundred and fifty dollars.

Samuel Sterling was hot, rich and had class.

I got his number from Ty and phoned him to ask him to dinner that weekend. Considering he was in Paris, he couldn't make it but said he'd take a rain check.

Paris.

Totally, the dude had class.

Ty

A week and a half later…

Ty's phone rang, he stepped away from the bike he was working on and pulled it out of his back pocket.

The number on the screen said it was withheld. He hesitated, opened it and put it to his ear.

"Yo."

"Is this Mr. Tyrell Walker?"

"You first," Ty ordered.

"Angela Buttner, California Attorney General's office."

"Restitution discussion goes through my attorney, Nina Maxwell."

"Mr. Walker, I'm not calling about restitution. I'm calling you to explain we've had a request from Mrs. Jolinda Hayes. She'd like your contact information."

"Who's Jolinda Hayes?" Ty asked.

"She's the mother of Shaun Hayes, the other man framed by Detectives Fuller and Palmer. The man who committed suicide three days prior to going to trial."

Fuck.

Ty pulled in breath. Then he asked, "Why does she wanna talk to me?"

"She hasn't explained that, sir. She just requested your contact number. Obviously, we can't give her that information unless you agree."

"Give it," Ty stated.

"Sorry?"

"Give it to her."

Pause then, "Oh. Okay, well, thank you—"

Ty flipped his phone shut.

An hour and a half later, it rang again. He pulled it out of his pocket, looked at the display and saw an LA area code.

He sucked in breath.

Then he flipped it open and put it to his ear.

"Walker."

"Tyrell Walker?"

"Yep."

Pause then, "This is Jolinda Hayes. I'm—"

"Know who you are."

Silence from Jolinda Hayes.

Ty wasn't silent. "Know what he lived through, all of it, bein' inside and not wantin' to go back, bein' framed, knowin' he was goin' down and why. Don't know you. Don't know the kind of life you've lived but I do know it's doubtful you lived through somethin' like that. I know why he did what he did too. It was his choice. It was him takin' his power back. It was him doin' what he could to save you from livin' through that hell with him. It was not the right choice but it was a compassionate one."

When he stopped speaking, he heard quiet tears and he silently listened to them for a fuck of a long time.

Then he was done listening so he called, "Mrs. Hayes."

A tearful hiccough then, "Yes, Mr. Walker?"

"Ty," he corrected then didn't hesitate and continued. "It's too late but that doesn't mean it isn't there to savor. Your son got his shit together and died a good man and everyone in the country knows it. That's worth somethin' so savor it."

"R-r-right."

"Right. Now, get a piece of paper and a pen. I'm gonna give you my wife's number. You wanna talk, she'll listen. You wanna laugh, she's fuckin' funny. You never call her, that's your choice. But way I see it, we're family and my wife does the welcoming."

Another hiccough, some noise then, "I, um...Ty, I have a piece of paper."

Ty gave her Lexie's phone number and name.

Jolinda Hayes pulled it together and said quietly, "Thank you, Ty, for taking my call."

"Lady Luck finally saw fit to shine her light on me but life taught me to share. Welcome to the light." That got him a quiet sob into which he said quietly, "Mrs. Hayes, call my wife."

"R-r-right."

"Take care."

"You... you too, Ty."

He flipped his phone shut, opened it, called his woman and told her she might get a call from Jolinda Hayes and why at the same time he hoped to fuck she wouldn't burst into tears again.

She didn't. She asked him what he wanted for dinner.

He told her he'd eat whatever she made and flipped the phone shut after hearing her tell him she loved him and returning the sentiment. Then he got back to work.

* * *

Four weeks later...

Ty stood at the basin brushing his teeth wondering where the fuck his wife was.

It was time to shower.

Unusually, as in, for the first time ever, when they got up, he went to their bathroom, she wandered down the stairs.

He was about to bend, spit, rinse and go find her when he saw her in the mirror. She was wandering in the door behind him, her eyes on him, her body in a pair of loose drawstring shorts and a tight little tee, her arms behind her back, her face wearing an expression he couldn't read.

He continued to brush as through the mirror he watched her slowly make her way across the bathroom to him. He lost sight of her when she fitted herself to his back.

He felt her lips move on his skin and he knew she was tracing his tat.

He put a hand to the edge of the vanity counter, bent his neck, spit, rinsed, shoved his toothbrush in the holder, looked at himself in the mirror and rumbled, "Lexie."

Her hand appeared, coming around his side and his eyes dropped to see she was holding a white stick. She placed it on the counter by the sink.

There was a little window in the stick.

And there was a little pink plus sign in the window.

His body went still.

He felt her lips move against the skin of his back as she whispered, "I'm pregnant, honey."

Ty Walker closed his eyes because he couldn't bear it. He couldn't even see her and her light was shining so bright, it seared his retinas, beat through his skin, his tissue, warming him straight to the marrow of his bones.

When he felt her movement, his eyes opened and Ty watched as her other arm snaked around his waist, her fingers light on the skin of his abs when he felt her lips go away and her chin rest gentle on his back and she called, "Ty?"

"Boy, Julius Tatum. Girl, Ella Alexi," Ty declared and felt his wife still at his back.

Then she asked, "Did you just name our future child?"

"Yep."

"Uh, honey lumpkins, that's the kinda thing that's discussed."

"You get the next one."

Silence.

Then, "All right, baby, I can live with that."

His gaze moved to his eyes in the mirror.

Then he smiled.

Then he moved and he moved in order to take a shower with his wife.

Lexie

Two weeks later…

I walked into the diner, already knowing what I was going to order.

And it was a miracle when my step didn't stutter when I saw Detective Chace Keaton sitting at the booth at the back.

It was the first time I'd seen him since that day in my closet except once when he was on television, caught by the news reporters walking into Carnal Police Department.

The media circus had died down, the reporters moving on to feed on fresher meat.

But things in Carnal were still shifting and hopefully this was in order to settle and not to rock again.

There were four police officers who kept their jobs at CPD. Chace and Frank were two of those four. Three had been indicted, as had a clerk and the secretary who worked for Fuller and the detective pool. The rest of the Carnal Police Force had been discharged. Detective Darren Newcomb was one who'd been discharged, but he bought this rather than an indictment because he made a deal and was turning evidence.

Arnold Fuller had been stripped of his position due to multiple counts of corruption and mishandling the investigation of a local serial killer, including delayed responses to dispatch his officers when two of his female citizens were reported missing. He also had pending indictments for corruption, conspiracy and providing false evidence during an out-of-state murder investigation.

Officers from other stations around the county were covering as the Town Council went through a massive hiring process.

The framing of Ty and subsequent harassment, the bungling of the serial killer case that had swept up Laurie, Tate and Jim-Billy as well as inquiries into the death of Misty Keaton were the focal point of the charges brought and reasons for discharge. This was also primarily what the media fed on. There was more, of course, and many Carnal citizens had no problems standing in front of a camera or with a reporter taking notes and letting them know what went down in Carnal.

It was all out there.

Except whoever financed, covered up and protected Fuller and his men's activities.

In other words, nothing on any powerful men, including Trane Keaton, had leaked.

I didn't know if this meant another shoe was going to drop or if they were just powerful and rich enough to make their problems go away. All I knew was that Ty was so famous, it was very doubtful anyone would touch him or me. The reporters might have gone away but the story hadn't. Ty even had a listing in an on-line encyclopedia. Laurie called me, told me to fire up my computer and showed it to me. The pictures they included were hot. The fact it existed was not.

But…whatever.

I was married to the man I loved. His name was clear. He was free. I was carrying his baby. And the restitution Nina negotiated meant we didn't have to worry too much about their college educations *and* I could get my reading area in our bedroom (which I did *plus* a rug for under the bed).

So all was good in my world.

But there were loose ends in Carnal.

Rowdy Crabtree had not been found.

And Misty Keaton's murder had so far gone unsolved.

I had been right. Misty's friend in Maryland, Tate discovered, *was* indeed the woman in the tape. She was also, back then, the mother of a three-year-old boy and the woman whose ex was a serious asshole. She'd kicked him out and divorced his ass but he was the kind of man who felt he could come over whenever he wanted, shout the house down, slap her around and take stuff, such as the money in her wallet or things of value he could sell.

She had a job as a waitress in a bar in Gnaw Bone called The Dog, was not close with her family as in, she never spoke to them, and her ex kept stealing all her tips. Therefore she needed out and to get out she needed money, and it was the kind of money she didn't have and had no hope of getting especially when her ex-husband kept taking the little she had.

So she got that money by doing sick-ass shit with Trane Keaton. In fact, she got two hundred thousand dollars for doing it, blackmail money direct from Trane, which I didn't think was enough but that's just me.

Still, it got her out of Colorado and nearly a continent away, it set her up and her ex, being an asshole *and* lazy, didn't put up the effort to trail her and continue making her life miserable so it also bought her peace.

Until Misty died.

She confirmed to Tate that Misty was as messed up as Misty was. Misty had doting parents, good looks and had grown up wild because her folks didn't know how to say no. So she pretty much did whatever she wanted to do whenever she wanted to do it. She wasn't used to getting no for an answer so she didn't mind doing what she had to do to get what she wanted.

And she wanted Chace. Like, *a lot* (obviously).

And he made it clear he wanted only one thing from her and that was only part of what she wanted from him.

Seeing as she'd convinced herself her talents in bed (something for which he kept coming back for more) and her looks would eventually win him around, she successfully set about trapping him, thinking, insanely, that he'd eventually get over her sick, twisted power play and fall head over heels in love with her.

This was not a lie. This was what Miss Maryland told Tate, straight out.

It was a fucked-up play by a pretty spoiled girl who, personally, I thought needed mental help.

But she was dead so that was impossible.

Though I did make a point of noting this. I had no blood family, didn't have a mother figure until I was thirteen and could see myself falling in the trap of giving a child I loved everything she or he wanted because I had to wade through a whole lot of shit to get what I wanted and it took thirty-four years. Upon learning this about Misty, I decided on the motherhood course of Do What Ella Would Do in order not to fuck up my kid by loving them so much it made me weak and them stupid.

Misty's friend, by the way, was terrified. Tate, by the way, was a straight talker and told her she had reason to be and if she had any of that two hundred grand left, she needed to get herself safe.

Being Tate and checking up, the next time he called, her number was disconnected.

No more was heard from Misty Keaton's friend. Arnie Fuller was out on bail and keeping his head down, as in, no one saw him *ever.* Gossip was dying down and the Town Council was acting fast to clean up. But people weren't used to living out from under small-town tyranny. They were guardedly happy yet braced. The boat had rocked and only those who deserved to get thrown in the water got drenched.

But after what happened to Ty, Misty and Rowdy, everyone knew anything could happen.

So they were breathing easier but that didn't mean they weren't prepared.

Chace Keaton had weathered the storm. What he did was known, very much so. Handsome, well dressed and having a confident manner, he was the poster boy for the IA and pushed in front of the cameras to show that Carnal wasn't entirely infested. There were good brave men serving the community. You could tell he didn't like it but again, as it seemed was his curse, he put up with it.

I just hoped for him, like it had for Ty and me, it would eventually die down.

In the diner that day, I quickly looked away from Chace and walked to the counter, taking a stool so I could do what I did when I picked the diner for lunch. Order takeaway and take it back to the salon so I could gab with Dominic, Kayeleen and their clients as I ate lunch. I knew exactly what I wanted so I waited for the busy waitress behind the counter to get to me. And while I waited, my eyes went everywhere to avoid going to Chace.

Then they honed in.

And they honed in on a woman I knew. She was the librarian in town. She went to see Dominic and Dominic declared that her hair was the third best head of hair in Carnal behind Lauren Jackson's and my own (though I wondered if he was being nice, still, he said it like he meant it). It was a thick, shining sheet of real auburn, dark, hints and highlights of red and rust, it was gorgeous. And with her pale skin, bright blue eyes, fantastic cheekbones and that hair, she was extremely pretty.

But she was a total librarian. To my recollection, I'd seen her four times, twice at the salon, once at La-La Land and once at the grocery store. Each time she was in a dress, nice, stylish, hinting at her figure which was curvy and sweet but by no means showing off or doing anything to get even a little attention. And this was because she was shy, *super* shy. When you were talking to her, she often didn't meet your eyes, she smiled in a way you could swear it was an illusion (which, incidentally, I thought was cool) and she had a melodic voice that was nevertheless very quiet, like a librarian's voice should be.

And her name was Faye. Faye Goodknight.

Really, that was her name. Faye Goodknight.

Totally awesome name.

And just then, as my eyes honed in on her, she was staring at Chace Keaton.

No, not staring at him. She was gazing at him *longingly.*

Hmm. I liked that.

I watched her body jerk, her eyes cut to me, feeling mine on her. But before I could smile, her face flamed and she looked away.

Totally shy.

I chanced a glance at Chace. He had an open file folder on the table beside him, head bent to it, pen scribbling on it, plate set aside, finished eating but not done with what he was doing.

A very pretty woman who was into him had been staring at him and he didn't know she existed.

I didn't like that.

His wife had recently died, but still, he didn't like her and eventually he had to get back up on that horse.

The waitress came, took my order and when I was done, movement caught my eye and I watched Faye carrying her bag of takeaway coming my way to pass me to go to the door.

"Hey, Faye," I called when she got close. Her eyes tipped up, skimmed through me and she lifted her hand to tuck a shining sheath of hair behind her ear.

"Uh, hey, Lexie," she murmured then hurried by me.

I lost sight of her and was going to turn to watch her go but for some reason my eyes went to Chace and my body went still.

He was staring after Faye. I knew it. And he not only knew she existed, he *really* knew she existed.

And the expression on his face hurt to witness.

I'd never seen anything like that before but I figured it would be what a starving man looked like when he saw a plate of bread in front of him but he was too weak and it was too far for him to get to. He'd never make it so he was going to waste away without trying.

He wasn't even going to reach.

Yes, that was what his expression looked like.

I knew it because I'd never seen that expression on my face but I felt that feeling for weeks when Ty and I were apart.

I tore my eyes from him and caught the eyes of the waitress. She tipped up her chin, finished refilling the coffee cup she was filling and came to me.

"Somethin' else you need?" she asked.

"Yes, um... do you know Faye Goodknight?"

"Uh, yeah. Known her since she was about three. Lived here all her life, same's me."

"Is she married?"

The waitress, whose nameplate said Poppy, burst out laughing.

I waited for her to be done but I did it with a smile so she wouldn't think I was rude.

She quit laughing and said, "No, hon, Faye ain't married. Reason she's a librarian. She lives in a book... *all the time.* Life goes on around her, she has no clue. Head in the clouds, rest a' her wrapped in a cocoon. Don't know if she's ever even dated."

That was just plain weird.

Therefore I pointed out this weirdness. "But, that's weird. She's very pretty."

"Yup," Poppy agreed.

"So, you would think..." I started to deduce then quit and asked quietly, "Did something happen to her?"

Poppy's brows went up. "To Faye?"

I nodded.

She shook her head. "Nope. No way. Nothin' ever happens to Faye. Not one thing. Some folks are just that way. She's always been quiet. She's always liked fantasy worlds better'n real ones. Just her way. She's a sweet little thing. Comes from a good family she's close to. She's just..." Poppy shrugged, "Faye."

Very pretty. Good family. Librarian. Very possibly a virgin. Just the woman you'd set up in a house behind a white picket fence who would bake pies, be the leader of your daughter's Brownie troop who you could train to give world-class head.

Her looks, her demeanor, her age, which I figured was not far off mine, and her possible virgin status meaning she was probably one of two of her type in the entire state of Colorado. Which made her, at my approximation, one of maybe one hundred in the entire United States of America.

Worth hanging around Carnal for, let her sit waiting in the wings as you sowed your wild oats, even if your boss was dirty stinking filth.

Then suddenly she's completely out of your reach when you're forced to marry the town's crazy-playing slut, your father is a sleazebag, albeit a rich one, and even though you were shoved in the mud but risked a lot to pull yourself out and get clean, you'd never quit feeling dirty.

I nodded to Poppy again and asked, "Can you do me a favor?"

"Sure," she replied.

"Can you change my order from takeaway and serve it at Detective Keaton's table?"

She blinked before her mouth dropped open. Then her eyes darted back and forth between me and Chace's table. I came in relatively frequently but never chitchatted with her because she was always busy. Still, she knew me. She knew Chace. She knew Misty. She knew Ty. And she knew our intermingling history.

This wasn't a surprise. Everyone did.

Hesitantly she repeated, "Uh... sure."

"Thanks," I whispered, sucked in air, turned from the counter and walked on my high heels through the diner toward Chace's table.

His eyes were on me when I was ten feet away.

I didn't stop until my ass was planted across from him.

He held my eyes a moment and then said low, "Lexie."

"Hi," I replied softly.

"Somethin' I can do for you?"

"Yeah, sit there and listen to me say thank you for helping me and Ty."

He said nothing, just held my eyes.

So I said, "Thank you."

"My job," he replied.

"No it wasn't," I whispered. "What you did was beyond the call of duty and we both know it."

He again said nothing but his gaze never left mine.

"So, thank you."

He jerked up his chin then muttered, "Don't mention it."

I smiled and reminded him, "I just did, like three times."

Chace Keaton did not smile.

So I stopped smiling then started quietly to say, "I think you know that I know—"

Chace interrupted me. "Do me a favor, Lexie, and don't talk about it."

I shut my mouth.

"Move on," he stated. "It's a small town but big enough that you and Walker can go your way, I'll go mine."

"I can't do that."

He dropped his pen, sat back and lost what I suspected was one of his many cop faces. This one was carefully composed to look polite, mildly interested but mostly detached and communicating the minute you were done with him, he'd move on and not think about you again. What came up was impatient and annoyed which I suspected was not a cop face.

"Why?" he asked.

I leaned forward and explained, "Because I have a husband whose power was stripped from him and I lived a life that offered limited choices and the ones it offered weren't very good. So I kinda know what you're going through."

"You have no clue."

"I do."

He leaned forward too. "All right, Lexie, then how's this? No offense, but I don't give a fuck if you do."

To that, I informed him, "She was staring at you."

He did a slow blink at the change in subject, the anger that had edged into his annoyed impatience changed to mystification and he asked, "What?"

"Faye Goodknight," I answered, and I got surprise then more than an edge of anger.

"Don't even—" he began but I cut him off.

"My guess? Romance novels. My guess? She started reading them early. My guess? She started them at a time where they made a huge impression on her and changed her perceptions. She isn't cocooned, she pays attention and she knows there are no men out there like the men in those books she reads so she prefers being with them than trying to find someone like them, which, she thinks, is a fruitless endeavor. That fantasy is far better than any reality and, you know what? She's right. Men are a pain in the ass and a lot of them are dicks who cause heartbreak. And her, a girl like Faye? Well, she knows she's the kind of girl men like that will chew up and spit out. So she's smart and she's not going to go there."

Chace opened his mouth to speak but I kept talking, not giving him the opportunity.

"But you know something else? Lady Luck can sometimes be generous to people who deserve it and right in her hometown is a man who she doesn't know but he gave up everything to look after his father but what she *does* know is he was brave enough to put his ass out there to save an entire…fucking…*town.* And, bonus, he's hot, dresses nice and has a great body. So don't piss away your life, Detective Keaton, because I learned, no matter how shitty it is, no matter how many times you got slapped back, no matter how much that shit stings, you have to keep reaching for what you want. Never give up. If you don't, you'll find happiness. I know. I got slapped back so many times it isn't funny. Now I'm in love and pregnant and the sun shines on me all the time. Even when I'm asleep. If you don't give up and keep reaching, you can feel that sunshine too. But better than that, you ask her out and find out she's the one, you can give *her* that sunshine and she'll make sure you'll never regret you did it."

He stared at me without a word.

Well, there you go. I didn't get through but at least I tried.

It was time to cut my losses.

I turned my head and shouted, "Poppy!" which got her attention as anyone would, shouting across a diner so I shouted again, "Take that back, it's going to be takeaway."

"No it isn't, Poppy," Chace called after me, and my head shot around to look at him. "Serve Lexie's lunch here."

"You got it, Chace," Poppy shouted back.

Chace looked at me. "Sit. Eat your lunch. But please, fuck, no more life lectures. Can you do that for me?"

I grinned and said, "Sure."

He stared at me. Then he shook his head.

He went back to scribbling on his paper.

I watched.

Then I asked, "So, are you gonna ask Faye out?"

His neck bent so just his head tipped back and he skewered me with his blue eyes.

"Okay, okay," I muttered. "Yeesh."

He looked back at his papers and kept scribbling.

Poppy served my cheeseburger, curly fries and diet at the table.

I squirted an enormous mound of ketchup on my plate while commenting, "By the way, you're hot but you're super hot when you get angry."

His neck bent so his head tipped back again and he scowled at me.

"Just sayin'," I muttered, digging a fry into my ketchup, popping it into my mouth and deciding against telling him his scowl proved my point.

I continued to do this and after I picked up my burger and took a big bite, Chace spoke and he did this to his papers.

"Walker gonna lose his mind, find me and rip my head off when he finds out you were sittin' here with me?"

"Nope," I said through half-munched burger.

His neck bent and head tipped back again. "Nope?"

I shook my head, swallowed and grinned. "Well, he might not invite you to our child's christening but, like me, he's grateful for what you did. If you're not thinking that and instead thinking he's jealous, nope again. You're not my type. I'm not into blonds. But you know who is?" I asked.

"Lex—" he started.

I finished quickly, "Faye Goodknight."

He sat back again but this time his eyes rolled to the ceiling.

"You do know I'm on a mission," I informed him then took another bite of burger.

His eyes came back to me.

I chewed, swallowed and explained, "When women get all loved up, they do this. They want to spread the joy."

He just stared at me.

"They get obsessed with it," I went on.

Chace sighed.

"So you should probably just give in," I finished.

He shook his head then bent it back to his papers again but I could swear he did it while his lips twitched.

Good.

I finished my lunch in silence while Chace Keaton scribbled, moved papers around, studied some photos and scribbled some more. When I was done, I opened my purse, pulled out money to cover my lunch and the tip and tucked it under my plate.

Then I announced, "Well! Off to get a library card. See you later, Chace."

Before he could say anything, I slid out of the booth.

But when I was out of the diner and walking along the sidewalk in front of it, I looked into the window to the back booth and saw a pair of attractive blue eyes on me.

And they were smiling.

And it wasn't the only thing on Chace Keaton's face that was smiling.

So when I lost sight of him, it was my turn to smile.

Angel

One and a half weeks later…

"You are fuckin' shittin' me," Angel Peña clipped to the DA.

"Nope, failure to appear. Jumped bond," the DA replied.

Angel shook his head.

Duane "Shift" Martinez. A pain in his ass.

"Means your afternoon is free, Angel," the DA went on.

Angel didn't want a free afternoon. He wanted to sit in the courtroom and watch then testify at Martinez's preliminary hearing.

Shit.

"Heads up, you need to make sure the paperwork is processed so his bondsman knows real fuckin' quick that he's FTA. He doesn't get someone out on this guy's ass right away, he can kiss his bail money good-bye," Angel advised.

"No bondsman posts bail without collateral," the DA returned.

"Martinez is known to fib about collateral. The bondsman got dibs on Shift's momma's house, he's gonna learn soon Shift has no momma. I don't know what he put up. I just know there's a twenty-eighty chance he don't got it."

"No bondsman is that dumb," the DA replied.

"The one who bonded out Martinez is. He's already kissin' ten percent of his bond good-bye 'cause he needs a bounty hunter to round him up. Shift was a huge flight risk. He took flight. This is not a surprise. Martinez perpetrated the ultimate fuck to his best fuckin' friend. You think he won't fuck his bondsman on collateral, you're whacked. The longer this shit is delayed, the more chance Martinez has to get to Mexico."

Or Colorado but, pray God, Angel hoped not.

He watched the DA's mouth get tight.

Then he watched him pull out his phone.

Message received.

Angel jerked up his chin and walked on his cowboy boots out of the courtroom and through the halls of the courthouse automatically listing in his head who would get calls and their priority.

First, Ty Walker.

He was pushing through the front doors of the courthouse, pulling his phone from his inside jacket pocket when the drive-by happened.

The automatic weapon fire took down three innocent bystanders.

It also drilled four rounds into Detective Angel Peña, the intended target.

CHAPTER TWENTY-ONE

He Took That Too

Ty

Ty stood, hip against the kitchen counter, eating oatmeal and watching his wife shuffle around the kitchen fixing her own oatmeal and a travel mug of coffee for him.

His eyes slid from her, his torso twisting, his gaze moving to the latest addition in their house.

Next to the fireplace, a black frame, in it two sheets of glass and pressed between that glass side by side were two pieces of paper with the logo of the hotel in Vegas where they'd stayed when they were married. The first was her note to him and the second was his note to her the next day.

For reasons he didn't know and didn't process mostly because they were obvious and didn't need processing, he carried her note with him every day, in the morning with his wallet and phone, shoving it in his pocket so his was ragged and worn. A little over a week ago, Lexie had discovered it. He was taking a shower after coming back from the gym. She was sorting out his gym bag after setting his protein shake on the vanity.

She'd probably handled it numerous times but his woman gave him privacy, one of the multitudes of things he loved about her. When he was ready to share, she was there. Until that time, she gave him space.

Why she unfolded it that night, he didn't know or ask. But when he came out of the shower with a towel around his hips, she was sitting on their bed. Without delay or words, she lifted up the unfolded note, words out and showed it to him.

Then her other hand came up and she lifted up an identical piece of paper, this had folds in but it was not worn and it was his much shorter message.

She'd kept his note too. It only had one word and two letters on it but she'd kept it.

He felt the roots of that thing inside him dig deeper. It was embedded in a way it would never go away but that didn't mean, frequently, it didn't push deeper, swell and spread.

His eyes went from the notes to her.

"I carry it in my wallet," she whispered, her head tipped back, her face soft and he knew in about five seconds she would start bawling.

So he walked to her, carefully pulled the pieces of paper out of her hand, set them on the nightstand, bent deep, wrapped his arms around his wife picking her up, planting her deeper in the bed and he pulled off his towel.

Then he took his time fucking her.

This was his means to the end of stopping his woman from crying. It was also, as it usually was, fucking brilliant.

She didn't tell him she was taking it to the frame shop but he came home the night before to see it mounted on the wall. No one would get it and most would probably look at it and think it was whacked.

He didn't give a fuck.

When she wrote her note to him, she was already falling in love with him. When he'd written hers, he was already gone. They'd known each other days but, keeping those notes, they knew. And that frame was a reminder of what they knew and when they knew it.

Ty fucking loved it.

He didn't use words to tell her that because he didn't need to. He'd frozen when he saw it and when his body was at his command again, his eyes found hers. He said nothing but held her eyes until she smiled. He smiled back. Then he went up the stairs to take a shower and she went to the blender.

"Okay," she said, and he twisted back to see her screwing the lid on his travel mug, "your assignment today is to think about something."

Ty made no response, just shoveled in more oatmeal.

She grabbed his mug, picked up her bowl of oatmeal and moved to him, standing close, smack in his space, as she always did, setting his mug by his hip, as she always did and lifting her bowl up in front of her, which was new.

He didn't know if his baby inside her was changing her program or the onset of winter was. She was eating more. Most nights, she stretched out beside him to watch TV and crashed within minutes. That was to say, around seven thirty. Instead of just pulling on her panties when she'd cleaned up after they were done at night, she tugged on drawstring shorts and a tee or a nightie and climbed in beside him. She had on a nightie now and thick slouchy socks. It was November and they'd already had snow that didn't go away. She was from Dallas. Dallas didn't get snow and the temperatures rarely fell below freezing. Her blood was thin. She wasn't used to it. She also didn't complain. She knew she would get used to it.

She kept talking.

"Supply is exceeding demand for Dominic at the spa. He rents out his rooms in the back to the massage therapist and skin technician. The massage therapist only works part time and her appointments are now six weeks out. The skin technician is a little flaky and it isn't unheard of that she misses appointments and when she comes in, nearly every day, she's usually late so her appointments run late. That reflects on Nic, not her, and he's not a big fan of that."

She stopped talking. Ty swallowed the last mouthful of oatmeal and set his bowl on the counter.

Then he prompted, "You're telling me this because…?"

"I think I want to go to school to do one or the other or maybe even both. They make three times as much as I make, I'd never screw over Dominic and they have it sweet. It's like, the best job in the world. A woman looks forward to a massage or a facial. It's the highlight of her day so, in a way, you giving it to her makes *you* the highlight of her day. It'd be cool getting paid to do something people look forward to, being the highlight of their day and, when they leave you, they feel relaxed and peaceful. I think that would be awesome."

"Do it," Ty replied, and Lexie blinked.

"Uh...maybe you should think about it. First, it costs money to go to school. Second, it'll mean me being away in the evenings, third—"

Ty cut her off. "Babe, do it."

"But, we have—"

He lifted a hand, wrapped it around the side of her neck and asked, "You wanna do this?"

She nodded.

"Do it."

His woman held his eyes. Then she grinned.

Then she said, "Okay, I'll do it."

He gave her neck a squeeze before he released it but only to move his arm to slide around her waist and bring her closer, muttering, "Payback is me gettin' rubdowns from my wife when I get back from the gym."

She set her bowl aside, lifted her hands to rest them on his chest, rolled her eyes and said to the ceiling. "I'm not even enrolled in classes yet and he expects freebies."

"God don't care about me expecting freebies."

She rolled her eyes back and retorted, "God cares about everything."

That was the damned truth, fortunately.

"All right," Ty changed the subject, "somethin' for you to think about today."

Lexie tipped her head to the side and asked, "What?"

"We got a kid comin', we got a shitload of money in the bank and still not a small amount of cash in the safe. The first one comes, we lose our guest room. The next one comes, you lose your craft room. They get to the point where they can cogitate, my woman is not gonna let me fuck her the way I like anywhere but the bathroom. This does not work for me. We need a new house."

Her eyes got big and her lips parted before she whispered, "But I love our house."

"I do too but it isn't gonna fit four kids, us and our sex life."

It was then her eyes slid to the side and she murmured, "This is true."

Ty pulled her closer, her eyes slid back and her hands slid up to round his neck. "This does not have to happen now but it has to happen. You need to think about what you want. We do this, we do it once and settle. We don't need to be movin' our brood all over Carnal as it grows. So you find what you like in a way that you're gonna like it a good long while."

"What about what you like?" Lexie asked.

"I got one condition and that is, your ass in my bed every night. Since that's gonna happen anywhere we're gonna be, the rest of it, I don't give a fuck."

That was when he got her soft face, warm eyes and a sweet, quiet, "Ty."

"We do it before the first one comes then we do it soon. It's your first, you advance, I want you worried about our kid, not movin'. Yeah?"

"Yeah," she whispered, her arms around his neck getting tighter, her body moving up because she rolled up on her toes.

"Now I gotta get to work," he said quietly.

She nodded and, still whispering, replied, "Okay, honey."

He bent his neck and touched his mouth to hers. After that, he dropped his forehead and touched that to hers. Then he released her, tagged his travel mug but wrapped his hand around her hip and gave her a squeeze before he let her go again and started moving away.

"Later, mama," he said to the back door and heard said to his back, "Later, baby."

Ty walked out the back door, down the stairs, got in his Cruiser and went to work.

* * *

Three and a half hours later…

Ty's cell rang. He did the drill, looked at the display, flipped it open and put it to his ear.

"Champ," he greeted.

"Where are you?" Julius asked quickly, his voice strange, urgent, and Ty felt a whisper of dread snake up his spine.

"At work," he answered.

"You haven't heard," Julius stated.

"Heard what?"

Julius sucked in breath.

Then he told Ty, "Day before yesterday, Shift was FTA at his prelim hearing." Pause then, "My man, this kicks me in the balls to tell you this shit because I know you got a relationship with that cop but he was there, Peña, at the courthouse. When the hearing was cancelled, he walked out right into a drive-by. He took four. He's alive but they are not thinkin' good things and when I say that, he's already received last rites. Him still breathin' is a miracle and that miracle is aided by a machine."

Ty was already on the move through the garage to the office where Wood was in with Stella and Pop.

"Shift do it?" he barked into the phone.

"Was mayhem, the shooter took out three other people. Two survived. One got one right in the neck, bled out before help arrived. Bystanders were freaked, it happened fast, but they said it was a black man though further descriptions aren't great. My guess is, Peña's got more enemies than just Shift. But you gotta have this heads-up."

"Right," Ty muttered, climbing the stairs to the office.

"Sorry, brother, wish you and Lexie had a longer run without shit news comin' at you," Julius said quietly.

"Me too. Thanks for callin' to tell me, brother," Ty replied, opening the door to the office.

"I'll call, I get any more," Julius told him. "Later."

"Later," Ty said into the phone, flipped it shut, looked through the office to see all eyes on him, his intent to tell them he had to walk to the salon to deliver shit news to his wife. Lexie'd be pissed if he waited until that night. Peña's position elevated significantly in

Lexie's mind since he'd gone all out for Ty so that meant Lexie'd want their asses on a plane and she wouldn't want a delay in that.

But before he could open his mouth, his phone rang in his hand. He looked at the display and felt his brows draw together at a number that was local but one he didn't know.

His gaze went through the room, he muttered, "Somethin's up but hang on." He flipped his phone open, put it to his ear and greeted, "Yo."

"Ty?" He heard a familiar voice that made his blood run cold. "Sorry to bug you but I called Lexie's cell and at home, no answer. She hasn't come into work yet. Half an hour late. This isn't like her. Is something up? Is she unwell?"

Dominic.

Lexie hadn't gone to work yet.

Shift was FTA.

Peña was delivered last rites.

All the air in Ty's lungs squeezed out, leaving his body void of oxygen.

Without answering and saying not one word, he flipped his phone shut and his long legs took him through the office to the front door and out of it. He flat-out ran down the steps and to the Cruiser, pulling his keys out and beeping the locks on the run. Tearing open the door, he folded in, started it up and screeched out of his parking spot, through the forecourt and out into the road.

He was at home in half the time it normally took and he bolted up the outside stairs taking them three at a time. His heart squeezed when he saw the back door hanging open but he didn't hesitate running through it. Then his heart twisted when he saw the state of the house. Struggle, evidence of it everywhere, oatmeal on the wall, a broken bowl on the floor under it, a shattered glass, a stool overturned. He didn't look closely, didn't give it time as he raced through the house up the stairs and to their bedroom.

Bed unmade.

Clothes on the floor.

Not unusual.

But no nightie tossed anywhere.

And no Lexie.

His feet took him to the closet because the light was on. He looked down and saw it.

The safe open, cleaned out. Her jewelry boxes gone, the cash gone.

His gun, the clips and ammo gone.

He turned and sprinted down the stairs, through the living room, down the stairs to the utility room, opening the door.

Snake and Charger there.

He had no fucking clue what Shift was driving.

He just knew Shift had his money, the jewelry, his gun and his fucking wife.

"This isn't happening," he whispered to the cars, his chest expanding and contracting so big, so deep it was painful. He felt it in his gut, his throat, that burn searing through him. "This isn't happening," he repeated.

He hit the button on the wall to open the garage and ran through, ducking low because the door hadn't fully opened. He cleared it and ran to the Cruiser. He yanked open the door, leaned in and grabbed his phone he'd thrown on the passenger seat.

He flipped it open, found Julius and hit go.

It rang once after he put it to his ear.

"You okay, my man?" Julius answered.

"Shift has my wife. What was he driving and was there someone with him?"

Silence.

"*Julius!*" Ty roared. "*That piece of shit has my wife!* What car was he *fucking* in when the drive-by happened, and was there someone with him?"

"No partner, Walk. Don't know the car," Julius answered as Ty turned and saw Wood's truck approaching the condo at high speed. "But I'll find out."

"Do it fast," Ty ordered.

"You know I will," Julius replied then there was a disconnect.

Wood was parked and out of his truck, eyes on Ty, body and mouth already moving. "Talk to me."

"Lexie's gone. The man Tate and I visited in Dallas shot Angel Peña and headed up here. He has my wife."

Wood stopped close and pulled out his phone, saying, "You call Tate. I'll call the CPD."

"Tate's after a skip," Ty told him, and Wood's eyes lifted from his keypad to Ty.

"I think he'll come back." Then he put the phone to his ear.

Ty made his call and got Tate's voicemail.

"Tate, Duane Martinez skipped bond. He took care of business in Dallas and shot Peña. Now he's taking care of business in Colorado and he's got Lexie. Fuck, fuck, *fuck*..." He lost it, pulled it together and then said in a whisper, "I need you again, man."

He flipped his phone shut.

As Wood muttered on his phone, it hit him.

The air.

He looked around.

The sky was bright and blue. The sun shining.

But no snowmelt.

It was below freezing.

He turned and sprinted back up the steps, checking behind the door where there were hooks where they kept their jackets and coats. He stared at it, never paying much attention, not knowing if she hooked hers there last night but she usually did and it was there. In fact, all three of them were there. Two of her heavy but stylish jackets and her new winter coat.

His heart twisted again and, fuck, that shit hurt.

Wood walked in, eyes on Ty. "CPD on its way but what spooked you?"

Ty looked to Wood. "She's in her nightie."

Wood held Ty's eyes and started carefully, "Ty—"

Ty leaned toward him bent at the waist and thundered, "My *fucking* wife is with a *fucking* piece of *fucking* shit. It's *fucking* freezing. She's *fucking* carrying my child and she's in her goddamned *fucking* nightie and all I can *fucking* do is stand here and wait for a goddamned *fucking* phone call so I can know what *the fuck* I'm lookin' for."

Wood took one step toward him and said quietly, "Man, you have got to calm down."

"Maggie was with a drug-dealin' pimp with vengeance on his mind, she was pregnant, in a fuckin' nightie and socks when there's snow on the ground, would you be calm?" Ty clipped.

"You've had your blowout, now you gotta get a handle on it, Ty. You losin' your mind is not gonna help Lexie."

This, fuck him, was fucking true.

His phone rang in his hand, he didn't even look at the display before flipping it open and putting it to his ear.

"Talk," he barked.

"Brother, I'm headin' home right now. Just outside Denver, should be there in two hours."

It was Tate.

"Right," Ty replied.

"Keep your head. You call CPD?" Tate asked.

"Wood's here. He did. They're on their way."

"Peña?"

"Given last rites."

Silence then, "Fuck."

"Right. Fuck," Ty bit off.

"Keep your head, Ty."

"You beat the shit outta the man who kidnapped and stuck your woman, Tate. You know where I am right now."

Silence then, "Right. I need to get home."

"Fast," Ty grunted.

"She'll be okay, brother," Tate said softly.

"We had a winning streak for a while now, Tate. Lady Luck does not like me that much and she's played with Lexie since my woman was born. Time for her to remind me and my wife, like she always does, that good comes with bad."

"Keep your head, brother."

Impossible.

"Right," he whispered.

"Be there soon."

Ty flipped his phone shut.

Then he heard the sirens.

His phone rang again.

He listened to Julius telling him the drive-by was perpetrated by a lone black man with an automatic weapon in a blue, 2010 Nissan Pathfinder.

Chace

Chace Keaton approached Ty Walker, who was standing in his kitchen looking ready to commit murder.

Justifiable homicide.

It was the only time in his life he'd had that thought. And he had it because Lexie Walker had lunch with him twice.

Once, when she broke the deep, impenetrable layer of ice between them he never thought would even crack and she did it being honest, friendly, fucking funny and very cute even though, or maybe because, she was a little bit of a goof.

The second time a week later, when she happened on him again at the diner, sat right across from him without invitation and ordered her food. She'd gabbed. He'd worked and pretended to ignore her. Then, when she went for her wallet, he told her that if she tried to pay for her lunch, he'd walk straight to the garage and tell her husband they were having an affair.

She'd laughed hard and long. Then she'd reached out and touched his hand.

Then she'd whispered, "Until next time, Chace," and he watched her strut away in her high-heeled shoes knowing she was very taken, pregnant and wishing she wasn't either.

He stopped three feet from Walker and he spoke.

"We have an APB out on the vehicle. What you need to get right now is that there's no blood. There was a struggle but that was limited to the kitchen so we think she realized the smarter play was to do what he said and she was right, that was the smarter play. Your explanation of his motive is another thing we got goin' for us. He wanted to exact vengeance and he was on a different path, he would not take her. He would have done what he intended to do the minute he found her. This means hope, Walker."

Ty Walker held his eyes and made not a sound.

"How well do you know this guy?" Chace asked.

"I played poker with him once. I beat the shit outta him twice. He deals drugs. He pimps women. He was not gentle with his girls. He's a liar. He ordered a hit on his best friend. He shot a cop in Dallas. This is all I know," Walker rumbled.

"And he's pissed at you because you kicked his ass, is that correct?"

Walker jerked up his chin then went on, "This is not a man who likes to get bested. He's small but not in body, in mind. He's stupid. He's greedy. He's mean. Normal human shit in him was disconnected a long fuckin' time ago. He thinks of one thing, himself."

"So you'd have no idea where he's going?" Chace asked.

"No fuckin' clue," Walker answered in a way that the words were quick but forced. He did not like to say them. He did not like what was happening. He did not like the feelings he was feeling. And he did not like that he was again powerless in a way that someone else made him be and not in a way where he fucked up himself.

Then his body jerked and he pulled out his phone.

"What?" Chace asked.

"Ella," Walker muttered.

"Who?"

Walker's eyes came to him. "Ella. Woman who took Lexie on when she was thirteen. She's known Shift since he was little. She might know."

"Good," Chace murmured. "Call her. I'll need to speak with her."

"It is not good I call her," Walker returned quietly. "She thinks of Lexie as blood, a daughter. I did not want her to know this until I know what I gotta tell her."

Chace held his eyes as Walker put the phone to his ear, not envious of Walker having to make this call, not envious of anything Walker had going on right now.

"Ella?" he heard. "Ty. Where are you?" Pause then, "Sit down, honey." Another pause then, "No, do that for me now. Sit down and don't delay. I gotta talk to you a minute then I gotta pass you to someone who you gotta talk to." Another pause, "You sittin'?" Pause then, "Yeah, honey, it's Lexie. Shift jumped bond, came up and kidnapped her from the house this morning. Cops are lookin' for her but they got no clue about this guy and the man knows him best in Dallas is not doin' too good and can't talk. So, I need you to tell the police here all you know about Shift, where he might go, what he might do. Can you do that?"

Chace watched him listen, close his eyes then open them.

"Right, here he is. His name is Detective Keaton, yeah? You talk, you need me, I'm right here."

Then Walker held out his phone.

Chace took it and put it to his ear. "This is Detective Keaton. I'm talking to Ella?"

Nothing.

He put his hand over the receiver and asked Walker, "What's her last name?"

"Rodriguez."

Chace nodded, took his hand away and said, "Ms. Rodriguez, I need you to talk to me."

"Won't do her." He heard in a voice that was completely and alarmingly dead.

"Sorry?"

"Don't have it in him, that boy. Don't got nothin' in him. No brains. No feelin's. No courage. Won't do her. But he'll take her to someone who will."

Chace's gut twisted at her words and her tone. It was as good as done for her. She was already preparing to grieve.

And because of this and for other reasons, he didn't tell her that Duane Martinez had already "done" four people, three in the hospital, one dead.

Instead, he asked, "Does he have any connections in Colorado?"

"Not that I know," she answered.

"So, will he take her to Dallas?"

"My guess? Yes," she replied.

"Then we have time," he carefully assured her.

Silence.

"I need to let you go now, Ms. Rodriguez. Would you like to talk to Ty again?"

"No, tell him we're prayin' but he's got better things to do than try to make me feel better."

"Right," Chace mumbled. "Thank you for your time."

"I'll be here," she replied.

"All right. Good-bye, Ms. Rodriguez."

"Good-bye, Detective Keaton."

He heard her disconnect, his eyes went from where they wandered to the counter back to Walker to see he had his home phone to his ear.

"Tate?" Walker said. "Ella says he's takin' her to Dallas. In about three seconds I'm in the Snake."

He touched a button on the phone, tossed it on the counter, leaned forward, pulled his phone out of Chace's hand and moved.

Chace called after him, "Walker, let the police deal with this."

"You tell your brothers, they find me, flip on their sirens, I ain't stoppin'," Walker said to the stairs then he jogged down them.

"Fuck," Chace whispered, dug his own phone out, flipped it open, called the station and told them to inform local departments and the Highway Patrol that a black Dodge Viper with silver racing stripes would likely be detected greatly exceeding the speed limit and if they caught him on radar they followed him but let him be.

Then he turned his eyes to Frank who was staring down the stairs and called his name.

"Guy's headin' to Dallas. Tate Jackson is heading to Dallas and Ty Walker is heading to Dallas and so am I," he told Frank, and Frank jerked up his chin.

Chace Keaton walked swiftly out the back door but not so swiftly he didn't see the photo in the windowsill of Walker and Lexie standing close, arms around each other, beautiful landscape in the back, Lexie Walker smiling bright and happy at the camera, clearly exactly where she wanted to be and where that was was not standing in front of beautiful landscape.

The image burned in his brain, he made it through the door, jogged to his SUV, swung in and headed out.

Tate

His cell beside him rang, he nabbed it, looked at the display, flipped it open and put it to his ear.

"Keaton," he greeted.

"News just in, Tate. Duane Martinez was picked up yesterday in Oklahoma."

Tate blinked at his windshield then asked, "What?"

"Highway Patrol caught him speeding. He didn't stop. Fifteen-minute high-speed chase, he crashed but was unharmed, took off on foot, they got him. Since he freaked, he luckily left the weapon that did Peña in his SUV and didn't have a chance to use it again. Took some time to process him, run his prints, find out they'd get to prosecute him after Dallas did and they informed Dallas. Dallas sent boys out to get him. This we just got. He never made it to Colorado."

"Then who has Lexie?" Tate asked.

Keaton was silent a moment then, his voice deeper, pissed but controlled, "One, Rowdy Crabtree. Two, Arnie Fuller. Or three, my father."

Fucking hell.

"Break that down for me, Chace," Tate ordered, searching for an exit sign to turn the fuck around a-fucking-gain.

"Rowdy is freaked and fucked. Arnie is missing. And I know Newcomb slipped that video to Walker and Lexie so it stands to reason that my father would find out that same thing. He'll want Walker to collect all copies and return them to him and he'll want to ensure Walker and Lexie do not talk. And he'll do what he can to make that happen."

"You talk to your dad?" Tate asked.

"Called four times. He's not answering. Called my mom, she says he's at work. I don't want to worry her so I left it at that."

"He usually take your calls?"

"Not even close. Then again, I got nothin' to say to the man so I don't usually call him."

Tate thought that was likely the fucking truth.

"Why Arnie? He did this, it would be a serious fucked play."

"Arnie hates Ty Walker."

"Think that's been established, Chace, but the man's not dumb. I'll repeat, he did this, it would be a serious fucked play. He's already a national pariah and he's an ex-cop. He wants to do everything he can to avoid jail time, not buy himself more."

"Arnie hates Ty Walker, Tate, but he hates Irving Walker more."

Tate spotted the exit sign, one mile ahead, he processed that but his mind was on the conversation.

"What?"

"For Arnie, black doesn't mix with white, *ever.* And, for Arnie, black *definitely* does not mix with Reece Rayner. The woman he had his eye on. The woman whose pants he wanted into before or after he put his ring on her finger. The woman who said no to him more than once and the woman who ended up knocked up by and married to a black guy."

Tate stared at the road and whispered, "You are fuckin' shittin' me."

"Nope," Keaton told him. "Ty Walker never committed a crime in or around Carnal that I knew of but he had a file in the office, in Arnie's desk, thick and always gettin' thicker. Arnie kept his eye on Ty while Arnie nursed his vengeance and bided his time. He wanted to fuck father and son, put both in their place and remind Reece of her mistake all at the same time. What happened to Walker was not random. Not by a long shot."

Tate knew what this meant. And Tate knew this was not good.

"So, Ty bests him, publicly humiliates him in a huge way, he breaks and now he's unpredictable," Tate deduced.

"My guess, yes. I don't put anything past my father but he usually throws money at shit so this is not his style. If Rowdy Crabtree has one working brain cell, he's in Brazil by now. Arnie Fuller is fucked, his brother is fucked, both are goin' down and both are goin' somewhere they do not want to go and very well might not make it back from. He has nothin' to lose."

Arnold Fuller had nothing to lose but Alexa Berry Walker, and her husband Tyrell had everything to lose.

Including the child Ty told him a couple of days ago his wife was carrying.

Fuck.

Chace spoke in his ear. "Tate, I'm tellin' you this and not Walker because he's on his way to Dallas. My opinion, what Fuller's already done to him coupled with this, that may be the best thing while we round Fuller up and get Lexie. Give him time to cool down before he gets back. Wouldn't matter if it was Fuller or anyone did it, gives him time to cool down. But it is not my pregnant wife who's missin' and you got experience with that so I'm handin' you the ball to make the call. Whatever you decide, you take that man's back, I'll do what I can to take it too if he hits Carnal and he's close when we get her back to him and catch the fucker who took her."

"I'm callin' him, Chace. No fuckin' way I'm sittin' on this. Anyone did that to me with Laurie or Jonas, they'd buy what I dished out to whoever hurt 'em."

"Like I said, you make the call. Now I got work to do."

Tate pulled off at the exit and decelerated, saying, "Me too."

Then he heard said quietly, "I'll find her, Tate."

"Do it while she's breathin' and that baby's still safe."

"Right."

Disconnect.

Tate flipped his phone closed, flipped it open and did this while he maneuvered the overpass and re-entered the highway going the other way.

Then he called Ty.

Lexie

"You like black cock?"

I stared at him.

I was freezing. So fucking cold. So fucking cold.

His arm flashed out, he caught me with the butt of Ty's gun and I went flying to the side.

"*You like black cock?*" he screamed.

I pushed myself up on a hand, feeling the blood seeping into my eye. I turned my head, looked through the red and locked eyes with Arnold Fuller.

Then I whispered, "I love it."

I watched him lift the gun and take aim.

Irving

"You like black cock?"

He heard it.

That motherfucker. That fucking motherfucker.

That fucking motherfucker.

He burst through the door, Arnie Fuller turned on him. Gun in his hand already up, he didn't hesitate to fire.

Irving took the bullet but he was on the move. All six-foot-six, two hundred and twenty pounds of him, he tackled Fuller who went flying back, hit the wall at the side of the hunting cabin and Irv heard the gun go flying.

He grappled with Fuller but his eyes went to his bleeding daughter-in-law.

"Go," he ordered.

She scrambled to her feet, eyes on him and started, "Irv—"

"*Get the gun and go!*" he shouted.

She moved.

He fought Fuller until the blood leaking from him meant he couldn't fight anymore.

But before he slumped to the ground, took five boot kicks from that fucking motherfucker and lost consciousness, he knew Lexie was gone.

Lexie

The keys were not in Fuller's truck so I had no choice but to run.

And I ran.

I started down the lane but then I thought, Irv was wounded, if Fuller got away, he might take his truck and to take his truck, he'd need road and even on this pitted, frozen, mud, one-lane road, he'd get to me quickly. So I should get off the road.

But Irv had to get there somehow, which meant there had to be a car or something that also needed road.

I just didn't see it.

So I kept to the road until I heard the truck behind me. Then I veered into the forest.

We were far from home. Far. Very far. Two hours away. That far. I was in a nightie and socks. We were at even higher elevation than Carnal. It was freezing. I had no idea where we were or what was close.

So I just ran.

Then I heard him on foot coming after me.

Oh God. Oh God.

I had to get away.

My feet slipped and slid on the ice and snow and I was thankful my socks were thick wool. No traction but plenty of cushioning.

I kept going.

I stopped abruptly as the forest suddenly opened up. I slid across a sheet of ice on top of a huge red Colorado boulder that led straight to a cliff.

Panting, I looked over the cliff.

Shit. Shit. *Fucking shit.*

I had no idea how far down that was, I just knew it was far.

I looked left. I looked right. I waited too fucking long to make a decision.

He crashed out of the forest. I whirled and lifted the gun.

He didn't hesitate, he came right at me.

I had nowhere to back up but cliff. I had nowhere to run.

And I had two lives to save.

In a nanosecond, the name Tuku flashed in my mind.

So, actually, I knew I had *three* lives to save.

So, to do that, I made the decision to take one.

I pulled the trigger, eyes open but mind blanked to the sprays of hideous red and I kept doing it until he went down.

Then I stood on a cliff in the middle of fucking nowhere staring at a dead man while breathing hard and freezing my ass off.

I ran to him and checked his pockets.

No fucking phone. No fucking keys.

Shit, shit, *fucking shit*!

I kept my eyes to the ground to follow my tracks in the snow back to the road, moving fast and keeping moving. I needed my heart pumping and blood rushing, warming my body, keeping my baby safe. When I got to the road, the door was hanging open on his truck and I heard the dings.

The keys were in it.

I climbed in and forced my frozen, trembling fingers and equally frozen, trembling legs to do what I commanded but they were really fucking frozen and trembling a fuck of a lot. My three-point turn took seven points. But I got it turned around, raced up the road and stopped outside the tiny one-room cabin, got out of the truck and ran inside.

Irv was not moving. I ran to him, got to my knees and felt for a pulse. The red was seeping from his chest, pooling around his body.

"Stick with me, Irv," I whispered, checking his pockets. "Please, honey, stick with me."

Back pocket, phone. Just like his son.

I flipped it open and my thumb moved over it.

Stupid. Stupid. Automatically, I called Ty.

It rang once then, "Dad, I do not—"

My stomach clenched, my heart flipped and I cut him off with, "Baby."

Silence then a muttered, "Thank fuck, thank fuck," pause then, "are you safe?"

"M-m-mostly."

"Right," he clipped then, "mama, where are you?"

"Two . . . two . . . about two hours out of Carnal. North. Hunting cabin. Mountains. Ty, I don't know. We're high. I tried to keep track of all the twists and turns but I couldn't. There were too many. It's in the middle of nowhere. But your dad found it and he took on Fuller so I could get away. He's been shot and, honey, he's losing a lot of blood. I have to get in Fuller's truck. I'm too cold and I don't know if I can move your dad or if I should and I don't—"

"Get in the truck, get somewhere, leave Dad," he ordered.

My hand was on Irv, curled around his neck and I whispered, "I can't leave him. He saved—"

"Yes, babe, he did. Do not pay him back by losin' digits or our child by freezin' your ass off. Get in the *fucking* truck and get to *fucking* safety. Now."

Okay, someone was freaked and freaked made him bossy and impatient.

Understandable.

So I whispered, "Okay."

"I'm lettin' you go now. I'll get him help but I want you callin' me frequently, even if you're just drivin'. Got me?"

"Yes, baby."

"Good. Get in the truck, mama."

"Ty?" I called.

"Baby, get in the truck."

I ignored him and whispered, "I killed Fuller."

Silence then, gently, "Mama, please, fuck, get in the truck."

"Okay." I was still whispering.

"Okay," my husband whispered back.

Then he was gone.

I went to the truck that I'd left idling, blasted the heat and searched it. I found a first aid kit and two blankets. Rifling through it, I found it was a regular first aid kit, nothing to help with a bleeding gunshot wound.

I grabbed the blankets, ran back to Irv and did my best to wrap him as tight as I could with blanket one then covered him with blanket two, tucking him tight all around. He moaned a couple of times while I did this but didn't regain consciousness. Still, moans were good. Moans meant alive. I'd take moans.

I bent, kissed his cheek quickly, whispered in his ear, "Thank you, hold tight, stay alive and we'll get you help as soon as we can."

Belatedly, though I'd never fucking tell Ty in a million fucking years that I had delayed, I ran to the truck, jumped in, closed the doors, locked them, put that fucker in gear and raced the fuck away.

Ty

His phone rang, it was in his hand, he hadn't had a call from his wife for twenty fucking minutes so he flipped it open without looking at his display and said, "Talk."

"Tate," he heard. "Aspen Valley Hospital. Both your father and Lexie are here. He's in surgery, she's getting checked over."

"Right," Ty said, his heart, lungs and gut not loosening even a little.

"How far out are you?" Tate asked.

He looked at his speedometer. Then he looked in the rearview mirror and saw the highway patrolman who had been on his ass but keeping a distance for the last hour and a half.

Then he said to Tate, "Half an hour."

"Okay, brother," Tate said quietly. "Quick brief. You need this now and you need to keep yourself safe drivin' that fuckin' car while I tell it to you. Then you need to process it. Then you need to bury it because you gotta have your shit together when you get here. This was all about you but now it isn't. Now you gotta look after your wife."

"Tate—" Ty growled.

Tate didn't delay. "I've seen Lexie. She's got some bruises, she's trembling like a motherfucker, scrapes from a dash through the forest and Fuller clocked her with a gun butt so looks like you two'll have matchin' scars."

Fuck, fuck, fucking *motherfucker.*

Tate kept going. "They're worried about shock. She killed that fuckwad and no matter why she did it and she had no choice, she is *freaking out*. Her drama that she endured probably isn't helping. Seein' your dad the way he was also isn't helping. She's a fuckin' mess. I got Laurie on gettin' to your house and gettin' her some clothes. She's all over it."

"Right," Ty bit off.

Silence then, cautiously, "Okay, now, your father came in flatline."

Ty stared at the road but his hand on the steering wheel tightened.

Tate continued, "They shocked him, got a weak heartbeat, rushed him into surgery. But, brother, that is not lookin' good."

"Right," Ty whispered.

"Maggie is goin' to Reece as we speak."

"Right," Ty repeated on a whisper.

"Keaton is locating your brother."

Ty didn't respond.

Silence then, quietly, "Where's your head?"

"I'm good."

Again quietly he got, "Good. See you in half an hour."

"Right."

He flipped his phone closed.

Then he made a one-hour journey in half an hour.

Angel

Angel Peña opened his eyes and felt someone in the room.

He didn't turn his head because, no matter the fucking painkillers they were pumping into him, he'd learned movement didn't feel too good.

So he shifted his eyes and saw Ty Walker standing three feet away.

Fuck him.

He shifted his eyes further and saw Lexie asleep in an armchair, knees to her chest, the arm that had been holding them had fallen so her hand was at her ankle, her head was turned, chin tucked in, cheek to the back of the chair.

But she had a black eye and a thin strip of white holding together an angry red-and-purple gash.

His eyes went back to Ty who had moved to the side of the bed.

"Shift?" he asked, and his voice was a harsh rasp. This was mostly because he hadn't used it much. It was also because the day before they'd yanked the tube that had been down his throat for four days.

Ty shook his head and answered, "Fuller."

He forgot not to move and his eyebrows shot up.

Good news. That didn't hurt. Maybe he was getting better.

"Fuller?"

"Lost his shit, kidnapped my wife, took her to a hunting cabin for reasons we'll never know, got her with the butt of my gun before my dad stormed in. Lexie got away but tagged my gun before she went. Dad took a bullet to the chest. He died twice but now he's in better shape than you. Fuller went after her. On a cliff in a nightgown, Lexie drilled him with six. He's very dead. She's very alive." He paused, held Angel's eyes and whispered, "Now back to sunshine."

Angel tried another movement and found it didn't hurt to smile.

Then he heard, "Angel?"

His eyes shifted again to watch Lexie folding out of the chair.

Shit, but only Lexie Walker could have a black eye and an angry gash on her eyebrow and still look beautiful.

She moved to him and Ty shifted slightly so Lexie could get in there and she did, immediately curling her fingers around his hand.

Her blue-gray eyes held his. "How are you, honey?"

He held her blue-gray eyes. They were warm, concerned, searching and he felt her lightly squeeze his hand.

That was all he was ever going to get. All he was ever going to get from Lexie Walker.

And he'd take it.

"Better now," he answered then she proved him wrong.

She gave him a bright smile and her light shone down on him, bright, blinding, beautiful.

He took that too.

EPILOGUE

Catching Up

Five years later…

Forearms in the bed, my husband's big hands spanning my hips lifting them up, my knees were inches off the bed. I'd pushed my thighs back and pressed their insides to the outsides of his as I took his driving cock.

If he wanted to take me from behind, he was so tall, his legs so long, this was how we had to do it unless he stood by the side of the bed.

I liked it, like, *a lot.* That power, the reminder of how big he was, the strength that was at his command. It was a huge, freaking turn-on.

I was close, God, I was close. I slid an arm out in front of me, under the pillows, pressing my hand into the headboard. I tilted my ass up half an inch to get more, held on tighter with my thighs and pressed into my hand to give me leverage to push back.

Ty pulled out and dropped me to my knees.

My head shot back and my neck twisted, my mouth opening to protest but he was leaning over me, his arms circling, one at my belly, one slanting across my chest. He pulled me up on my knees and one hand immediately went to my breast, fingers rolling my nipple, the other hand moved instantly downward, finger rolling my clit.

My head fell back, colliding with him. I turned it and begged. "Want your cock back, baby."

He didn't respond. He never responded. He just kept doing what he wanted to do.

And it felt *way* nice.

Still.

My hips moved with his hand, my hand moved to cover his at my breast, my other one curled behind me and wrapped around his cock.

"Honey," I breathed.

He didn't stop.

I started stroking, gripping hard, pulling, sliding, moving fast.

Ty growled in his throat.

I tipped my head back to see what I could of his face but didn't get the chance, his mouth came down on mine and his tongue darted in and out, matching my strokes on his cock.

I gripped harder and moved faster, as did my hips and his tongue.

There I was again, God, so close. I reached for it and my hand gripped tight but stopped as he gave it to me and it was so good, my entire body shook with it.

Then I was on my back, my husband on top of me, driving deep, grunting with each stroke, his hands at my hips yanking me down as he thrust up. I had nearly all of his weight. I was hazy from a really fucking good orgasm that hindered my breathing and his weight hindered it more. I didn't care. This happened, not often, only when I wound Ty up. Therefore, I liked it, snapping his control. And he never did it long. He only did it when he was close.

And he was close.

Then he was there.

I felt it, watched it, listened to it and loved it.

He'd shoved my knees up high at his sides and I pressed them in and wrapped my arms around his shoulders as he shifted his weight to a forearm in the bed, the other arm moving to curl around my lower back as his hips continued to move. He was gliding. He did this too, and often, taking me gentle after he took me hard.

I liked that too.

When our breath settled and while he was still gliding, I turned my head, found his ear with my lips and whispered, "I'm pregnant."

His body stilled, mid-glide, half in, half out.

Then he slid fully in and stayed there but lifted his head and caught my eyes.

"Seriously?" he rumbled.

I grinned. "Seriously."

"Babe, we've been tryin' for like, two days."

I bit my lip not to giggle, succeeded, let it go and informed him, "More like a month."

His eyes drifted over my head and he muttered, "Feels like two days."

"It's been a month, hubby."

It hadn't. It had been six weeks but I decided not to say that.

His eyes came back to mine. "Jesus. Your fuckin' womb's more fertile than the heartland."

I felt my body shake but quelled my verbal laughter.

"Maybe it's your swimmers," I suggested, my voice shaking with laughter I hadn't unleashed. "Maybe they have Mr. Humongo's superpowers."

Ty didn't find anything funny. He didn't laugh. He didn't smile. Instead, he bent his neck back, looked at the ceiling and said an audible prayer.

"Please, God, this time, give me a fuckin' son."

My body shook more.

"I'm not sure God likes the word 'fuck,' honey," I told him and his head dropped.

"He knows me. He's answered my prayers before and trust me, mama, He doesn't give a shit."

I burst out laughing.

Ty pulled out slowly, rolled mostly off me, got up on an elbow in the bed, his long, heavy legs tangled with mine, body pressed the length of me, hand at my belly, eyes watching me laugh.

I turned slightly to him as my laughter waned and sought to assure him, "I feel it. This one's a boy."

"You said that last time. You were wrong," he reminded me.

"I *really* feel it coming through strong, Ty. He's speaking to me," I promised him.

"Babe, you said *that* the *first* time. You were wrong then too."

I decided to be quiet since he was not lying.

Ty wasn't quiet.

"Lex, Lella's four and a half and I had to paint the living room last weekend because she got in your fingernail polish and painted her fingernails, her fingers, her hands, her toes, her toenails, her calves, her belly and a three-foot-square space of wall with that shit."

I bit my lip because he was still not lying.

He wasn't done.

"And Vivian's two and a half and she was screamin' just last night 'cause she got hold of one of your hoops and was trying to shove that fucker through her earlobe. She was in pain but, fuck me, she didn't quit. My baby girl was *determined* and she didn't care if it ended in carnage."

My body started shaking again because he was *still* not lying.

He wasn't finished.

"And she pitches a fit every time she sees a game on television."

I pressed my lips together hard and rolled into him, wrapping my arm around his waist and holding tight, my body still shaking because he was *still* not lying.

"I need another dick in this house and soon before the whole fuckin' place is painted pink and I slip on a glitter pen and break my neck."

I swallowed laughter and promised him, "You won't slip on a glitter pen."

"I will, you don't quit buyin' that shit for Lell. How many does she have now, a thousand?"

It was more like nine hundred and twenty-five. But I decided not to quibble and instead change the subject.

"We should probably get up and shower. I have to start cooking."

He held my eyes. Then his big, warm hand pressed lightly into my belly and his gaze moved there.

When his touch didn't ease and his gaze didn't shift for some time, I called softly, "Ty?" and his eyes, those beautiful, light brown eyes with their thick, black, curly lashes came to me.

"Proof," he whispered.

"What?" I whispered back, lost in his eyes, over five years with my man and, still, I frequently got lost in those eyes.

"Proof," he repeated then explained, "Lady Luck likes us."

I grinned because she did. I'd had five beautiful years and I wasn't sure but I was thinking we were favorites.

"Yeah," I said softly.

His hand pressed slightly deeper as his head bent so he could touch his mouth to mine. Then his lips went away but his forehead touched mine.

Then he was out of bed but reaching in and I was out of bed.

Then we were in the shower.

It was a long one.

Seriously, if my man didn't want so many kids, he should probably stop fucking me so much.

Then again, at that point, the damage was done so we might as well have fun.

* * *

The doorbell rang and there were three "I'll get its," one from Bess, one from Honey and a deep, rumbling one from Ty.

Ty won and I knew this because Bess and Honey didn't stop what they were doing and Ty moved.

At his rumble, I had looked over the counter and I saw Bess's man, Roland, and Honey's man, Zander, sitting in armchairs but I watched my husband appear from behind the couch in our sunken family room. Ella Alexi was on his back. We called her "Lella" or "Lell" because, when she started speaking, that was how she referred to herself.

She called my other Ella gramma.

My husband shifted to his feet with his daughter on his back with practiced ease. This was because both Lell and Vivie considered their father's large frame their own personal jungle gym and treated it as such.

He didn't complain. Not once.

Lell locked her arms around his neck, her little legs not long enough to surround his chest (even though she was well off the charts for height, still, she wasn't even five) but they still clutched tight. Ty helped, curving a long arm behind him under her bottom.

Lell secure on his back, I watched as he bent then I heard a squeal and he came up with Vivian Bess, our Vivie, carrying her under his free arm like a sack of grain. She kept squealing but it wasn't her pissed-off squeal. It was her giggly squeal.

He strode to the four steps then up them carrying his daughters while his head turned and his eyes slid to me. I grinned at him. He grinned back. Vivie squealed again. His grin turned into a smile.

Then I lost sight of him as he headed to the front door.

I looked back to the sunken living room, which had floor-to-ceiling windows out in a point that were nearly a story-and-a-half tall and gave a view of the hill, Carnal and the hills and mountains beyond. The family room was vast. Up the four steps it opened into an almost equally vast kitchen that sat at the heart of the house and faced the family room over a high counter with stools.

Off to one side and up two steps was a circular room that was a dining room that had huge windows and French doors to a deck.

Off to the other side and down two steps was a square room that was an office, ditto with the windows, doors and deck.

Down the wide side hall to the front door at the front of the house was a more formal living room and a set of stairs that led to the top floor.

Down the other wide, side hall off the office that also eventually led to the living room was a smaller opening that included a butler's pantry and an area the developers called a "Mom's Unit," which included cupboards and a long counter with a cutout at one end that gave space for a chair. That was where I had my sewing machine and did my craft stuff.

Farther down that hall on one side was a half bath, on the other side was the door to a three-car garage.

On top of all this vast space was another, smaller, open family room, five bedrooms and three full baths, one of those full baths being in Ty's and my gigantic master suite that also faced front in a point with floor-to-ceiling windows to our spectacular view and off the side opposite the bath there was a private deck.

I found the house about three weeks after our ordeal finally ended for good. It was in a cushy development up a hill off the north side of Carnal. The houses were few and very far apart. Ours had been ordered by a family whose father unfortunately and unexpectedly lost his high-paying job so they had to back out. The good news about that was, they'd gone for the gusto on build with all the upgrades they could order and the developers were scrambling to find someone who'd take it off their hands. So we got it for a song though that song was still a whack.

Once I saw it, I went back with Laurie, Wendy, Betty and Maggie who all agreed it was the shit then I went back with Dominic and Kayeleen and they told me I *had* to have it so I took my husband there thinking he'd say no way.

It was huge. It was pricey.

But it was us.

Ty, being Ty, walked through without comment then stood in the empty space of the master suite that had only two weeks before been carpeted and had criss-cross stripes of tape on the massive windows. He stared out the windows for three seconds then looked down at me and muttered, "Get it, mama."

I didn't demur. I got it.

We made a whack on the condo, we had a whack in the bank and we recovered the whack that Arnold Fuller stole from our safe. Our mortgage ended up being the same as the condo, and we still had money in the bank.

I had Ella Alexi and finished my massage therapy certification, which didn't triple my salary, it quadrupled it. Not to mention, I loved being a massage therapist because I was right, people loved coming to see me. I was the highlight of their day.

So it was all good.

I heard movement and mutterings and looked to the side, my hands on a rolling pin rolling pie dough, and I saw Laurie, Tate, Ty and my daughters emerge from the hall. Lella was still on her daddy's back but now Vivie had her little arms wrapped around Tate's neck, one of his arms was behind him supporting her booty, the other hand lifted and holding onto her forearm.

I smiled at him then looked to Laurie, who was talking.

"Hey, guys," she greeted Ella, Bessie, Honey and me, all of us in the kitchen cooking, something Ty told me I should not allow (except Bess and me) but something, since it was Thanksgiving, I really couldn't stop them from doing.

Laurie got heys back and walked into the kitchen, dumping bags on the counter beside me and saying, "Sorry, honey, but Jonas is a no-show. This week he and his girl have decided it's forever and he's at her parents' house for dinner. We didn't get the news until about an hour ago and thus ensued a father–son talk that I was dragged into as an innocent but silent bystander, silent because I couldn't get a word in edgewise. So I didn't have a chance to warn you." Then she leaned in and said quietly, "This has not made his father happy."

I looked in her eyes and asked a surprised, "Tate doesn't like Jonas's girlfriend?" And I was surprised because I'd met her more than once. She was cute, she was sweet, she was a cheerleader and since Jonas was the captain of the football team, handsome, smart, funny and doting, they fit.

"Tate doesn't like Jonas bailing on his family on a family holiday at the last minute for some girl," she replied then told me something I already knew. "Though, they've been together now for three years so she isn't exactly some girl. But Tate also doesn't like them being together for three years. He does not want his son to make his father's mistakes. That said, she's really sweet and not exactly like Tate's high school girlfriend but he's having flashbacks. Neeta flashbacks have a way of grabbing hold and not letting go. So, I've said my piece on the way here and now I'm being neutral. They'll have to figure it out."

I was filing this away to tell Ty later as proof that sons might not always be easier than daughters when Laurie gave me more fodder.

"Jonas looks just like his dad and acts just like his dad. This is not lost on Tate. Though Tate doesn't see that Jonas has skipped the twenty-five years his father lived through hell with Neeta. I've also explained this to him and he's ignored me so he'll have to figure *that* out too."

This was good stuff and I wanted her to tell me more but she shut it down.

"Now." She clapped her hands. "What can I do?"

"You know how to make sweet potato pie?" Ella chimed in readily.

"Of course," Laurie said. "That's my favorite."

"Stuff's all set out." Ella jerked her head to another counter across the kitchen where the stuff was, indeed, all set out. "Have at it."

Laurie moved to the sweet potato pie station and Honey moved to Laurie's bags and unearthed a six-pack of beer, two bottles of wine, the chocolate pecan pie Laurie promised to bring, a gallon of ice cream and three cans of spray whipping cream, the best kind.

Vivie suddenly shrieked, my head snapped up and I saw that Ty had switched the channel from the parade to a game to watch with Tate, Roland and Zander.

His eyes came over the back of the couch to me and they spoke volumes. I looked down to my pie crust and kept rolling while grinning.

At shriek two from Vivie, which included actual words this time and they were, "*No footbaw, Daddy!*" Bessie forged into the opening breach, calling while walking toward the living room, "Vivie, girl, get in here, baby, you too, Lellie, honey. Girls get to be in the kitchen doing the fun stuff."

Lell appeared instantly, dashing in quickly but quietly.

My firstborn was like her father. She had a lot to say and a lot of ways to communicate but not all those were with words.

Vivie made a mad, boisterous dash, screeching, "*Fun stuff!*" and shaking her hands over her head.

And it was obvious who my secondborn took after.

Lell attacked her grandmother's legs, wrapped her arms around, tipped her head way back and smiled up at Ella. Ella instantly bent and lifted her, depositing her bottom on the counter and explaining she was peeling potatoes so we could mash them later. Lell listened with rapt attention and stared with absorption at her grandmother's hands.

Bessie swung Vivie up in her arms while Vivie still shrieked, "*Fun stuff! Fun stuff! Fun stuff!*" as Bess carried her into the kitchen and then this chant changed to, "*Pie! Pie! Pie!*" when she spotted Laurie's pie.

"That's for dessert, baby," Bess murmured to her.

"*Pie, Auntie Bess!*" Vivie squealed.

I ignored my daughter squealing and could do this because I had a great deal of practice because she rarely spoke in any other tone and I turned to Honey and asked, "Can you get Tate a beer and see if the boys need a fresh one? Game's on."

Honey grinned at me and rushed to the fridge.

I rolled the pie crust over the rolling pin then rolled it over the pie dish.

"*Pie!*" my daughter shrieked.

The doorbell rang.

My eyes went back to the family room to see Ty fold off the couch. Then I looked back at my crust.

One minute later, I heard called, "Where are my ragamuffins!"

"Grandpa," Lell whispered, her eyes moving across Ella to me and they were alight.

"*Grandpa!*" Vivie squealed and fought Bess's arms.

Bess let her down and Vivie raced out of the kitchen. Then she moved to Lell and let her down and she raced out too.

Thirty seconds later, Irv appeared with both girls riding his legs, their bottoms skimming the floor as he walked.

More greetings which Irv returned but he came right to me, my daughters still riding his calves, ankles and feet. He wrapped his hand around the back of my neck, bent in and kissed my temple.

I closed my eyes.

"Hey, Irv," I whispered.

"Beautiful," he whispered back and squeezed my neck.

I opened my eyes and tipped them back to look up at him.

He smiled at me.

I smiled back.

Then, with some effort and not very quickly, he shuffled out of the kitchen with my girls still attached to his legs.

"You want a beer, Irv?" Honey called and my eyes shot to Ty.

"Coke," Irv called back with zero hesitation. "Thanks, Honey-hon."

Jeez, I loved it when Irv called Honey "Honey-hon."

I let out a breath. Ty followed his dad. Honey raced out with Irv's soda like she'd get to stand on a podium and have a medal draped around her neck if she got the fastest time. That was Honey. She'd definitely win gold for being sweet.

I started to cut the overhang off the pie crust around the edge.

The doorbell rang again. Ty went after it again.

One minute later, we heard Julius shout, "That fuckin' pool at the hotel is *heated*. My man, I took a dip at nine thirty at night, in the mountains, snow all around, and it was *the shit*!"

"*Unkul Juujuu!*" Vivie shrieked. I could hear her little feet on the go and I was loving every minute of my daughter's excitement. Mostly this was because she was excited. She had a lot of love to give and enjoyed spreading it around so she was in heaven. But also this was because this meant that later, she'd be out like a light.

I looked into the family room and saw Lell on her grandfather's lap. Her head was turned to her sister but it quickly turned back. This was not because she didn't love her Uncle Julius. This was because she absolutely freaking adored her granddad.

I watched as she tipped her head back and lifted her little hand to put it to her grandfather's throat. That was her thing these days. She liked the vibrations she could feel when people talked.

As for me, I liked to feel my daughter's hand on my throat when I was talking to her.

"That man needs to watch his mouth," Ella muttered.

I didn't respond. Five years and the big family Ty and I somehow managed to acquire that was close and stayed close because they'd endured multiple dramas, the aftermath of tragedy and the lingering fear that never really went away of thwarted tragedy. This meant we didn't stay apart long and paths crossed often, holidays, birthdays, vacations. Everyone knew everyone else very well. And most everyone got along.

But Ella wasn't a big fan of Julius's profession or the fact that he had three women. I'd talked to her about this repeatedly and did not change her mind. Julius being Julius, therefore not only likable but lovable, also did not manage to change her mind. Bess and Honey adored him. So did my daughters. Ella was just going to have to suck it up.

More people, more greetings, these with Julius, Anana and her daughter with Julius, Ilori, who was nearly eight and closing on the beauty of her mother. Anana joined the women in the kitchen. Ilori went with her dad to join the men. Honey unveiled the Julius family offering. More beer. More wine. A bottle of top-shelf vodka. A bunch of flowers.

The doorbell rang again. Ty moved to it again.

I was pouring pumpkin pie stuff in my crust and didn't hear anything but boots hitting tile then I felt a hand at the small of my back. I stopped, turned my head and looked slightly down.

"Angel," I whispered.

"*Hola, mi querida.*"

I smiled. Angel smiled back.

"How is Carnal Hotel?" I asked.

"The pool is heated," Angel answered.

My smile got bigger. So did his.

"Though, thinkin' I took a swim last night with a big black guy who boosts cars," he added. "You won't tell my cap, will you?"

He totally knew he'd taken a swim with a big black guy who boosts cars considering this wasn't the first time he'd been around Julius. This, too, had been an uneasy alliance at first. But Angel's love for me and subsequent actions for Ty and Julius's love for Ty and subsequent actions for me meant they moved beyond uneasy because they had common ground. I suspected when they went their separate ways, they didn't talk about their association with their crews at home. That said, I knew Julius sent Angel a premium bottle of tequila for his birthday this year and I also knew Angel sent Julius a premium bottle of Hennessy for his.

"Your secret is safe with me," I whispered, and that got me a bigger smile.

Then he put slight pressure on my back before his hand fell away.

I looked around him and smiled again at Angel's very pregnant wife, "Hey there, Rosalia."

"Hey, Lexie. Hey, y'all." She dumped bags on the counter. "Anything I can do?"

Ella, the oldest, the grandmother therefore not being in her house but still being the boss, gave out instructions.

Rosalia got busy.

Angel moved toward a couch.

Ty moved behind him.

Vivie caught sight of Angel and dissed Julius to shriek, "*Unkul Anhay!*" and throw herself bodily from Julius to Angel, who was not prepared but fortunately caught her after she launched herself off the arm of a chair before Julius could stop her. Angel lifted her up, threw her in the air, caught her then pulled her close and blew a raspberry in her neck all the while my daughter emitted shrieking giggles.

Rosalia emitted a quiet giggle beside me.

My eyes slid to Lella and Irv and I saw their heads bent to their hands. They were playing thumb war, my daughter's tiny fingers curled around her grandfather's very not tiny fingers. I watched him let her win. I listened to her soft giggle. My eyes moved to my husband to see he was also watching, his face in profile but I could still see it was soft.

Then I went back to pouring pumpkin stuff in the pie shell.

Lots of people, lots of mouths to feed.

I had to get my shit together so I could feed my family.

* * *

Just to explain and update a few things...

* * *

That day five years ago, Irv knew how to find me because Irv knew that hunting cabin. Every black man and woman in the tri-county area did. And they did because Arnold Fuller was what he was because his daddy and granddaddy taught him how to be that way. And, back in the day when they could get away with it, any black man who stepped outside of what the Fullers and their brethren felt was their place, Fuller's daddy, granddaddy and their brethren took them to that cabin and taught them their place.

And Irv explained this to Ty and the police after he explained that a buddy of his who had the pastime of listening to police band radio called to let him know I was taken. He remembered that cabin. He knew Arnold Fuller. He figured he'd hold a nasty grudge and he knew, if Fuller did, he'd act on it.

Going to that cabin was a long shot, but he took it and it turned out he was right.

He should have called the police.

He didn't because he had a son to win and a score to settle.

It was a decision based solely on emotion, which made it not wrong but also not right.

What it was, was understandable.

Like father, like son.

And in the end, he saved my life.

* * *

Three months after Fuller kidnapped me, my husband disappeared in the night and he didn't come home until the early hours and when he did, he took a shower before coming to bed.

I didn't ask.

He didn't tell.

The next day at the salon, as it does, word spread that someone torched that hunting cabin in the night. Luckily, they doused all around with water so the flames didn't spread and it was so old, it went up like a light and burned fast.

And then it was gone.

An ugly piece of history up in smoke, and generations to come would never know it existed at all.

It would be a long time later, at his pace, when Ty told me what he did and explained he wasn't alone. Dewey, Tate, Deke, Wood, Pop, Shambles, Ned, Irv and Jim-Billy went with him.

So did Chace Keaton.

Yes, straight-arrow Chace Keaton.

Then again, Chace was a man in the business of righting wrongs. He'd put his ass out there to do it before so I guess it wasn't surprising he'd do it again regardless of the methods he needed to use.

I thought the building might be gone but the ghosts probably remained.

I also thought those ghosts probably got a kick out of watching those men burn that shithole to the ground.

* * *

Ty talked to me. Tate talked to me. Chace talked to me. Even Officer Frank popped by the house one afternoon to talk to me about shooting Arnold Fuller. They thought I'd freak considering the fact that I did at the hospital. Delayed reaction to Irv going down, me being kidnapped and me taking Arnie out.

I was fine.

Until one day, I wasn't.

Driving home from the grocery store on my Monday off, I got the shakes.

And my hands on the steering wheel guided the Charger to Carnal Police Department. I walked on shaky legs inside and asked to talk to Detective Keaton.

He came right out.

He held me while I lost it in an interrogation room and when I say lost it, I mean *I lost it.* Then, when he calmed me, he got me Kleenex. Then he sent an officer out to get me a latte from La-La Land.

He sat with me while I drank it.

Then he followed me home to make sure I got there okay.

He went straight to the garage and told Ty what happened. He also explained to Ty that I didn't go to him because I didn't want him to see that, that last piece of me that Fuller took since Fuller took so much from Ty already.

From the time Chace left me to the time Ty got home, I was a nervous wreck. I thought he'd get pissed, thinking I'd gone behind his back, not liking that I shared that with another man. I was such a mess, I didn't even phone him to attempt to detect his mood because, if he was going to lose it, I didn't want it to come sooner rather than later.

But Ty didn't get pissed.

He just came home from the gym as usual but did a thorough scan the minute he saw me. I knew he saw I was anxious and my anxiety had hit the red zone. But he just walked to me, wrapped his hand around the back of my head, gave me a kiss, touched my forehead with his and asked me to make him a shake. Then he went up to take a shower.

I made his shake and I did it grateful that he got it and didn't get pissed.

He never spoke of it, neither did I.

But he watched me closely after that and he did it for weeks. He didn't hide it but I didn't mention it. Our daughter was growing inside of me, he was concerned and he kept his finger on the pulse.

So did Tate. So did Chace. So did Officer Frank. Jim-Billy. Deke. Wood. Pop. Krystal. Laurie, Maggie, Stella, Dominic . . . everybody.

But I got rid of it that day. I gave it to Chace and he took it from me.

He'd taken his own load from Fuller so I knew it was selfish.

But I also was grateful and would be eternally.

To let me show this, Chace allowed me to buy his lunch one of the days we shared it at the diner instead of what usually happened, him buying mine.

He allowed me to do this once.

It wasn't much but at least it was something.

* * *

Three and a half weeks after my kidnapping, Rowdy Crabtree was detained in Arizona on the US side of the US/Mexican border trying to cross. He was arrested and transported back to Carnal.

He stood trial in Chantelle for Misty Keaton's murder. He was not offered bond because he was a flight risk.

He was acquitted and instantly moved out of state. I didn't know where.

I also didn't care.

Misty Keaton's murder was never solved.

Chace Keaton may not have liked his wife but he liked the way she died less.

So her murder had not been solved but that didn't mean Chace still wasn't looking for her killer.

* * *

Shift, being Shift, therefore stupid but not knowing it, tried to cop a plea.

Yes, he was a drug-dealing pimp who ordered the hit on his best friend and personally executed a drive-by that killed one and wounded three and he tried to cop a plea.

The DA drove a hard bargain.

Shift's currently enjoying his stay in a Texas penitentiary and would until he died. Life with no chance of parole.

It was up in the air whether it was a good bargain or not that the DA didn't push the death penalty.

* * *

And thus endeth the shadows.

Now it's all sunshine.

* * *

And two hours after Angel and Rosalia arrived, I sat at my dining room table which was stuffed full of the people I loved, my hands slightly out to the sides, my wrists resting on the edge of the table, my right fingers curled around Angel's, my left fingers curled around Irv's as I listened with bowed head to Ella saying our Thanksgiving prayer.

Then she was done but before I released the hands I held, I squeezed them tight at the same time they squeezed mine the same exact way.

I looked up and down the table and saw my husband's eyes on me and in them I read it all, everything, all he needed to say, all I loved to hear.

Five Thanksgivings he'd lost to a nightmare.

Five Thanksgivings I'd given him different versions of this.

Looking in his eyes I could see, finally, I was catching up.

Ty

"You sure?"

"Sam, I'm not sittin' a game," Ty said into his phone, his body moving through his house. Familiar movements, the same every night, these movements to shut it down, lock his girls in, make sure they were safe.

"I'll cover your buy-in," Samuel Sterling said in his ear.

Ty turned out the lights under the cabinets of Lexie's kitchen and asked, "Someone you wanna teach a lesson?"

"Three someones," Sam answered.

"How bad do they need this lesson?" Ty asked, moving out of the kitchen into the sunken family room to turn off the lamp that was sitting on a side table there.

Lex had a shitload of furniture in that area. Two full couches, four armchairs, two big footstools, four side tables and a coffee table.

When she filled that space, he thought she'd temporarily gone insane.

He'd been wrong.

Between her and her girls sucking back wine while cackling over what he suspected was not the books they were supposed to be reading (he thought this primarily because Krystal was a member of Lexie's book club and Krystal was not a woman to belong to a book club but she *was* a woman to cackle over wine) and him having the men over for beer and games, that furniture saw a lot of use.

"Some might not think they need this lesson badly," Sam replied, then said quietly, "a brother would disagree."

Ty straightened from the lamp and looked out at the lights of Carnal.

He didn't reply.

Sam kept talking.

"It's in Hawaii. I'll send the jet for you, Lexie and the girls. I've got a house here, you can stay there. They get a vacation, you do too except you take time out to sit the game and take their money, give me back my buy-in, put the rest in Lella and Vivie's college fund." He paused, "Though, it probably wouldn't hurt to use some to buy Lexie more diamonds."

Suddenly, Ty's eyes didn't see Carnal. His mind had a vision of his wife cooking, eating and being with their family that day in her clingy wraparound dress, high-heeled boots and the diamonds he gave her last Christmas in her ears and at her neck.

Ty gave Lexie diamonds for her birthday, Christmas and their anniversary, every year. He worked overtime to do it. And he never fucked around. She didn't get earrings or a necklace or a bracelet. She got a set. Sometimes a couple of pieces, sometimes three.

For their fifth wedding anniversary that year, though, Bessie and Roland came up from Miami to watch the girls for a long weekend while Ty took his wife back to Vegas where they stayed in the same hotel but in a better room. There he topped her wedding rings with a wide band set all around with diamonds. It cost a fucking whack and the stack of rings nearly covered her finger to her knuckle.

She took them off to clean them every day and she took them off to give her massages.

Other than that, they were never off. Not when she was showering, cooking, bathing the girls.

Never.

"When is this?" he asked Sam, eyes on Carnal.

"Two weeks."

Two weeks. They hadn't had a real vacation since April when they went to Ella's for a week over Easter.

He bent his neck and looked at his feet, muttering, "I'll talk to Lex."

He heard Sam's chuckle then, "All right then, see you in two weeks."

Then he had nothing but dead air.

He flipped his phone shut and shoved it in his back pocket knowing Sam was right. Hawaii, a private jet, money in the bank and diamonds, his woman would not be hard to convince, especially since this was his first game since the one he sat two days after he met her.

He'd stuck to his vow.

Until now.

He moved through the house, seeing the shadowed pieces on the walls.

Lex was a regular at the frame shop in Chantelle, such a regular, they sent Christmas cards. Glitter pen art done by Lell framed like it was executed by a master. Unusual multi-frames holding family snapshots. Two small shadow boxes displaying their daughter's tiny hospital bracelets, two others that held the first lock of their hair cut by Dominic, Lell's tied in a little, pale yellow ribbon, Vivie's with a pale pink one. Down the main hall, a double line of black-framed, cream-matted, black-ink, tiny but slowly getting bigger handprints.

Five of Lell's, one Lexie did two days after Lella came home from the hospital and one for each birthday. Three of Vivie's little hand.

There'd be another row there soon or she might branch out to the opposite wall and he liked that, he liked a décor based in comfort and family but he loved the home his wife made for them.

He checked the outer doors one last time to make sure they were locked, engaged the alarm then he went to the stairs.

But he stopped dead at the foot when he saw the shadowed figure sitting halfway up.

Ella.

He felt her eyes in the dark and gave her his.

She was silent.

He was too.

Then she whispered, "Love you, Ty."

It was the first time she'd said it even after years of her acting it and Jesus, God, it felt fucking good.

"Same," he rumbled, his voice rough.

He saw the shadow of her head nod then she got up and he watched her walk up the stairs and turn right.

He sucked in breath. Then he followed her.

As he did every night, he looked in on Lella and Vivie, who shared a room at Lexie's demand. She wanted them to grow up close, like Bessie and Honey did. She wanted them to have girlie nighttime chats. She wanted them to have togetherness.

She got what she wanted. Ty didn't argue. There was no reason, her motives were sound.

Both his girls were out. Not a surprise. They'd had a full day.

Then, quietly, because Ella, Bess and Roland and Honey and Zander were staying with them, he went to his wife.

He barely got the doors closed before she looked at him from her place sitting cross-legged on the bed and said, "The answer is yes."

He stopped and stared at her.

Then he guessed, "Sam called you before he called me."

She threw her arms in the air and, in a muted shout, cried, "Hawaii!"

Jesus. His wife was a goof.

He walked to the end of the bed, trying and failing not to let the scar marring her left dark arched eyebrow penetrate. He could ignore it in the day. It was the night, when the rest of the world faded and it was him and Lex in their room, their bed, when he couldn't. It was a constant reminder of that day where he lived for agonizing hours with the possibility that he could lose her, he would never have Lell or Vivie, when he couldn't ignore it.

It wasn't identical to his, slightly off to the outer edge whereas Ty's was in the middle. He didn't mind matching Team Walker t-shirts (something, now, both his daughters had, his wife and his daughters wore them often, he wore his solely at the gym).

He did mind semi-matching scars.

This had got so deep under his skin, he'd eventually talked about it with Tate, considering Laurie bore her own scar after being stuck by a serial killer and Tate had to see that shit every day. Tate had words of wisdom, they helped but not enough.

So, in the end, he had to suck it up and remind himself she was in their room, their bed, their daughters down the hall and now his, hope to God, son in her belly. She'd endured a nightmare and killed a man so she could end up breathing and save him from the lonely, lost life Tuku had led.

And he absolutely could live with that.

But he wished like fuck one of the many times he swept his thumb along that scar, when he was done, he'd make a miracle and it would go away.

So far this had not happened but he didn't stop trying.

He made it to the end of the bed and put his hands to his hips. She pushed forward and crawled on all fours to him. His cock started getting hard watching her and kept doing it when she made it to him, got up on her knees and slid her hands up his chest as she pressed close to him.

"Nic already gave me the time off," she told him.

"I'm thinkin' you chattin' with Sam behind my back is somethin' I should be pissed about."

Her head tipped to the side and her lips twitched. "Why?"

"Uh…Lex, you and Sam are playin' me," he informed her.

"Right, so you can beat the pants off stodgy old farts that Sam heard saying the n-word," she returned. "It's worth it."

And there it was. It was gone. Any wound he left after tearing her apart five years ago hadn't just healed over. It was gone. He knew it because she didn't blink before playing him. No uncertainty. She knew he'd do nothing, not one thing, to harm what they had.

But fuck, assholes said that shit all the time.

"When did I become a crusader for black justice?" he asked.

"You're not. Sam is. It's just that, this time, Mr. Humongo is his wingman."

He stared down at his woman and shook his head because, serious as fuck, she was a goof.

She pressed closer and coaxed in a soft voice, "Come on, honey. Sam says his house is right on the ocean. The girls'll love the beach."

The beach.

Hawaii had beaches.

"I'll do it," he stated and watched his wife smile. Then he asked, "Can you tell me why you keep puttin' clothes on before you go to bed?"

"It's November. It's cold."

Not in the house it wasn't. He had three girls to look after. He never jacked down the heat. He wanted them to be comfortable at all times so he saw to that, including paying a whack on heating their huge fucking house. Something else he spent a whack on to keep them comfortable.

"Lex, fuck you before we go to sleep," Ty pointed out. "You puttin' on pajamas is a ridiculous obstacle."

She pressed closer and her hands slid down and around his back to hold him tight.

"I like the ways you take them off," she whispered.

"That's good, mama, but it's *me* who's gotta take them off."

She pulled back and asked, "Is it that much of a pain in the ass?"

Ty moved and he did this quickly and efficiently, and in less than thirty seconds his wife was on her ass and naked in their bed.

Then he answered, "No."

She grinned. Then she found her knees again. Then she lunged.

Fuck, his woman was a wildcat.

He let her pull him to the bed not about to complain mostly because, seeing his wife naked in their bed, his cock was no longer getting hard.

It was there.

* * *

"Good day," she whispered into his chest.

Ty didn't reply but she was wrong. It wasn't good. It was fantastic.

"Love the way Irv is with the girls, especially Lell," she went on.

Ty again didn't reply but he did too. His father and his girl had a bond, thick as thieves. Irv loved Vivie but he had a connection with Lell, one she'd cherish for always and never forget, even years after he was gone. Ty did not have that. Neither did Lexie. But his daughter would.

And he liked that.

His relationship with his father had obviously improved significantly after his dad saved Lexie's life at the same time nearly losing his and, with Irv now off the booze entirely, it kept getting better.

His mom never entered their lives, not anymore. She'd had a variety of run-ins with Lexie in town *and* at the house that set Lex to throwing some serious sass and bought his mother a visit from her son communicating her ban. His father might catch it when he got home after a visit but he never said. Ty didn't ask. But when Irv came over, which was frequently, he never acted like he did, so it was likely he hid it. It was a little late for Irv Walker to shield the ones he loved but it was better late than never.

Ty liked that too.

Lex gave his gut a squeeze and muttered, "'Night, baby."

"'Night, mama."

She sighed.

Five minutes later he took her weight.

Five minutes after that, she rolled away.

When she did, he rolled into her, curled his arm around her belly that was carrying, hope to God, his son and pulled her close.

She snuggled closer.

Then he tipped his chin and smelled her hair and two seconds later, Ty Walker fell asleep with his wife tucked close and the lights of the small, quiet, safe Colorado town of Carnal shining through their huge-ass windows.

* * *

Eight months later, Lady Luck was still feeling in a generous mood.

Ty knew this because it was then, Julius Tatum Walker was born.

* * *

And twenty months after that, she was still feeling the same way.

Ty knew this because it was then, Elijah Irving Walker was born.